THE
MIDDLE
HEART

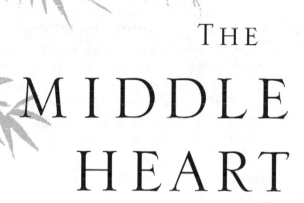

THE
MIDDLE
HEART

BETTE BAO LORD

ALFRED A. KNOPF   NEW YORK

1996

THIS IS A BORZOI BOOK
PUBLISHED BY ALFRED A. KNOPF, INC.

Grateful acknowledgment is made to the following for permission to reprint previously published material:

Farrar, Straus & Giroux, Inc.: The poem "At a Banquet in the House of the Taoist Priest Mei" from *The Chinese Translations* by Witter Bynner, copyright © 1978 by Witter Bynner. Reprinted by permission of Farrar, Straus & Giroux, Inc.

Penguin Books Ltd.: Excerpt from the poem "Hard Is the Journey" by Li Po from *Li Po and Tu Fu,* translated by Arthur Cooper, copyright © 1973 by Arthur Cooper. Reprinted by permission of Penguin Books Ltd., London.

Stanford University Press: Adapted form of poem "The Same Illness Has Been with Me . . ." from *Yuan Mei: Eighteenth-Century Chinese Poet* by Arthur Waley. Adapted by permission of Stanford University Press.

Library of Congress Cataloging-in-Publication Data

Lord, Bette.
    The middle heart : a novel / by Bette Bao Lord. — 1st. ed.
        p.   cm.
    ISBN 0-394-53432-8 (hardcover)
    1. China—History—20th century—Fiction.
    2. Friendship—China—Fiction.   I. Title.
PS3562.O678M53   1996
813'.54—dc20
                                                                    95-36165
                                                                    CIP

Manufactured in the United States of America
Published February 14, 1996
Second Printing Before Publication

For
Swifty, Corona and Winston

CONTENTS

PART ONE

JADE

BINDINGS

(1919)

Stone guardian's footsteps sounded beneath her window
like the clapper of a blind fortuneteller. Was he still hoping that she
would change her mind, lose heart, not go through with it? Foolish man!
Jade lingered in bed, toying with the bracelets that always circled her
wrists, taking pleasure in the smoothness of her arms, as white and cool
as the Yongle vase her husband caressed when he replaced the flowers
each morning before the portrait of his first wife.

Why could he never see beyond the pockmarks on her face? Ten
years under the same roof and still he failed to appreciate her many virtues.
Only a dreamer with eyes fixed on top of his head would have expected
beauty as well as a handsome dowry. Anyone else would have thanked
the gods for a match so dispassionately arranged, so equitable. Had her
skin been unblemished, she would never have become a room filler for
any widower, much less a bankrupt one with an insolent son. She would
have been the mistress of a great clan, not this sorry House whose land
had been pawned like articles of clothing until only a few tattered courts
in provincial Wen Shui remained. She would have been the . . .

Ai ya! What was she doing, indulging in fantasies? That was his
failing, not hers. Impatiently she threw off the quilt and crossed the bare
floor to perform the ritual that had begun each of her days since the

illness left her forever scarred. Seated at the dressing table, she poured hot water from the thermos bottle into the shallow bowl, soaked the silk handkerchief and placed it steaming upon her face. Three times she did this and then, while her skin was still warm, she covered it with an expensive paste made of secret ingredients but smelling of honey. Only when this had been accomplished did she look into the mirror. Carefully she applied the rice powder and rouge, then lacquered her hair into a bun, hiding her forehead with long bangs. Now strangers at a distance would see a face that, if not pretty, was unblemished.

Satisfied at last, she unlocked the sandalwood trunk at the foot of her bed and took from it the pillow stuffed with scarves. She grimaced. Even now, with only days remaining before she would be done with the deception, she resisted. Her figure was slender as a reed and moved as gracefully. What a shame to spoil it! But the disguise was critical and, holding the pillow to her waist, she reached into the chest again for the long sash and wound it around her body as tightly as her amah had wound the bindings that, when she was a child of seven, had shaped her feet into golden lilies. Once the ends were tucked away, no movement could work them loose.

There was no pleasure in choosing among the cotton gowns borrowed from her portly sister-in-law, so once the pillow was in place Jade dressed quickly, then proceeded to the altar in the far corner of the room. She lit a stick of incense and placed it in the censer before the porcelain image of the Goddess of Mercy. Head bowed, she sank to her knees and prayed.

"O merciful Kwan Yin, let the child be a boy. For without a son, how can I hope to fulfill my responsibilities to the House of Li? How can I be worthy?"

More importantly, how could she ever hope to hold her head high? When she first came to the House of Li, the studied slights of the women had been endurable. After all, every new bride was put on trial in her husband's home, especially one who, like herself, had had to kowtow at her wedding to a portrait of his first wife. Even now Jade could see the dead woman's wretched amah weeping as she prepared the bridal chamber, as if the newcomer had murdered her former mistress.

All this she had accepted with resolute pragmatism, a trait inherited from her father, the shrewdest of merchants. But after ten years, the arrogant Li women still set the tradesman's daughter apart, and no matter how long she continued to live among them or how much of her father's money they spent, without a son she could never expect more than polite disdain from her social superiors.

"O Kwan Yin," she cried, "give me a son and I vow to make him a leader of men, so that he may in turn honor you." She kowtowed nine times, then waited a decent interval before rising to her feet to unlatch the shutters and let in the revealing light.

*

A WEEK LATER, Stone Guardian shared a rickshaw with his wife, as the coolie, cursing the noisy mobs that forced him to detour down one street, then another, trudged from their hotel toward the hospital. For once he regretted his economies. If only he had hired a second rickshaw he would at least be free of the cloying smell of honey that soured the air when Jade was about.

He fixed his gaze upon a tall girl with bobbed hair who stood on a makeshift platform, gesturing like a soldier as she shouted into a megaphone. "China, awake!" she cried. And hundreds of boys and girls— the entire student body of every middle school in Shanghai, it seemed— roared in response: "China, awake!" Fools, he thought, you have as much chance of prevailing over the imperialists as I have of prevailing over this malevolent wife of mine. Nothing can save us. We are too poor. We are too weak. Foreigners shackle our country just as Jade shackles the Patriarch of the House of Li. There is no way out, not for China, not for me.

At the hospital, Jade hurried to the nursery, leaving him free to slip inside the girl's room. It was actually quite small, but the whitewashed walls and tiled floors, uncluttered except for the single iron bed, lent a spaciousness that belied its dimensions. Amber Willows did not stir. How young she looks, he thought. Younger than her seventeen years. Her hair, the color of ink, was loose and trailed across the white sheets like the finishing stroke in the word "eternity." He leaned toward her, then resisted the temptation to caress her cheek.

Somewhere, in another room, a baby began to cry. The girl's eyes opened. "Is that my . . . baby crying?" she whispered.

"Don't excite yourself. Rest, rest."

For a brief moment he thought her trembling hands were reaching out for him, but before he could clasp them they dropped as from their own weight, and he heard her ask, "Where is my baby? Where is—"

"The baby is with Jade."

The lights in Amber Willows' eyes faded. He bent to kiss the furrows from her brow, but again drew back. Why didn't she shed tears like other women? Tears could be wiped away, but not that opaque look, without will, without want. He had noticed it the night they met at the House of Midnight Scholars, when he had paid generously to be her first; and later, in the west chamber, when he had been in no hurry to see her disrobe, content merely to feel the smoothness of her face; and again when he had paid the proprietress still more to reserve Amber Willows for him alone. In time the lights had returned to her eyes, as she learned that he, too, was caught in heaven's web, that he meant her no harm, that he needed someone as helpless as she to love.

Suddenly, like an overwound toy, Jade spun into the room, trilling, "My son is beautiful, so beautiful! His eyes are bright as lanterns and his skin is smooth, unblemished as the tenderest bean curd."

Turning his back to her, Stone Guardian mumbled under his breath, "That's not what the nurses say."

Jade made a dismissive gesture. "Oh, if you mean the birthmark— it's beautiful too. A tiny kingfisher next to a well, which is his navel—a sign of good luck if ever there was one. Why, I've already sent word to my father to have kingfisher jewelry made for me. And all my new dresses will . . ."

Sickened by the thought of seeing kingfishers and smelling honey every day for the rest of his life, Stone Guardian wanted to spit, but knew nothing would come of it. His mouth was dirt dry.

Now Jade commanded him and Amber Willows to attention, to look her way. He counted to ten, but when at last he obeyed she proceeded merely to lick a finger, then used it to smooth her long bangs again and again, until every strand was arranged to her satisfaction.

Finally, she cleared her throat and addressed them. "Many months ago . . ."

Not again, he thought. He could anticipate every word, every gesture, and indeed, the wretched woman was now shutting her eyes and drawing a deep breath, as if to summon the courage to speak, even in passing, of the House where he had found solace in Amber Willows' arms. How could he have imagined then that the price for beauty would be so high?

"Had the child been a girl . . ."

Yes, yes, we know. Had the child been a girl, you, my dearest wife, would not have cared whether she was kept or killed, abandoned at the nearest baby tower or sold. His eyes were on Amber Willows, who stared at the ceiling as if momentarily it would give way. How could they live the future Jade had planned?

"But my prayers have been answered. The child is a boy, a healthy, beautiful boy, my son. And he will grow up to be an official. Yes, yes, an official as mighty as the Li ancestor you all claim forced the ouster of the chief eunuch in the Forbidden City. Then we'll see how those fine, upstanding relatives of yours will grovel. Meanwhile . . ."

Meanwhile, Stone Guardian thought, Amber Willows and I will be trapped in a nightmare beyond the powers of the young to imagine and the old to endure, a nightmare that is your dream.

Pointing to Amber Willows, Jade declared, "You will be wet nurse to my baby, and to show how generous I am to those who vow loyalty to their mistress, you may bring along that crippled brother of yours to live off me as well."

So Jade had decided to take the brother hostage too. Her father's daughter, she would leave nothing to chance.

Pointing to him, she declared, "And you, my husband, will be a loving father to our son."

"What do I want with him? I already have an heir," he retorted, then added, mimicking her, "A healthy, beautiful boy."

For a moment, Jade didn't look so smug, and he took satisfaction in having given her pause. It did not last. Changing the subject, she commanded their silence. Forever. She needn't worry, he thought. He would die before revealing his shameful, unconditional surrender.

"With Amber Willows registered under my name, our secret will go with us to the grave." She paused dramatically, then flashed a smile that cracked the makeup on her face. "You see, I've thought of everything."

Everything except . . . What did the pockmarked bitch know of a man's hunger for beauty? The torment of having it near and not possessing it? Far better to lose Amber Willows as he had lost his proper wife than be forced to bury her anew, day after day, in his heart.

He walked to the window. There was no view. A wall. With his back to them, he said, "My wife, as you know all too well, I had no choice but to agree to this grotesque charade. My debts are many. My means are gone. But why must you keep her around? Wet nurses are plentiful, servants too. Take the baby, but let her go."

"No . . . no, please." Amber Willows struggled to push herself upright. "Master—please, Master, I want to wait on her. I want to. I must be with my . . . the boy."

Her voice was no stronger than the rustle of fallen leaves, but her words killed his spirit as surely as if they had been the sword of heaven and this the appointed hour.

The Grasping Ceremony

(1920)

ON THE DAY of the Grasping Ceremony, when a child's fate was foretold, Amber Willows tied the tuft of hair that had been left on the baby's shaven head with red silk, as tradition demanded, and stepped back to admire him. His vest of red brocade was embroidered with lambs in token of the Year of the Sheep, 1919, the year of his mother's suffering. His pants were as green as the trees had been on the fourth of May, when he was born. It was a suit befitting the son of an emperor.

She felt a surge of pride so intense that tears leapt to her eyes. One fell, and with it the weariness that had weighed upon her during weeks of embroidering by the light of a smoky lamp also fell away. She had selected threads as fine as a single strand from the silkworm's cocoon and a needle no thicker than a hair, so that the stitches might be as true as the weave in the brocade. And so they were.

Now, carrying her treasure, she walked gingerly around the rotten slats in the floor of the gallery and down the steps to the stone garden. There, despite the lateness of the hour, she paused at the great rock in its center that had been hauled four hundred years before from the bottom of Wuxi Lake and presented to the House, at the Emperor's command, in honor of the extensive system of dikes the Lis had built. The rock was prized for evoking an endless variety of sculptures. Surely it would be a lamb today. And so it was.

She turned to go. Stone Guardian blocked her path, in his eyes the same yearning and anger she saw there whenever they happened upon each other alone. Lowering her gaze to the hem of his blue gown, which was stained with the mud of last week's rain, she said, "I beg your pardon, Master, but you must hurry and dress. The guests are arriving."

"Guests?"

"In honor of our boy's birthday." She held out the baby to him.

Stone Guardian glared at the child as he would a usurper. "Not ours! *Her* boy. And I have no intention of playing host for her or hers on this or any other day."

She squeezed the baby tight, wringing out the courage to ask what she must, and yet knew she ought not, ask: "How can a father's heart not have room for his own son?"

Before he could respond, she slipped past him and hurried toward the moongate, and not until she was safe in the next court did she look back. Though he was nowhere to be seen, his shadow continued to trail her, as it always did, like an abandoned dog. She could hear it sighing, feel the cold wetness of its nose nudging her hand, see it circling before it settled down at the foot of her bed for the night. Even when she slept, the master pursued her, howling, "Not ours. Hers. That boy is no son of mine!"

Near the main hall her six-year-old brother, Mountain Pine, drew himself up as straight as his lame leg would allow and waved. The baby, as usual, wanted to be carried by the boy who rocked as he walked, and squirmed like a giant carp caught in a net until she relented and handed him over.

Waiting for permission to enter, she marveled at the scene in the hall. Except for the dark hues worn by the four Li widows, who sat on chairs set against the walls, flanked by their personal servants, the qi-paos of the assembled ladies were as colorful as a field of wildflowers. At the center of each cluster, a clanswoman hosted guests of her generation. The crimson rug, gift of a village saved from extinction by the courageous judgments of a Li patriarch in the Ming Dynasty, had been cleared of furniture. The scrolls, painted by admirers of the House in the Qing Dynasty and, with the rug, among the very few family heirlooms that remained unsold, dressed up the tired walls with lotus ponds, dragonflies and cherry blossoms. Beside the altar of the ancestors stood a table bearing the tray upon which were displayed the toy implements of the noble professions. All this was for the boy. Her boy. Jade's son.

Suddenly a chorus of delight erupted. Mountain Pine, holding the baby, had stepped into the room. At once, Jade snatched her son away to parade him from guest to guest, pretending humility while gushing over their gifts. "You spoil us so. Such extravagance for this worthless nobody of mine."

Not yours, mine, Amber Willows thought, and again tears came to her eyes. She shook her head, willing them away, but must have made some sound, for Mountain Pine squeezed her hand. She looked at his upturned face. It was flushed with the joy of anticipation. Ashamed, she scolded herself for vain yearnings. After all, what stars in one's heavenly chart could be recast? What lifelines could be redrawn? As she made her way through the room, hearing the ladies talk of the striking resemblance between Jade and her son, as she offered them candies and nuts, sesame and almond cakes, an assortment of dried and fresh fruits, Amber Willows, the true mother, nodded and smiled.

At long last, Jade, still carrying the baby, took his tiny hand in hers to light the incense on the altar. Then, having executed three deep bows before the ancestral tablets, she minced on her golden lilies to the center of the room and, in a voice shrill with pride, ordered everyone to form a circle, as large as could be, around them. Finally, nodding to her son's wet nurse and to his young servant, she announced the start of the Grasping Ceremony.

Amber Willows fetched the tray of toy implements. "Remember what we practiced yesterday," she whispered to her brother as together they walked to the center of the circle and bowed, first to Jade, then to the guests, who were cheerfully accusing one another of neglecting decorum while inching surreptitiously nearer for a better look. With a finger upon her lips, Jade shushed them. The giggling subsided.

Mountain Pine took the toy sword from the tray, held it aloft for all to see, then placed it on the rug.

In unison the ladies chanted, "Grasp the sword, this hour, this date, and a soldier's life will be your fate."

Next came the hoe. "Grasp the hoe, this hour, this date, and a farmer's life will be your fate."

Then the hammer, the inkstone, the brush, until all the toys but one formed a small circle within that made by the ladies.

Only the official's seal remained on the tray. To this object and this object alone Jade had attached a red ribbon and silver bells, and when Mountain Pine took it in his hand, he waved it enticingly just beyond the baby's reach before setting it on the floor to complete the circle of toys.

"Grasp the seal, this hour, this date . . ."

Their part in the ceremony over, Amber Willows and her brother retreated through a gap in the circle of ladies to stand a discreet half-step behind them.

". . . and an official's life will be your fate."

A hush fell over the room, and Amber Willows sensed that even those who scoffed at such rituals were suddenly uncertain, wondering if destinies could somehow be fixed by trifles.

Jade set the baby down on the rug, then hastened to the place in the outer circle closest to the seal and knelt. "Come over here, come to Mother," she called. "Take the seal, my son. Take the seal."

But the baby remained where he was, blinking solemnly.

Jade made a clucking sound. He looked her way, then surveyed the faces smiling down at him.

Jade pounded the floor. He made a move toward her, then changed his mind and sat back, tugging on his shoes.

Suddenly, he was scuttling across the floor.

For a moment Amber Willows could only stand staring at the ring of toys. Nothing had been disturbed.

"Why didn't you stop him?"

"Why didn't you?"

"I never saw a mouse move as fast."

Merciful Kwan Yin, Amber Willows thought, what made my boy go to Mountain Pine?

Jade clapped her hands once.

Quickly Amber Willows freed her brother's ankle from the baby's grasp and sent the boy fleeing from the room. Then she placed Jade's son once more in the center of the rug.

At last the baby grasped the seal. At last all was well.

THE RIVER

(1932)

ON AN UNSEASONABLY warm day, when the sun bleached the skies, a playful wind off the Yangzi River lured Steel Hope to its banks. He sat with his servant on the top of a crumbling levee that was part of the elaborate network of dikes built by his ancestors centuries before—the reason their hometown had been named Wen Shui, Civilized Waters. Once the levee had held back floods; now it was merely his favorite lookout. He shut his eyes, trying to picture the grandeur of the dikes when new, but all he could see was the ebony coffin that last year's angry floodwaters had gouged from the earth somewhere upstream and flung into the top of a drowned mulberry tree. It had stayed there for weeks, while the survivors keened for the millions lost, their voices piercing the heavens. Their robes of coarse white hemp had transformed the landscape into an endless, ashen shroud. . . .

He shook the memory away. Sad thoughts, always unwelcome, were especially so on this unexpected holiday, and once more he tried coaxing Mountain Pine into a game. It was useless. When reading, as now, the servant could sit longer than a chair. Ignored again, Steel Hope was about to snatch the book away when he was distracted by the music of the pigeons flying overhead. They were his, a gift from Amber Willows, who, with her dexterous fingers, had tied the reed whistles to their tails.

As the birds swooped toward the river the sound of the flutes grew deeper; as they rose into the heavens the pitch rose too. He filled his lungs and thought how good it was to be idling in the sun. Indeed, anything was better than being imprisoned in that dingy schoolroom and stuffed like a duck with ancient homilies.

He nudged Mountain Pine. "Hey, how long to repair the school roof?"

Mountain Pine straightened his glasses, but otherwise seemed not to hear. On his lips was that smile of indomitable serenity he always wore when reading.

"A week? A month? A year?"

Still that Buddha smile. Always that Buddha smile. Ai ya! It had been the same for six years, ever since his mother made Mountain Pine his bookmate. Steel Hope would rather have endured the canings his father administered for poor grades and misdeeds than be tied to the scrawny scholar every minute of the day. Not that he couldn't get free. Flying Feet, though five years younger, against Shriveled Leg, though a head taller, was no contest. But that was the trouble—no contest. Besides, the one time Steel Hope had yielded to temptation and escaped, Jade had had Mountain Pine caned. Was the second son of the Patriarch of the House of Li the kind of warrior who would send a cripple to do battle in his stead? The answer was obvious. It was just his bad luck that his mother knew it too!

Sighing, he watched the smoke from a decrepit steamship paint the wind black. Its transit revealed another vessel, a patrol boat flying the Japanese flag. The very sight of the white and red banner infuriated him. It mocked the greatness of his country and his clan. It made him feel small. It reminded him of his father, who, as a young official at the time of China's humiliating defeat in the war of 1895, had had to preside over ceremony after ceremony at which the Imperial Flag was lowered to yield to the Rising Sun. If not for that unutterable degradation, he thought, Stone Guardian would still be the admirable man everyone said he had been up to that time, and not the failed Patriarch and heartless father Steel Hope knew. If not for that, Stone Guardian would care for his second son.

To stop the tears from flowing, Steel Hope flopped onto his stomach and took aim. "Bang, bang, bang . . ." That was for seizing China's lands. "Pow, pow . . ." That was for stealing China's wealth. "Bang, bang . . ." He leaped up and scrambled from one imaginary machine gun to another, firing round after round. Finally, the last Japanese vessel left afloat, a passenger ship tied up at the dock, took blasts until the hull was riddled with holes and it sank. The hero, gasping for breath, collapsed beside Mountain Pine.

"Hey, I could've used some help," he said when he could speak again. He expected no reply, but this time his bookmate surprised him.

"Look at that! Over there!" Mountain Pine pointed toward the quay.

Steel Hope shot upright, but saw nothing unusual. "Look at what?"

"That boy. There he goes again."

Now Steel Hope saw him, an urchin darting stealthily among the half-naked coolies hawking rickshaw rides, the peddlers of souvenirs, the beggars scrambling for coppers tossed by foreigners. He seemed to be moving in on a very fat man who was bowing like a piston to the puny Japanese captain standing at the head of the passenger ship's gangplank. Steel Hope blinked. Yes! So much flesh could only belong to Watermelon Wu, their land-grabbing neighbor, who prospered by being as cozy as lips to teeth with the imperialists.

As Wu turned to face shore, the sly one darted forth again. Quick as an adder he stuck a paper with a big black X drawn on it to the fat man's back, then as quickly vanished. Not until the bystanders began laughing and pointing at him did Wu realize he'd been marked. Even Mountain Pine laughed, as the traitor, twisting and thrusting like a pregnant sow, tried to snatch the sign from his back but succeeded only in losing his Panama hat.

"I'm going after that boy," Steel Hope said, and raced toward the quay, keeping an eye on the pair of grimy feet he could just see behind the line of rickshaws. As he rounded the last sedan he executed a combination of Swooping Scissors and Throttle the Tiger and pounced.

"Friend!" he whispered, to avoid giving the wrong impression. The boy wasn't convinced. So violently did he kick and punch that Steel Hope was forced to tighten his grip. "Keep still," he hissed.

The boy made a strangling sound.

"Stop that!" It was Mountain Pine.

Steel Hope let go. The boy keeled over in a heap.

"You must forgive my young master," Mountain Pine said courteously, helping him up. "I'm Mountain Pine. He is Steel Hope. What's your name?"

"Firecrackers."

Steel Hope had never heard of such a name and started to laugh, but thought better of it when confronted by a pair of fierce black eyes. "Hate toadies, do you?" he said instead.

"Only a traitor wouldn't!"

Steel Hope nodded appreciatively. "How'd you get the paper to stick?"

"Cockleburs."

"Cockleburs?"

"Cockleburs," repeated Firecrackers, grinning, and without further conversation the guttersnipe, the lame servant, and the young master of a noble house strolled off together toward the broken levee, where they sat dangling their feet above the water. Steel Hope removed his shoes and socks and regretted the cleanness of his toes. "I'm the second son of the Patriarch of the House of Li," he announced.

Firecrackers' mouth fell open. "The famous House of Li?"

"None other."

Scratching his armpits, Firecrackers assessed this information, then said, "Got anything to eat?"

Steel Hope shook his head.

Firecrackers pointed. "What's that in your pocket?"

"That's not for eating," said Steel Hope, showing him the old rice, which he had kneaded into a compact ball. "It's what I feed the goldfish."

"I've got goldfish too," Firecrackers declared. "Big ones."

Before the young master could let out an incredulous hoot, Mountain Pine had snatched the rice ball from his hand and given it to the braggart. "Try feeding them some of this," he said.

The boy pocketed the rice.

Steel Hope shook his head. His bookmate might know lots of things, but clearly he knew nothing about boys like this one. "Show me your fish," he demanded. "Where do you live?"

"On a boat, a yaolu."

He was impressed. "Take us there."

"I can't. I mean, I would, but . . . it's not here, it's gone downriver."

Steel Hope rolled his eyes heavenward, but noting that fierce look again, he decided against calling Firecrackers a liar and wracked his brains for a more congenial subject. "Like games?" he asked finally.

"Who doesn't!"

"*He* doesn't!" Steel Hope, scratching a sudden itch, nodded toward his bookmate.

Firecrackers asked, "Like races?"

"Sure. I always win."

"You do not."

"Yes, I do."

Louder and louder they each insisted until Firecrackers poked the young master in the ribs and said, "Prove it. Last one across the river is a turtle's egg."

Steel Hope gulped. It was not yet spring and, despite the sun, the river, which was lis and lis wide and only the gods knew how deep, would freeze his nuts off. More to the point, he couldn't swim. But then . . . neither could Mountain Pine. Cupping Firecrackers' ear, the young master sadly imparted this most unfortunate fact and, without thinking, added that ever-handy excuse, "He's got one long leg and one that's short, you see."

Halfway through the sentence, Steel Hope realized how feeble an excuse this was and how quickly he must come up with something else or be laughed at. By the time he finished the sentence, Merciful Kwan Yin had told him exactly what to do. Before Firecrackers could react, he was off, shouting, "Come on or forfeit the contest!" The others had no choice but to follow.

At a deserted spot along the shore, where fish nets were drying, he drew a straight line in the dirt, then paced its length and, with mathematical precision, determined its midpoint. Straddling it, he bent down and traced his feet. Next, at each end of the line he drew two more pairs of feet. By now Firecrackers and Mountain Pine were looking at each other for a clue. Steel Hope marched to the center position, cleared his throat, and commanded his companions to take their places.

Mountain Pine, sighing wearily, took the spot nearest him and asked, "What next?"

Steel Hope wouldn't be rushed. He stretched, rolled his head, rippled his muscles, shook out his legs, and cleared his throat again, but just as he was about to speak, Firecrackers, who had taken his assigned place but had been watching this performance suspiciously, shouted, "You've got to make it fair."

Steel Hope was insulted. "I'm no cheat," he said. Then, to reinstate the proper mood, he repeated his entire warm-up before proclaiming, "For this competition Mountain Pine's leg being short an inch or so doesn't matter. Neither does your being small and skinny or me being strong and fast.

"But before we can begin . . ." He paused. "Get ready . . ." He untied his trousers. "Get set . . ." He dropped them. "For a pissing contest!"

Suddenly, there was laughter.

Steel Hope turned. Mountain Pine was doubled over, pointing to the pair of feet traced in the dirt where, a moment before, Firecrackers had stood.

"Where did he go?" Steel Hope asked.

The servant shook his head, still laughing. "Who knows? Maybe I'm not the only one who's short an inch!"

PURE BRIGHTNESS

O N THE DAY of Pure Brightness, when willows are in bud
and clans gather to unite past and posterity, the members of the House
of Li knelt among the family graves to perform the ancient rites. Solemnly
the Patriarch, Stone Guardian, intoned the words that since the Ming
Dynasty had been said in this place on the third day of the third month
of the lunar calendar: "O Spirits of our Noble Ancestors, we, your children,
have traveled from near and far to attend your needs in the afterlife, to
venerate your memory, to enshrine forever your legacy of honor and
attainments in our hearts.

"We who still dwell in the earthly realm beseech you who abide in
the netherworld to intercede on our behalf. . . ."

Barely listening, Steel Hope examined his palms. The red welts were
still there. Spirits, he cried silently, why don't you ever intercede for me?
You must know that Father punishes me for no reason at all. The splotches
of ink on the cuffs of his new silk jacket accused him, however, and he
hastened to hide them from view. Well, maybe there had been a reason
for the punishment this time. But the spirits might at least have alerted
the Patriarch when the promised five strokes had been delivered.

O Spirits, he prayed, soften Father's heart and I will be as obedient
as Mountain Pine. And should you have time left over, please, please stop

Mother from devoting every moment to making an official of me. Jade had feigned illness to avoid seeing her husband make a spectacle of himself at his first wife's grave, but even in her absence her son could hear her voice. "Now, now, don't disappoint me," she clucked, at least once a week. "You know that I live only for the day when the splendor of your achievements will lend a glow to my dark existence."

And I live only for the day when you stop nagging me. . . .

Suddenly there was a silence. Had others heard her voice and his unfilial thoughts? Steel Hope's eyes swept the scene. All heads were solemnly bowed, even those of his four grandaunts, who always whispered among themselves. He could never imagine what these women, cloistered together since widowhood, had to say to each other that they hadn't said a thousand times before. Nearby were the shy maiden cousins, who lived in the innermost courts but whom he wouldn't recognize if one ever let go of the other's hand.

His gaze settled on his brother, Grand Hope, whose Western suit, spats and Panama hat marked the twenty-four-year-old as a sophisticate from the Foreign Concessions. Truly, Steel Hope didn't mind half as much as Jade that Grand Hope gambled, dropped foreign words that no other Li understood into every conversation and boasted of his success in the Shanghai Stock Market—or even that Stone Guardian never mentioned the countless times the clan had had to pay his elder son's debts but now recalled at least once a day the one time, about three weeks ago, when Grand Hope had paid the clan back. Since all fathers traditionally indulged their firstborn, such partiality was bearable. But the way Stone Guardian, who loathed the Japanese, pretended ignorance of Grand Hope's blatant admiration of Japanese power, efficiency and modernity— even of his visit to Tokyo without permission last year—did rile him. And why should it be that Grand Hope, who never cared whether he pleased their father, could make him laugh? On Steel Hope, the Patriarch wouldn't spend a smile.

". . . In victory, our ancestors were magnanimous. Never did they strip any man of face, least of all those who were vanquished. And so must we do the same. Remember our ancestor who not only spared the surviving son of his bitterest enemy, but provided funds throughout his life for his welfare.

"In defeat, our ancestors upheld honor. And so must we do the same. Remember our ancestor who, having lost favor in court, trekked ten thousand lis into exile rather than disavow the words he had written. . . ."

When he was younger Steel Hope had loved hearing about these heroic ancestors, but lately he'd found himself comparing the great deeds his ancestors had performed for the Empire with the empty words his clansmen mouthed every day. Once the Lis had been renowned for sacrificing themselves to save the lives of strangers; now they seldom bothered to be kind even to one another. Hardly an hour went by when his parents didn't quarrel.

"... Thus we who bear the honored name of Li shall never forget what the great sage taught us, that civilization began with filial piety...."

After Stone Guardian had led the nine kowtows before the monument, the collective ceremony was over, and the clansmen scattered to honor those who had ridden the stork. They ranged leisurely over the hillside, placing upon the graves of their most direct ancestors willow branches to ward off evil spirits and bowls of fruit, plates of cold food and cups of wine to feed both the living and the dead. Steel Hope trailed behind his brother.

Halfway down the hill, they stopped at the grave of the first wife of the Patriarch, where Stone Guardian was already on his knees, weeding the mound. Suddenly Steel Hope felt as if he were intruding, as if he had happened upon an intimacy, a tenderness, not meant for him to see. The weeds his father pulled were not weeds, but stray threads from the gown of a beloved.

As his brother knelt alongside Stone Guardian, Steel Hope backed away. He drifted, hesitantly at first. Then, like a boulder loosened by seasons of rain and snow, he hurtled down the hill, racing headlong until finally the land met a stream, and the thought of muddying the hem of his new gown stopped him. For a few minutes he looked for a crossing. Then, ashamed of thinking like an old woman, he jumped into the slime at the water's edge.

He shaded his eyes and looked about for a companion, but on the Day of Pure Brightness no one worked the fields. He listened, but heard only the wind. Masking his disappointment, he shrugged and proceeded to shadowbox down the path until the gravekeeper's hut came into view. Perhaps he was at home and wished for company, though from a distance the hut looked deserted. Close up, it was positively derelict, with large cracks patched with straw in walls that would have collapsed long ago but for crutches made of bamboo. Had it always been this way? Only the rags and bones drying on mats strewn about the yard and the row of scallions planted by the doorway, surprisingly beautiful amidst the squalor, affirmed that someone did live here.

The door was ajar, and he called into the darkness within. "Wei? Wei?"

No one answered.

He tried again. Again there was no response, and he was turning away when he thought he heard a faint coughing.

"Is . . . anybody home?" He could see nothing. Was the house inhabited by ghosts? "I'm from the House of Li. . . ." Yes, there was coughing. It sounded human enough, and seemed to come from a far corner of the room. Still, Steel Hope hesitated. The place had a sour smell. Mountain Pine, who had memorized all the maxims all the sages ever uttered, said that men were more fearsome than ghosts. What if the gravekeeper was drunk? What if, disturbed, he flew into a murderous rage?

Finally his eyes became accustomed to the gloom, and he saw two cots against the back wall of the room, one empty, the other heaped with straw and—there was an arm attached to—what? Was a corpse buried in that mound of hay? The arm twitched. He flinched and edged back. He was almost out the door when the coughing started again, a dry hacking that sent bits of straw floating to the ground.

He stopped in his tracks. What if the gravekeeper was deathly ill? Mountain Pine also said that within the four seas, all men are brothers. Surely the coughing man could use a brother now. Besides, it would be cowardly to leave him, and no Li was a coward.

Breathing through his mouth, Steel Hope stood tall and boldly approached the cot. There he discerned, almost buried in the straw, a face greasy with sweat, a man too weak to be dangerous. "Are . . . are you all right?" he asked.

The man gulped for air like a fish on shore. "Wa . . ."

Steel Hope leaned closer.

"Water . . ."

He nodded and searched the room, at last finding a cup in a niche above the stove. But when he peered into it he found it filled with cockleburs. What would anyone want with those? he wondered. Then, suddenly, he knew, and pursed his lips slightly to draw out a big, slow smile. He'd been right. That liar Firecrackers didn't live on a yaolu. He lived in this very hut, and the gravekeeper must be his father. No, from the look of him, grandfather.

"Water . . ."

He snatched a jug and ran to the stream, scooped up some water and raced back.

The gravekeeper swallowed with difficulty.

"More?"

When there was no reply, Steel Hope decided the man was hungry and began searching for food in the jars and baskets scattered about the room. Finding nothing except some dried beans and uncooked rice, he regretted not having stuffed his sleeves with his share of the feast before leaving the ceremony. By now, all that remained uneaten would belong to the ancestors. Still ... the food would just be sitting there—and no Li, as far as he knew, had ever gone hungry. "I'm going but I'm coming back," he said, and sprinted off, out the door and up the hill to the graveyard, where his clansmen, living and dead, having enjoyed their annual picnic together, were now gathered around the Patriarch, who had begun recounting the tale of the ancestor who designed the dikes.

From behind a tree, Steel Hope waited for the right moment. Finally, as Stone Guardian approached the climax of the story, he saw his chance and tiptoed to the grave of Great-Grandfather. "Noble Ancestor," he prayed, "don't be angry. One offering among so many means nothing to you, but it will make all the difference to a starving man." Then, glancing about to make sure he was still unobserved, he snatched a dumpling. Nothing untoward happened. Perhaps Great-Grandfather didn't disapprove—after all, hadn't he extended credit to his tenants for seedlings and then destroyed the notes when there was a drought? Keeping a wary eye on his kinsmen, Steel Hope slipped from one ancestral mound to another, snatching bits of food. Finally, sleeves full, he scrambled back down the hill and burst into the hut.

The gravekeeper was in a deep sleep. He cursed. A benefactor should be hailed with praise, not snores. There was nothing to do but leave the food and rejoin the clan.

He was setting the last of the cakes on the brick stove when suddenly the hairs on the back of his neck bristled. Someone else was in the room. He froze. For robbing the ancestral graves, his father would chop off his hand. He saw his inky fingers twitching in a pool of blood, the jagged stump ...

"What ... are you doing here?" The voice sounded nothing like Stone Guardian's. It belonged to someone much younger. Bravely Steel Hope swung about.

Firecrackers stood in the doorway.

When the boy repeated the question, but with even less authority, Steel Hope's eyes narrowed. "I could ask you the same question, but you'd just tell me more lies. Besides ..." He paused, then announced triumphantly, "I know."

Firecrackers shot a fearful glance at the sleeping gravekeeper and turned as pale as a bone.

Was whatever ailed the old man catching? Steel Hope took a half-step toward the door, then thought better of it and fixed his gaze on the tabletop, with its splinters and pits. If only Mountain Pine were here.

"Please don't tell," Firecrackers begged. "No one must know that the gravekeeper is sick and a girl is doing his job. We have nowhere to go. Swear, Steel Hope. Swear, no matter what, that you won't tell."

Who was Firecrackers talking about? "What girl?"

"Me."

He burst out laughing. When he'd caught his breath, he thumped his chest and shouted, "I'm no dummy. I know the difference between a girl and a boy. Why do you tell such ridiculous lies?"

"But . . . but you said you knew. You mean Father didn't—" Firecrackers stopped short.

Suddenly Steel Hope recalled the pissing contest. Suddenly he couldn't close his mouth or make a sound, or stop the blood that must have colored his face like a repulsive rash. He bolted toward the door. Firecrackers blocked the way. They wrestled fiercely, and for a long time, because Steel Hope, though far stronger, couldn't bring himself to punch a girl, even a girl who looked and fought and smelled like a boy. In the end, he pinned her down.

When he saw her tears, he let go. "I didn't mean to twist your neck so hard. Are you all right?"

"Yes, Young Master," she said, and he stood and once more started for the door. Firecrackers grabbed the hem of his gown. "Please, Young Master," she begged. "You've got to stay and hear me out. No lies, I swear. The truth. Please, Young Master, please?"

Mulling it over, he found his curiosity was stronger than his embarrassment. She seemed so desperate. What did she have to tell him? "Make it quick," he said.

She began to brush the dirt from his clothes and he retreated from her touch. Since he'd turned twelve, the year before, not even Amber Willows had been allowed to fuss over him. "Not here," he said. "Outside." Outside, she couldn't block the way when he decided to leave.

Sitting by the scallions as far from the door and the girl as he could get and still be within earshot, without making a move or saying a word, or even looking at her, he listened.

"My father wasn't always a gravekeeper," she said. "Before the spells came on him, he was an agent boater with a yaolu of his own. He was strong then. He could push and pull the long oar all day, every day, going from town to town, from village to village. He could call every customer by name. He knew every order by heart, no matter how large or how small—what color, what size, what grade—everything. He could locate the right basket or jug or bag faster than the owners themselves. Customers trusted him. The shopkeepers who paid him to sell their specialties in the villages did too. Happy faces greeted us everywhere.

"Now, even beggars spit on him. Who wants a gravekeeper around? If only I'd never been born. If only I wasn't cursed. . . ."

She stopped. How could she tell this boy of the happy times, of the day when her mischievous brother, proclaiming he was a spirit sent from the deep to capture wicked little girls, and wailing like a ghost, had crept up on her, coming closer, closer, until her mother, laughing affectionately, lifted the corner of the oilcloth she was mending to envelop her frightened daughter in the safety of its folds? How could she tell him of the disaster that had ruined their lives and was all her fault? How could she?

But Steel Hope had drawn nearer to her. "Please, go on," he said softly. "Don't be afraid to tell me." She only glanced at him, but even so she saw so much caring in his eyes that she felt safe. And she did tell, choked with tears, speaking in fits and starts, like someone desperately trying to piece together a shattered mirror by seizing a shard here, a shard there. Steel Hope, listening, was afraid for her. He didn't dare interrupt. Fixing his attention on every utterance, he managed to discern the essentials, but even then, he wondered if the events so real to her had happened at all.

Her mother had given birth to twins. First, a healthy boy child. Then, a stillborn girl child. There was nothing to be done, so the agent boater lowered the dead baby over the side. But as the body slipped into the water, suddenly there were cries, cries as loud as firecrackers. The girl lived.

Growing up, Firecrackers wanted to be just like her twin, to be as audacious and fearless and carefree as he, to do all the things he did, but of course, being a girl, she couldn't. While he climbed, swam and fished, she washed, cooked and mended. While he roamed as he pleased in towns and villages, she had to remain on the yaolu, waiting to hear about his adventures. Someday he would be an agent boater like their father. Someday she would have to leave them to join her husband's family. How she envied him.

One afternoon, when her parents were busy settling accounts, she followed her brother into town. With so much to see, she kept bumping into people. Most of them just kept on walking. A few cursed. She was too happy to mind.

There was much to buy, and she had only a few coins left from her New Year's red envelope. Keeping her brother in sight, she hurried along the street trying to choose, and finally decided on an orange.

A motorcar passed. It was green and shiny, and she turned to watch it, walking backwards.

Again she bumped into someone. The man's Panama hat went flying and the half-eaten orange in her hand was mashed against his white suit. Though she immediately brushed off the seeds and tried to wipe away the stain, her efforts only made matters worse. He shoved her away. His friends shouted angrily, but she didn't understand a word. When she stooped to pick up the uneaten sections of her orange, he kicked her.

She let out a howl. Her brother rushed to her aid. The man struck him. Another hit him with an umbrella. He stumbled backwards and fell. His head hit a rock. The man and his friends disappeared. Bystanders crowded around, all talking at once.

"Japs!"

"What can you do?"

"To Brown Dwarfs, a dead Chinese means less than a dung fly."

Firecrackers watched with horror as her parents mourned—her father as wooden as a plank, her mother at first wailing, then keeping silent and refusing to eat. That neither ever questioned her presence at the scene made her wish even more that she could trade places with her brother. With each passing day she became increasingly certain that the gods had never meant her to survive her birth. They would continue to exact retribution until the heavenly accounts were settled.

One morning her mother, now bedridden, awoke and thought her daughter was her son. When Firecrackers instinctively answered to her brother's name, the grieving woman smiled and, for the first time since the tragedy, ate some noodles. That day Firecrackers cut her hair, put on boys' clothing, and became her twin brother. Thus she might please her mother and, more importantly, fool the gods.

Now and then her mother would sense that something was wrong and test her. "Climb the mast, son," she would say. So Firecrackers climbed. "Go for a swim, son," she would say. "Fish would be nice." So Firecrackers swam and fished.

Then, on the night of the Mid-Autumn Festival, when they were about to eat the mooncakes, her mother suddenly asked, "Where's Firecrackers? How can we celebrate the bond of all bonds when one of us is missing? I must go after her." She left the table, calling her daughter's name.

Her father waited for Firecrackers to do something, but she couldn't think what. No matter who she was, her twin or herself, they were only three. She didn't hear the splash, or see her mother again.

Thereafter the agent boater succumbed to spells that came and went without warning; he lost his route and, to pay his debts, the yaolu was sold. Before long they had no roof and little to eat. Then one day, not long before the New Year, while making the rounds from servant gate to servant gate begging for leftovers, they happened upon the House of Li. When the second cook recognized the agent boater who had serviced him so honestly and diligently, he took pity and, knowing that his relative was retiring as gravekeeper, offered the mistress another to take his place. The mistress agreed. . . .

There was a long silence. Now Firecrackers' eyes were dry, and it was Steel Hope who blinked away tears. He ached for her and the family she had lost. He ached for the family he had never had. While the difference between their lives was as great as the difference between a boy and a girl, somehow the hollow they shared was real. Finally he asked, "But why do you go on with the masquerade?"

"Don't you understand?" she cried. "Father stands for hours just moving the broom back and forth over the same spot. So when he's asleep I pretend I'm as fearless as my brother and tend the graves. If the House of Li ever knew a dirty girl was looking after their ancestors, they'd throw us out. Then where would we go?

"I also work mornings at a teahouse. If Old Yang knew I was a dirty girl, he'd throw me out of there too. Then how would we live?"

Steel Hope didn't have an answer. Firecrackers was right: If his clansmen knew about her, they'd never let her and her father stay. "You must have relatives," he said.

She nodded.

"Go to them! They'll give you a home."

She shook her head. "Only Father knew where they live, and he's forgotten that, too."

He must help her. He must find a way. But what did he know about girls? All he knew for sure was that they got married, and without stopping to think, he blurted, "What if I made Mountain Pine marry you?"

Firecrackers broke down and sobbed.

Steel Hope was bewildered. What had he said that was so wrong? "Mountain Pine would be a good husband," he argued. "He's kind and loyal and the smartest one in school. . . ."

Firecrackers shook her head violently.

"He is, I tell you!" Then, suddenly, he realized that his mother would never permit his bookmate to marry before her son graduated, and he refrained from saying any more.

"Oh, please keep my secret anyway," she begged. "Say you'll help. Say you'll be my friend."

For a long moment, he didn't know what to do. Then he spotted a cocklebur on the ground, and in a flash it occurred to him that they shared a common enemy. Had it not been for those sneaky dwarfs, her brother wouldn't have died and his father wouldn't have lost his pride. And what true son of the House of Li would forsake an ally in need?

Of course, it was outrageous that a boy would befriend a girl. But with her hair even shorter than his, her feet as calloused as a rickshaw driver's, who would ever suspect? And if nobody else guessed, what did he care? Naturally Mountain Pine would have to know, but he'd never tell. Mountain Pine's failing wasn't telling secrets, it was avoiding games.

At the thought of games, Steel Hope grinned. What game could possibly be better than helping this wretched girl and, in the bargain, fooling the whole town?

"You swear never to grow your hair long?"

"I swear."

"You swear never to wear a qi-pao?"

"I swear."

"You swear never to wash your feet?"

"I swear."

Racing away, he shouted over his shoulder, "Wait for us at the dike tomorrow afternoon."

THE MIDDLE HEART

ALONG A SECLUDED stretch of an ancient canal, there was a deserted dwelling, no more substantial than a watchman's hut thrown up at harvest time. Everyone knew its story. Years before, the pretty young tenant, cursing all men who ever bedded an unwilling woman, had stabbed herself in the heart. Thereafter, it was said, any trespasser woke to discover his member gone, replaced by a small green caterpillar.

Steel Hope had long dreamed of appropriating the hut, which was only a short walk from school, for his headquarters, but having known just two females well, he feared that if the ghost had the spleen of his mother instead of the kind heart of Amber Willows, it might pick a quarrel even with such innocents as he and Mountain Pine. Now he wondered. What harm could come to a girl? None, he decided, and so, on the day after Pure Brightness, he dared Firecrackers to go inside. When she walked out as she had walked in, only dirtier, if that was possible, he concluded that the prior occupant must have had a gentle nature. From then on, when he and Mountain Pine had finished at school, and Firecrackers had turned her mop over to Old Yang's nephew, who took her place in the afternoon to serve wage earners with money for tips, the three of them convened at the haunted spot to carry out the young master's plans.

At their first meeting, they cleaned the place. At their second, Steel

Hope cut their thumbs and mixed their blood, and together they swore the legendary oath taken by Liu Pei, the remote relative of the Emperor; Kuan Yu, the warrior; and Zhang Fei, the butcher of pigs, as described in every boy's favorite tale, *The Romance of the Three Kingdoms*: "We three, though of different clans, bind ourselves to one end. We swear to defend our country and save our people. We cannot undo our separate births, but on the same day we mean to die. May Heaven, all-ruling, and Earth, all-producing, read our hearts! And should we turn aside loyalty and forsake duty, may the gods and man smite us."

Then, as Mountain Pine and Firecrackers looked on, Steel Hope painstakingly carved a giant ideogram on the blackened wall—the character for loyalty. When it was finished, he slashed a horizontal line through the center of it. To Firecrackers, who couldn't read, he explained that now there were not one but two words. Together they meant "center." But the top alone was the word "middle," as in the Middle Kingdom, the hub of civilization, China; and the bottom alone was "heart," as in the truest and bravest of all hearts, the heart of a Chinese patriot.

Firecrackers gaped, then looked to Mountain Pine, who nodded to confirm that these claims were true, and asked wearily, "What now?"

Steel Hope rubbed his hands together in sly anticipation. "We'll go collect some cockleburs and tag every last Jap from here to Shanghai!"

Firecrackers clapped her hands and shouted "Yea!" at this proposal, but Mountain Pine said, "That's certainly tempting, though I'm told Japs, unlike Watermelon Wu, are more likely to carry guns than fat. Of course, there's always a chance even an expert marksman might miss, so give it a try. I prefer to watch. Somebody's got to be alive to scoop up your guts."

"Are you a coward?" asked Steel Hope.

Without the slightest hesitation, Mountain Pine replied, "Now and always."

"And you, Firecrackers?"

Firecrackers scratched thoughtfully, then stepped forward to stand shoulder to shoulder with Steel Hope.

Outnumbered, Mountain Pine began to speak in that distinctive, hushed voice that he only employed to command his young master's attention—as effective as yanking him off the ground by the scruff of the neck. "Remember what the ancients said about the art of war. Victories are won only with the aid of the people. Without it, even the most brilliant generals and the most fearsome warriors will fail. Before doing battle, you must first make yourselves heroes to the people."

"How?" Firecrackers asked, scratching again.

Only a dumb girl would ask such a question, thought Steel Hope. "By doing good deeds, of course," he said. When Firecrackers still looked doubtful, he added, "Like my ancestors." Which explained everything to anyone born and raised in the vicinity of Wen Shui.

Good deeds proved hard to do, however. One look at the ragamuffin, the cripple, and the fast talker whose fine clothes could only be stolen, and people shooed them away. To be rid of them the faster, some even tossed coins at Mountain Pine, who could tolerate anything except being an object of pity, and spurned them. But Firecrackers had no such compunction, and pocketed them gladly, thus offending the sensibilities of the beggars, who, as members of a time-honored guild, abhorred nonprofessionals. When their king, having decided to teach the insolent amateurs a lesson, charged the do-gooders, brandishing a cleaver in his one and only hand, they barely escaped. And the coolies were no kinder. Spitting and cursing, they hurled rocks at those who threatened their livelihood by offering to do for free what the coolies did to feed their families.

After these misadventures, Mountain Pine, not built for quick get-aways, suggested that perhaps it wasn't wise to foist themselves even on the needy. Regardless, Steel Hope, racing ahead, shouted, "Would Kuan Yu give up?" And, gaining on him, Firecrackers echoed his cry. The servant had no choice but to follow; and so it went, until one afternoon, in yet another headlong flight from the King of Beggars, Steel Hope smashed into Teacher, knocking him into a food stand, which collapsed and sent the neat piles of dough balls bouncing down the street. It took all Firecrackers' quickness to nab the wayward sweets, all Steel Hope's strength to prop up the stand and all Mountain Pine's skills at preserving harmony to placate the injured parties. But the price was high. The servant had to promise that the young master would never again be seen dashing about town like a hooligan. The incentive to comply was considerable. Next time, Teacher would report their crimes to the Patriarch of the House of Li.

As Teacher rode away on his bicycle, Mountain Pine sighed with relief. Firecrackers looked to the young master. Steel Hope, secretly bored with doing good deeds, saw the injunction as a way of saving face and leaped into the air to execute a series of triumphant kicks; then, throwing his arms around his companions and pulling them close, he announced that the time had come to embark on the next phase of his master plan. From now on, they would devote themselves to training their bodies and honing their skills in preparation for battle with the real enemy, the Japanese. They would devote themselves to a program of self-strengthening.

And so, at each meeting, they added another stone to the pouches made from old stockings tied around their arms and ankles before moving slowly and smoothly through the exercises of t'ai chi. As one they grasped the bird's tail, played the guitar, brought the tiger to the mountain, repulsed the monkey, crept like the snake and threaded a needle at the bottom of the sea. At all these drills Mountain Pine excelled, for they required balance, harmony and a mind free of distractions.

Next came the races, and these, inevitably, Firecrackers won. Whether sprinting toward the bridge or jumping up and down steps or leaping from stone to stone across water, she always stood at the goal to welcome her rivals.

Tests of stamina were Steel Hope's favorites. Long after the others lay breathless and immobile, he went on with more sit-ups and chin-ups, more climbing and carrying.

But if Mountain Pine was the champion of control and Firecrackers of agility and Steel Hope of will, as the weeks went by, all three brothers of the Middle Heart became stronger, and their spirits more resolute.

And after each session of self-strengthening, while the sun eased down between the hilltops, they lolled about like lazy dragons, eating leftovers from the House of Li.

Sometimes Mountain Pine recited poems.

> You rode a yellow horse
> I rode a white one
> Horses, two colors
> but our boyish hearts were one.

Sometimes he told stories. Steel Hope fancied those in which generals led men into battle. Firecrackers favored those in which a stranger suddenly appeared, to alter fate. And Mountain Pine told many of these. But he himself favored morality tales, in particular the one about the phoenix that alighted in the garden of a prince. So charmed was the nobleman by his visitor that he called for artisans to build it the finest cage and his secretaries to prepare a banquet of welcome. Dignitaries by the hundreds came, wearing robes of silver and gold. Delicacies cooked by the finest chefs were served. Songs composed by the most talented musicians were played. No effort or expense was spared. All thought it was the grandest of gestures. All but the phoenix, which perished.

Steel Hope shivered as he stood at the bow of the ferry that was taking him on his annual visit to see his grandfather and wondered why the arrangements this year were different. Normally on his birthday he would be seated with his mother in the warm cabin, dreaming of how to spend the contents of the red envelope that would soon be his. Today, his father, who never took his second son anywhere, had come instead, and then insisted that they stand on the deck in the rain.

Wrestling with the umbrella, which he tried in vain to hold steady against the gusts of wind and the pitching of the boat, Steel Hope wished bandits had waylaid the messenger who changed their plans. The man had ruined his birthday. But why hadn't Stone Guardian declined his father-in-law's invitation, when in the past he'd done so as a rule? Perhaps the merchant had invited someone important. But Father knew everybody and didn't need introductions; if anyone did, it was Grandfather.

Distracted by these thoughts, Steel Hope almost lost his hold on the umbrella. Then, wiping away the rain with a sleeve, he thought he saw something in the distance. Yes, it was the wharf. Thank heaven, thank earth.

But even after everyone else had disembarked, Stone Guardian refused to budge. They were not to step ashore until the car arrived, he said. Minutes passed, and still there was no sign of the stately black Ford. Perhaps, Steel Hope thought, Grandfather didn't permit his most precious possession to be driven in the rain.

Finally, as the ferry crew was making ready to haul in the gangplank for the return trip, a mule-drawn delivery wagon with "Prosperity Emporium" painted on its sides meandered into view. The driver, huddled under a canopy, pulled to a halt, then glanced their way. So he'd been right; the car hadn't been allowed out. Steel Hope looked expectantly at Stone Guardian, who stood as still as the marble lions that flanked the gates of the House of Li. The ferry's whistle screeched. "Father, please," Steel Hope begged. Only then did the Patriarch move, marching straight into the downpour.

By the time Steel Hope caught up, Stone Guardian was already seated in the wagon—alone. Where was Grandfather? Could it be that the store was no longer prospering and the merchant, having sold the Ford and let the help go, had had to stay behind? But if that was so . . . would the red envelope for his grandson's birthday still be forthcoming?

Rainwater from Stone Guardian's robe dripped onto the floor of the wagon, making a sound as unpredictable and as irritating as a hiccup. Stone Guardian, though, revealed no discomfort. He sat straight, on his face an expression that recalled one Steel Hope had seen pictured in a book. It was the expression of a prisoner facing execution, willing himself not to flinch when the bullets pierced his heart. But that notion was ridiculous. Grandfather, a man of uncertain ancestry, treasured every hair on the head of the Patriarch of the ancient House of Li and, to the dismay of all the clansmen, delighted in introducing himself as Stone Guardian's father-in-law.

When the wagon stopped, Steel Hope hastened to unlatch the doors and, expecting to see his grandfather smiling beneath the neon sign that flashed above the open storefront, waved at a figure in the shadows. As soon as he had done this, however, he realized that the figure was only a life-size doll dressed up to look like a man. The sight so intrigued him that he didn't notice that his father had once again marched through the rain and was now well inside the store. Steel Hope ran after him, but as he passed the shutter doors, now folded open, he paused again to inspect the doll. It wore a black Western suit, wire spectacles with real glass, brown leather shoes, and a Panama hat like Grand Hope's. He was about to raise a trouser cuff to see if it was fitted with socks as well when he heard a voice greeting his father and snapped to attention. The head clerk had come from behind one of the six counters that ran the length of the store to bar Stone Guardian's way to the proprietor's office. "Good afternoon, Mr. Li," he said, tipping his Panama hat.

At least, Steel Hope thought, Grand Hope had the sense not to wear *his* hat indoors.

"Venerable Proprietor begs your understanding," the clerk was saying. "He has urgent business. He asks that you sit here and enjoy some tea." He gestured toward a square wooden table that was set just inside the store's entrance, barely out of the rain.

Steel Hope was certain his father would turn on his heel and leave. Not to be properly received after so long a trip, when only a door separated relatives, was unpardonable. Even strangers with nothing to recommend them but the calling card of a long-forgotten acquaintance were made welcome at the House of Li. Amazingly, however, Stone Guardian sat down.

Steel Hope felt doubly humiliated; both his elders had lost face. But what could he do except pretend that nothing had happened? So he took a seat as well and, noting the plate of stale cakes on the table, recalled the twelve-course feasts he and his mother had enjoyed on previous trips. Even imminent bankruptcy wouldn't excuse such uninviting fare, and Steel Hope saw no evidence of that. Indeed, he was certain that since last year the store's ceilings had been raised and the walls pushed back to make it bigger. True, at the moment there were hardly any shoppers, but the storm had probably kept them away; the few women trying on jewelry and fingering bolts of wool had their chauffeurs in tow. And there were more clerks than ever. They stood in clusters and whispered, their sidelong glances attesting to the fact that the merchant's rebuff to his wellborn son-in-law had removed any inhibitions they might have had about savoring the distress of their superiors.

At last the office door opened and the merchant emerged. He was wearing a shiny black suit and sported a polka-dot bow tie. In his hand was a fistful of papers, which he proceeded to deal out to the clerks, who trailed after him like a gaggle of goslings.

Steel Hope jumped to his feet. "Good day, Grandfather," he said, bowing. "Mother sends good wishes."

Without a nod to Stone Guardian, who was also standing, the merchant patted his grandson on the head. "Tell her I'm doing fine. Beautifully, in fact. Not just here, but in my other ventures as well."

"Other ventures?"

"Hasn't Grand Hope told you?"

Steel Hope shook his head. Though the two brothers saw each other every day, they hadn't spoken to each other for the last month; not since he accused Grand Hope of kowtowing to the Japanese and Grand Hope accused him of worshiping backwardness.

"Transport, real estate." The merchant spoke loudly. "The bankers squabble among themselves over the chance to finance my every whim. There's even talk of putting me in charge of a most profitable export-and-import business." He probed an ear with his pinkie, whose nail had been grown and shaped for the purpose. "But enough about me. What about you?"

As he answered his grandfather's queries, Steel Hope became increasingly anxious. The merchant had yet to acknowledge his son-in-law. Repeatedly he glanced from elder to elder, until Stone Guardian took his seat again. At last, seeking a way to bridge the distance between the two men, he blurted out, "Grandfather, please sit and let me serve you tea."

The merchant burst into laughter. Steel Hope was puzzled. What was so funny about offering to pour tea?

"By all means, serve the tea," said the merchant, still not looking at Stone Guardian. "It soothes the throat quite nicely when there is pleading for money to be done. Ask your father—better yet, your brother—to teach you about such things."

Steel Hope was more puzzled than ever. As far as he knew, Grand Hope had never set foot in the store.

"Grandson," the old man said, still chuckling, "you're going to make a fine merchant someday." He glanced at his clerks. "Isn't that so?"

In chorus, they replied, "A fine merchant, Venerable Proprietor."

What were they talking about? A merchant was the last thing he would be. For a son of the House of Li, Jade had far grander plans.

"Yes indeed," the merchant went on. "How very, very gratifying it is to have a relative at last who instinctively understands the cardinal rule of commerce: that favors pave the way to success. . . ." Throwing up his arms dramatically, he sighed and addressed the head clerk in particular. "How utterly stupid are those who refuse the simple requests of their benefactors. How much more stupid it is to expect those benefactors to treat them as kindly as before. . . ."

The boy blushed for his grandfather, who didn't have the good manners not to lecture even a gosling in public, especially when the reprimand was gratuitous. This head clerk would sooner rob his ancestors' graves than displease his boss.

For the first time since he had emerged from his office, the merchant looked at Stone Guardian. "Well, perhaps someday such people will realize that nothing stays the same, that those who succeed are those who change with the times. . . ."

Steel Hope no longer felt so superior. Could it be that the lecture was not meant for the head clerk after all?

"Even emperors sitting on the dragon throne were not above granting favors. Even the dumbest donkey knows not to kick the man who feeds it. . . ."

Why didn't his father say something? Wasn't he listening?

"But then, I'm always surprised at how many snobs there are in this world, aren't you, Steel Hope?"

He was caught off guard.

Pinching his grandson's cheek, the merchant repeated the question.

"I . . . I'm not . . . no, I mean . . ." Steel Hope mumbled. Then, seeing the smirk on the head clerk's face, he said defiantly, "I don't know so many snobs."

"Perhaps you should study the people around you. Some of the oldest and most respectable of clans live off the generosity of relations. No doubt it's part of a grand tradition. . . ."

Steel Hope stole a glance at Stone Guardian, who was fixed in that same prisoner's pose. Was the merchant talking about the House of Li? Until that moment, Steel Hope had given little thought to how his father managed the clan's expenses. He knew that there were economies and that several courts had been sold to Watermelon Wu and that the excitement of the venture into silk had not lasted long; but no one within the walls of the compound, including the talkative gatekeeper, had ever gossiped to him about money. It was not done.

A flush of shame surged through him now, as his grandfather actually began to tout his own cleverness in one transaction after another. Didn't the merchant understand how uncivilized it was to boast?

Had he spoken this last thought aloud? he wondered. His grandfather was now speaking of breeding. "I fear I lack it. I fear I can't pretend that money isn't important, that it falls from the heavens without ever having passed through other people's hands. If the money is good, what difference does it make who has touched it before? Right, Steel Hope?"

Why ask me? Steel Hope wanted to say, but he refrained, remembering how he had longed for his red envelope.

Again Grandfather seemed to read his mind. "I bet you don't care who has fingered your birthday money, do you?"

Steel Hope smiled weakly.

The merchant tapped his teacup, which the boy had yet to fill, then went on. "I'm in business. I'm not particular about who I do it with. What's the difference so long as the money is good?"

Stone Guardian finally spoke up. "Whom you do it with, I presume, includes the Japanese."

Unperturbed by this accusation, the merchant merely stuck his pinkie in his ear again and shrugged. "Why not? Their money's good. Besides, they've cornered so many markets nowadays that there's no avoiding them. Like it or not, my business is to stay in business, and unfortunately I don't have helpful relatives. With, of course, one outstanding exception— a young man with grand hopes who has his eyes on the future. Don't you agree, my daughter's husband?"

The insolent clerk snickered, then twirled his Panama hat on a finger the way Grand Hope did, and suddenly Steel Hope wanted to grab his father's hand, to beg him to explain away what he now knew in his heart to be true: that Grandfather's good fortune had something to do with the Japanese—that Grand Hope, his father's beloved son, was involved with China's enemy as well—that Stone Guardian had answered the old man's summons because he needed money and had no other choice—that by the presence of the Patriarch here every member of the House of Li was dishonored.

Father, tell me I'm wrong, he wanted to cry out. But how could he? He looked away.

Stone Guardian ignored his father-in-law's question, staring out at the rain as if everything depended on making an accurate accounting of the drops.

The merchant snapped his fingers. At once the head clerk came bowing. "Fetch the box that my new assistant, Grand Hope, brought back from Shanghai yesterday."

To keep from crying, Steel Hope fixed his eyes on the clerk, who dashed into the office and then, lugging a small chest, slowly made his way back. The chest was no bigger than a footstool, but the beads of sweat oozing from the clerk's forehead attested to its weight. Steel Hope was certain it contained gold.

Minutes passed. The merchant took his time removing the key from his watch chain, took his time unlocking the brass padlock and even more opening the box and removing from it the red envelope that always before had been the sole purpose of Steel Hope's journey.

But this envelope couldn't be for him. It was too thick. And indeed, before he could reach for it, the merchant tossed it at Stone Guardian, as he would toss coppers into a begging bowl. When it landed, in Stone Guardian's lap, it burst open.

"No!" Steel Hope cried. Then, quicker than thought, he scooped up the bills and held them aloft. "Thank you, Grandfather!" he shouted. "Thank you for my birthday gift!"

I T W A S still raining. Once more the deck of the ferry was empty except for Stone Guardian and Steel Hope. Once more the father stood in silence, his eyes fixed on something he alone could see.

They were well out into the river when a huge transport flying the Rising Sun suddenly loomed ahead, steaming toward them as if bent on ramming the ferry. At the last moment it veered away, to leave the smaller craft tossing like a wood chip in its wake.

Gripping the rail with both hands, Stone Guardian shouted, "Brown Dwarfs, die and go to hell!"

Suddenly Steel Hope's eyes filled with tears. Through their veil, he saw his father as he had been only a few weeks before, standing among the graves, recounting the history of their ancestors. When, on some future Day of Pure Brightness, the clan gathered to sweep Stone Guardian's grave, what glories would be recounted then? That the Patriarch had stood at attention when the Imperial Flag was lowered, yielding to the Rising Sun? That he had sat in silence while a mere tradesman insulted the House of Li? That he had doted on a son who allied himself with his father's enemy?

Sobbing, Steel Hope let go of the umbrella. It grazed Stone Guardian's back. The Patriarch swung around. His hand flew up. "How dare you cry!" he shouted as the blow fell. "How dare you pity me!"

The Full Moon

FIRECRACKERS SPLASHED the last of the water over the
scallions, then lifted her gaze heavenward. Once she could have traced
the moon's inhabitants with a finger pointed at the sky, so clearly did
she see them silhouetted there—the cassia tree and, beneath its boughs,
the hare, working the pestle and mortar with which it compounded the
elixir of immortality. But since that night of the full moon when the gods
took her mother in her place, all she had seen were smudges that tarnished
the glow. Lately its appearance seemed to change ever faster. So, day to
day, did hers. And no matter how good and diligent the worker, how
loyal and amusing the friend, a girl would never do.

With each new face, the moon seemed to ask, How much longer
can Firecrackers be who she chooses to be? Bowing her head, she prayed,
as she did every night, to the Goddess of Mercy, Kwan Yin, to be able
to keep for a while longer a figure that was as straight as bamboo.

Had Steel Hope also been wondering, How much longer? Was that
why he'd been so moody? Though the sun shone, the day after his birthday
he'd refused to budge from the hut or tell her and Mountain Pine what
the matter was. He'd just sat in a corner hugging his knees, and no
amount of pleading, coaxing or cajoling had helped. Mountain Pine had

told her to save her breath, adding, "Young masters are like buffalos, born difficult."

Then, when she licked a finger to remove a spot of dirt from his black leather shoes, Steel Hope had shoved her away. She hadn't minded, but Mountain Pine had. "Is that your good deed for the day?" he asked.

What happened next was awful. The young master took off one shoe and shied it at her, then the other, but twice she ducked and twice he missed the mark. "Put them on. Your feet stink up the place!" he said then and, holding his nose, stomped out of the hut. If Mountain Pine hadn't assured her that the next time they met, Steel Hope would act as if none of this had taken place, she would never have stopped weeping.

As it happened, the young master had actually apologized to her, and for some reason this made her sad. And now, looking at the moon, she wondered if the reason he had acted so strangely was to anger her enough so that the fake boy would leave the Middle Heart before the good-hearted young master was forced to end their friendship.

*

THE ONLY distinguishing feature of the Teahouse of the Mongol's Boots was its name. And even that was seldom appreciated by those who frequented the place, for only scholars familiar with Lu Yu's classic *The Book of Tea* would recognize the allusion. The peddlers and petty merchants who were regular customers simply called it Old Yang's, and the vagabonds who rested at its five rickety tables before continuing their search for an army to serve never bothered to call it by any name at all.

Today was Market Day in another part of town, and only one table was taken—by the uncles of the owner's late wife, who presumed on family ties and played mah-jongg while drinking for free. Old Yang never complained. Firecrackers grumbled under her breath. They were not her relations, and all they ever left for her was deposits in the honeypot.

When three real customers finally came through the door, however, they were not the sort Old Yang cared to have about. Unshaven, filthy and reeking of themselves, the strangers carried rifles slung across their backs.

"Quick, quick, the stove," shouted Old Yang, and then, whispering, informed her that they were bandits.

She felt a thrill of fear. Bandits terrorized the countryside, robbing travelers and then vanishing into the sorghum fields; if caught, they spent a night or two in jail, until their brothers could bribe the guards to set them free. As she tossed kindling onto the fire she couldn't take her eyes off them.

"Hey, where's our tea?" shouted the biggest bandit, banging the table. "We've waited long enough to plant and harvest a crop."

"Right away, right away." She pumped the bellows faster.

While the bandits drank she swept the floor nearby, hoping to hear a story to tell the others. They said nothing, however, merely blowing noisily into their steaming cups and slurping until they were empty.

"More tea?"

The bandits laughed.

"You call this tea?" said the big one, who seemed to be the leader. "Jail juice was better." Without warning, he grabbed her arm. "Boy, give us a dance or a song! Getting out of jail calls for a celebration."

Firecrackers looked around for help, but the relations had stitched their eyeballs to their mah-jongg tiles, and Old Yang nodded, urging her to obey. If there was one person she mustn't offend, it was he. She would sing. She didn't know how to dance. Clearing her throat, she sang the only song she knew.

Even before the end of the first line, the big bandit was pounding on the table. "Boy, you must ache to join your ancestors," he shouted. "First that filthy drink. Now this."

The others had covered their ears.

She didn't understand. She had a good voice. They must not care for the song. "I don't know any other tunes," she said.

"You and that ape's abortion in the next cell. All night, he sang it over and over and over."

Suddenly, she knew fear. The song was her mother's. No one was left in this world to sing it except her father and herself. What had happened to him? Yes, his cot hadn't been slept in, but on hot nights the river often called the sleepless agent boater to its shores. Had he caught a spell there? "Please, sir . . ." she cried, tugging urgently at the head bandit's shirt. "You must tell me. What did the singer look like? Was he tall and a little bald?"

Rather than giving her the blow she half expected, the bandit only stared at her, on his face a look poised uneasily between anger and astonishment.

"Please, tell me. You've got to tell me. Was the singer tall and—?"

The man's stare squeezed into a squint. "The boy's loony," he said.

"Let's go," said one of his companions. "You know I can't stand loonies. They remind me of home."

The head bandit tried to pry loose her fingers, but no sooner had he freed one than the others gripped even harder. His friends hooted, calling him no match for a girl, and suddenly she feared for her life. What if they guessed the truth? But she had to know. "Was the singer—?"

The bandit opened his mouth wide, bared his teeth and bit her hand. Still she wouldn't let go.

He flung her to the floor, along with some coins for Old Yang. Before she could get to her feet, they were gone. Before Old Yang could stop her, she had followed them out the door.

Someone called her name. She turned to see Steel Hope and Mountain Pine waiting for her across the street.

"Help me!" she yelled, and bolted down the alley toward the jail, toward the river flashing in the distance, slick and glinting, as if the angry gods had dashed a giant oil lamp to the ground. She didn't have to look behind her. Steel Hope's moods these days might be uncertain, but he would never hesitate to come to her rescue. Firecrackers ran faster than she had ever run, yet the sensation she had was not that of racing; her feet belonged to someone else, they were much too big and heavy. The road was a slippery sewer of mud. Why was there no air?

She stopped to catch her breath.

"What's happened? What's going on?" Steel Hope had caught up.

Unable to speak, she raced on.

Within view of the jail, however, some force suddenly held her back, slowing her down as if, despite her effort, she didn't want to reach her destination. She remembered. She had been here before. No, not here, farther downriver, but a place like this one, two-storied and brick, belted with a double row of windows—no, not windows, slits, each no wider than a palm. Inside there was a long, narrow table. It was made of enamel and gleamed like frost. On it lay a boy her size. His eyes were closed. From somewhere down the hall came the sound of footsteps, stiff leather shoes.

Firecrackers shook her head, dislodging the memory. The image vanished but not the footsteps, coming closer. Glancing to her right, she saw a work gang advancing from the docks. She went on.

As she started through the gate, a hand grabbed her. It belonged to a guard. "Hey! You can't go in."

Then Steel Hope was there. Pulling her free, he lost his balance and they tumbled to the ground.

The guard spat. "Out of my sight before I break your scrawny necks."

Firecrackers scrambled up. "Please, sir, let me in. I'm looking for my father."

"Why here? Is your father a thief?"

"Oh no, sir." Still panting, she said whatever came into her mind. "My father used to be an agent boater. People trusted him. They pitched their coins onto our deck as we sailed by. They trusted—"

"Why isn't he an agent boater anymore?"

"He began to forget things. . . ."

"Other people's things?"

"No! He was sick. He couldn't remember."

"What thief doesn't have a bushel of excuses?" The man held out a hand. "You want in?"

For a moment, she didn't understand. When she realized he wanted money, she looked to Steel Hope, who dug in his pockets. He shook his head, then ran to meet Mountain Pine, who had only now reached the jailhouse square. But Mountain Pine's pockets were empty too.

Firecrackers wiped her eyes.

Steel Hope looked toward the guard, who was now sharing a cigarette and chatting with the work gang's armed escort, and saw their chance. He signaled. Firecrackers and Mountain Pine nodded. So did the prisoners, who immediately closed ranks so the three could sneak unnoticed through the gate.

Something drew Firecrackers down the hall to an open door. The room beyond was empty except for a few chairs. She went to the window. It looked out on the inner courtyard. By the far wall, her father sat in the dirt. His neck and arms were locked in a wooden stock. His head hung down like a peony on a broken stem.

She scrambled through the window and ran, calling, "Father! Father!" He didn't look up. She threw her arms about him. Then she screamed.

T HAT NIGHT Steel Hope tossed in his bed. Never had he felt so unlike a hero. He had been detained at the jail while Firecrackers accompanied her father's body to the paupers' graveyard and Mountain Pine was sent to fetch Stone Guardian. He had been grilled by the guards and rebuked by the warden for insolence, for brawling, for accusing them all of murder, when it was obvious that the gravekeeper's heart had given out. He had been caned hard by Stone Guardian, then a second time when he tried to prevent the Patriarch from caning Mountain Pine. His mother's pleas had compounded his father's fury. It was only after Amber Willows fell to her knees before the Patriarch, her arms hanging helplessly, her eyes raised to meet his, that Stone Guardian had flung the stick across the room and turned on his heels.

While others wailed, Steel Hope hadn't shed a tear. Now he wept. Why had the gravekeeper found the pin he had intended as a gift for Firecrackers and tried to sell it? He had meant to help his friend, not make her an orphan.

He could still hear her weeping for her father, just as he had heard the sound of her anguish for hours on the day when he threw his shoes at her. It had followed him everywhere, until the remorse that had lighted on his shoulders weighed like a boulder, and the cobblestones that cut ever deeper into his bare feet had forced him home. There he had found his birthday shoes inside the door and a note from Mountain Pine: *Only you fit your shoes, only you can make amends.*

He had burned with shame and thought for a long time, recalling how he felt when he was wronged, recalling as well how Amber Willows, who was always there to wipe away his tears when he was a child, would distract him from his troubles with a toy. Finally he knew what he must do. He must give Firecrackers a present. But where would he get the money to buy it? Stone Guardian had his red envelope. Stealing money was too risky. Stealing something that nobody would miss was not, however, and his mother had more pieces of kingfisher jewelry than she could count.

He banged his fist on the headboard. Why hadn't he pawned the pin himself and given Firecrackers the money? Why did he have to hide it in the jar of cockleburs?

He was afraid to close his eyes. Each time he tried to sleep he saw Firecrackers hugging the dead man and crying, over and over, "My father is not a thief. My father is not a thief. . . ."

He could have explained away the undeniable evidence then, but had said nothing. And later, during the police interrogation, a part of him had wanted to confess, but he had kept silent. The truth, he decided, wouldn't bring the gravekeeper back. At best, it would produce a tiny notice posted on some government building attesting to the honesty of a dead man nobody but his daughter cared about. Besides, Firecrackers was alive and needed a friend, not a pea-brained princeling who, however unintentionally, had caused her father's death.

Over and over he told himself that he had made the right choice in keeping silent. And yet . . . now he wondered. Could it be that his father had somehow known all along that his second son was unworthy and, being unworthy, didn't deserve his affections?

THE NEXT MORNING Stone Guardian ordered Mountain Pine to go and evict Firecrackers from the gravekeeper's hut. Despite the risk of angering the Patriarch irrevocably, the servant took Steel Hope along to bid their friend a proper farewell.

Silently, they watched her put on, over her own jacket and pants, all the clothing the gravekeeper had left. When that was done, she went about the hut gathering objects—a chipped bowl, a toy yaolu made of matchsticks, a tattered quilt. These she placed in a small basket, more oval than round, the kind farmers used to carry eggs. They had brought her some food and a little money and a pair of new shoes Amber Willows had sewn for herself but gladly gave to Steel Hope. The food Firecrackers insisted on sharing as usual. The coins she pocketed. The shoes, with a strap across the arch, were too good for walking, Firecrackers said, and she set them on her cot to admire until the last moment.

Silently, they watched her dust, then sweep. The broom made a scratching sound and left a trail on the dirt floor.

At first Steel Hope thought he was imagining the song, so softly was it being sung. Phrase by phrase her voice grew stronger, never faltering, until, after a while, it pushed back the walls and filled the room with music, all the more poignant because each note was colored with despair.

Then, facing the door with her palms held together above her head, she cried out in an unearthly voice keen with longing that, though Steel Hope had never heard it before, he knew. The older servants had told him many times how they had heard it coming from the Patriarch's chamber after the death of his first wife. The husband had been praying aloud then, as the daughter was praying now, for one last visit with the most beloved, which people believed was allowed. But no matter how fervently and how long Firecrackers prayed, the ghost of the gravekeeper refused to return to the hut. And as her voice grew faint, Steel Hope wondered if it was his presence that caused the agent boater to stay away, for he had heard that after three days and three nights in seclusion, Stone Guardian had emerged clutching a piece of blue silk torn from his wife's burial robes.

At last, with her voice barely a whisper, Firecrackers went limp, as if her spirit had left her to go in search of the gravekeeper.

As minutes passed, Steel Hope grew more and more anxious. Was she ever coming back? He looked to Mountain Pine for a sign, and his bookmate nodded imperceptibly and mouthed the familiar words "Patience, Young Master, patience."

Finally she stiffened as if jabbed by a pin, then moved past them, groping like a sleepwalker. From behind the stove, she retrieved an old newspaper and a piece of burnt kindling. She smoothed out the paper and, handing Mountain Pine the kindling, asked him to write for her.

"What shall I write?"

" 'Small Village by Big River.' Baby Wang lives there."

"Who's Baby Wang?" Steel Hope asked.

"He's the one I'm promised to."

"You are?"

Her shoulders began to shake uncontrollably. Steel Hope took hold of her arm. Staring down at his hand, she spoke without inflection, as if her voice belonged to someone else. "One day, not long before we came here, Father and I stopped to beg at a peasant's home. When the man went to get us something to eat, he handed me the screaming baby he was carrying. When he returned with two corn buns, the baby was asleep. The peasant said the baby's mother had died. He didn't want to marry again, and he didn't have any money to hire an amah. If he was going to tend his fields, he'd have to find a wife for his motherless child. I would do. He promised my father that I would have a good home and would never go hungry. My father agreed to the match. He said a daughter would have to be married sooner or later, and with no dowry I couldn't expect to do better. I said I'd run away. That's when the baby started screaming again, and I did too, even louder. Finally Father took me with him, but the farmer said that if things didn't work out, I could still return and marry Baby Wang."

Steel Hope tilted his head back to keep from spilling a tear of his own. Was it worse to be married off by a destitute father or to be nothing to a father?

When Mountain Pine had written the name of the town, Firecrackers studied the characters, as if making certain that each stroke was correct. Then she placed the yellowed paper on the stove and knelt.

She was so still for so long that by the time she struck the flint, the motion was startling. Finally the flint sparked, and she lit the paper. As it burned, she cried hoarsely, "O my father! O my mother! O my brother! Do not leave me alone in this world. Please, please follow me to this place."

Steel Hope couldn't bear to see her grief and retreated outside. Was the shame his father had felt on the ferry equal to the shame he felt now? The helplessness too? Was this what it was like to be a man? He scooped up a handful of pebbles and hurled them with all his might, one after another, into the air. If only he could throw one far enough to reach the heavens and wake the sleeping gods, then surely they would show compassion and make things right again.

Driven by that notion, he continued to scoop and hurl, and the stones flew up and fell to the ground around him, until one struck him on the head.

He touched the wound. The gods were no longer asleep. They were angry at him. With good reason. He deserved punishment. He resumed throwing the stones, higher and higher, until, doubled over from the exertion, he sensed that Mountain Pine and Firecrackers were standing at the door watching him. Quickly he wiped his face. No one must mistake his sweat for tears.

He went to join them and for what seemed a long time they stood shoulder to shoulder like Liu Pei, Kuan Yu, and Zhang Fei, as if the three sworn brothers of the Middle Heart were about to march off again adventuring. But their days together were over. There was nothing to say and nowhere they dared look except down at the row of scallions. Eventually, Firecrackers went inside and returned with her basket. The toes of her new shoes, tucked safe in the layers of her clothing, peeked out between the buttons of her jacket. With a shake of her head she refused their company and walked away, leaving only the prints of her bare feet in the path.

THAT NIGHT, afraid of nightmares, Steel Hope circled the rock garden as wearily as a yoked animal, until the overpowering need for his bookmate drew him toward the servants' quarters. They were just a short stroll away from the Patriarch's compound, but he had never been there before. While other members of the Li family, including Grand Hope, occasionally visited the retainers, his mother, not caring who heard, had strictly forbidden her husband and her son to set foot beyond the kitchen walk. "Lis are Lis, servants servants," she said. "Dragons have no place in sparrows' nests."

Once in the back compound, he realized he didn't know which door opened into Mountain Pine's room, and proceeded to the nearest window. It was shut. He licked his finger and wet the rice paper so that he could see through it. There were two shadows, one large, the other slender, tossing and turning in the bed. Or was it struggling? He couldn't be certain until he heard Amber Willows whimper helplessly, "No— please, no—you mustn't."

Was her attacker a thief? A murderer? What difference did it make? He must rescue his beloved amah.

He burst inside—and froze. Crouched on the bed, half-naked, his trousers bunched at the ankles, was the Patriarch of the House of Li.

With an inchoate shout of rage, Stone Guardian pushed himself upright, exposing as he did a disheveled Amber Willows, who immediately rolled out of view onto the floor. He staggered toward his son. He was drunk. "You bastard, I'll have your life. I gave you life and I'll take it back, take everything back . . . everything. . . ." He swung at Steel Hope and missed, then fell at his feet.

Steel Hope wanted to run away, run as fast as he could and never come back, but not a muscle in his body would move.

Silently the Patriarch struggled to his feet, then straightened himself to his full height before negotiating the three steps to the threshold, where suddenly he retched. As the stench of vomit filled the room, he closed the door behind him, so gently, so carefully that it was almost as if he knew the wood was not wood, but the thinnest glass.

Steel Hope found himself drifting backwards and, without thinking, he started to sit down on Amber Willows' bed, but at the feel of the warm sheets he recoiled and, gasping for air, lurched toward the window. It was still shut. Unlatching it was beyond his powers. His legs buckled and he braced his back against the wall.

How could his father have imposed himself on her? How could such a man be the Patriarch of the House of Li? No one must ever know. No one! The weight of yet another secret broke him and he sank to the floor.

". . . don't hate him." She must have been speaking for some time.

"What?"

"Don't hate him. He's not a bad man, just an unhappy one."

"Who?"

"Your father."

"What are you to him?"

She made no reply, but stretched her arms out to him, and for a moment he was again the child who feared the dark and she the loving amah who kept watch. He longed to go to her, to be a child again, frightened only of phantoms that vanished with the dawn. But he could not.

He asked once more, louder, "What are you to him?"

This time she answered. "Nothing. Can't you see? His only wish is to die."

"I don't believe you."

"You must."

*

JADE THREATENED to kill herself unless her son remained by her side. But when Steel Hope threatened to do likewise unless he was permitted to attend the Yong Kuang boarding school in Nanjing, she relented, and secured a teaching position for Mountain Pine at the Christian Mission for Orphans in the same city, so that the servant could continue to keep an eye on his young master.

Upon his arrival at the school, Steel Hope found among his belongings a parcel tied with silk. It contained a red envelope filled with money from his mother; an apple, whose homonym is peace, from Amber Willows; and a letter from Stone Guardian that read:

Son,

Ministers may admonish the Emperor but never desert him.
For by virtue of his station, the sovereign commands
unswerving loyalty. If Chinese had served only those who
were pure and just and true of heart, the Middle Kingdom
would not have endured.

May we live in harmony,
FATHER

PART TWO

DESTINY

SUMMER WISHES

(1939)

Y EARS AFTER the gravekeeper died, Firecrackers would often
wake and for a moment think her family together again aboard the yaolu.
Side by side just beyond reach they would stand, silent and expressionless—
three spare figures browned by the sun and swathed in shrouds of white
hemp. Sometimes they were caked with dust, as after a hard journey;
sometimes their skin glistened, as after a swim. In the beginning she had
feared they came to reproach an unfilial daughter for neglecting their graves,
but as time passed, she realized they were there to signal their arrival at the
port of call into which she herself had just sailed, and she would smile. And
though, always, the deck of the boat would pitch, her kinsmen never stumbled, sustaining dignity by gracefully floating upwards in a perfect row.
Always she studied their toes. They were familiar, long and tapered, like
her own.

At the first sign that another passenger aboard the vessel was waking,
they would vanish. Only the boat itself was real—not a yaolu, but a junk
called the *Pavilion of Fairies* that plied the Yangzi as her childhood home
had done, though it peddled entertainment rather than goods. Firecrackers
had been an apprentice of the *Pavilion*'s Xiaoxing Opera Troupe ever
since the day when, on the road from Wen Shui to the village of Baby
Wang, she had encountered the giant of a woman named Mushroom,

who had persuaded her to audition. Big Boss had approved of her voice but little else. Her name, in particular, would not do, and as a first step toward the goal of transforming the filthy urchin into a beautiful actress, he had decreed that henceforth she would be Summer Wishes. That had been seven years ago, and now she was Firecrackers rarely, even to herself, but still she rebelled against calling the *Pavilion of Fairies* her home.

As she did every morning when the junk was in port, Summer Wishes rose in the dark. Seated on the edge of her bed, she rubbed her aching body; it had grown, but the four-foot plank set catty corner in the bow that she had slept on since she joined the troupe had not. Carefully she pulled her dress from beneath the straw pallet and stepped into it. Then, carrying her shoes and mindful of those sleeping on the floor, she tiptoed around Mushroom and the fourteen other actresses in the big cabin that served as both bedroom and rehearsal hall and climbed the steps leading to the deck, where she dipped her hand in a bucket of rainwater and splashed her face. Then in the wan light before dawn she crept down the gangplank and set off for the pine grove at the summit of the hill that sheltered the village.

The air was still cool, and tendrils of violet streaked the sky. Where the road veered toward the fields, she slipped off her shoes and, hitching up her skirt, stepped into the meadow. Its dewy grass tickled her bare feet, and suddenly she was running, loping up the hill as if she were her twin again, dashing ahead, then stopping to discern if anyone was following, like a deer that has just escaped from its pen. An occasional bird took flight, and two scrawny goats bristled as she passed, but she saw no other creatures. She was safe. She was free. Free to romp, to strut like Big Boss, to let her long hair fly like the tail of a kite, to slouch like that hunchback at the fairgrounds in last week's village who couldn't lie flat and so slept upright.

She was even tempted to cross her eyes. But what if "Once crossed, always crossed" was true? Then all those hours she'd spent rolling, narrowing, widening her eyes; staring at the lighted tip of an incense stick, looking over it, under it, to each side of it, would have been wasted.

Hungry, she conjured up a hot bowl of millet to sustain her on the climb, thick as dough and salted by crunchy turnips. Even better, how about a duck egg with two lucky yolks, fried in the finest pepper oil; or a ham hock stewed overnight until it melted in the mouth like tofu? Her stomach moaned: not even a sip of water would pass her lips for hours. She had work to do.

At the summit, where veils of fog were caught in the branches of the trees, she put on her shoes and plaited her hair, using a blade of grass to tie up the end of the braid. Then, standing as still as the pines that towered overhead, she banished Firecrackers and, with slow and evenly timed deep breaths, summoned to attention every particle of the actress Summer Wishes.

Though Big Boss ordered his girls to strengthen their voices by vocalizing at full volume facing a wall, a river or the wind, Mushroom recommended singing amid dawn's dewy vapors, and despite the inevitable quarrels with the man who employed them both, Summer Wishes obeyed the woman who had befriended her so long ago.

Lifting her gaze, she began to sing. The songs were arias she had copied from the performances of others. All the girls copied. How else could they memorize the lines or understand the story, when none of them could read? Imitating others who sang and danced had come so naturally to Firecrackers that at first she had assumed doing so was no different from speaking or walking, abilities shared by all. Now she took pains to hide the ease with which she mastered her roles, for actresses were more jealous than the gods and more superstitious than widows. She must be a fox spirit, they would say, watching her. Only a demon could mimic another as quickly and as truly as an echo.

Big Boss, on the other hand, accused her of being an ingrate. In return for providing them with scanty meals and a place to curl up for the night, he expected the girls in his troupe to obey his every command with a smile. But Summer Wishes seldom obeyed, and never smiled. Had it not been for Mushroom, who did all his work, from selling the tickets to staging the performances, while he took his ease, the slothful miser would have booted the apprentice out. Still, he refused to cast her in the best parts, putting her on stage as a last-minute fill-in or, worse, dispatching her with the girls willing to perform at private parties where men expected sexual favors. But because Mushroom was always at hand and bigger than the sons of turtles and didn't give a damn whom she walloped on the nose or in the nuts, Summer Wishes continued to escape with her virtue.

As the hour passed and the fog lifted, she noticed that the older woman was sitting on a nearby rock. Her face beamed with approval of the protégée whose talent she deemed equal to the ambitions that had ruled Mushroom ever since her father sold his bulky sixth daughter to the father of Big Boss for a few bags of rice. Now, without a word of greeting, she sidled into a dance, holding a bough aloft as lightly as if it were one of the tasseled switches that in operas signified a horse. Her movements were at once artistic and absurd. Extravagant whimsy, she had long ago decided, diverted attention from nature's flaws.

In a moment Summer Wishes had joined in the impromptu parody—juxtaposing to the verses Mushroom sang snippets of arias from the most unlikely of roles. Then, as if they had crossed a magic threshold, the two began to sing in earnest, a passage from *Longing for the Joys of the Laity*.

> I'll shed my nun's robe
> I'll bury the scriptures of Buddha
> I'll fling away the wooden fish
> I'll cast aside the cymbals . . .

And as their voices, so pure and yet so distinct, mingled, Summer Wishes could know once more that joy was more than a trick among the many tricks she had learned to display.

> Oh not for me,
> the life of a holy woman
> Oh not for me,
> the life of a Bodhisattva of the Southern Seas.

When the last of the fog had lifted the two women made their way down the hill, and then, trailed by children, dogs and the village idiot, they walked up and down the main street announcing the performances to be held later on the wharf. Mushroom beamed, waved and shouted. Summer Wishes followed within the shadow cast by her companion, never saying a word or lifting her gaze from the ground as she prayed for the taunting voices of the villagers to stop. Unfailingly the men leered, trading lewd tales of triumph over the likes of her. The women gaped and hurled insults or spat. Mushroom ignored these inevitable assaults; to her they were as natural and impersonal as thunder and lightning. Summer Wishes felt that she had no right to breathe.

When the villagers finally scattered, heading home to eat their first meal of the day, Mushroom started for the docks, but Summer Wishes, appetite gone now, chose a longer, out-of-the way route through a gully, where sheaves of rice hung from trees to dry, and her friend, as always, yielded. Ahead lay the Bridge of Womanly Virtues. Dedicated to a local widow who upon the death of her husband had never again left the women's rooms, or spoken to anyone outside the family, or touched any object ever held by a man, the marble span seemed to call to Summer Wishes today.

"What's wrong?" asked Mushroom. "Has Big Boss been after you again?"

"No more than usual."

"Then what?"

Summer Wishes shrugged.

"You're not still thinking of leaving the troupe, are you? Of refusing to sign up? I promise you, the worst is over. Now that you're a trained actress and no longer an apprentice, Big Boss can't get away with treating you like a barren daughter-in-law. Now he must pay you—not much, I know, but pay you nonetheless. And with coins knotted in your handkerchief you'll see how different life can be. Child, you must sign!"

Summer Wishes looked away. The seven interminable years of apprenticeship had indeed passed, but the thought of spending another seven with Big Boss, even as a paid performer, terrified her. She had changed in ways infinitely more mysterious than becoming a son to her mother. She had become a stranger to herself. After seven more years, even that stranger might be gone.

"What's going to happen to me if I stay, Elder Sister?"

Mushroom cupped the younger woman's face and spoke as if to a child—the child she had never dared hope to have. "Good things, wonderful things. You'll be famous and rich. You'll be the Beauty of the Yangzi Delta, the greatest star of Xiaoxing Opera there ever was or will be."

"I don't want to be a star." As Summer Wishes spoke these words, she wished them back, for Mushroom flinched, knifed by the one person in the world who could wound her.

"Don't speak such lies," whispered Mushroom. "Lies overheard come true. I know you. I know you want to be a star. If you didn't, why would you practice day and night, night and day . . . ?"

When she shrugged again, Mushroom grabbed her and shook her, demanding to know why, why, until Summer Wishes stammered: "S-s-so the people who insult me on the street won't laugh at me when I'm on stage too."

"I don't believe you. You work because you want to be the best. Besides, you love the opera, don't you?"

Summer Wishes didn't know the answer. To live at least part of every day in another place, another time; to wear gowns fashioned for women sheltered like prized blossoms behind high garden walls, was to lose herself in a dream, and seemed at times as vital to her well-being as food or sleep. On stage, she knew what to say and how to say it, what to do and when. She rescued parents and brothers, kingdoms and dynasties. She was praised. But what of the price she paid in humiliation and hurts, when the show was over? She searched for an answer in Mushroom's eyes. They brimmed with unshed tears.

"What could you possibly want more than to sing, my precious?"

Before she could stop herself, Summer Wishes blurted, "I want them to invite me to tea."

Mushroom hesitated, then chose to play the dolt, and let out a hoot. "Is that all? Come," she said, seizing Summer Wishes' hand. "I'll invite you to tea—green tea, black tea, jasmine tea, chrysanthemum tea, dragonwell tea. . . ."

Summer Wishes broke away. "Don't pretend you don't understand," she cried. "What mother ever allowed even her white-haired moron of a son to bring an actress home?"

For once, Mushroom was speechless.

"You see?" Summer Wishes said, and asked again, "What will happen to me if I stay?"

"Child, I can teach you to sing like a flute, dance like water, act every role from maiden to warrior, but I can't read fates."

"If only someone could."

Mushroom said no more then, but as they made their way along the footpath that edged the canal, suddenly she tittered. "Remember the seer?" she asked.

Feeling a thrill of fear, Summer Wishes nodded. She recalled all too vividly Mushroom's account of the necromancer from this village, whose magic had decided the fate of the butcher, accused of beheading his wife and her lover. "Fill this tub," the seer had commanded the villagers. "Fill it half with well water, for that which is calm and yin, and half with river water, for that which speeds along and is yang." The villagers obeyed. Then, floating the severed heads in the pot, she stirred the brew with her cane nine times and announced as the ripples began to subside, "If the heads face each another, they were adulterers and the husband should go free. Otherwise, he must lose his head as well."

The seer still lived in the village—as did the butcher. Summoning her courage, Summer Wishes said, "Please take me to her, Elder Sister."

The hut was little more than a heap of mud, but planted along the path were bamboo stakes flying banners of yellow and orange inscribed with endorsements of the seer's skill, dated and signed by grateful customers. No doubt the mud heap was a lucky one and mustn't be disturbed. As Summer Wishes and Mushroom approached, the seer appeared at the threshold to wave them in. Her features were squashed. Her complexion resembled cork. Her white hair clung like moss to her humped back, on which perched a black rooster.

Mushroom started to explain. The hag put up a finger and looked toward Summer Wishes, then disappeared into the dim interior. The two friends followed. The door shut itself.

The seer squatted on the floor and motioned for them to do the same. By the time they had done so, she was already in a trance. Summer Wishes didn't dare speak for fear of disturbing her, didn't dare look about for fear of offending her, didn't dare breathe for fear of inhaling the miasma that seemed to emanate from her and fill the room. She stared at the rooster, which stared back.

Suddenly the seer jerked as if prodded by a sword. Her lids opened. Only the whites of her eyes were visible. The pupils had disappeared.

Summer Wishes grabbed Mushroom's arm.

"I know. I know," the seer chanted.

The lids closed. There was another shudder, longer this time. Then she spoke again.

> Voice of thunder,
> life of flashes.
> Still sparkling,
> ashes, ashes.

Summer Wishes felt as if her heart were in her throat and gulped. The life of flashes must signify her own life, Firecrackers' life. But what of the ashes?

"I know. I know," the seer said again. "Do you believe? Truly believe?"

"Oh yes, yes. I believe."

"Show me your palms."

Summer Wishes wiped her hands and held them out. Mushroom placed a coin in each. Without a glance the seer pocketed them; then, carefully and silently, she studied the left hand and the right, passing an index finger along the lines. Several times she nodded. Once she frowned. Suddenly Summer Wishes wasn't so sure that she wanted her future revealed. What if death was to come tomorrow? What if she was destined to be a—

"Make fists." The seer studied the folds of the skin, then slowly unbent each finger until all were extended.

"Put them away. The answer to your question is, Go."

"Go?" Yes, that was the answer, the best answer, Summer Wishes thought, seizing the idea. But where? "Go where?" she asked, suddenly emboldened.

"To the mountains where pines grow. There you will find hope. Though poor, you will not be without friends. Though lowly, you will be

admired. But remember what I said—'Voice of thunder, life of flashes . . .'"
Her voice trailed off.

Summer Wishes wanted to probe further, but the seer had apparently
fallen asleep. Mushroom got up first, then pulled Summer Wishes to her
feet.

"But . . ."

"Come, Little Sister."

Outside, the sun was at its zenith and from far away came the cries
of children. Summer Wishes peered in the direction of the sound, hoping
for a glimpse of a barefoot boy sprinting ahead, pursued by a young master
and his bookmate, until the sounds of merriment grew so faint that she
wondered if the three of them had existed at all.

"Well?" Mushroom asked. "Well?"

Caught up in the past, Summer Wishes didn't reply. Once again she
was on her way to Baby Wang's, not knowing whether, by then, someone
else had already become his wife; hoping at the same time that it was and
was not so. The journey had taken longer by two days than she had money
or provisions for, and hungry and exhausted, she sat down by the side of
the road to rest. As she had done many times, she pulled out the shoes, still
nestled inside her shirt, to admire them. The stitching on the white soles
had been done by a hand as skilled as a foreign machine; the buttons were
round and shiny as pearls; the cloth as soft and smooth as—

"Hey, how much for the shoes?"

Looking up to see the tallest woman in the world biting into a thick,
fragrant pancake, she said, "They're not for sale, not for all I can eat in a
year."

In one quick, smooth motion the woman sat down beside her. Holding
out the pancake, she asked, "Want it? No charge. Just sing me a song."

Summer Wishes could still recall the flaky crust of that pancake and
its chewy, lightly salted center, but had no idea why she had begun confiding
her troubles to a stranger or why, despite the sadness that lodged like a
cleaver in her chest, she had gone off with her to audition for Big Boss.
Perhaps what people believed was true: Even upon meeting, strangers who
belong together sense that together they are whole.

Still, every step of the way to the *Pavilion of Fairies*, she had thought
despairingly what she now knew to be so: that an actress, however accomplished, however virtuous, was regarded as no better than the rouged women
who entertained men in the flower boats, no better than those who carved
corns from any pair of passing feet—the lowest of the low.

A Good Night

(1940)

T H E R E W A S no moon above Chongqing, only tentacles of lightning in the distant skies followed by the rumble of thunder echoing from mountain to mountain. It was a good night, a rare night. For so long as the storm cloaked the wartime capital the Japanese bombers would stay in Hankow, and no warning balloons would be hung or sirens sounded. Tonight, along the riverbanks, clusters of men and women stood silhouetted by small fires, burning spirit money for all the luckless ones condemned to wander the earth because they had been slain by the invaders and their bodies lost; all the luckless ones whose souls could not be hailed by their rightful names.

Steel Hope and Mountain Pine leaned on the rails of a jetty, watching the bits of gold and silver foil blaze and dim, and their embers, scattered by the sultry breeze, sink into the river like spent fireflies. After a long silence, Steel Hope heard his friend, the aspiring poet, recite:

> A legion of silent apparitions wait,
> wait toe to heel and arms outstretched,
> for the hand of a kinsman
> to guide them home.

Steel Hope wasn't moved by the poem, but irked, and then irked at himself for being irked. Had four years as an engineering student turned him into such a creature of science that he was able to conceive of life only in terms of tensile strength and millimeters? No, damn it, the fault wasn't his but the poet's. Mountain Pine's imagery smacked of the fatalism of the Chinese, a subject of nonstop debate among his classmates that never failed to anger him. Lincoln Chen said that fatalism had been so artfully cultivated from generation to generation that it was now a latent cancer, inbred in all Chinese. If his favorite teacher was right, then sooner or later Steel Hope too would succumb, and the thought of that was unbearable.

He shot an accusing glance at Mountain Pine. "How can you speak of the poor bastards as if they were phantoms in some folk romance?" he demanded. "They didn't die in their sleep, you know. Think of the people we left behind in Nanjing. The women raped—again and again, by whole battalions of Japs. The men buried alive and the babies tossed like pebbles down wells. No one—"

Suddenly he stopped, his anger overtaken by frustration. Throughout his outburst Mountain Pine hadn't moved. Smiling that Buddha smile, he continued to gaze across the river as if he were an indifferent visitor from some land of dreams instead of a Chinese. "Don't think you can keep on ignoring me, Mountain Pine! The day will come when you'll have to give me a fight."

With equal measures of benevolence and scorn, the servant replied, "No doubt, my Young Master. No doubt."

Steel Hope smiled despite himself. Though he had received his degree in yesterday's mail and Mountain Pine hadn't attended a single college class, once a bookmate, always a bookmate. What had he expected? An exchange of curses or blows? No, that would have been impossible, and much too satisfying. And not for the first time he wondered, How could someone born a servant and as devoted to service as Mountain Pine be so unservile? To watch him scrape the shit from the honeypot was to witness an emperor performing a sacred ritual. His sleeves, however threadbare, were always rolled just so. His implements, however repellent, were always placed on the gutter beside the open drain just so. There were mornings when Steel Hope wanted to snatch the toothbrush out of his hand before the fifty strokes were done. He sighed. What would that accomplish? When both of them were toothless, Mountain Pine would still possess the power to disable him like a child.

A strong wind, as fiery as dragon's breath, rose from behind them, lifting matted hair. It was not at all like the playful breezes that used to lure the young master to the banks of the Yangzi, but Steel Hope suddenly saw in the window of his mind three sworn brothers perched side by side on the crumbling levee, dangling their bare feet above the water. He and Mountain Pine had never returned to the Middle Heart once Firecrackers had gone, and after he got caught up in the anti-Japanese demonstrations in Nanjing, he'd rarely thought of it. Eventually even the recurring nightmare, in which he locked Firecrackers in a stock, fed her dumplings and then shot her dead, had stopped.

Now he found himself regretting the cleanliness of his toes. He laughed out loud.

"What's so funny?" asked Mountain Pine.

"I was thinking about Firecrackers and how I envied her filthy feet. What a fool I was!"

"You were a fool all right," said Mountain Pine. "Who else would think that determination and exercise can work miracles, like growing my lame leg another inch?" Never would he admit that whenever those silly stone-filled socks tied around his ankles were removed, he had walked with a new ease. Nor would he admit how thoroughly he'd enjoyed the Bible stories he'd read to the orphans at the Christian Mission School in Nanjing, which told of even greater miracles—or that the Christians too had prized willpower above brainpower and calisthenics above calculus. The similarity, however, ended there. Only the demanding Steel Hope could make him feel as if he belonged.

Out of nowhere a woman appeared alongside them—an older woman, slim, pockmarked, with thick bangs and her arms outstretched. Mountain Pine blinked. Jade? Had she been murdered by the occupation forces? Had her apparition come searching for her son?

No, the woman was speaking, and in a strange dialect. Her voice was throaty, not at all like Jade's. This was no ghost. Yet he could see from the expression on Steel Hope's face that the son, too, had mistaken the stranger for his mother. As one, they stopped lounging on the rail and drew themselves up to attend to her respectfully.

Oblivious of them, the woman continued to address the heavens. They didn't understand the words, but their meaning was all too clear—mothers who had outlived their children had sounded the same lament in Wen Shui after the Big Flood.

Minutes passed and then, as suddenly as she had come, the woman turned to go. Wordlessly they watched her recede into the night, going farther and farther, until she had stepped back into the dream they had forgotten they dreamed, of a faraway place called home.

Gazing again at the reflection of the small fires flaring and dying in the river, Mountain Pine thought, So it is true that everyone has a twin somewhere, and wished that he could meet his and ask him for a lesson on how a servant inextricably bound to his master could live a different life. He almost laughed. It would be just his luck that, like Jade and the grieving mother, they would not be able to understand each other's speech.

He had last seen the mistress three years before, on the eve of Steel Hope's and his departure for Chongqing, where all skilled and educated patriots were headed to help Chiang's government unite the country when war seemed inevitable. Awakened in the middle of the night by his sister, he had followed her to Jade's chamber. Not since he was a young boy had he been permitted beyond its threshold, but he remembered the cloying smell of honey.

For a moment, upon entering, he thought that the porcelain Kwan Yin had somehow been set on fire. The entire altar was ablaze with candles. Then he saw Jade, crouched in a kowtow amid the jittery shadows.

When Amber Willows knelt beside her, what choice did he have? He knelt as well. But no sooner had he done so than Jade sat up and, hissing like the sputtering flames, commanded him to look after Steel Hope. "Mountain Pine, swear to the Goddess of Mercy that no matter what, you will see to the welfare of my son throughout his absence from home. And I shall swear to see to the welfare of your sister throughout that same time, no matter what."

Never had he been so offended. Commanding someone to swear to do what she must have known full well he was gladly going to do was worse than blackmail. He should have had the honor of displaying loyalty without having loyalty thus demeaned. And the way she had done it, complete with a none-too-subtle threat—a swift kick would have been kinder. How could such a fool have given birth to his friend? He pitied her. He cursed her. He was in awe of her. At once, in turn, and more. Jade never forgave an offense. Jade never forgot a vow.

Now, looking at Steel Hope sifting through memories of his own, he felt a wave of gratitude for the mistress. It was true that if her son hadn't dug him out from under the rubble after the library roof caved in, someone else probably would have. But only Steel Hope could have known how to halt the panic that had robbed him of reason and was about to change him into a sniveling, quivering animal. "Damn it, Mountain Pine," the young master had said when he broke through, his face, framed in the opening, as filthy as it often was when he was a child. "Must you always bury yourself in books?!"

He had never thanked Steel Hope for saving his life, nor was it expected; as far as the young master was concerned, the episode was closed. Mountain Pine couldn't be as cavalier, however; for this debt, on top of all the others he owed the House of Li, weighed heavily, and had kept him at Steel Hope's side as no vow made to his mother could. Still, he had lived as a retainer for so long that he rarely entertained a thought of another life, except at odd moments when he would come upon a man his age, strolling with his family, and wonder, Will I ever marry?

A voice answered, "Yes." Startled, Mountain Pine turned to see Steel Hope nodding as he muttered to himself. "Yes, we must!" he exclaimed.

"Must what?"

"Light an offering too."

"How? We came unprepared."

Steel Hope prodded him with a friendly jab. "You're forever jotting thoughts down on paper. See if you've got a scrap on you somewhere."

Mindful of the opera tickets in his pocket, Mountain Pine hesitated. They were to be a surprise. Revealing them now would spoil the evening he'd planned tomorrow in honor of Steel Hope's graduation. For surely the hero in the young master would insist on making a grand gesture, and the precious tickets would be burned to please the theatergoers among the dead.

But Mountain Pine was no hero. He was that slave chained to a battered bamboo desk in the alley behind their apartment house who had labored to pay the graduate's tuition and their expenses while children jumped rope and chased stray cats and elderly strollers huddled around him to study his calligraphy. Copying didn't pay much, but luckily, for a copier as meticulous as he, there was plenty of work. Specialized books were hard to obtain. Had he and Steel Hope, along with thousands of other volunteers, not lugged the libraries of a half-dozen universities the three thousand lis from the coastal cities to this inland capital, there would be none even to copy from. And now, with the Japanese blockade, the originals were irreplaceable.

So were the opera tickets.

"What's the matter?" Steel Hope teased. "Can't the great writer spare a page or two?"

The great writer could spare an entire manuscript. But not the tickets. He would not sacrifice the climax of their long-awaited celebration, marking, he realized now, not only Steel Hope's graduation but the end of his tenure as bookmate—the fulfillment of a promise he had made not to Jade but to himself.

"Well, don't just stand there," the young master snapped. "Start looking through your pockets, or I swear I will."

So much for his new life. Smiling ruefully, Mountain Pine looked.
"Well, did you find anything?"

"Not a scrap, just this box of matches."

Searching his own pockets again, Steel Hope still came up only with
a few coins and the cigarette case that had been a gift to his father from
his first wife. It was the work of a master artisan, worth a hundred times
its weight in silver, but however high his debts and however low he had to
crawl for money, Stone Guardian had never pawned it. On his deathbed,
a year after Steel Hope had gone off to boarding school, he had presented
the case to Amber Willows; and, just before their trek to Chongqing, she,
in turn, had presented it to Steel Hope.

"Your father gave it to me only because he was certain that I would
give it to you when enough time had passed and you were older," she said.
"You must believe me. You must understand why he didn't offer it to his
second son himself. He was afraid to take your look of disgust with him to
the grave."

Since that day he had kept the case always with him, though he still
couldn't decide if her words were true. Perhaps, if he had returned to kneel
by his dying father's bed or had been there to set fire to the paper ingots
of silver and gold at the Patriarch's funeral, he could have found it easier
to believe her. But when the telegram came informing him that Stone
Guardian was dying, he had pretended that the school doctor had quarantined
him for a mysterious illness.

Opening the silver case now, he removed the cigarette. Cigarettes made
with real tobacco and tipped in gold foil had long been a luxury he couldn't
afford, but this one hadn't been bought. It had come with the case. At first
he hadn't smoked it because he preferred other brands. But later, in the
presence of Mountain Pine, he would claim that since Amber Willows didn't
smoke, the only legacy the Patriarch of the House of Li had left to his
second son was a cigarette that had been overlooked. He wouldn't touch it.
He couldn't toss it away. Never did it fail to remind him of the bitterness
of their past.

As he fingered it, he wondered why he neglected the long, weekly
letters that Jade sent and he received in timely fashion, despite the war,
while he kept in his wallet the only one he'd ever received from his father,
which, counting the salutation and valediction, came to a sum total of forty-
nine words, and whose meaning he pondered endlessly. That hers were
written by some professional writer whose skills were limited to expressing
how he was missed, how he must sleep well and eat well, how everyone
wished him good fortune, long life and happiness in a thousand florid ways

was a good excuse, but an excuse just the same. Was it a question of rarity? Of perversity? Remembering, he imagined his father, hunched over his desk, writing, "May we live in harmony."

Holding up the gold-tipped 999, he said, "What about this?"

To Steel Hope's surprise Mountain Pine was visibly moved. "Are you quite sure?"

He nodded. "It's time. It is a good night."

In silence he and Mountain Pine made their way slowly down the uneven stone steps to reach the riverbank, stopping now and then as though to let pass phantom mothers making the journey on their knees. Now and then lightning revealed tangles of straw-and-mud shacks perched like the nests of prehistoric birds on the cliffs. How much nicer Chongqing was by night, Steel Hope thought. By day, from October to May thick slime and mist slithered into the crevices of the rocky bluffs, and in summer clothing was soaked with sweat the moment it was worn and the streets oozed filth. In all seasons, the rats were fearless. And yet, despite everything, and especially at moments like this, when its citizens were of one mind, no patriot could fail to be filled with pride in and affection for the flotsam of humanity who had fled the occupied territories to make a home in this wretched place; who had rebuilt it again and again out of rubble.

Let the planes come! he almost shouted. For every bomb that fell, his countrymen would grow more defiant; and his country would endure.

When they reached the shore, Steel Hope tapped the gold tip of the cigarette on the case, drawing out the moment until this tangible reminder of the rift between father and son would be gone forever. Finally, he nodded. As he put the cigarette to his lips, Mountain Pine struck the match. Inhaling once, Steel Hope savored the taste, bitter with age, then gave it to his friend, who did the same before returning the token to Steel Hope. With both hands he proffered the sacrifice to the darkness, then cast the cigarette into the Yangzi for the pleasure of all those who had been lost.

THE OPERA

THE NEXT EVENING, after gorging at the Hazy City Cafe on skewers of tripe and greens dipped in a hot pot of chili, spices and oil, washed down with several bottles of cheap wine, Mountain Pine and Steel Hope staggered up what was a thoroughfare by day, and by night a bazaar lined with lantern-lit stalls that sold everything from common cabbage to golden-haired monkeys. Suppressing guffaws, each accused the other of undermining dignity.

"You ordered the last bottle."

"And you drank it up."

Shoppers scrambled out of their way. There were a good number of them, but fewer than if there had been a breeze and thick clouds weren't trapped by the mountains, for newcomers to the city, unaccustomed to the suffocating humidity and heat, chose to lie on straw mats in front of their apartment houses, reserving places on the sidewalks for the night. A beggar squatting in the gutter turned his back on the disreputable pair. A woman intent on the eggs piled high in the baskets she carried stopped just short of a head-on collision. Shifting awkwardly, like a trio of neophyte dancers with their eyes trained on menacing feet, they tried to step clear of one another without success until, in a voice taut with frustration, the woman squawked, "Stand still!"

At once Steel Hope and Mountain Pine stood at attention like wooden clothespins. Then the new graduate saluted. And kept on saluting as she scurried away, until her shrill curses could no longer be heard above the peddlers hawking their wares.

"Knives, knives!"

"Beans, beans!"

"Shoes, shoes! Shoes that won't slip. Shoes that won't slide. Shoes that won't take you for a ride. Shoes . . ."

Steel Hope dragged Mountain Pine to the shoe seller's stall, no wider than a tray, and pointing to the shoes made from discarded tires, exclaimed, "Look! Look! Just what I need! If I don't stop wearing these soggy cloth soles, my feet'll grow moss."

"We can't afford them."

"Who says?"

"Your host says. Move those damp feet, or we'll be late for the performance."

Steel Hope didn't seem to care, for he stopped at the next wine stall and refused to budge until his bookmate had toasted him many times, each time more extravagantly than before. Only after the half-empty bottle slipped from Mountain Pine's hand and broke did they hook arms and stagger on uphill past houses interspersed with bombed-out lots.

Cheered by the traces of ancient creativity that had somehow survived modern destruction, Steel Hope paused to admire the work of a Qin Dynasty architect who had placed his moongate so that a young cypress, after generations of reaching for the sun, would in maturity be perfectly framed. He grinned in anticipation. Soon, he would be designing bridges that would also stand triumphant over time.

Suddenly Mountain Pine guffawed.

"What's so funny?"

"I . . . was just remembering"—he pointed ahead to a boy relieving himself in a pile of rubble—"the first time a female . . . vanished when you dropped your pants."

Swaying, Steel Hope scratched his head and pursed his lips in concentration; then, after a while, he grinned. "Hey, how about a pissing contest now?" he said, reaching for the buttons on his trousers.

The bookmate in Mountain Pine smacked the fumbling hands and hissed, "Stop! Stop that this minute or you'll recite all the Tang poets."

When Steel Hope looked as if he was going to cry, Mountain Pine quickly pointed up the hill to the flickering neon sign on the roof of a two-story stucco building. "There it is. Downriver Xiaoxing Opera Upriver."

"That rickety place! Let's find another." Steel Hope about-turned, but his body made a full circle. "As a certified structural engineer and a soon-to-be official of the Ministry of Roads and Communications, I'd rather condemn it than set a toe in there."

Mountain Pine stopped in his tracks. Might he be buried alive again? At the thought, his throat tightened and he could feel his heart pounding, pushing what air there was out of his lungs. Suddenly he was sober as a condemned prisoner. Steel Hope was right. What miracle had kept the place standing when all about was rubble?

Steel Hope must have sensed his anxiety and been sobered as well, for when he spoke again his words were no longer slurred. "To hell with right angles. I haven't been to the opera for ages."

Mountain Pine wasn't persuaded. "Perhaps we should sell the tickets and go back for those shoes," he said.

Steel Hope took him by the shoulders and, staring into his eyes with a look as compassionate as Amber Willows' when she first measured her little brother's withered leg for long pants, said, "My dear friend, you've worked too hard and too long to spoil the celebration you planned now."

Sincerely touched, Mountain Pine swallowed his fears. More determined than ever to show Steel Hope a good time, he bought him a pack of Double Lucks at the door. "Here, fill that empty case!" he said.

"What's come over you?"

"Don't get excited. Everyone claims they're made of sawdust."

Inside, Mountain Pine almost fell, so intent was he on studying the ceiling, until Steel Hope assured him the cracks were superficial. They hurried down a dim passageway lined with tiny rooms, in which recent graduates like Steel Hope toasted one another merrily, to a large hall where even more rambunctious people of all ages, stations and attire jammed benches, fanning furiously. Simultaneously they spotted a side bench that was not quite filled and scrambled to claim seats, ducking the steamed towels thrown by ushers to waving spectators impatient to mop their sweaty brows.

Seated at last, Mountain Pine turned to his immediate neighbor to inquire about the next opera, since shows ran continuously from morning to midnight. No sooner had he done so than he regretted it. Only too willing to oblige, the old man proceeded to tell Mountain Pine more than he wanted to know, while gassing him with the odor of the garlic cloves he was eating like kumquats.

"The eight cyclic characters of your birthdate must be most fortuitous. They've finished with the patriotic skits and all those homely girls

and pimply boys in everyday clothes who can't sing or dance or act...."
The man paused to offer him a clove from his bottle of Longevity
Buds, which Mountain Pine politely declined. "I don't doubt these college
students' sincerity, but what do the higher-ups take us for? Only a
simpleton would buy more war bonds. I'd rather shove my money directly
up their sleeves and save myself the paperwork...."

Mountain Pine pointed out that the musicians seated at the side of
the stage were now playing, though they were hardly audible above the
din. The man nodded and went on talking and chomping as before. "But
that's not what you asked me about and heaven knows that's not what
I want to talk about. My lucky man, you are about to enjoy a performance
that cowards would die for. Summer Wishes singing Zhu Yingtai....
It's enough to make this old fortuneteller wish he could relive his life of
unending sorrows."

Having finished the garlic, the old man was now gulping the Longevity
brine. "Wait till you hear her sing of dreams as she marches off to school
disguised as a boy, observe the subtlety with which she hints of her true sex
to the roommate she loves, and mark my words, you'll weep when she stops,
on the way to her wedding, at the grave of her true—"

The boisterous audience hushed. Thanks to Buddha, Mountain Pine
thought, and then, like the others, found himself transfixed as Summer
Wishes floated onto the stage. Like the others, he leaned forward to catch
her every word, every note, studying her almond-shaped face and luminous
eyes as if he had never seen a beautiful woman before. It must be the
wine, he told himself. Yes, that was it, the wine. Ogling pretty girls wasn't
his habit, though he'd come to accept it in Steel Hope, who claimed that
his bookmate was more proper than a eunuch with his balls in a jar. Was
what the matchmakers said true—that men as self-contained as he were
lone trees in the grasslands, magnets for lightning?

He forced himself to look away. Summer Wishes' voice as she sang
of yearning was so sublime yet so sincere, so pure yet so passionate, that
for once words, however poetic, didn't matter.

He started. Steel Hope's cigarette had singed his hand. When he
pushed it away and his friend never noticed, he thought, Summer Wishes
has bewitched him, too, and he felt a twinge of loss. His eyes returned
to the stage.

The heroine was about to throw herself into the open grave of her
beloved when the air-raid siren sounded, an impossible noise that resembled at once the roar of demented bears and the squeal of scalded
pigs. Only when Summer Wishes had left the stage, however, did the

audience groan and reluctantly get to their feet, as children do when, playing happily in the schoolyard, they are called back to class. The ushers shouted, "This way! Shelter nearby. This way!"

Mountain Pine and Steel Hope helped the old fortuneteller to his feet, but lost him as they were propelled toward the exits. There was no panic: familiarity had made air raids almost routine. Still, everyone whispered, as if the noise of people talking would enable the enemy to discover their whereabouts.

Outside, the clouds had been blown away, and the moon was near and bright. In its light the rivers wrapped around Chongqing glittered like shining gold ribbons, making of the city a gift to the bombers.

The entrance of the cave in the towering cliff loomed just ahead now. Once again, Mountain Pine's throat tightened. Once again, his heart pounded the air out of his lungs. He wanted to stop, turn back, run, but others with no such qualms pressed him inside. The air was fetid. Droplets of water seeped through the rock walls, soaking hair and skin, even shoes, so that the onrush of footsteps made a disquieting, squishing sound. Still, relentlessly, he was propelled onward, past the benches already crowded with people, deeper and deeper into the cavern. The light from the oil lamps in their stone niches seemed to grow feebler. His mouth tasted of mildew. He suffered one of his coughing fits.

Steel Hope rubbed Mountain Pine's back and waited patiently for the hacking to end, and when it did, he gave him an encouraging smile. "Only books can do you in, my friend, and there's not one in sight."

Mountain Pine managed a nod.

At last the crowd began to thin and they found seats. Mountain Pine strained to hear the second alert, announcing the actual sighting of Japanese planes over Chongqing. The sooner it came, the sooner the raid would be over. Sometimes it never came and the whole night would pass without relief. Steel Hope was already asleep. Mountain Pine envied him.

Surely it was not death he feared. Death extracted all memory, but there was nothing from his days on earth to remember. What then? More likely that his life would end without his having lived. When the library roof collapsed, it had been days since the last raid. He'd been alone. The place had looked no different than it always did—austere yet handsome with its vaulted ceilings and gray steel shelves crammed with books, the older ones bound in soft covers lying on their sides, the new ones standing upright. Once he had remarked to Steel Hope that the wooden rafters looked as sturdy as the crossbeams on the great boat that Admiral Cheng Ho sailed to Madagascar almost a century before the first voyage of

Columbus. Then, without warning—one moment they were crossbeams, and the next, down they came.

Disbelief suspended even gravity, for the books cast from the uppermost shelves seemed to hover in the air like the first innocent flurries of a blinding snowstorm. He had simply watched as they floated toward him. If he felt any emotion at all it was a bittersweet pang for the green apple he had set beside the inkstone to reward himself for working through the night, and for the cascading volumes—old and new, thick and thin—that now he would never read. One finally landed nearby. Another. The apple tumbled out of reach.

When he realized that he could neither see nor move, he wondered mildly if he was dead, and decided he was not. He could hear. He was certain the groaning sound came from the thick oak desk that had temporarily saved his life. With no more dread than he would feel when anticipating the eager embrace of an onrushing child, he waited for his chest to be crushed.

The terror had come only when he heard the voices of his rescuers, and again later, hours after Steel Hope found him. But since then, it had never left him, not completely. True, it was no longer the panic that had seized him when he saw his friend peering down at him and grasped for the first time how close he had come to never seeing a human face again; usually a tightening of his throat and chest, a sudden urge to move about, little more. . . .

Silently he began to recite poetry, as he had always done to calm himself. This time, though, it was not the beloved lines of Tu Fu or Li Po, but the ones he had heard Summer Wishes sing, and then it came to him that this was the nearest shelter to the opera house and all the performers would be here. Summer Wishes would be here.

He got to his feet. A hand stopped him. "You're not thinking of leaving, are you?" Steel Hope asked.

"Just going to the entrance for a breath of air," he said, and wondered why he lied. "Don't worry."

As he passed the rows of benches, he looked for her first among the women in stage dress, but none remotely resembled her. Had she taken the time to change out of her costume? He retraced his steps, looking for her among the women hidden in the shadows. Where could she have gone? Perhaps she too needed air. As he neared the entrance, the warden reminded him not to step outside. He nodded absently, wondering what he would say if she did appear.

He debated whether to go back to his seat, but the air was refreshing and the city still peaceful in the moonlight. He sensed someone watching him, shook the feeling off as a fancy. Would this day of foolishness never end?

*

LISTENING FOR the second alert, Summer Wishes wrapped the blanket tighter about her head. It was an ugly gray, but the magic markings stamped in one corner possessed the power to deflect bombs more assuredly than the hardest mountain rock. Of this she was almost certain. It didn't make any difference to her that the fortuneteller had identified them as a stamp signifying the blanket was the property of the United States of America.

If the talisman were just fraying wool, why had the coolie, hungry enough to eat dirt, demanded such an exorbitant price? And if he was lying, why such outlandish lies? Perhaps the man knew that show people like her harbored as many superstitions as beggars harbored lice and could never resist buying luck. Then again, perhaps he had told the truth about being among the very few who had escaped the Nanjing massacre— and all because some foreign devils had handed him a blanket. As he said, "One look at that powerful bird and the fiercest warrior lopping off the heads of the most sacred Buddhas would run away."

Summer Wishes hoped his words were true, but in any case had long ago decided that anything lending comfort, whether it was a talisman or not, was good.

She closed her eyes, hoping to doze through the hours that stretched ahead. Instead, questions burst into her mind. How long must they hide? Had Mushroom bothered to go to a shelter or had she stayed in bed? Could the theater survive another bombing? How many more raids before they would end? One unanswerable query led to another. On ordinary nights the energy that galvanized her for a performance would still churn hours after her last bow, delaying sleep. Tonight sleep was impossible.

For want of something better to do she studied the people around her. There was the father who wore a calm face for his children but couldn't stop twirling the ring on his finger; the man who limped past her, heading for the entrance of the cave, his eyes hardly blinking as they swept the aisles; the old widow who fussed because she had missed another night of sleep, but who reveled in the company of—

Her attention was drawn back to the man who had hurt his leg, perhaps in his rush to get to the shelter. For whom was he searching? And why should she care?

Something compelled her to rise and approach him. It was so unlike her. However lonely, she kept to herself, for those who would befriend an actress she rebuffed, and those she would befriend rebuffed her.

Could he be a student? Perhaps he had accompanied the three smart college girls from the best families in Chongqing who had performed at her theater that night, though not painted, of course, nor at the same time as she. His glasses and pallor and the faded clothes he wore fit nicely with the characteristics of the students she'd seen in films or from afar, but not knowing more than this about such a grand class of people, she couldn't be certain. And if his lameness weren't from a recent injury—would a cripple be allowed to attend a university?

She edged herself into the space alongside him. His profile looked vaguely familiar. She willed him to turn around, and in time he did. Their eyes met for a moment; then he fixed his gaze on his feet.

She had never before spoken first to a strange man, but again something compelled her, and she ventured, "Are you from downriver?"

He nodded, but said nothing. Was he dismissing her? No, she was quite certain he acted out of shyness.

"I am, too," she said. "Near Shanghai."

Clearing his throat, he said, "I recognize you."

"Yes? From where?"

"Tonight. At the theater."

"Oh." Was that all? She turned to leave.

"Please don't go. You were wonderful."

Suddenly she knew him. "Mountain Pine?"

"Yes?" His tone was as before. Had he been so enchanted by the actress that he didn't realize she'd called him by name? Laughing, she grabbed his sleeve. "Don't you know me?"

He stared speechless at her hand.

"Look at me!" she cried.

Lifting his gaze, he said, "You are Summer Wishes."

"No, no . . ." She tugged harder. "Of course I am. But I have another name. Think back. Long ago when you were—" She stopped in mid-sentence. Could he have forgotten? No, that was impossible. "Listen, listen," she urged, still laughing, still tugging at his sleeve. " 'We cannot undo our separate births—' "

" '—but on the same day we mean to die.' "

She jumped. The speaker wasn't Mountain Pine. The voice came from somewhere behind her. She turned. Even in the dim light, she could see that he was a most handsome young man.

D A W N   I N C H E D across the horizon. The fires in the northern part of town still smoldered, but the bombers had long since returned to their base and the people to bed. Already the coolies who supplied the city with water were dipping their buckets into the river to begin their ceaseless shuttle up and down the cliffs, and the hawkers of breakfast noodles were twirling their dough. Already the clean-up teams were gathering with their picks and shovels and wheelbarrows. The city was eager to start rebuilding again.

Enveloped in darkness except for the circle of light shed by a single naked bulb, the three childhood friends lolled about like sunbathers, seated at a gaming table set up on the opera-house stage. The urgency of speaking had eased, and they savored the wonder of their reunion. Again and again, for no apparent reason, there was a shake of the head, a smile. Occasionally one yawned, but none made a move to go. When words failed, silence, warm and easy, recaptured the days along the river where affections, as fine as they were inexplicable, once flowed. When words returned, chatter, disjointed and nonsensical, redeemed the youth they had lost when young. Recalling bits and pieces of that spring the young master, his bookmate and the gravekeeper's son had shared, they exclaimed over them, admired them, extolled them, like panners of gold who, upon scooping up water to splash the dust from their faces, find shimmering nuggets cupped in their hands.

"Remember when you overturned—"

"How could I forget? And what about—"

"—the afternoon we—"

Like the scores of colored scarfs a trio of magicians might pluck from a hidden source and toss skyward, their snippets of memories knotted together in midair.

Suddenly a gaunt old man carrying a broom appeared out of the darkness and, after begging their pardon, began to sweep the stage. Except for asking them to lift their feet, the intruder didn't speak, yet the three friends sat staring as though mesmerized by the stroking of the broom, attending to every sound it made until finally the task was done and, bowing, the man backed into the gloom and a door opened and closed.

Now the silence was different. It erected a wall that hid secrets, awkward and painful.

Summer Wishes searched for another "remember when" to restore gaiety, but all those she could think of were tinged with sadness. Desperate, she asked Steel Hope to tell her more about his and Mountain Pine's journey to Chongqing, but even before he could answer, she regretted her words. What if, in return, he asked her to do the same? What might he think of the foul-smelling beggar who, day after day at inns and eateries, had lapped up the leavings in customers' bowls before the proprietors could give chase; someone whose shame had damned her as surely as filth had caked her throughout the miserable year during which she and Mushroom had followed the seer's injunction to go to the mountains? If Steel Hope knew, what would he think of tonight tomorrow?

"Well . . ." Steel Hope grinned, rubbing his hands together. "For the first twelve hundred lis from Nanjing to Hankow, we traveled by steamer. I think. How would I know what was propelling us? We were packed in so tight among bodies and boxes of books I didn't see my fingers or toes for two weeks. Afterwards, though, I could still walk, and that was too bad, because we two scholars from Nanjing then *walked* a good deal more than twelve hundred lis and worked like coolies every step of the way, pushing and pulling and dragging those damned boxes of books up and down mountains from one sorry village to the next. We all did—students and professors alike. . . ." He paused, savoring the pride of accomplishment he had felt leading the column of students from his school. Though they had numbered only twenty out of the thousands charged with the critical mission of transporting China's great centers of learning inland to safety, they had carried the books and laboratory equipment that were essential to educating the engineers who would be indispensable to repairing the damage done and to restoring the Middle Kingdom to its rightful place as a country so respected and so powerful that no other country would ever again dare invade.

Summer Wishes almost wept. Begging was unbearable, but the young master doing the work of a coolie was worse. She'd had no choice: foul-smelling beggars repelled unwanted attentions. But had he wished, he could have flown to Chongqing in an airplane.

"Don't look so sad," Steel Hope said. "Everywhere we went the people cheered us. Isn't that right, Bookmate?"

Mountain Pine frowned. "Just tell her what she wants to know," he said. "And for heaven's sake, spare us that web of colorful yarns you spin whenever women, young and old, suitable or unsuitable, are around." The words were out and at once he was sorry. Even to his own ears they sounded churlish. Did he think that by warning her, he could make her think better of Mountain Pine or change the way she looked at Steel Hope, who attracted attention effortlessly? It was not so much his features, which were fine enough, as that restless ardor of his, even when at rest, that distinguished the young master.

"This time," Steel Hope was saying, "we were heroes, real heroes." Summer Wishes lowered her gaze. She mustn't stare at him.

"But enough of that," he said. "What about you? You've certainly changed for the better." He grinned. "What a fright you were then. Now you're a dream come true. Isn't that so, Mountain Pine?"

"Stop talking nonsense." Again Mountain Pine hadn't meant to sound so peevish. But Summer Wishes must realize that compliments were the young master's specialty.

Steel Hope took no offense and said, "I know better than to try to dazzle a brilliant actress—not to mention that brat Firecrackers, who was hardly the type to be impressed."

You are mistaken, she thought.

There was another silence. She could feel his eyes on her. Why didn't he say something? If he didn't, she must. But what? She couldn't tell him about her life as an actress. Her mind was a blank. Why didn't she know what to do except on stage? . . . Yes, that was it. She could dazzle him as the actress would with flamboyant gestures, mocking eyes and a song, beseeching the hero to tell his tale. And she did.

Mountain Pine burst into applause. When Steel Hope raised his hands in capitulation, she sang a final trill of triumph and gracefully extended a palm, inviting him to take the floor.

Steel Hope scratched his head. "You'll have to help me out. Tell me what you'd like to know."

"Weren't you homesick in Nanjing?"

"Why? Nanjing was where I chose to be. Besides, I was too busy thinking about the future to think about the past."

Summer Wishes swallowed her disappointment. She thought about the past they'd shared all the time. Her most precious possession was still that pair of shoes. The buttons no longer shone and the cloth was torn, not from wear but from her sleeping with them under her pillow for seven years on the *Pavilion of Fairies*, because the other girls, who'd been sold by their parents for less than the price of those shoes, would have stolen them if they could.

"Don't look so upset, Summer Wishes. Our Loyal Goodness Mountain Pine was equally glad to be gone. Isn't that right?"

"Right."

"How could anyone with a home not miss it?" asked Summer Wishes. "Especially one as grand as the House of Li." Closing her eyes she saw again the garden walls and arching roofs that the agent boater and Firecrackers had gawked at while gathering the courage to knock at the back gate. "Townspeople never stopped talking about how beautiful it is. . . ."

Was, thought Steel Hope. Was even then a remnant. And now? Now that the House of Li was in occupied territory, and that traitor of a half-brother of his was the Japs' favorite go-between in Wen Shui in all matters having to do with administration and commerce, he wouldn't be surprised if his ancestral home had been turned into a whorehouse for the Brown Dwarfs. Hadn't Grand Hope already been entertaining them at the Prosperity Emporium before Wen Shui was lost? He could just see him toasting them in the hall where their ancestor had planned the building of the great dikes. As Summer Wishes prattled on and on about the virtues of the House of Li, suddenly he couldn't sit and listen a minute longer, and got to his feet and strolled to the edge of the shallow stage. Turning, he retraced his steps, slowly at first, then quicker and quicker, until he was pacing like a tiger thwarted by the confines of its cage.

Summer Wishes' voice trailed off. His pacing frightened her.

Seeing her distress, Mountain Pine caught Steel Hope's arm and yanked him back into his seat. "You'll have a lifetime to think unsavory thoughts," he said. "No more now."

His former bookmate was right, as usual. Steel Hope took a deep breath and pulled on a smile. "I must apologize. Firecrackers, you know how happy, truly happy, I am that we've found one another again."

There it is, she thought. The same caring look that for eight interminable years she hadn't been able to dismiss. Or forget. Or outgrow. Now it was too late. She had seen it again. It existed after all.

Self-consciously she withdrew her hand to tuck away a strand of hair, and another, and even one that hadn't strayed. She laced her fingers tightly and put them in her lap, afraid that if she didn't, they would claim a life of their own and seize his and not let go. And this must not happen. Steel Hope would expect such forwardness from an actress. She must never be perceived to be someone who exacted and extended favors, like others in the troupe. Not by him. She must never be perceived to be someone who could blink stars or tears into her eyes at will. Not by him. She must—

Abruptly Mountain Pine stood up. "It's almost nine," he said. "I have lots of copying to do."

"Don't go, you can't go!" she cried. What if, alone with Steel Hope, she couldn't subdue her hands and they broke free?

"Steel Hope doesn't have to start making a living for a couple of weeks yet. He's welcome to stay."

"Please."

This time it was Steel Hope who yanked Mountain Pine back into his seat, and to engage him, Summer Wishes asked if it was too late to take him up on the offer he'd made once a day at the Middle Heart. When Mountain Pine said nothing, she asked, "Don't you remember offering to teach me to read?"

"So I did."

Before anything could go wrong again, she eagerly urged him to fix a time and a place for the lessons. They were still working out a schedule when, without warning, Steel Hope interrupted.

"This is a celebration. Let's dance."

She was afraid. Before she knew it, she had exclaimed, much too loudly, "The Guomindang forbids it!"

"The Party forbids a lot of things. People go on doing them just the same." Steel Hope pulled her to her feet and waltzed her around the table, in and out of the circle of light, singing lustily an old foreign tune everyone loved and could la-la-la.

She followed his lead effortlessly. This was not at all like dancing with Mushroom, to whom dancing was an act of war—a means of fending off the clutches of the sons of turtles. Unlike Mushroom, Steel Hope was not too tall, nor did he hold her at arm's length. She felt as though they were waltzing into one of the stories she loved, where a stranger changes all.

How long had they been dancing? She couldn't judge. If only for a few turns, why was she out of breath? If for an entire song, why had the dance seemed so short? His eyes were as she remembered, glinting with mischief, but were they laughing at her or inviting her to laugh?

Mountain Pine was slumped in his chair, head bowed. "He's asleep!" she exclaimed, afraid again.

"Looks like it."

She called his name. The servant didn't move.

"Let him sleep. What were we talking about?"

She had no idea. Again they danced.

Her hands were cold. With great effort she managed to release herself from his arms to make a fuss of spreading her blanket over Mountain Pine to keep him warm. Only when she was safely seated again did she realize that it was summer, and the day was hot.

Steel Hope drew his chair up next to hers.

Why must you stare so? she thought.

Reading her mind, he answered, "I'm not used to seeing you like this. As I said, you've changed, really changed."

"I have?"

He nodded gravely. He looked into her eyes as if searching to see where the actress had stored the stars and the tears. Suddenly he threw his head back and laughed. "Oh yes, you've changed. For one thing, you haven't scratched yourself all night."

Once more he pulled her to her feet and took her in his arms. This time he didn't sing or hum. This time they danced to a tune yet to be composed, to which their bodies swayed in languid synchrony until, entering the shadows, they barely moved at all. He placed her cheek on his shoulder. He gently tucked a stray strand of hair behind her ear.

Resting against him, she recalled the warmth of the sun when Firecrackers still took afternoon naps on the deck of the yaolu and, without moving, could touch someone with whom she had shared a home even before either was born. She had feared that the feelings she had once been allowed, and had lost, were gone forever. Now she thought that never even in the happiest dreams of her childhood had she felt so deliciously alive.

Suddenly Steel Hope let her go and shoved his hands into his pockets.

He didn't walk away, however, and though he cleared his throat, his voice was still hoarse when he began insisting on hearing more about what life was like for a star.

She had little choice but to entertain him, and recounted a series of droll mishaps in the theater—some that had happened to her, others that she'd only heard of. . . . She couldn't stop, in case he should ask other questions, questions she didn't want to answer. She told of the time the darkness fell when it was supposed to be noon, the time ramparts appeared in the middle of the sea, the time the page was garroted instead of the king. Eventually, hearing her own words, she realized that these incidents no longer seemed strange; resting her cheek on his shoulder had been stranger still.

Bewildered, she forgot her lines.

"Summer Wishes?"

"Yes."

"Did you ever try to see us?"

She shook her head, thinking of how, whenever Big Boss's disobedient apprentice was made to perform for brigands at fairgrounds alongside dancing monkeys and bare-chested wrestlers, Firecrackers had looked for her two sworn brothers in the crowd—yet prayed they wouldn't see her.

"We never stopped wondering what became of you. We couldn't believe you no longer cared. We weren't wrong, were we?"

Not wrong. But she mustn't say so. Her voice would betray her and reveal how much and for how long she had cared, that she still cared. Shaking her head ever so slightly, she managed, "We were only children. . . ."

"Were we?"

"Only children?"

"No. Were we wrong to think you would care?"

How simple he had made everything seem that summer, she thought. But Mountain Pine still limped, and she—

"Answer me. Were we wrong?"

"I . . . cared. . . ." She was about to say more, but he no longer seemed interested, for suddenly he scooped her into his arms and they were dancing again, whirling faster and faster until she was certain they would crash into the table or overturn a chair. As suddenly he stopped.

She thought that perhaps Mountain Pine was awake, and looked his way. He hadn't moved.

Reaching into his pocket, Steel Hope took out his cigarette case and, after several attempts to strike a match, lit up. She wondered whether he would offer her one. Ladies of repute never smoked, but did Summer Wishes?

"What would your fans think," he asked, "if they could see you as you were then: a bundle of rags and a pair of dirty feet?"

Firecrackers snatched his cigarette and inhaled deeply. She made a face.

"Sorry about the sawdust."

She didn't understand.

"I should've warned you. Whoever labeled that thing a cigarette should be shot."

She threw it away.

Steel Hope retrieved it, and began to tell another story, something that made little sense, about a last cigarette. She pretended to listen. She heard the waves lapping against the yaolu and her mother's song, a lullaby. Quickly she folded her hands tight.

FOG

(1942)

STEEL HOPE HURRIED from corridor to corridor, office to office, cubbyhole to cubbyhole, searching. On every wall, in every niche was a portrait of Stone Guardian. His father's eyes bored into him. He must find it. What? Expectantly he opened a door. The room was empty. Expectantly he opened another and another. . . .

When he finally escaped those eyes and woke, it was dawn, and the room that inflation had forced them to keep even after there was no more tuition to pay felt as cold as the caves.

He sat up and looked about. Damn Mountain Pine! His roommate was gone and there was no hot breakfast ready to ease the start of another bone-chilling day. Damn the weather! He pulled the quilts up to his chin and stared vacantly at the bamboo furnishings, so weary they whined; the plaster walls, dingy with soot and streaked with the bloody remains of mosquitoes and flies; the drafty window, which they had boarded up, since glass panes, like everything else these days, were substandard, too thin to withstand a sneeze, much less the slightest hint of a bomb; the second hand of the clock, shifting from numeral to numeral . . . until finally, teeth chattering, he couldn't stand the place a moment longer and leaped out of bed.

A few minutes later, bundled in a long padded coat, scarf and hat, he walked quickly to keep his blood from congealing. He walked not caring where, so long as it wasn't to the Ministry of Roads and Communications. The thought of joining the ranks of his fellow bureaucrats in the central courtyard and shouting with them at the top of his lungs, "With one mind, we strive! With one heart, we fight!" made him physically ill. And afterwards, standing there at attention freezing his butt off while the disembodied voice in the loudspeaker spewed static and one of those pedantic, puerile, polemical speeches that went on and on and robbed him, for want of another vocabulary, of words to express his patriotism.

He climbed the steep stone steps that served Chongqing's pedestrians on streets that ascended and descended as sharply as roofs, past vacant lot after vacant lot and piles of rubble where temples once stood, past charred facades and chimneys and crumbling walls, and here and there a defiant new stucco house—climbed until he was out of breath and the accursed sky seemed only a fingertip away.

He ached for the sun. So what if its rays signaled a clear night and invited the Jap bombers to fly? The cost to the enemy of the planes, parts, fuel and ammunition expended on a raid far exceeded the cost of rebuilding Chongqing. Only last week he had done the calculations for amusement as he sat in his windowless cubicle surrounded by musty boxes stacked to the ceiling. Besides the occasional bureaucrat demanding some blueprint from the dead files, his only human contact had been with the half-witted janitor, who feared for his lunch of smelly fish heads and hid it on the floor beneath Steel Hope's kneehole desk. So it had been throughout his two years at the Ministry of Roads and Communications. There was nothing to do, nothing that meant anything, certainly nothing that had anything to do with building bridges.

He had deliberately left out of his calculus of costs the lives lost in the raids. In his present mood, war was war, and death its price.

He stepped into a doorway to light a cigarette, but not a single match in the entire box sparked. They were as damp and as useless as he. The need to smoke became overpowering and he joined the queue at the nearest hole in the wall, but when the line of frostbitten customers only stomped in place without advancing, he was reminded again of the rally at the Ministry and, half expecting to hear the hectoring voice from the loudspeaker, shuddered and walked on.

A truck, smack in the middle of the intersection, blocked traffic and his way. He yelled at the driver. Without looking up from his comic book, the man pointed to his partner, who was pasting up a poster on the traffic island: "Citizens, observe cleanliness!" Another of Chiang Kai-shek's commandments that mocked reality. Water was scarce. Hot water costly. Soap unobtainable except in exchange for its weight in gold. But no matter how many critical tasks went undone, Chiang's New Life Movement, with its dos and don'ts culled from his Methodism and Confucianism, took precedence. Every week without fail virgin posters replaced the old. Once he had regarded such zany efficiency as a lark. Now it infuriated him.

He was tempted to scissor kick the worker out of his way and deface the poster with a sketch of Emperor Hirohito, up to his ears in soapsuds. Only his inability to draw and the likelihood that his frozen fingers would snap off stopped him. Besides, what would such efforts accomplish except to land him in jail? The Japanese weren't the object of the Generalissimo's attentions anymore. No sooner had America joined the battle and the bombings eased than the Guomindang had taken victory for granted and resumed the fight against the Communists. No sooner had survival been forecast than the powerful had become profiteers. Corruption unchecked at the top was now to be found everywhere: generals pocketed payrolls; quartermasters pilfered rations; soldiers made off with anything portable. Better the Jap planes. At least when they were overhead, he knew the enemy.

Once he was moving again, Steel Hope realized that his feet were automatically taking him in the direction of Summer Wishes' place. Apparently they knew where he could shake his foul mood. For no matter how many times he visited the attic room she shared with Mushroom, each time he experienced the same surprise—of someone who, within a blink, saw that Chongqing could be painted in colors, not just chiaroscuro. Suspended from the rafters on bamboo poles were silk and satin costumes in lush hues of lime and persimmon, plum and pomegranate, all exquisitely enhanced with beads, sequins and pearls. The apartment was not simply a contrast to the relentless gray of the city. It was a sanctuary for souls starved of gladness.

And the keeper of that sanctuary, scurrying here and there in a flurry of activity, stirring the gowns to life until everywhere he looked there would be phantom maidens dancing, was Summer Wishes. She was unlike any other woman he knew. She greeted happy subjects the way a bird with muddied wings greets water, and unpleasant ones with flights of fancy so bewildering that rational beings were awed by their own willingness to see the world through her eyes.

But when he heard a newsboy cry "Buy your Monday papers! Papers here!" he stopped. Of course, Mountain Pine would be there, and, worse,

Monday was the day he and Summer Wishes played at school. Damn it! On top of everything else, the thought of seeing the two of them hunched over a child's text was enough to drive him to suicide. The interminable lessons were not only a waste of time; lately it seemed all the two of them did was talk about him and what a boor he'd become.

At the newsstand, he spotted Lincoln Chen's picture in the *Chongqing Daily*. He didn't bother to buy a copy. Depending on the writer's views on how best to boost support for government policies—whether by shunning intellectuals or by seducing them—the article would characterize his favorite professor's activities as nefarious or praiseworthy. But suddenly he felt an urgent need to talk to the man who had named him the leader of their column on the trek to Chongqing and whose company, rather than that of his cliquish classmates, he had sought throughout his college years. At the corner, he bulled his way through the crowd penned between the iron railings of the bus stop and squeezed onto the next crosstown bus. He might as well have walked. It stopped at every stop and between stops. Several blocks from his destination he gave up and got off.

Turning into East Wind Alley, he stopped short. Two burly men with identical dark caps pulled low paced in front of the familiar two-storied house marked by pots of red peppers set on its balcony. Guomindang thugs! When had they been installed? There was never money to pay the soldiers at the front; but to pay spies at home—always. In Nanjing scum like them had beaten him and other student demonstrators senseless. Scum like them had shoved his boarding school comrades into the arms of the Communists. Unlike his friends, he'd stayed politically neutral, hoping for a united China. Now . . .

What did he have to lose? His job? He marched straight toward the two men and asked them for a match. Startled, the older one fished out a lighter, an expensive one. Steel Hope bowed. He removed his hat. He displayed his full face, his left and right profiles. He volunteered his name and age, the addresses of office and home. "And so as not to tax your paltry sum of brain cells, here's my card," he added; then, feeling that the day hadn't been wasted after all, he bounded up the steps.

At the top, however, he hesitated. What if the house was full of worshipful students, as it often was? He listened. All was quiet. He dropped his cigarette and knocked.

The door opened. A man in his fifties, dressed in a quilted gown so faded and patched that it would be impossible to guess its original color, Chen could have stepped from an ancient scroll depicting a hermit scholar who had abandoned all earthly ties to live alone on a mountaintop.

"Good morning, Teacher," Steel Hope said.

Squinting, Chen leaned so close that his thick glasses touched Steel Hope's chin. "Steel Hope?" Cataracts had robbed the professor of most of his sight, but somehow faulty vision had quickened his step. Already he was hurrying toward his study, with its bookcases, like a coach after a soccer ball. "Good, good, good. Just a moment while I finish collecting what I need from my files."

Steel Hope took a seat opposite the desk in the immaculate room where everything had an assigned place, and watched his teacher bob up and down as he pressed his nose to the rows of books lining the walls, taking down this one and that to remove clipping after clipping that he had filed between their pages. As many times as Steel Hope had watched this process, he was still unable to decipher the professor's system, unless, of course, Chen depended on smell. At this thought, he smiled for the first time that day. The professor amused and amazed him.

"Steel Hope, your timing couldn't be better. My latest reader decided that the climate disagreed with him and left town last night."

Steel Hope thought, No doubt for Yenan, that garden spot where only communism grows, but all he said was, "How many does that make?"

"Twenty, thirty. Who counts?"

"The thugs outside?"

Chen waved his hand dismissively. "I picked them myself, personally."

Steel Hope burst out laughing. "And I suppose to save them the trouble you write their reports for them?"

The professor tugged his beard, as was his custom when he was especially pleased with himself. Then, looking about, he asked where his guest had put his coat.

"Nowhere. I'm keeping it on."

This declaration precipitated a lecture on the wisdom of discriminating between outdoors and indoors, with the emphasis on discrimination. "For one of my most promising students to ignore that critical aspect of life would be most short-sighted. In case you haven't noticed, there's a difference between being inside and being outside. How big a difference depends on the season. And I do believe the season is changing fast. Don't think you can stay aloof from the climate, my dear fellow."

It was true, he had stayed aloof. Even during his years in Nanjing, when he had been a leader of student demonstrations against the government's do-nothing policy, he had prided himself on being a patriot who judged people and politics solely on their merits, whatever their party.

To be accurate, he held both the Nationalists and the Communists responsible for China's plight. One minute they were pledging a united front; the next it seemed they were at each other's throats again, quarreling over arms, territory, commands and, of course, funds. And the next, yet again, brother was killing brother for the seat at the head of the table while the enemy set their home on fire. Besides, ideology bored him.

But Chiang Kai-shek spoke for China on the world stage, and here in Chongqing the Guomindang ruled. With them, at least, he would have the chance to build something, to redeem honor. Or so he had thought throughout his college years, and when he first went to work at the Ministry. Now . . .

Looking out the window, he saw that the fog had thickened. Now he was desperate for a change. Any change. He had kept his promise to his mother by graduating and becoming an official, but even she would be ashamed of one who left his footprints only on salted fish. Try as he might, he couldn't think of any way to change his job for the better. Better, then, to change jobs.

He jumped to his feet. "Professor, how would you like a new reader—someone who'll be at your permanent beck and call?"

"If you mean yourself, I'd have to say no."

He was stunned. Only a minute ago he'd been one of Chen's most promising students. Angry, he barked, "But why?"

"You're not ready to take on such an onerous responsibility. Work at the Ministry a while longer."

"Work? What work? All I do is sit around, doodling to keep awake." He was going to add that after hearing Chen talk, on his last visit, about the digging of tunnels in Communist territory, he'd been doodling an entire network, then realized how ridiculous this would sound.

"Keep your eyes open a little longer," said Chen, turning back to the bookcase. "Sort the clippings while I finish collecting what I need for you to read. And from now on, think of enduring boredom and cultivating patience as a part of your education."

Steel Hope cursed under his breath but did as he was told. When he saw an antique cricket cage on the desk, almost identical to the one made from a gourd that Stone Guardian had always kept on his, it and Chen's lecturing took him back to childhood and his mood became even darker.

His father's study had been much smaller than this one. For generations it had been part of the receiving room, but as courtyards were sold, halls had been subdivided. The result was a room with a single window in which the oversized display case and the desk squeezed up against the wall offended symmetry. Unruly stacks of books sprouted from the floor. In winter, the air smelled of marsh; in summer, of mold, though if Stone Guardian noticed, he never spoke of it.

Standing in Lincoln Chen's study, Steel Hope saw himself in that room, kneeling on a washboard as he had done so many times: taut and still, an inkstone balanced on his head. Even now he could feel the weight growing, his muscles straining, the splinters from the washboard stinging his shins; hear the chirruping from the patriarch's antique cricket cage as he watched the smoking stick of incense in the censer. When it had burned completely to ash, his punishment would end.

Throughout his ordeal, Stone Guardian sat on the opposite side of the large desk, hunched over his abacus as if he were alone, as if totaling debits were all that mattered, as if the study were the throne room of the Emperor, his every word the law. Who had decreed that he should rule? Who?

Steel Hope had focused his anger on the prized cricket, which his father had spent hours trapping. He didn't dare hurt its cage; the gourd the color of cinnabar, with a lid of imperial jade, was an heirloom that had been passed from patriarch to patriarch. But the cricket, as indifferent to his suffering as its owner—that was a different story. In one quick motion, right under Stone Guardian's nose and without disturbing the inkstone on his head, he grabbed the cage and held his hand over the air holes. It didn't take long for the chirruping to stop. By the time Stone Guardian noticed the silence, the cricket cage was back in its rightful place. . . .

Lincoln Chen pushed him gently aside, interrupting Steel Hope's reverie. "Don't just stand there, Steel Hope," Chen said. "Start reading. And when you're done, go back to work!"

WHEN STEEL HOPE reached the Ministry, after dawdling as long as he could at a cheap but busy restaurant, an attractive woman dressed in a stylish and obviously expensive red coat was gesticulating wildly at the guard posted at the gatehouse. To no avail. Guards were trained to stand like trees. Steel Hope couldn't resist coming to the aid of any damsel in distress, and in no time he was doffing his cap, bowing slightly. "May I be of help?"

"Oh yes, please. This man understands none of the dialects I speak. How do I get to the offices of Deputy Minister Tang?"

Tang! He had been trying to see Tang for the past month about getting some meaningful work. If this rich girl was a relative of his, the day might turn out fine after all. Politely he introduced himself and, composing his most charming smile, held out a hand. "I'll be most happy to escort you."

She hesitated, then, glancing around the compound of identical squat gray buildings, removed the glove from her right hand and consented to shake his.

To coax her from silence as they walked together down the seemingly endless corridors, he borrowed from Mountain Pine's conversations to give a running commentary on an imaginary gallery of priceless paintings. Several times, he invited her to stop for a better look at the blank wall.

"Notice how Huang Kung-wang has drawn the three distances in this painting to emphasize the level, the removed, and the high. . . .

"The secret in this painting is its spiritual consonance, though that quality, of course, is beyond the capacity of words to capture. . . .

"And this is my favorite. Can anyone show me one that even comes close to its subtlety?"

The girl was obviously amused, for while she didn't encourage him with questions, she also gave no sign of a desire to hasten the end of the tour.

The receptionist in the outer office ignored him. "Miss Tang, your father has been called to a meeting and regrets that he can't go to tea."

A daughter was much better than a mere relative, and immediately Steel Hope said, "Miss Tang, would you do me the honor—?"

She was shaking her head no before he could finish, and the appearance of Office Director Ling, one of the Deputy Minister's watchdogs, put a stop to his gallantry.

"Cassia?" Ling was obviously astonished to see her there.

"Such a nice surprise, Uncle Ling."

Steel Hope nodded to the honorific uncle and stood his ground while the two exchanged news of their families. He cleared his throat. Only then did Ling acknowledge him, asking, none too politely, why he hadn't been at the rally that morning. When Steel Hope offered no excuse, he began ranting about discipline and devotion and setting the proper example, taking no notice of the obvious embarrassment not only of the delinquent junior official but of the boss's daughter. To escape, Cassia pretended interest in the only picture that hung in the room, the same unyielding Chiang Kai-shek that graced all government offices, while Steel Hope debated doing something foolish like a scissor kick. No wrong deserved such a public scolding.

Abruptly Cassia turned and, for the first time looking boldly into Steel Hope's eyes, she took his arm. Steel Hope was astonished. What was she up to? Interrupting Ling's lecture, she spoke playfully, yet with just the proper dash of authority to remind her father's subordinate who she was. "Oh, you mustn't hold today's absence against Steel Hope. It was my fault. Something came up unexpectedly and I had need of him."

Bewildered by her interest in so unlikely a suitor, Ling nonetheless gave the correct reply: "Of course, of course. Believe it or not, I was young once myself."

Equally bewildered, by her evident change of heart, Steel Hope was also quick-witted enough to seize the opportunity she had offered him. "Sir, you won't mind, then, if I take the rest of the day off?" he said, patting her hand. "Cassia has asked me to tea and a show."

Ling smiled grimly. "Yes, of course," he said again. "But Cassia, do see that he is present for next week's rally."

"He will be," Steel Hope graciously replied for her. Then, before the man could say another word, he swept Miss Tang out the door.

Her revenge for his impudence was to empty his wallet. After ordering a tray of sandwiches and cakes at the American Hotel, her favorite and also the most expensive in Chongqing, she barely touched them. He pretended not to notice. Whatever the cost, it would be worth it. A word from her to the Deputy Minister and he could stop doodling and start designing the bridges and tunnels his country so urgently needed.

But before he could initiate the intricate maneuver that would obtain her intercession in his behalf, Cassia suggested going on to the theater for a foreign movie. Given the state of his finances, he had no choice but to cajole the high-born lady into accepting a more amusing, though less prepossessing, destination, a seedy place to be sure, but one that offered what no other theater did—the sensation of the Xiaoxing Opera, his friend Summer Wishes.

At the word "friend," Cassia flashed a knowing look, which slowly settled into a tolerant smile; the same look Steel Hope's social peers all flashed upon being introduced to the beautiful actress he escorted, to show their sophistication and their appreciation for how one among them had managed to satisfy his sexual appetites without compromising his desirability as a suitor whenever a wife-to-be, less accommodating and comely but infinitely more eligible, should come along. Steel Hope despised that look almost as much as Summer Wishes did. His reasons, however, were complicated. Loyalty to his childhood friend had forced him to prove these sophisticates wrong by honoring her virtue. But in doing so, he proved nothing except what a fool he was—to himself. Who but a fool would refrain from helping himself to magnificent fare to prove a point that must inevitably be lost on those who couldn't possibly realize he was trying to prove one at all?

Now, however, he returned Cassia's knowing look. This was not the time to solve his romantic problems. He must talk Tang's daughter into going to the opera without divulging the fact that it was the only place in town that accepted his chits.

After the performance was over, Cassia suggested that they go backstage "to meet your . . . friend, the star."

It was a terrible idea. Summer Wishes would welcome the well-born intruder by throwing a tantrum, as she had done more and more often lately to compensate for the ambiguity of their long friendship and the reality that fame couldn't alter her status as a mere entertainer. But what choice did he have? He smiled grimly and led the way.

Backstage was even more chaotic and cacophonous than usual. Summer Wishes was dashing about, overturning props and burrowing in lockers, frantically searching for her talisman. "When I get my hands on the thieving bitch I'll pull out her hair strand by strand!" she shrieked. "That lice nest of hers is going to look so much like an egg you'll have to crack it open to tell them apart!"

He tried to remove Cassia from this mad scene, but she was amused and drew him behind a screen so their presence wouldn't interfere. Stifling giggles, she whispered, "Whatever is she looking for?"

"A blanket."

Her laughter now was unrepressed, and he didn't like her manner; indeed, he liked it even less than that of Summer Wishes.

"Let's go," he said.

"Let's not," she replied as Summer Wishes backed into the cymbals, knocked them off their stand, and burst into tears. Steel Hope, still behind the screen, almost kowtowed when Mountain Pine limped into the room with the missing blanket wrapped around his shoulders.

"What's the matter?" Mountain Pine asked sleepily.

At once Summer Wishes adopted the demeanor of a perfectly rational person and replied, "Nothing," upon which Cassia applauded, revealing her presence and Steel Hope's.

He felt as if he were crossing a room carpeted with poisonous spiders as he tried to select the proper tone and words for introducing the haughty daughter of the Deputy Minister to the actress . . . as if such introductions were a common occurrence. Mountain Pine was no help. He threaded his hands into the sleeves of his jacket and bowed deeply in the traditional manner—a sign that he had taken an instant dislike to Cassia and preferred not to give her any chance to offer her hand to shake—then busied himself picking up the wreckage and putting things back where they belonged.

"You gave a performance to end all performances," Cassia said to Summer Wishes. The words were polite enough, but the tone was condescending.

"Then you must not go to the opera very often," replied the actress, feigning the customary modesty while studying the only woman Steel Hope had ever brought to the theater.

"On the contrary, I make it a point to see everything, from Shakespeare to the organ grinder's monkey."

"I've seen Shake—" Summer Wishes paused a beat, then started over again: "I've seen my good friend Old Sha perform so many times that I've lost count. Which of his roles do you prefer?"

Steel Hope was mortified, but smiled on. Cassia was enjoying the encounter, and it didn't surprise him when she had another terrible idea— a late supper at her home.

Summer Wishes accepted without the customary excuses.

"And of course my invitation includes"—Cassia paused to award Steel Hope a smile—"my host, who promised me an amusing time and has succeeded beyond measure, and"—again she paused and, turning to Mountain Pine, added too kindly—"this person to whom I have not yet had the honor of being introduced."

Before Mountain Pine could refuse the invitation, Steel Hope pulled him aside. "Summer Wishes needs a friend. You have to go."

"The hell I will. You got her into this. You get her out."

Summer Wishes settled their dispute. "Mountain Pine eats with me after every show," she announced. "If I go, he'll go. . . ."

The Deputy Minister's house had arching roofs and was surrounded by garden walls; along its entranceway dwarf trees planted in shallow clay pots were set upon stone pedestals that led to a veranda decorated with colorful crossbeams. It recalled the paintings of a Li ancestor who had served in Sichuan over a hundred years ago.

To the servant who waited dutifully at the door, Cassia said, "Please tell Father we have guests for supper and ask if he will join us."

Steel Hope brightened. Perhaps coming here wasn't such a bad idea after all.

The receiving hall was furnished simply: Western sofas contrasted tastefully with antique rosewood. On the walls hung scrolls, gifts from noted artists who had penned poems to commemorate their meetings with the Deputy Minister. A grand piano stood in one corner. On the music stand lay a flute.

As tea was being served, a tall man entered, dressed in a fur-lined gown of maroon silk. Steel Hope hardly recognized the Deputy Minister out of uniform, and only at that moment did he become aware that Mountain Pine's pants were an old pair of his that Mushroom had lengthened by turning down the cuffs; that Summer Wishes' outfit, except for her bright red pumps, was almost identical to the tunic and pants worn by the maid.

Tang, however, was gracious, accustomed, no doubt, to entertaining unexpected guests, though his smile was reserved for Cassia as she made the introductions.

At a first meeting it was customary for the elder to pursue the obligatory search for a familiar name among the guests' clansmen. While staying clear of any who lived in occupied territory and might know Grand Hope as an open collaborator, Steel Hope finally succeeded in naming a distant relative the Deputy Minister had met, if only briefly; he neglected to mention, of course, that he himself had not yet had the pleasure. From there, they probed further, this time among the dead, and Steel Hope breathed easier. He had no trouble impressing his host with illustrious ancestors. Pleased, the Deputy Minister paid him the honor of offering him a cigarette.

At dinner, however, sitting before an array of wineglasses and an abundance of tableware, the conversation became awkward once their host cut off Steel Hope's query by stating that he preferred not to discuss the Ministry at home. Steel Hope tried to recover by bemoaning the dreary weather, but that topic was soon exhausted. Cassia, he thought, did her valiant best to make conversation, but Mountain Pine remained as silent as a shadow and Summer Wishes, unwilling to do anything that might dishonor him in front of his boss, was reduced to lavishing praise on one dish after another. Her extravagant enthusiasm embarrassed them all.

Cassia tried once more. "How long have you known Steel Hope?" she asked Mountain Pine.

Mountain Pine hesitated. Only after the Deputy Minister had repeated the question did Steel Hope realize that his friend was reluctant to reveal the truth. He sought to close the subject by saying, "Forever."

Surprisingly, Mountain Pine's expression became even darker. Had his bookmate mistaken his intentions? Could he possibly think that the young master was ashamed of him? Before this night such a notion would have been inconceivable. Now Steel Hope quickly tried to undo the damage by touting Mountain Pine's learning, the elegance of his verses.

No one at the table could have missed how Cassia's eyes narrowed. Clearly she doubted his veracity, and Steel Hope quickly added that his friend would soon be writing for the very best magazines.

At this, Mountain Pine interrupted. "To be precise, I've known Steel

Hope since he was born. My sister was his wet nurse, and I his servant boy."

Even Cassia, the accomplished hostess, had nothing to say to this.

As they got up from the table, Steel Hope longed to suggest that the visitors take their leave, but didn't dare while the air was still so intractable, though no doubt everyone wished for just that. The distance between the dining room and the receiving hall seemed much greater than before. The soles of Mountain Pine's shoes squeaked. Summer Wishes' high heels echoed.

At last they resumed their seats on the sofas. Steel Hope shifted uneasily. Father and daughter focused on an invisible wall in the middle distance. Summer Wishes avoided Steel Hope's eyes. Mountain Pine sat with his arms crossed. Servants appeared at the threshold, then, without entering, scurried away. Steel Hope took his cigarette case from his pocket and opened it. It was empty. This time his host didn't offer him one.

As the silence stretched to an intolerable fineness, Steel Hope wished he were anywhere but here, even in his smelly cubbyhole of an office.

Suddenly Summer Wishes pointed to the piano. "Who plays?" she asked.

"We both do," Cassia replied. "Father, the piano; and I, the flute."

"Won't you play something, please? I love music. We all do."

"If you'd like."

The Deputy Minister was aghast at the idea, but at the urging of his daughter he relented. In yielding, he exhibited the terrible politeness of a mandarin discharging an odious task.

Cassia fussed over the selection of the music, rejecting one familiar piece after another. The tune she finally chose was a plaintive one, especially suited to the flute. Father and daughter played well, and when Cassia glanced his way, Steel Hope smiled gratefully and pantomimed clapping. He didn't notice Summer Wishes rise to her feet, only her grace as she joined the other two at the piano. At first he thought he was imagining the song, so softly was it being sung. Then slowly, artfully, her voice soared until it transformed the dank night into day, letting in the rays of the sun to warm him. Once again, she was Summer Wishes, the actress. She gave him a prideful look. She was singing in English. He didn't understand how.

THE TEMPLE

WHEN THE FOG lifted to make room for the heat of spring, ice cream parlors—some barely a stall, others spacious storefronts—sprouted throughout Chongqing, as, surprisingly, there was a lull in the bombing. Summer Wishes was jubilant and, with her penchant for analyzing serendipity, almost at once discovered how these two happy events were inexorably linked.

That powerful forces must have diverted the enemy was incontestable. But these had to be mightier than the reasons Steel Hope cited—that the planes now targeted American soldiers, ships and planes, and the field of war had widened. What could these forces be? To Summer Wishes the answer was obvious. What else but the cosmic energies inherent in the wind and the water—feng shui? The presence of the new ice cream parlors had altered the earthly course of these elements, and this in turn had realigned the city with its natural surroundings, producing greater harmony, which brought good luck.

Her explanation made abundant sense. It also had ample precedent. Before locating any canal or dam, the Emperors had never failed to consult diviners concerning the feng shui of the proposed sites. So did everyone else, from the poorest peddler to the wealthiest banker, consult them before establishing any business or building a home, whether rude shack or resplendent compound. So did every filial son before buying a grave site for his father. So did Summer Wishes before renting a room or placing her bed within it.

The ice cream parlors, then, were essential to preserving the lull and the luck; and to ensure their continued existence, she took it upon herself to frequent these vital establishments as devoutly as if they were temples. To her, the ceiling fans, the striped canopies and the scratchy tunes emanating from gramophones assumed the role of incense, holy shawls and the chanting of sutras. The students studying at tables ascended to the status of revered luohans, whose learning penetrated the mysteries of heaven and earth, and so she emulated them by sporting rimless spectacles, a loose blue cotton qi-pao, white socks folded neatly at the ankles and sturdy black shoes. The price of two scoops of orange ice served as alms, but eating them was all too pleasurable, hardly a sacrifice, and so she dispensed inordinate tips as well.

Mushroom, normally indulgent, fretted. At current prices, what she had paid for a yard of brocade five years ago now bought a spool of thread. Their budget was stretched, and frozen treats two or three times a day hardly qualified as a necessity. With new shows added twice a year, and the next one due to open in less than eight weeks, where was the money for her charge's new costumes to come from? But no matter how gentle or how shrill the plea for some fiscal restraint, Summer Wishes recoiled with the stunned horror of a Buddhist nun asked to dine on greasy ham hock.

"I'll wear the old costumes," she said firmly.

"You can't! You're the star."

She pouted. "Then you work it out, Mushroom. You always do."

Mushroom threw up her hands. "What's the use? You can't help being a superstitious spendthrift. And I can't help being so capable."

Now, with Mountain Pine and Steel Hope, the two women were strolling toward the bus stop to catch the Number Three, which would bring them to the edge of an open-air market near the countryside, and yet another ice cream parlor, one of the few that they had neglected. Just the four of them on a pilgrimage, as Summer Wishes had planned. Not Cassia. Above all, not that she-devil whose presence disturbed her harmony and luck. Sharing Steel Hope with any other woman was like sharing the stage with a mouse, but sharing him with Cassia was like performing opposite a pack of rats. She was a matchmaker's dream. Not only had she been physically blessed with all five skull openings in perfect alignment, but she came with enough dowry boxes to sink a caravan of camels in the sand; and, most worrisome of all for Summer Wishes, the ancestral doors of the Tangs were equal in height to those of the House of Li.

To top it off, the matchmaker's dream had a father who starred in Steel Hope's dreams.

Ever since that late supper at the Deputy Minister's house, Steel Hope had played the attentive suitor, while Cassia had been inviting all her friends to the opera for the sole purpose of showing off Steel Hope, who lacked the money to entertain the woman elsewhere. If that wasn't bad enough, after the last act the crowd would troop backstage, where they attended the performance of her most challenging role—as Cassia's faithful go-between—at no expense.

What choice did she have? They were the darlings of the most famous and the most powerful, if not the wealthiest, families in China, be it Nationalist, Communist or Occupied. But she was also to blame. Unable herself to help Steel Hope become the man he'd always wanted to be, she had forever been urging him to enlist the favor of those who could. Now, night after night, she gushed, playing hostess to her rival while seething inside. What if Cassia favored her pet prince too much and too well? What if Steel Hope found such favors to his liking?

Today was one of her rare days off. Today, Cassia would have to do without Summer Wishes' hero.

Now, seated at an outdoor table with an excellent view of the market, its myriad amusements and parade of passersby, she reminded the others that the day belonged to Summer Wishes, and thus they must abide by her rules: No talk of opera; no talk of budgets; no talk of books; no talk of anyone remotely connected to the Ministry of Roads and Communications; no talk of work or the lack thereof; no talk of spies, corruption, traitors, politics or war.

Her companions demanded to know what topic was left.

She thought for a moment; then, fingering the packet of gold-tipped 999s in her pocket, which she planned to give to Steel Hope at some auspicious moment, she suggested the subject of her fans, in particular, the old fortuneteller, whose gift the cigarettes were.

Mountain Pine, recalling the first and last time he had sat beside the man who chomped on Longevity Buds and never missed a performance, pinched his nose. "What about him?" he asked.

"Well . . ." whispered Summer Wishes, motioning for everyone to lean closer. "He predicted that I'll be coming into some money."

Mushroom's eyes rounded like coins. "In time to pay for your new costumes?"

Steel Hope rapped the table. "You're out of order, Mushroom," he said. "No budgets, remember? And no talk of that fortuneteller either, unless the money he predicted is in your pocket."

Mushroom groaned. "What then can we talk about?"

"We can talk about *my* fans—in particular, the Tagalong Triplicates. Yesterday, they asked me to choose which nuts to buy. . . ."

Silently Summer Wishes cursed. Banning any talk of the Ministry, she had taken care of Cassia and her gang, but not the three classmates, pretty in dresses of the same style and curly hairdos, who were forever waylaying Steel Hope. Last week, when he and Mountain Pine as well as Mushroom escorted the star to the theater, the girls had come upon them by scheduled chance, and had asked him to choose melons for them. When he gleefully began to juggle three green ones, she had pushed Mushroom forward, proclaiming melons were her specialty. Mushroom, who had taught Steel Hope how to juggle, had snatched the melons from him one by one and, holding them at arm's length, pronounced them the best there was—for bellyaches—then sent the three shameless flirts on their way, each hugging a consolation prize.

This time they had made sure Summer Wishes wasn't there. . . .

". . . So, blindfolded, I circled the cart tasting the peanuts, walnuts, hazelnuts and chestnuts, and some nuts so exotic that I'd never tasted them before. And if Kwan Yin is at all merciful, I'll never have to taste them again. They were like stone. I almost broke my jaw. . . ."

Seeing the storm clouds gathering in Summer Wishes' eyes, Mountain Pine peered around for a waiter to take their orders and end this monologue. In truth, he wanted to end it on his own account as well, though it was the young master's ease he was jealous of, not his admirers. He didn't want to be reminded of his own awkwardness, of being introduced and then ignored. Steel Hope's flirts always made him feel like a dung-colored snail watching cardinals flit from tree to tree.

". . . The peddler informed me that the exotic nuts were called dried beans!"

With that punch line the fun-loving bachelor served himself up as buffoon. Summer Wishes and Mushroom burst into laughter, and even Mountain Pine couldn't help smiling. Steel Hope could charm the feathers off a peacock.

The waiter, stifling a grin, appeared.

They were just finishing their ice cream when a woman no bigger than a monkey, who was pulling by the ear a youth the size of a bear, drew their attention. Round and round she scooted and round and round he lumbered, until suddenly she shouted, "Oh pity me, having to marry a suckling boy! Oh pity me, having to teach a husband how to say 'Mama' and 'Papa'! Oh pity me, having to wait fourteen autumns and winters, fourteen summers and springs, for his chin to sprout a single hair!"

No longer did Summer Wishes find the couple amusing. They could have been Firecrackers and Baby Wang. She was about to suggest leaving when the husband reared back and smacked his wife hard.

Everyone gasped, but the woman wept with joy. "Oh, Kwan Yin is merciful," she cried. "At long last my husband is a man!"

Summer Wishes clapped at the happy ending. "What a scene!" she declared, then, lowering her voice to a conspiratorial whisper, added, "You must write about it, Mountain Pine."

Others had beaten him to the subject, thought Mountain Pine, at least once every few years for the last two thousand. But, as always, he was touched by her kind suggestion, however naive. "Only if you play the lead," he said.

"Why not me?" asked Mushroom.

"Because, my good woman, the man who dares to strike you hasn't been born yet!"

When everyone burst out laughing, Steel Hope loudest of all, Mountain Pine suddenly felt as if the snail had sprouted wings, and immediately motioned for a second round of ice cream.

While the others concentrated on eating before their portions melted, Summer Wishes, who preferred her ice cream soft, eyed two portly women dressed in sheaths so snug that their numerous rolls of fat seemed individually wrapped. They were pushing and pulling at a bolt of gold and black fabric, each squalling that her hand had made the first contact. The pattern was distinctive and Summer Wishes sighed wistfully. "Mushroom, how much better that fabric would look on us," she said.

At her words Steel Hope glanced up and, recognizing the Japanese motif, was suddenly furious. Enemy goods smuggled through the lines were on sale everywhere, it seemed, reminding him of Grand Hope and the Emporium and his own continued impotence, despite his attentions to Cassia. "It's shit. Japanese shit smuggled through the lines by traitorous shits for greedy shits to sell to don't-give-a-damn shits," he pronounced, and then, swiping his hand across the table, added, "I bet the machine for making ice cream comes from Japan too!"

His unfinished bowl of ice cream landed in the dirt.

The others at the table pretended not to notice. Ignoring such sudden rages, quick to come and quick to go, was always the wisest course.

Besides, they'd heard his speeches before. Only the waiter reacted. He came running to rescue the bowl, but retreated when, in conclusion, Steel Hope snarled at his beautiful companion, "Let others shame themselves."

"And what's so shameful about wearing something new?" Mushroom aimed her eyes at him like cannons.

Mushroom was the one person Steel Hope couldn't afford to cross. He threw up his hands in mock surrender. "Nothing, nothing whatsoever. Only not that fabric, please."

But Summer Wishes was no longer listening. "I hear drums," she said, and stood up.

"And violins and horns and flutes," said Steel Hope, wanting to make up for his churlishness. All about them gramophones spinning in various stalls produced a cacophony of sound, like an orchestra of musicians each blissfully playing his own favorite song.

"No. Real drums. It must be a wedding!" Summer Wishes loved weddings. "Let's go and see!"

Mushroom groaned. "My feet like it right here."

"Mine too," said Mountain Pine. Being a fourth was one thing, being a third quite another.

Summer Wishes folded her hands in prayer. "Steel Hope?"

He hesitated.

"Please. It's my day off."

Who could resist a supplicant as lovely and needful as she? Certainly Steel Hope couldn't, and together they darted through the crowd, past the vendors of crabs and eels, the herbalist, the locksmith and the weaver of baskets, heading toward the sound of the drums.

At the crossroads, Summer Wishes pointed to the right. "Look, over there." On the narrow dirt path that curled up the mountain, just beyond the terraced paddies, shimmering like magic carpets quickening for flight, they could see the brightly painted red and gold sedan chair carrying the bride, concealed within the windowless compartment whose door was sealed with strips of crimson paper. The procession wasn't a grand affair: just two men banging on kettledrums, two more shouldering a pole from which dangled a dowry trunk, and a small band of well-wishers.

Summer Wishes and Steel Hope made their way along the towpaths that crisscrossed the paddies, moving swiftly until a rocky incline leading to a bamboo grove slowed their pace. By then the procession had disappeared and the drums were barely audible.

Welcoming the shade of the bamboo, Summer Wishes tarried. For once, she and Steel Hope were alone, and suddenly she didn't care about the wedding. It wasn't her own, after all. "I'm too tired to run after the procession anymore," she said, telling an obvious lie that she hoped would please him. "Besides, we can see brides any day in spring. Let's just enjoy ourselves."

Smiling, he opened his cigarette case. It was empty.

She pulled out the pack of gold-tipped 999s and offered it to him.

"You shouldn't have done it," he said. "These cost a fortune."

"I didn't buy them, they were a gift from—" As soon as she spoke, she wanted the words back. His face had turned to stone.

He walked on, leaving her holding the cigarettes.

Doing her best to keep up, she thought how unfair he was. Of the many presents sent backstage by admirers, she made Mushroom return them all except for the occasional gift from the old fortuneteller, who, even a most suspicious mother-in-law could see, was harmless. His offerings were tokens of esteem, not costly enticements of silks or jewels. Certainly nothing he couldn't afford. In these uncertain times, didn't just about everyone pay to have his fortune told?

When Steel Hope had to step aside for a boy leading several donkeys laden with firewood, she was able to grab his sleeve. "I didn't do anything wrong. I didn't."

He removed her hand and hurried ahead.

She went after him, but was unable keep up the pace, and the distance between them grew. She must do something. A tantrum of her own perhaps? No, he was no stagehand or musician, easily cowed. She must appeal to his gentler instincts. On a soft patch of grass, she fell, then moaned. "Steel Hope, come back! Help! I tripped."

He stopped but didn't go to her, thinking, An accident of convenience, no doubt.

"Please help me, Steel Hope."

The pathos in her voice would have moved the keepers of hell. He turned to find her seated on the ground, rubbing an ankle, and looking as helpless as a sparrow with a broken wing. Perhaps he had misjudged her. He ambled back. As he was helping her to her feet, she shoved the cigarettes into his pocket. "I only kept the fortuneteller's gift for you."

"And what does that make me?"

Summer Wishes thought for a moment. "My friend?"

He shook his head in disgust.

"But we *are* friends, everybody knows that. And what are presents for but to give to friends?"

"Other men's presents?"

"What's wrong with that?"

He threw the cigarettes away and walked on. She started after him, then raced back to retrieve the gift and, dusting the dirt off the cellophane wrapper, resumed her pursuit. "I'm not like the others . . . I'm not," she insisted.

"Neither am I."

She trailed him into a wood, where trees of every variety were tall and their branches long. He didn't speak and she didn't know what to say. The light filtering through the panoply of leafy parasols was tinted a tender green, a light more like the moon's than the sun's. The air no longer tasted of dust, but was as crisp as water from a bottomless well. An unseen thrush trilled. The path was deserted.

He slowed, permitting her to catch up.

"Truly, I didn't mean to make you unhappy," she said, attempting a smile. "I was thinking only of you."

"I know."

Soon they were strolling through a region of the forest studded with eucalyptus and pine, and the lush fragrance of the trees' mingled scents took her breath away. Helping her over a difficult stretch, he put his arm around her. His face was so close to hers it was a blur. The wedding drums had been silenced altogether now by the sounds of the woodland; yet she heard them as clearly as she heard the orchestra when she sang. The beating, ever faster and louder, became unbearable. She feared she might faint.

"Why are you so quiet, Summer Wishes?" he asked.

"Why are you?"

He had taken his arm away, and they were walking again, but now hand in hand.

This is not a dream, she thought. In her dreams she knew exactly what he would do and what he would say. The scenes never varied, not even as little as an opera's story varied from one performance to another. He would declare his love. He would write to his mother. After a few days a kindly man wearing a cap with brass buttons would appear at her door. In his hand would be no mere letter, but a costly telegram: "The House of Li welcomes Summer Wishes."

A twig snapped. Birds darted through the air, trading branches.

She must have stopped walking, because he asked if she was too weary to continue.

How could she be weary of walking on air?

"Remember, the farther we go, the longer our way back."

His concern made much less sense than all the notions of hers at which he scoffed. What foolishness! Laughing, she tugged him along. He laughed too. How could he not? Against the arsenal of happiness she had marshaled there was no defense.

They passed a patch of wild lilies not yet in bloom, and she thought of the scallions that had once grown at the door of the gravekeeper's hut, and the changing moon and its constant passage and knew that somehow everything that had ever happened to her was converging on this day and from this day everything to come would flow.

As this realization grew ever stronger, there appeared off to the right a trail where overgrown weeds had been trampled flat, and without a word they chose to follow it. Soon they found themselves in a grove of stately pines as perfectly spaced as the rails in a balustrade, and, rounding a massive boulder, they came upon a small deserted temple. The sight was so startling that even as they approached it she could hardly believe the edifice was real . . . and yet so holy was the shrine that priests in their topknots and flowing saffron robes were bowing to welcome them.

The ancient steps had sunk partially into the earth, but the graceful roof still arched heavenward, draped in a mantle of dappled light. Fearful that any word or gesture might break the enchantment, she refrained from calling his attention to the tiny fawn, surely a descendant of the herd of deer the priests had once tended, that was just slipping out of view.

They stepped lightly, as if it were important not to disturb even a pebble or a blade of grass. The temple door, carved from the trunks of giant oak trees, was thick and solid, but it swung open at her touch, and for the longest moment they stood at the threshold. We are standing at the boundary, Summer Wishes thought, the boundary between the wing and the stage, the past and the future, one lifetime and the next. She closed her eyes, so that she might store forever in her heart the feeling she was certain he shared—an exquisite anticipation, at once unbearable and sublime.

Without a sign but as if on cue, they stepped inside. Strangely, there were no cobwebs or dust in the empty hall, now divided by a single shaft of light. How could that be? Perhaps her eyes were seeing what they wanted to see. Perhaps the debris had been cleared away by a novice who had remained faithful through the years.

So moved was she by such loyalty that she fell to her knees before the altar. "O Kwan Yin," she prayed silently. "How can I thank you for giving me this day?"

She heard a sound, a moaning, almost human. Steel Hope was closing the door.

Unable to discern any form in the darkness, she nevertheless sensed that he was coming closer, and as she waited breathlessly for him to walk the few feet to join her, the distance between them seemed a thousand lis.

Why wasn't she anxious? Afraid? They were the same questions others asked her each time she took the stage. She never had an answer, except to say that it was always so. But now she understood: Such serenity belonged to the province of dreamers where anonymity, not reality, ruled. In the theater, she fulfilled other people's dreams; here, a dream of her own.

With the sound of the first drops of rain hitting the temple roof, she knew that long after the shower had passed, they would still be locked in each other's arms. She also knew that as inevitable as the shedding of restraint and the gathering of tangled embraces would be the terrible price exacted by the god who had once dwelt on the altar where they made love, and that her dream would be lost . . . *still sparkling, ashes, ashes.*

IT WAS DARK, and for a long while he had been cradling her wordlessly, his breathing and hers indistinguishable, equally attenuated as if to prolong the interval between the beats of their hearts. Never had he felt so aware, so content.

Tenderly he traced her features with his fingertips, trying to see her face when there was no light, and, to his wonder, he discovered that the actress, whom he had known as a girl and had seen almost every day for the last two years, and the woman whom he perceived in his heart were not one and the same. Her loveliness had so beguiled him that only now was he seeing Summer Wishes with clarity. Searching for the words to describe his love, he found himself recalling the title of the poem that Mountain Pine had begun immediately after their reunion and never completed: "A pearl, a splendor, a grain of sand . . ."

Without warning, their synergy broke. For a moment, he couldn't decide whether it was she or he who had shuddered. Then he understood: She was afraid. He was too. She dared not speak. She dared not move. Her body no longer seemed as tangible. Somehow it was lighter, much lighter.

He pulled her close. He held her tight. He felt as if her ribs were laced with his like fingers clasped together—and yet she was slipping away.

Quick! He must summon her back. He whispered. The words sounded so foreign to him, as foreign as some forgotten language, even though the youngest child used them every day. He whispered that from now on, if she laughed, he would laugh; if she wept, he would weep; if she were to go away, a part of him would be lost.

Why did she still seem so distant?

She doesn't believe me, he thought. Yet how could she not? This time his words were true. . . .

His sleeve was damp.

She claimed her tears were tears of happiness. He knew she lied.

How could he make her understand what he himself did not? He couldn't. He only knew that affections never questioned for half a lifetime had in an afternoon turned into love. Perhaps love in the guise of affections had been there all the while. Perhaps love, unnamed and unexpressed, was not yet love.

Hoping that if his words couldn't convince her, his ardor would, he kissed her long and hard. Then he whispered, "Please believe me, my dearest love. What must I do? How else can I show you my heart?"

For a long time she held on to her silence and her stillness, and it took him almost as long before he finally realized that she had stopped distancing herself from him and was searching like a schoolgirl for the correct answer.

At last she tugged his sleeve excitedly, laughing with happiness and pride. She told him that he must save one of her gold-tipped 999s and keep it in his silver case for even longer than he had kept the one belonging to his father.

He laughed with her, and then he vowed. He would keep her gift until he was too old to stay the hour of his passage beyond the Yellow Springs. Only then would he smoke it, and with each puff recall all the goodness he had known in this life.

A Wedding

Two days later, Steel Hope leaned on the fender of the Jeep parked outside the opera house, waiting for Summer Wishes. The vehicle was assigned to him—proof positive that befriending Cassia had enhanced his prospects. Tomorrow his career would start anew.

When he'd announced at lunch that he would be going to Kunming on important official business, Summer Wishes and Mushroom had acted as though he'd won a ticket to immortality. Mountain Pine alone hadn't patted him on the back. Perennially the pessimist, he'd warned of amusing a tigress and mistaking her for a cat, and added insult to injury by stating the obvious —that this time Steel Hope wasn't juggling green melons, but grenades.

He glanced at his watch. Why was the orchestra still playing? However chaotic rehearsals for a new opera were, this one should have ended by now, though admittedly, even at this distance and to his untrained ear, the music sounded as discordant as Mountain Pine's barbs had sounded earlier. Mountain Pine was right about one thing, however: the mission was hardly a challenge. Anyone who could count and drive could check an inventory. Still, the Deputy Minister had chosen him personally, and not because he had a driver's license or was the most junior member of the design staff, but because "You're the only person I can really trust."

He glanced at his watch again and decided to give the Jeep another dusting. Returned from battle and pocked with bullet holes, it wasn't much to look at, but what did that matter? With Summer Wishes in it, a broken-down wheelbarrow would be the envy of the gods. His heart smiled at the thought of her.

To think that he had almost spoiled the afternoon they'd spent together when he recognized the temple for what it was. Inside, empty but immaculate; outside, utterly deserted, with not a footprint anywhere closer than the path of trampled reeds almost a li away—what else could it be but a depot for smugglers or black marketeers? He had meant to stalk out, had actually made it to the opened door before he remembered that he hadn't come alone. But when he turned to find Summer Wishes on her knees praying at the empty altar, nothing else mattered except how lovely she looked, haloed by the sun.

With all his being, he hoped that Mushroom wouldn't show up to escort the star home as usual, but would stay put in the attic room stitching, as she had promised Summer Wishes she would do until the new costumes were finished. One look at the Jeep and the big woman would plop herself in the backseat, remarking yet again that, woods or no woods, she'd never heard of anyone who wasn't eyeless, earless or legless losing track of a bridal procession, unless his attentions were totally engaged otherwise. He peered up and down the street. There was no sign of her.

Giving the vehicle an affectionate pat, he silently thanked his traitor of a half-brother. If that cocky bastard hadn't bet his boss a year's worth of gas that he could lure anyone the merchant cared to name—and his grandfather had named Steel Hope—behind the wheel of his shiny new Mercedes, he would never have learned to drive. Of course he'd been very young then, but even now he squirmed to think how cheaply Grand Hope's worst enemy had been bought. That the gambler had had to travel all the way to Nanjing to win the bet had offered no consolation, since he visited the capital often to woo the beautiful daughter of a leading scholar. Fortunately she had refused him. Or unfortunately. Steel Hope didn't know which was worse: dying young as she had done during the rape of Nanjing or living long as the wife of a notorious traitor.

There was a flurry of activity when Summer Wishes came flying out of the theater pursued by several distraught musicians and clambered into the Jeep, but once she was squarely lodged in the seat, like an Empress on her throne, the star banished her clamoring colleagues, commanding them to return to their instruments and practice until they learned to play a tune.

As the men padded off, she tapped the horn and said, "Let's go. We must hurry to find the wedding before it gets dark."

Steel Hope was mystified. "Whose wedding?"

"It doesn't matter. Anyone's wedding will do. A wedding is such a happy occasion, and bound to bring you good luck for your journey and your future success and"—she paused, smiling at once shyly and slyly— "for us."

He gripped the wheel to keep from throttling her. Summer Wishes' superstitious fancies were one of her most endearing characteristics. But not today. Not on their last night before parting for weeks. Not after what had happened at the temple.

Prying free his hands, she held them next to her heart; then, searching his eyes gravely, she whispered, "Please, Steel Hope. How can I send you off without good luck? We were wrong to . . . We should have kept following that other bridal procession and not . . . stopped at the temple. But if we attend another wedding right away, today, the gods, being so busy, might confuse the dates or the names and faces of the bride and groom and not be angry with us."

From that willful gleam in her eyes he knew it would be useless trying to talk her out of this latest fixation. Appealing to logic wouldn't work, any more than it had worked to counter her faith in the powers of feng shui when, patiently and painstakingly, he had explained the strategic and tactical considerations that were manifestly at play behind the interruption in the bombing. Her response had been two more scoops of orange ice.

Squeezing his hand, she again whispered, "Please."

He heaved a sigh, then asked, "Where does one look for a wedding?"

"Not in the city. We must return to the countryside, where ceremonies are held outdoors, and to the vicinity of where we . . . the temple."

AT TWILIGHT, while the sun painted the heavens a victorious scarlet hue, and Steel Hope waited for Summer Wishes to choose the way at a fork in the dirt road with nothing in sight but trees, they finally heard the faint beating of drums. She rose to her feet and surveyed the landscape like a seasoned general, pointed to the right, down a twisting foot path, then leaned over to peck his cheek. Next time, my love, you ought to have more faith in me, she thought. She also prayed. Oh, let this be an omen, an omen of the bright future in store for us.

The drums stopped. So did her heart. Was the silence a sign that the gods were jealous after all? A prelude to revenge? Surely all gods must covet the unearthly happiness she stole.

Steel Hope must have sensed her fears, for he took her gently in his arms and told her that their love was blessed by heaven. And before she could ask "How do you know?" he drove the Jeep into the weeds and jumped out. "Hurry, we mustn't be late," he said.

They ran the rest of the way, stopping near enough to see but not so near as to intrude when the drums sounded. Happy again, Summer Wishes pulled him along to the foot of a mountain of straw. Nimble as a goat, she beat him to the top, where she then perched. The view was perfect. She could barely contain a shout of delight.

Lighted torches marked the perimeter of the village threshing ground, a concrete square the size of an inner court. In the background, doors taken from their hinges and placed on low trestles to serve as tables buckled under the weight of a dozen white enamel basins filled to overflowing with food. Pots upended and set around the tables as stools were yet to be occupied by the several dozen guests, who stood facing an altar covered in red cloth that was decorated with a giant gold-foil symbol of double happiness. Upon it lay a dozen porcelain bowls containing finer fare, offerings for the spirits.

An elderly man tore the paper seal from the bridal sedan and opened its door. With the help of the village women, a slim figure draped from head to toe in bright red stepped out. Summer Wishes sighed. Such a beautiful bride! To keep from fainting with joy she leaned against Steel Hope.

He chuckled. "One would think you'd been trapped in that suffocating box all day instead of her."

"Isn't she beautiful?"

"How can I tell? Not an inch of her is showing. Who knows what manner of—?"

"Isn't she beautiful?" Summer Wishes whispered again.

He knew she hadn't heard him. How precious she is to me, he thought, memorizing her profile. . . .

He could see that every step the bride took toward the altar, Summer Wishes took also. Each time the bride knelt before guests or members of her new family, Summer Wishes' knees bent. Each time the bride kowtowed, Summer Wishes touched her brow to the ground.

It was only when the bride knelt before the altar that they had any inkling something was wrong. The bride was still kowtowing. Again

Summer Wishes also knelt, but this time the ground, when she touched it, was unforgiving as ice. Suddenly the drums stopped.

Though she whispered, the words sounded in her ear like her mother's cry on that autumn night when she disappeared. "Steel Hope, where is the handsome groom?"

His arms tightened around her. "He's . . ."

Wiping her eyes, she peered at the scene below. There was no one alongside the bride, just a shadow. No, the torches were playing tricks. Not a shadow. It had substance, but it wasn't a man. It was a wooden tablet.

"Where is the . . . ?"

Instead of replying, he pressed his lips to her hair and held them there.

What did he not dare say? The figure in red was now obscured by her tears. She shook him. "What does it mean? You must tell me, what does it mean?"

He turned her head toward him, shielding her eyes, and said in a gentle voice, even gentler than the one she had heard as they lay on the sacred floor. "The groom is . . . gone."

"How can that be? This is his wedding day and there is his beautiful bride." She was weeping openly. "Tell me he's well."

"He is well."

"Tell me he's not in pain."

"He is not."

She couldn't bear to look at the figure in red again, or her heart would break too. She mustn't ask any more questions. She didn't want to hear him say what she knew to be the truth, that the groom had gone beyond the Yellow Springs.

He did say it. He told her that the handsome groom would wait as faithfully as the beautiful bride, and that someday they would be reunited and live happily forever as loving husband and wife.

Summer Wishes trembled.

Even an arsenal of happiness was useless against death.

HAND IN HAND they climbed the stairs leading to the attic, stopping along the way, now and then, to embrace. Opening its door, they saw that Mushroom had fallen asleep at the sewing table, and Summer Wishes whispered for him to wait.

When she returned, she carried her talisman, neatly folded, in both hands.

"Please take this along," she whispered, holding it out to him. "It will keep you safe from harm."

Of course, the notion was ludicrous. But no other gift from her would require a greater sacrifice. With both hands he accepted the gray, threadbare blanket and, in keeping with solemnity, bowed and departed in silence.

THE JOURNEY

It was dawn. A pale, bashful sun peeked from behind distant mountains. Whistling as he drove out of Chongqing, Steel Hope careened past the yawning mouth of an unmarked cave that sheltered some essential industry or munitions plant. Suspicious guards glared. Take a good look, he thought, you won't see another fellow as lucky as I all day. He waved.

The instant his hand went up, the cantankerous old Jeep, laden with the two full drums of gasoline needed for the journey, swerved toward the precipice. Wrestling the wheel with all his might, he managed somehow to negotiate the hairpin turn and avoid plunging over the cliff, but the sickening sensation that seized him when the centrifugal force flung open the door and dragged him to the edge of his seat didn't leave him even after the Jeep had slowed to a crawl up a long, steep incline. While he desperately needed a moment to pull himself together, he didn't stop. Braking now might stall the engine, and end his journey before it began. As he had discovered earlier, when he would have needed an ignominious push to get going if he hadn't by chance parked on an easy, downward slope, the Jeep's starter was capricious. Besides, if he didn't take it easy, the brakes might not last the distance to Kunming and back—over two thousand lis on the map, but many times more on the road that coiled around the mountains of the Daliang range. Breathless and sweat-soaked, he cursed himself. How could he have been so careless? How could he have jeopardized his life? Worse, his mission? From now on, he would keep both hands on the wheel and his mind on the road.

He drove steadily, stopping only to give the right of way to soldiers, peasant boys with almost no training, many drafted at gunpoint. Inevitably all were streaked with mud. Inevitably only the officers carried guns. Inevitably the troops were trailed by bearers, stooped under burdens shrouded with tarpaulins, and the wounded, hobbling as best they could. Whom had they been fighting? Nowadays, it could have been anyone.

He rested once, waiting for the Hejiang ferry. Peeling one of Mushroom's special eggs—hard-boiled in soy sauce, spices and tea—he watched a sampan on which a skinny little boy was giving chase to a hen. He grinned. If epithets plucked feathers, the fat bird would have passed for a cantaloupe. The child could have been Firecrackers.

Long after the sampan had sailed from view, he was still waving.

At twilight he pulled off the road and bedded down in a patch of wildflowers. His pillow was the suitcase Tang had asked him to deliver to a former servant in Kunming when he had a spare moment. It contained only discarded clothing; but unlike the Jeep itself or the drums of gasoline, it was easily stolen. Far more precious was the blanket that covered him, and as the stars—never so many or so near—grew brighter and brighter, he drifted off to sleep marveling at the unexpected amplitude of his life.

By dawn, he was on the road again. Ahead were the mountains of Guizhou, which seemed to spring straight from the valley floor like a battalion of granite warriors. Here the road, often hacked from solid rock, was more treacherous, but he made good time and even managed to enjoy himself on the downhill stretches, when the labored groaning of the Jeep's engine gave way to blessed silence as he coasted to conserve fuel.

Then, in late afternoon, on a straightaway where winds churned, sanding his throat and eyes, he failed to notice an obstacle in the road until it was too late to stop. He jerked the wheel. The Jeep veered sharply, narrowly missing the ditch before screeching to a halt, miraculously without stalling. Glancing back, he saw what looked like a large bundle of rags and surmised that it must have fallen from some passing vehicle. He had yet to see a wheelbarrow, a wagon, a car or bus or truck that wasn't stuffed to overflowing with refugee families and what few belongings they still had.

Then the bundle moved. The motion was slight, but he shivered as if the ground were shaking under the Jeep, remembering stories of the baby tower where infants were left to die. Could there be a child in that bundle of rags? He jumped out and sprinted toward it. As he approached, he could indeed make out a human face—not of a child but of a man sitting in the dust.

Kneeling beside him, Steel Hope saw that he was about his own age, and had only stubs for legs.

"Are you all right?" Steel Hope asked.

There was no reply. The man was breathing as imperceptibly as a yogi. "Are you all right?" he asked again. The half-closed lids widened. The eyes had no pupils, only scar tissue.

Steel Hope glanced about, but saw no one else along the road. The man's poor family must have abandoned him to the gods, but not because they wished to; though his clothing was patched, it was spotless. For a moment, he didn't know whom he pitied more—the man who had no place to go or the man who had such a place, but couldn't proceed on his way and leave the other to his fate.

"Wait here!" he said. "I'll get you some food and water." He ran back to the Jeep. Only upon reaching it did he realize how ridiculous the directive to wait had been.

When he put Summer Wishes' blanket around his shoulders, the man nodded. When he put the canteen to his lips, however, he shook his head, then seized the canteen and, upending it, proceeded to wash his hands in the stream. Before Steel Hope knew what was happening, the outstretched hands had already been wiped dry on his shirt. In two gulps the last of Mushroom's eggs were gone.

"Got more?" the man asked.

"You can speak."

"So you'd have the sons of turtles cut out my tongue too? Good eggs. Got more?"

The voice was so commanding that Steel Hope automatically apologized. "I'm sorry," he said abjectly. "That's all the food I had."

"Then let's get on with it."

Had he happened upon a lunatic? Get on with what?

The man let out a piercing whistle. At the sound, as if by magic, men scrambled up out of the ditch and came running. Before Steel Hope could get to his feet, he was surrounded. He didn't have time to be frightened. He only thought, Now I'll find out if what they say is true: that the whole of your life flashes before your eyes at the moment of death. . . .

To his astonishment, that moment was postponed. Not a man made a move to strike or search him. At least not yet. Numbering almost a dozen, they ranged in years from boys not much older than the child on the sampan yesterday to a few older than Professor Chen. Among them, there wasn't one with a full set of teeth, and like the cripple who was obviously their leader, they were dressed in an array of bits and pieces of clothes, collected no doubt from the homes and backs of their victims.

Suddenly he remembered Stone Guardian's silver cigarette case in his back pocket and the Jeep, still running; perhaps because the men hadn't attacked him, he foolishly tried to make a run for it. Fast as a lizard's tongue, the crippled man's arm shot out; his fingers gripped his victim's ankle like an iron cuff. "Wait here, wait here," he mimicked, sparking riotous laughter all around.

This can't be happening, thought Steel Hope. How could he have fallen for the oldest trick in the bandits' world? He willed himself to be calm, to think.

The cripple let out another piercing whistle. At once, there was silence. "With dinner over and my legs all present and accounted for"— he gestured at his comrades—"it's time to get you home," he said.

Steel Hope's head pounded with questions. Where were they planning to take him? Wouldn't it be much simpler just to rob him and leave him lying in the road? Were they going to hold him for ransom? Not likely. Kidnappers picked their victims with scrupulous care. These men had something else in mind.

Two of his captors adjusted the blanket, then carried their leader to the Jeep and placed him in the backseat, while a third, the only one with a gun, used it to prod Steel Hope to the driver's seat, trailed by loud cackling and even louder refrains of "Wait here, wait here," each step of the way. To his horror, every last bandit piled into the vehicle and hung on.

When the Jeep took off like a grumpy hound beset by bees, Steel Hope burst out laughing, but his passengers, too busy hooting and shouting, never noticed. Laughter somehow changed his plight into farce; it was almost as if Steel Hope were seated not in the Jeep but in the audience watching the play. From this vantage point and as critic, he judged that succumbing to fear was like loading the rifles for his own execution. He must take his cues from the bandit leader. He must be indomitable.

As they drove off, the half-man issued directions. "Go straight ahead for a li. When you see boulders piled up like cows' dung, turn left."

"Left? But that's off the road!"

"Turn left."

"But the Jeep'll never make it. Not with this many—"

"Are you questioning me?"

Steel Hope turned left. When the Jeep went in and out of the ditch without mishap, he realized that the blind man didn't need eyes. Not only could he navigate, he could see into the future.

After an interminable bumpy stretch, where one after another of the passengers bounced off until only Steel Hope, the gunman and the bandit chief were still riding, they entered a wood where low branches forced the three of them to bob and weave and duck. The chances of escape were better here, and Steel Hope tensed, wondering if he should risk it.

"Don't even think about taking a detour!" shouted the crippled mind-reader and then, as nonchalantly as a dowager directing her chauffeur, ordered him to turn right into the course of a dried-up rivulet, barely the width of the Jeep.

The pebbled streambed eventually ended. Ahead lay a clearing, where more bandits lounged about an abandoned watchtower built by some warlord before Steel Hope was born, to guard his domain against men just like these. At the sight of the Jeep, they wiggled their thumbs and hooted in triumph, but such booty must have been routine, for no one took the trouble to get a closer look.

"Park anywhere you please," said the bandit leader, and as Steel Hope braked and wiped the outpouring of sweat from his brow, he made a grand gesture and added, "Welcome to our humble home!"

Again prodded intermittently with the barrel of the gun, Steel Hope stumbled toward the tower behind the half-man and his four borrowed legs. Inside, the only source of light came from the small T-shaped slits where rifles had once reposed, and it took a while for his eyes to adjust to the murk.

Now propped between two sacks of rice on the dirt floor, the crippled man let the talisman fall from his shoulders and invited him to sit down. "I myself," he added, pausing to savor his joke, ". . . prefer standing."

Steel Hope, eyeing the gunmen posted in the doorway, made no move.

"Come, come, don't stand on ceremony." The bandit chief patted the floor. "Take a seat, any seat. Address me as Uncle."

Like hell I will, Steel Hope thought, but deducing that there was nothing to fear from the sentries while their chief remained in a jovial mood, eased himself down, keeping as far away from the bandit and his iron grip as the small circular room allowed. He longed for a smoke, but still feared for his silver case.

"Remind me never to play cards with you, my nephew. Even the shrewdest marriage broker would pay handsomely for your tips on driving a bargain. . . ."

"What bargain?"

Instead of answering, the man launched with gusto into a self-introduction. "Your uncle is a former Little Red Devil. Joined up in '33. Only thirteen then. Ran messages in and out of Guomindang territory for two years, before getting caught. Chiang's dung maggots poked out my eyes and chopped off my legs to ensure an early retirement. You Guomindang?"

"No."

"Nah, I didn't think so."

"I could be lying."

The bandit nodded thoughtfully.

Steel Hope had the feeling the man was testing him. For amusement alone? He didn't think so.

"Lying would be smart. Those fellows out there"—he nodded toward the door—"would like nothing better than to slurp Guomindang guts like noodles."

"Are they Red Devils too?"

"Mostly stragglers from the Long March and a few recent escapees from Chiang's army. But enough about us. Tell me about you."

When dealing with a mind reader like the former Little Red Devil, Steel Hope thought, it was best to stay close to the truth. "I'm an engineer," he said.

"Hey," the bandit shouted to the sentries. "Can you believe it? A shrewd hero of the masses like me outfoxed by a beardless scholar! Proves my point. We'll have more reading and writing around here from now on."

Steel Hope was stunned. "You have a school here?"

"Isn't one blind man enough?" The bandit pursed his lips and shook his head in mock dismay. "Just look at the bargain you've made, the way you've taken advantage of me."

What the hell was this exasperating man talking about? Steel Hope almost wished he'd get on with his nefarious business, whatever that was. "What bargain?" he asked again. "What advantage?"

"I'm getting to that. . . ." The bandit paused, then, in one continuous motion, snatched a fly in midair and slapped it onto the ground. Before Steel Hope had comprehended that this had indeed happened, a guard was pouring water over the man's outstretched hands. Drying them on the guard's pants, he went on as if nothing had occurred. "First, for coming to my rescue, you get to keep your life."

Despite himself, Steel Hope sighed audibly. So the cripple had in fact been testing him. But whatever for? He warned himself against another trick.

"Second, for that blanket, you get to keep your eyes and legs. Third, for that splash of water and a couple of eggs, you get to keep your Jeep and your gasoline." The bandit spat. "Damn! Have I gone crazy? A man in my position could use a Jeep."

Steel Hope, who an hour ago had been sure he was about to be murdered, could barely stop himself from begging, "Not the Jeep. Please not the Jeep."

The bandit shrugged. "Oh well. Once said, words can't be unsaid by a man of honor. Unless..." He paused, inclining his head like a dreamy maiden. "Unless, of course, you wish to insist."

Steel Hope decided instead to show the man some mettle of his own. "Before we finalize our bargain," he said, "please keep in mind that I could easily have run over you and kept everything. Isn't that right?"

"Wrong! My men would've buried you at my feet to serve me in the next life."

Steel Hope glanced at the guards. Nodding, they bared their gums in idiotic smiles. In return, he bared his teeth. The play was beginning to drag. He must bring it to a climax. "Why have you been testing me?" he asked.

"What do you take us for? Bandits?"

Steel Hope assumed the question was rhetorical, and said nothing.

"I asked, what do you take us for?" Suddenly there was an edge to the bandit's voice.

"I...you told me. You're soldiers in the Red Army."

"You bet your life we are." The guards, who had obviously executed more than a few hostages, thought this hilarious.

The bandit snapped his fingers in their direction. One of them ducked out the door and returned with Tang's suitcase, which he set on the ground in front of Steel Hope.

"Now, let's get back to business," said the bandit. "It's customary, I believe, for a guest to present a gift to his host, and I've set my heart on this suitcase of yours. How about it?"

In his astonishment, Steel Hope blurted out the truth. "The suitcase doesn't belong to me. I was carrying it for someone else."

The bandit went on as if his prisoner hadn't spoken. "And since we've decided not to stand on ceremony, we'll open my gift now if you don't mind," he said.

"But—"

"No buts." The cripple, no longer jovial, showed his palm. "The key."

Steel Hope shrugged. He wasn't going to cross the man over a suitcase full of old clothes. He took the envelope containing the key from his pocket and broke its wax seal. "Shall I unlock it?"

"And spoil my fun? You've done enough, leave the rest to me," said the bandit, pulling the case toward him. "By now you should know I love surprises." With the flourish of a master tea taster, he caressed the case, bent down to inhale its aroma. "Ahhh . . . genuine pigskin." He undid the lock, then opened the lid just enough to slip a hand inside. He beamed. "Oh, you shouldn't have. It's much too grand a gift. . . ."

Steel Hope took his cue. "On the contrary, it is most unworthy, Uncle. Forgive me, I must point out what you can't possibly know even with your expert touch—that the clothing isn't new, it's used, discards a friend is sending to a servant. Naturally, if you have a need for it even so, it's yours. But if you prefer cash, I'll gladly exchange what I've got for the suitcase."

The bandit reflected on this offer for what seemed an unnecessarily long time, then slammed his palms on the lid, closing it. He roared with laughter. Steel Hope was more bewildered than ever. What was so funny about old clothes?

"My nephew, some bugger's mistaken you for a sheep and rammed his tool so far up your ass that if you're not careful you'll end up with a forked tongue."

At this barnyard quip, the guards doubled over with laughter, and one of them took up his leader's metaphor. "Baaa baaaaa, baaa baaaaa . . ."

Steel Hope felt a chill. He should have known the case contained something besides old clothes. Why would anyone lock up old clothes in a genuine pigskin suitcase? "What's in that thing?" he asked.

"Baaa baaaaa . . ."

The bandit gave his head a thoughtful scratch, then said in a mocking falsetto, "Your dowry, perhaps, my lady?"

Again the guards laughed.

Steel Hope inched toward the suitcase. The bandit was quicker and scooped it up. "Shame on you. Even the oldest of old maids manage to hide their hots."

By this time Steel Hope didn't care if he was shot, he had to see what was in the Deputy Minister's case, how much of a fool he'd been. "Damn it, show me what's in that case!"

Laughing, the bandit hurled it at him, once again demonstrating his strength. Had Steel Hope not ducked, it would have sent him sprawling. The lid snapped open when it hit the ground, hiding the contents from view, and he gave it a kick, meaning to turn it around. Instead he sent tiny objects flying. One landed in his lap. He didn't have to inspect it more closely. He knew at once what it was. A quinine pill. There were thousands, worth a fortune on the black market—and an army in lives.

Not only was Tang lining his sleeves, he might as well be working for the enemy, loading their guns. Images shuffled through Steel Hope's mind like a deck of cards tumbling slowly through the air: Cassia taking off her glove to shake his hand; Tang offering him a cigarette; his grandfather tossing him his red envelope; Grand Hope opening the door of his Mercedes; the portrait of Stone Guardian in his recurrent dream, its eyes following him; his father as a young official watching the enemy hoist up the Rising Sun. . . .

Feeling a stab of pain as sharp as the point of a bayonet, Steel Hope doubled over, crying, "I'll kill him, I'll kill that corrupt bastard!"

AFTER THAT, he must have gone crazy, for the next thing he knew, he was soaked and filthy, his knuckles were bleeding and he was sitting at a table. Across from him sat the Red Devil, gulping from an old Carnation milk can. He could smell the cheap wine.

"Little Nephew, take it easy," the man said. "We have lots of planning to do."

"I'll kill—"

"If anyone's going to get killed, it'll be you if you go back."

It took a moment before Steel Hope realized that the man had spoken the truth. Even if he was permitted to leave here with the pills, he couldn't pretend nothing had happened, for upon delivery it would be obvious that the sealed envelope had been opened. If he went to the authorities, or was caught, how would he prove that the suitcase belonged to the Deputy Minister? Only the two of them knew about it. And even if he could somehow manage to establish that the pills were Tang's, how would he ever prove that he hadn't known about them or, worse, that he hadn't stolen them in the first place? With the best of luck, it would still come down to Tang's word against his. And who in authority would believe him? No one.

He reached for the wine, then put the can down. He mustn't make a fool of himself. He must keep a clear head. . . .

The bandit snapped his fingers. "May I make a suggestion?"

Steel Hope started. "Why not?"

The man assumed a most avuncular manner and said, "There's only one way out of this. You must kill yourself before they kill you."

This time Steel Hope understood at once. Running away would solve nothing. It would be proof of his guilt. And so he merely asked, "Will you help?"

"Ask around," the bandit said. "Solving problems is what I do."

IT WAS midnight. A sliver of a moon dominated the stars in a cloudless sky.

Steel Hope stood on a ledge and peered into the abyss. The fathomless dark mirrored his thoughts. The sorrow of vanishing without saying farewell to Mountain Pine and Summer Wishes eclipsed rage. Mountain Pine, who was blind to his excesses and had seen all his life unfold. Summer Wishes, who had offered him a love he could never hope to know again and to whom he had said, *From now on, if you laugh, I shall laugh; if you weep, I shall weep; if you go away, a part of me will be lost.* . . .

And yet, if he returned, they would be in danger, too. And if they were beside him now, what could he possibly say? That everything would be fine . . . that he would be back?

He took out the silver case. There were three cigarettes left, two cheap ones and the gold-tipped 999. He smoked one, then another, thinking of the promise he had made at the temple and how Summer Wishes had looked, haloed by the sun. He ran his hand over his sleeve, feeling the dampness of her tears, though it was dry.

When he took the last puff of the second cigarette, he held the smoke until his chest ached, then dropped the butt by his foot and watched the lighted tip grow dark. All the while, he prayed. Please take care of each other. For me. Please let her know that I haven't smoked this last cigarette. Please let me live on, so that I may come back.

He kissed the gold-tipped 999 and closed the case, and then, gazing for what could be the last time at the ideograms etched in the silver, he saw the Patriarch of the House of Li tending the grave of his first wife and whispered, "O my father, I understand."

As he walked back to the Jeep, one of the guards waved impatiently. "Hey, did you smoke a whole pack?"

"I needed a moment alone."

"You'll have plenty of time for that soon enough. Everything's set. The rest is up to you."

Removing his watch, pen, and belt, Steel Hope placed them with the cigarette case under the driver's seat. He hesitated about leaving his wallet. The money had already gone toward making arrangements; only keys and Stone Guardian's letter remained.

"Hey, what's the matter now?" said the same guard.

"Nothing," replied Steel Hope, tossing the wallet into the Jeep. Why take the chance of having it found on him? he thought. Didn't he know all forty-nine words by heart? Backing away, he smiled ruefully. Nothing, he thought, was what remained of the young engineer, except for the blanket the Little Red Devil was wearing as a cape—the talisman Summer Wishes had given to her love.

While one guard unscrewed the caps on the gasoline drums and the other lit and shielded a twist of straws from the wind, Steel Hope walked off.

He was still walking when the Jeep plunged down the cliff and exploded. He could see the path before him as clearly as if it were day.

FROM BEHIND a basketful of laundry, the landlady announced, "You're late! I let a guest into your room right after you went out. A nice-looking and beautifully dressed lady guest," she added meaningfully. Before the gossip could put down her basket and start interrogating him, Mountain Pine thanked her and made his escape, hurrying up the stairs despite the heavy books he carried. He wasn't expecting anyone, but perhaps that Ningbo banker with palsy had spilled tea on his papers again and sent his secretary over with them. When he saw that the door was closed, however, he slowed his pace. Obviously the guest, whoever it was, had left. He sighed. The banker paid well.

But as he set the books down to get his key, he heard a click. The door opened. Before him stood Cassia. If it had been Madame Chiang Kai-shek he couldn't have been more surprised. He managed to mumble a greeting and advised her that Steel Hope had gone out of town.

"I know," she said. Her voice sounded unsure.

It was only then that he noticed she looked nervous, and thought she must have heard that Steel Hope and Summer Wishes were more than ardent fan and star.

"I came . . . to see you, actually," she said. "May I sit down?"

He almost laughed. She had had the run of the place for hours.

"Of course," he said, gesturing toward one of the two chairs drawn up at the table. He noticed that she was carrying a small packet. She held it out to him.

"What's this?"

She hid her face in her hands and wept.

He was incensed. Being Steel Hope's bookmate for over twenty years was one thing; was he condemned to be his eunuch and look after his women too? No, my friend, he wanted to shout, you can tend to your rejects yourself! But Steel Hope wasn't there to be shouted at, and Cassia wouldn't stop crying; he had no choice but to offer his handkerchief.

"Thank you," she said when she regained control. "You're kind, most kind. I thought I should come myself. After all, you were his best friend."

"Were"? Had this woman and her father so poisoned Steel Hope's mind that he had taken his bookmate's insulting comments about tigress and melons to heart? No, that was impossible. What was entirely possible, however, was that Cassia was scheming to rid her suitor of an embarrassment. "What do you mean, 'were'?" he asked.

"There was an accident. . . ."

HALFWAY UP the stairs to the attic room, suddenly Mountain Pine felt as weak as he had ever felt after a prolonged coughing fit, when every ounce of strength had been expelled. He stopped climbing and slumped over the banister.

"Grandpa, are you sick?" It was a neighbor's child. "I'll go get Mother."

"Don't. I'm fine." With an effort, he straightened.

Seeing his face, the girl blushed. "Oh, Young Uncle, it's you. I thought . . . I mean . . . You looked so old."

"Go and play."

"Do you want me to help you? I'm very strong."

He shook his head and tried to smile. "Run along. It was my foot . . . it fell asleep."

The girl nodded her acceptance of this explanation, but kept an eye on him nonetheless as he pulled himself along by the handrail, until he made it to the third-floor landing. That sixth sense which warns speechless creatures of danger told him to look up. Summer Wishes was sitting at the top of the fourth flight, with her chin cupped in her hands, totally absorbed in "reading"; though she hadn't learned to read more than a few dozen characters, the actress could recite from memory whatever he had read to her. Seeing her now, he realized that it was Wednesday, the morning Mushroom set aside to bathe.

He considered fleeing. Yes, that would be better. He'd come back at a more convenient time.

He flattened himself against the wall to catch his breath before making his escape. But there was no escaping the fact that she was still sitting there, tracing the words with a finger, happy in her love.

For a moment, he accused her. Why did you have to be home? Don't you realize that I need more time, much more time?

When a voice within asked, And Steel Hope did not? he cringed with shame. Self-pity, always unseemly, was grotesque now. And yet the shame that self-pity sparked only fueled it. What right had he to take out his grief on her? No more right than he had had to take out his frustrations, his yearnings, his resentments, on his young master. Yet the admonition that had run through his mind constantly but had never been voiced, ever since the first night of their reunion when Steel Hope and Summer Wishes had danced together, sounded again in his head: "Young Master, leave her be, leave her be."

His legs failed him and he slid down the wall to rest on the steps. Their creaking betrayed his presence.

"Mountain Pine, is that you?"

He held his breath.

"Mountain Pine, is that you?" The same amiable eagerness was in her voice as always.

"No!" he wanted to shout. "Not yet!" She was coming down the stairs. By the lurid cover on the magazine in her hand, he knew that his pupil had been studying his latest story.

He had no choice now but to tell her. "Good morning," he said.

"You're early."

"No—I mean, yes! It doesn't matter."

She reached him and, smiling conspiratorially, glanced up at the closed door of her apartment. "It won't be long now. Much longer and she'd be as wrinkled as a dried jellyfish."

"Perhaps it would be best to come back later."

"No, don't go."

"But . . ." He blurted out the first excuse that came to mind. "I haven't had tea yet."

"I'll fix you some as soon as we're inside. Come and sit beside me."

The stairs were narrow and their knees touched. "Mountain Pine, are you ill? You're much too pale." She put a hand to his forehead.

He brushed it away more brusquely than he'd intended, and hastened to distract her. "How do you like my story?"

Usually he doted on her cheery words of praise, even as he realized how indiscriminate and excessive and ridiculous they were. Today, he was offended by them. How could she not recognize the work of a hack whose sole purpose was to humor the censors and fill his rice bowl? Every character was as thin as a paper doll; every scene, a vulgar plea for penny emotions. As for the plot, what was his didn't work; what did was borrowed.

He must have been frowning, for she began soothing his brow with her cool fingers. He brushed her hand away again. Still she smiled. Still she praised him. How could she be so blind? How could she be so ignorant as not to know that it was her imagination alone that transformed his rubbish into the stuff of dreams?

"... You'll see, our children's children and their children will be reading it at school."

He wished he were dead.

The door swung open. Mushroom, fully dressed in her usual black tunic and pants but with her hair still dripping wet, appeared at the head of the stairs. "Come on up," she boomed.

He turned away. Her loud voice hurt his ears.

"I didn't mean to keep you out here so long," she said, even louder. "It's just that these days charcoal is so expensive that I don't wash, I marinate."

For a moment, Mountain Pine considered giving Mushroom the terrible task, but even as the idea occurred to him he recoiled from it. He mustn't be cowardly. Steel Hope would have wanted him to be the one to tell Summer Wishes, and to do so when the two sworn brothers of the Middle Heart were alone.

While Summer Wishes put on the kettle and prepared lunch, Mountain Pine watched Mushroom as anxiously as a child watches his mother's back, though he hastily turned to the pulp magazine every time she faced him, pretending to be riveted by his own story. He must wait until she had completed her chores. Never one to waste a drop, she would use the bathwater to do the laundry and, when that was done, use it to wipe the furniture, and finally to mop the floors. Only then would she be going to the market. He willed her to stretch out her tasks to fill the hours until they had to go to the theater. He must have more time. He must.

The next thing he knew, his cup was empty, and Summer Wishes and he sat at the square table alone.

"Shall I read for you now?" she asked.

"What?"

"Read. My lesson . . ." Again she put her hand to his forehead. "I think you have a temperature."

"No, I'm fine." He wondered, Why does death always take the wrong man? In the past, he had wanted to exchange places with Steel Hope, but for different reasons. Swallowing hard, he said, "I have something to tell you." He took her hands in his. He had never done so before, and the gesture must have alarmed her, for she sat up straight, wide-eyed as a fawn startled by the footfall of a hunter.

"It's—it's Steel Hope," he stammered.

"He's back?"

"No."

"No, of course not. He's not due till next week."

He shook his head. "There was an . . . accident. The Jeep burned."

She freed her hands and forced a laugh, which went on and on until the sound, so unnatural and so insistent, seemed to be choking her. Finally, breathless, she said, "But of course Steel Hope escaped."

He shook his head.

"I don't believe you."

He reached into his pocket and brought out the packet Cassia had given him. His hands shook as he opened it and laid before her a watch and a buckle, which could have belonged to anyone, and a silver cigarette case, misshapen and scorched, and unmistakable.

For a long time, she stared hard at the objects, as if by force of will she could make them disappear. He thought that soon she must weep, but there were no tears. She touched the watch, then quickly withdrew her hand. He shut his eyes, praying for Mushroom to return.

When at last she spoke, the sound was barely a whisper. "May I keep them?"

"Of course. They belong to you."

"No, no, you don't understand," she said, smiling. It was the smile of an actress. "I'm going to hold these for him. I'll return them when he comes home."

At first he thought his ears had deceived him, but then he saw the look in her eyes, so vacuous and yet so crowded with phantoms, and he asked, "Haven't you understood? He's . . . not coming back."

She nodded. "I understand. You told me. Not today. And not next week. But he'll be back. He'll he back. He'll . . ."

Don't, he wanted to cry. This time you can't pretend. You mustn't. Not even for a little while.

She had put on a quizzical look, as though he were guilty of speaking nonsense.

How could he make her understand? Steel Hope was at peace. She was the one in danger now.

"Listen carefully, Summer Wishes. Steel Hope is . . ." It was no use; he couldn't say the word she could never bear to hear. Again he used the euphemism. "He's gone and he's never coming back."

"You lie!" she shouted. Her eyes were no longer blank, but feral. "You can't fool me. You've always wanted him gone. But he's coming back all the same. He's coming back. And I'll be waiting."

WHEN MUSHROOM returned, Summer Wishes was still polishing the misshapen cigarette case, rubbing it and rubbing it, even though it shone as it had never shone before. Without stopping, she looked up and smiled. "Oh, Mushroom, let's have noodles today, noodles for longevity. You like noodles, don't you, Mountain Pine?"

He saw that Mushroom didn't even dare to ask him what was wrong. There was a wildness in the room. She set down her basket and eased herself quietly onto a chair, as if terrified that any sudden move would tip Summer Wishes into the abyss that only those who loved her could see. On the surface, nothing unusual was happening. Beneath it, chaos. While she ladled water into the pot and set the table, she sang. It was a joyous song, about homecoming. But she sang it so slowly, so achingly, that it sounded otherworldly. When the water boiled, Mushroom automatically got up to fetch the noodles from the top shelf, too high for others to reach. Summer Wishes snatched them from her, shoving the big woman with such force that Mushroom almost fell.

"I'll do it. You're careless, always so careless about noodles. Don't you know that they must all be cooked intact? Don't you know that not one must be broken? You two are just alike. You don't really care about noodles. But I do. Oh yes I do."

Singing again, she selected a single noodle, the longest, and floated it gently into the pot.

PART THREE

FIDELITY

PUMPKIN FIELDS

(1944)

STEEL HOPE SAT in a field of pumpkins, watching as the village carter, perched on the roof of his hut, rotated through the points of the compass, pausing now and then to peer at something in the distance. In his hand was a megaphone stolen from the Japanese. Without it, Carter Zhou, who had the keenest eyes and strongest voice in East Village, but who feared, among many other things, heights, would never have volunteered for the post of singer. With it, he was a warning system.

Marveling at the skinny fellow, Steel Hope thought, as he had thought every day since the Party had sent him here from Yenan to shore up the tunnels after a cave-in, that were it not for Wispy Eyebrows, he'd be lost. Like most solutions to the cadre's problems, the megaphone had been the Headman's idea.

For the story behind the idea, however, he'd had to wait many months, piecing it together, as he'd pieced together everything he'd learned about these people and this place, from the odd phrase, if not monosyllable, dropped here and there as rarely as the heavens dropped snow south of the Yangzi. It had begun before the war, when, in his travels, Carter Zhou went to the cinema. The wonders he had seen had become district legend; above all, the pasty-faced foreigner with bumpy hair singing into a megaphone.

Who would have dreamed that a metal cone could mean life or death? When warned, the peasants would disappear into the tunnels, where they had also hidden the harvest, and escape capture during the enemy mop-up that had been under way in the area since the grain ripened. Even more unlikely, who would have dreamed that his journey in that cantankerous old Jeep would have brought the callow young engineer he had been to this post behind enemy lines? Or that he would be a leader of partisans, a Communist cadre responsible for the safety of ten villages in Hebei Province?

Suddenly Carter Zhou began singing at full voice a song of Hebei that electrified the hamlet, its warning carrying to the next village—even, it seemed, to where the vast plains merged with the cloudless blue sky. Peasants scrambled out of their homes. Some, carrying straw mats, buckets of dirt, brooms, and old truck tires, dashed toward the road. Others, hugging pumpkins so big that their arms could barely circle them, headed for the fields.

They worked quickly. Those with mats placed them over the holes in the road in which, the night before, they had laid homemade mines that exploded upon contact. Working behind them, those with dirt, which had come from the holes, dumped it on the mats, spread it and swept it smooth, then scored the pristine surface with tire tracks. In the fields, the men carrying pumpkins arranged them among smaller ones still attached to the vines, marking corridors planted with mines set to explode when detonated by the cadre.

As quickly as they had appeared, the villagers vanished from sight, though the enemy convoy, slowed by fear of traps along the way, had yet to come into the plain view of anyone except Carter Zhou.

Now Steel Hope sat hunched in a ditch facing the pumpkin patch, grinning with pleasure and pride. The whole operation had taken no more than eight minutes—three minutes less than the previous record. That had been several months ago, however; recent drills had been such dismal failures that he'd begun to think the villagers had lost heart and no longer cared what might happen to them. Now he realized they were only sick of practicing.

He checked the wires, each connected to a mine, that stuck out of the banks of the ditch like exposed roots against the map he'd drawn on a piece of sackcloth, with circles to indicate the locations of the bombs.

Unexpectedly, Wispy Eyebrows and four other men—all that was left of the local militia after seven years of war—joined him. He cursed. What the hell were they doing here? Everything was set. Everything had been agreed upon. All the villagers, including his present company, were supposed to hide in the tunnels until the enemy had gone.

He tried to persuade the five to follow the plan. None said a word or even looked his way. They merely squatted, peering intently through the bean trellises that screened them from the road. He smiled affectionately. Peasants! He might as well be addressing a row of stone frogs.

What were they now but targets anyway? Had been since their ammunition ran out and they'd buried their precious weapons—three rifles, five Mausers and a couple of old pistols, filched from dead bandits, Guomindang runaways, Japanese conscripts and puppet soldiers—in the tunnels along with the even more precious harvest. What if one of them got in his way and inadvertently betrayed their hiding place before the trap could be sprung? None of them was needed here. None of them was about to go away.

He checked his watch. It shouldn't be long now. He considered again urging the men to make a run for the tunnels before it was too late; but knowing it was futile, he refrained. He smiled once more, amused this time by his own behavior. After nearly two years of sleeping on their kangs, eating from their pots and working alongside them in their fields, he'd become as miserly with words as any peasant. Orders called for cadres to lead partisans in guerrilla warfare and convert villagers to communism. He did his best, but his best didn't go far. He himself had received only two weeks of instruction in Yenan before Lincoln Chen, whom he'd assumed was still in Chongqing, had suddenly turned up to dispatch him to this village to deal with the cave-in.

What did a spoiled young master with a degree in engineering know about being a district leader? The new cadre hadn't even known what to do with the flat stones the children presented to him when he arrived. He'd thought the paper substitutes were ornaments to decorate he couldn't guess what, until he came across some next to Wispy Eyebrows' honeypot.

But he had known how to shore up the tunnels with stolen railroad ties, which was more than his predecessor knew, and the villagers, seeing this, were willing to go along with his plans to turn what had been more of a snare than a refuge into a multi-leveled maze, replete with traps and mines, chambers for storing grain and safe havens, along with subterranean passageways to connect this village with the others in his district. Indeed, they treated him as reverently as they did their departed ancestors.

Their treatment of his tutelage was another matter. Those ideas that coincided with their own they embraced eagerly; those that didn't, they pretended to embrace eagerly as well—until moments like this when, without warning, they presented him with done deeds, unforeseen and unalterable.

At first, given his youth and sex and the former cadre's penchant for fondling women in the darkened tunnels during raids, they had shooed away all women flashing more than an upper and a lower tooth, married or not, whenever he was around. But that had changed as they realized he wasn't like his predecessor, but like the Communists in the stories people heard cadres tell—men who abstained from life's pleasures and devoted themselves wholeheartedly to revolution.

For in truth, the juggler of melons from Chongqing no longer existed. And at times like this, he could scarcely imagine him or conceive how Steel Hope could have assumed that Mountain Pine would always come when summoned, or that Summer Wishes would always lie beside him. Though they were never absent from his heart, they seemed as far away as the First Emperor.

Again he checked the detonating mechanism, and it occurred to him that, since they clearly had no intention of leaving, his companions might be of some use after all. He turned to the men. "Comrades," he said, "since you're staying, pay attention." One by one, he picked up the wires, pointed toward the sites of the mines in the field and at their locations on the map, then threaded the wires through the sackcloth. Now if he was hit, they could pull the right trigger wires at the right moment and blow the invaders away.

When Steel Hope had finished connecting the stand-in switchboard, Wispy Eyebrows grunted on behalf of the others, then returned to fixing his gaze on the empty road. As always, waiting was the hardest part of the operation, waiting and wondering if this would be the day the enemy would find the tunnels. It was always day. At night the Japs holed up in the cities or behind moats in guard towers. At night, he and the villagers went on the move, laying their traps. Once he had cried for Amber Willows to light the lamp by his bed and banish the beasts that sneaked into darkened rooms to steal little boys when they closed their eyes; now he prayed for the dark.

Reaching for a cigarette, he realized that his companions had been fingering their tobacco pouches. Were they empty? He held out his prized pack. To a man, they shook their heads no. He must have hesitated too long. Had they declined out of pride or out of kindness? Unable to read their faces, he lit a cigarette and joined their silence.

Who would have thought illiterate peasants could teach someone who Mountain Pine claimed could charm the fangs off a snake not to waste words? Of course, learning from the masses was a Communist tenet, but when he came here he'd never imagined it was anything but a useful slogan for winning their support. Perhaps degree holders like him were more of a product of their bourgeois upbringing than they cared to admit. Still, the Party welcomed them despite their failings. And what an eager convert he had been! One look at egalitarian Yenan and he'd decided. Nor was his reaction an exception. He hadn't realized it in Chongqing, but tens of thousands of China's intelligentsia, like Lincoln Chen's recruits, had forsaken their positions and comforts, homes and families to embark on a lonely life of discipline and hardship.

And if politics as such still bored him—at Party meetings, whenever the discussion turned to the thoughts of bearded foreigners he was as bothered as he had ever been by the hectoring voice at the rallies in the courtyard of the Ministry—the contrast between the corruption in the Nationalist capital and the fellowship he had found in the Communist one amazed him. People of high estate and low dressed simply and sacrificed. People of high estate and low worked the fields and the looms and lived side by side in caves carved out of the loess hills. Above all, people worked as one to win the war against the Japanese. Living among them had helped him stop thinking about the ignominious Tangs.

In Yenan his anger at all that the Ministry and the Deputy Minister had done to him, his sorrow at all that he had had to leave behind, his fears, his doubts, his loneliness—he had quenched them with the headiest of brews: hope.

It was a wonder the cadres hadn't taken him for an incompetent spy and locked him up when he arrived: after all, he was a highborn stranger claiming to be a renegade official from Chongqing. He wouldn't have blamed them if they had. To his surprise, however, someone in authority had already vouched for him—Lincoln Chen. What a wily one the half-blind professor had turned out to be! Not only had he escaped the sudden dragnet thrown up when those who had always regarded his activities as nefarious got the political upper hand, but he had beaten Steel Hope to Yenan, traveling the same route as his readers. It had taken only a word from Chen to open every door, including the one that led him to this district and meaningful work at last.

Slowly inhaling the bitter smoke of the Lucky Leaf, he, who winced whenever private faults were aired at Party meetings, secretly confessed to a weakness for some aspects of his former existence, such as store-bought cigarettes. At the same time, he found himself admiring his companions' fancy tobacco pouches, which hung around their necks. Each was unique, embroidered by a loving daughter and presented to her father before she stepped into her bridal sedan, or by the bride to her groom on their wedding night. He wished that Mushroom had taught Summer Wishes to sew.

In the distance, still nothing stirred, not even the tops of the twin poplars that caught the slightest breeze and lured the eye away from the monotonous, pale flatness of the land, and his thoughts turned, as they often did, to the lush mountains, and to the Bandit Chief, someone he cursed and blessed as he cursed and blessed the peasants. How strangely things had turned out.

"Stop shitting in your pants—I'll get you through," the legless Red Devil had boasted. "And for a joke I'll do it right under the noses of those Guomindang thugs and spies who lie in wait along the road between here and Yenan to chop off your legs."

"If you don't mind, I prefer arriving all at once, not in pieces like a certain Red Devil I know."

"For a scholar who's about to be barbecued to ash, you're mighty choosy. Oh, never mind, I'm feeling generous. Take my word for it, you'll arrive as unseen and untouched as those naked virgins that used to be bundled in a rug and delivered by eunuchs to the Emperor for the noble task of sucking the living juices out of him."

"Are you serious?"

"I'm always serious about honor."

"What do I have to do?"

"Take off your clothes!"

He must have laughed aloud at this memory, for Wispy Eyebrows shot him an anxious look. Reaching out to pat the Headman on his bony back, Steel Hope brushed his hand along the bank of the ditch and dirt trickled down his neck. Just his luck: only yesterday he'd had the rare pleasure of a bath. "Damn!" Again the sound brought anxious looks. What was the matter with them? Scanning the landscape, he found it as undisturbed as before.

Perhaps he should ease the waiting by telling them what was amusing him so. Surely even stone frogs would croak at the image of their revered cadre swathed in a red satin gown and layers of bridal veil, with dainty slippers on his toes and a jeweled headdress on his head, perched in a stolen sedan chair, sweating and panting like some giddy overpaid whore while being carried by foot, ferry and truck on the six-week journey from the watchtower in Guizhou to the outskirts of Xian.

Surely a laugh would do them no harm. But perhaps he'd better not. He'd never seen the men so tense. They were still nervously fingering their tobacco pouches. The muscles in their jaws throbbed. What had happened to these veterans, who were reputed to have snored through more than one such vigil?

Steel Hope began to suspect that they knew something he didn't know about the impending raid. They had a reason for being in the ditch, and keeping him company wasn't it. Damn peasants! What were they up to? What didn't they trust him to do? What more was there to see after what he'd already seen in this take-all, burn-all, kill-all war?

As quickly as it had flared, his fury fizzled. There was no blaming them. Their lives had been dogged by despair, deceit and disillusionment. How many times had he heard them sing of betrayal?

> If not the sun, the rain.
> If not the flood, the drought.
> If not the landlord, the warlord.
> If not the soldiers, the highwaymen.
> If not my chickens, my goat.
> If not my wife, my mother-in-law.

Life had taught them that blood was the only bond on which they could depend.

There was a tap on his shoulder. He turned. Pointing, Wispy Eyebrows shouted, much too loudly, "Look!"

He shaded his eyes. On the far side of the poplars was a trace of dust. Patiently he watched it darken and swell like a swarm of locusts gathering to devour every kernel in its path. As the churning cloud headed toward them, a distant hum became a rumble, a roar. His pulse quickened. Any minute now. He could almost hear the explosions, smell the sulfur. Instead, there was a deadly silence.

As the dust cloud dispersed, he couldn't quite decide if there were more than the two or three trucks they had expected parked by the poplars. Sentimental fool! Why had he ever allowed that delegation of crones to talk him into saving the old good-luck trees?

Now the militiamen were shoving him aside to take his place at the sackcloth switchboard. What the hell was going on?

Gritting his teeth, he said, "Get back where you were. Setting off mines is my job."

To a man, they shook their heads.

"Comrade," Wispy Eyebrows whispered hoarsely, "last week the Japs took our married daughters from the next village hostage. We knew the women would be forced to lead the way. So we told the puppets and they told the Japs about our mined road. Only the road." The Headman glanced toward the rows of pumpkins.

"Why didn't you tell me? Didn't you know I'd gladly cook the harvest and serve the entire Jap army and Hirohito before I'd think of harming innocents?"

The man nodded. "We knew."

Grabbing him, Steel Hope hissed, "What else?"

"We must pull the wires, not you. We must have our revenge."

Steel Hope didn't know whether to laugh or cry. He'd been right. They didn't trust him. "Be my guest. But don't pull any wire until your daughters have passed the last big pumpkin. No, no, better give them more room, be extra safe—until they've come abreast of the trellises. Got that? The trellises!"

The men nodded.

It'll be fine, he assured himself. Anticipating that the Japs might force natives to clear the way, the collectors of honeypots and manure had passed the word to everyone in the area to avoid the roads, to take to the fields, and if possible to lead the soldiers along the corridors, marked this month with oversized pumpkins, so that when all the Chinese had reached safety, the mines could be triggered to kill only their captors, who always trailed their hostages at a safe distance.

"They're moving."

Steel Hope watched intently as the doll-size figures climbed out of the truck, but he couldn't be sure if any of them were women. There didn't appear to be any struggle. They clustered into groups. Then these groups huddled together. They seemed to be consulting on what to do. They formed rows and marched into the pumpkin fields. It was only when he saw that all in the lead group were without rifles that he knew for certain that Chinese were among them.

He ached for those peasants. There was no knowing what tortures the sons of turtles had already inflicted on them.

As the lead group approached the bomb corridors, he saw that they were indeed women. The daughters were moving in lockstep, roped together at the waist. Relief swept over him when he realized that the rope between them was slack, allowing for adjustments.

Remember to lead the bastards between the big pumpkins! he exhorted them silently. Do that and we'll blow them back to Tokyo.

Slowly the women advanced, placing first the toe then the heel, taking tiny, delicate steps. A dozen Jap soldiers had followed them into the field, keeping their distance, carrying their rifles at the ready.

As the daughters approached the halfway point, Steel Hope could scarcely breathe, so overcome was he by their courage. It was true that they were in no danger from the explosives, but didn't they know that one false move or one fretful soldier could mean a barrage of bullets in the back? Of course they knew. Still, not one faltered. So graceful were their movements that the procession might have been a dance extolling the gods for blessings granted.

Now he could make out their sunburnt faces. Nothing about their features revealed their plight. No one wept. He glanced at his comrades. Their faces were expressionless. Yet all the women must have been their fathers' favorites, for they had chosen husbands for them who lived in the next hamlet, so that they would remain nearby.

Suddenly, the strange procession changed. It was as if the ropes that linked the women had become strings worked by a puppeteer and the eight magnificent marionettes were now performing a surprise variation. He blinked. As suddenly the daughters again walked as before.

Still lagging a dozen or so paces behind, the soldiers didn't appear alarmed. They too walked as before.

He must have been imagining things.

But when his attention was drawn back to the women, he saw that they were holding a shoe in each hand and that their feet were bare. So that was it. They'd been removing their shoes. Why? What the hell for?

He could ask them soon enough. They had almost reached the edge of the field. Their ordeal was coming to an end. Again he silently exhorted them: Just don't run. They'll shoot if you run. Don't run.

Then, only steps short of reaching safety, with their long soft shadows sliding over the vines in the field before them, all eight women suddenly let go of their shoes, fell to their knees, cried out, "O my father, please, you must, you must!" and kowtowed.

The explosions didn't come one by one, but simultaneously.

He sprang to his feet. He saw. He averted his eyes. His voice rang loudly in his ears. "No! No! No! . . ."

Shots came from the poplar trees.

He was being pushed out of the ditch, dragged away from the fields, hauled into Wispy Eyebrows' hut, pinned to the dirt floor. Dazed by the horror—flesh and bone and shoes tossed in the air like maple leaves blown by autumn gusts—he barely noticed two of the militiamen working the pulleys to move the false floor on which the brick stove with its fire and giant cauldron of hot water stood, and expose one of the entrances to the tunnels. Then he was being shoved inside.

He summoned all his strength and resisted, but they were strong, so strong. Peasants. He lost his grip and fell into the tunnel. The others followed.

He stared, accusing his rescuers. Only Wispy Eyebrows didn't weep. It was a minute or two before he had sucked enough air into his lungs to be able to speak. "Why? Why did you? Your own daughters! Tell me. Why?"

He searched the eyes of the Headman. They glistened. The lines in his face seemed to be etched deeper and deeper as Steel Hope watched. When he finally spoke, his voice had no life. "How could we not grant our own daughters their last wish? Death is a blessing to those who have been soiled like shoes."

STEEL HOPE STOOD in the feeder tunnel within earshot of the secret entrance under Wispy Eyebrows' stove. Again, there was nothing to do but wait. His comrades had joined the rest of the villagers in the holding chamber six hundred steps away, and since the enemy was bound to search every room in every house in the village, including the kitchen overhead, the only question was whether they'd find their way in.

Though he was accustomed to the blackness, it played tricks.

He could still see the bodies of the women strewn like home-stitched dolls among the pumpkins in the patch. A bloody hand twitching. So many black eyes staring. On the charred face of Wispy Eyebrows' eldest daughter a bright smile had lingered.

Increasingly edgy, he fingered the pack of cigarettes in his pocket. If only he could smoke, perhaps the terrible images would fade; the smell would waft up into the kitchen, though, and he mustn't.

He shut his eyes. But he couldn't shut out the visions coursing through his mind like the floodwaters of the Yangzi—visions from the past mingling with the bloody limbs and the yellow flesh of pumpkins and the blackness of his rage and sorrow, until Wispy Eyebrows' youngest daughter stood before him alone: a girl so shy that even now, in death, she dared not lift her gaze to look upon the man whose life she had saved. Hiding in the watery reeds, he had stared in horror as she ran, leading the enemy soldiers away from the pond, from the reeds, from him. With that look of forbearance centuries of enduring had bred into their genes, her clansmen and neighbors had watched her depart, watched her becoming smaller and smaller, as they had once watched her grow.

Now the blacksmith stood before him. The new cadre had been passing through the man's village on the way here, his first post, when the Japs rounded up all its inhabitants and threatened to bayonet their headman unless they turned in the stranger from Yenan hiding among them. Baring his chest, the blacksmith had stood as silent and sturdy as an anvil to receive the blow. He had died with his fierce eyes open. They were open now, but his voice was a ghostly whisper. "How can I rest when those barbarians still live? Avenge me . . . avenge me!"

The blacksmith vanished as mysteriously as he had come, and in his place, Steel Hope saw again the slim back of the shy girl, her long braid swinging as she ran. Unable to believe the Party could have foreseen this, he had tried to disobey orders and give himself up. But hands roughened by work until they felt more like pine cones than human flesh had grabbed him and pushed him underwater, and knees like boulders had pinned him in the mud. Even so he had heard the shots.

Long after the enemy was gone, he had knelt in the pond, emptied of tears, trying to express all that was in his heart, but the peasants had refused to let him shoulder the blame. "It must have been her time," they said. "It was fate."

He couldn't bear his pain in silence, however, and had foisted his words of regret upon them until one by one they dispersed, and only the girl's grandmother and he were left. When he tried to repeat his woeful refrain, the woman, with the face of a walnut and bound feet no longer than a pea pod, cried out, "Ai ya! Stop it. You didn't aim the gun. You didn't pull the trigger. You didn't kill her. In my lifetime I've had to drown two of my son's baby daughters so their brothers wouldn't starve. Have mercy, don't speak of regrets."

And he hadn't, not again—not on that day, or on the day when the militiamen's sons were flayed alive on the threshing square, or later when their young widows were marched away in a queue, their bodies as taut as clothing frozen on a wash line, pulled by the long length of wire that their captors had threaded through the same holes from which their gold earrings, treasured from generation to generation, still dangled.

He wanted revenge. Pressing his ear to the wall, he cursed. What was keeping the Japs? With three trucks, perhaps more, there were plenty of soldiers to have carried away the dead, taken care of the wounded and been in Wispy Eyebrows' kitchen by now.

Again the visions came. There was nothing to do but endure them as the villagers had endured the reality. . . .

Objects struck the ground overhead. The Japs had reached the kitchen. He listened for signs that the stove had attracted their interest. At the sound of water sloshing he flinched, bumping his head against one of the struts that reinforced the earthen roof. At the hiss of fire being extinguished, he was already scrambling, mentally counting the steps, as he made his way to a passage off to the left that led to a loop that wound down to a lower level and a straightaway, which would take him to the messenger posted by the opening to the crawl space that served the holding chamber.

. . . five hundred ninety-eight, five hundred ninety-nine, six hundred. This should be the spot. Yes, the man was there.

He tapped him on the shoulder three times, giving the signal to evacuate. Every second counted. The villagers must get to the intersection, then disperse, going their separate ways underground to exits lis away.

As the whispering of muffled footfalls faded, he about-faced and felt for the latch concealed in the tunnel roof directly outside the crawl space. There! He pulled. Earth fell until it walled off the opening, to the enemy and to himself.

He retraced his steps. After a hundred paces along the passage he began dragging his right foot, searching for the mud-caked hatch concealing the hideaway that was tucked into the tunnel wall five paces from the loop. There! Raising the hatch, he eased himself inside.

He removed the rags soaked in garlic water from the gourd tied at his waist and covered his face, in case the bastards used gas. Now there was nothing more to do again but wait.

Wait until all the Japs had passed his hiding place. Wait until he could safely sneak out, run the loop while setting fire to the straw tucked into its roof struts, and exit the way he had come—through the hole beneath the stove. Of course, there might be a Jap or two in Wispy Eyebrows' kitchen to greet him. What of it? He'd welcome a chance to kill them up close. Besides, better a bayonet or a bullet than choking to death on the smoke from the burning straw. Even the thought of it made him gag.

To calm himself, he pictured the groves of tranquil bamboo whose hollow roots had been cut to let air into the tunnels, and recited a poem by Wang Wei, a favorite of Mountain Pine's.

> In the bamboos
> Echoes the chatter of the washerwomen
> Returning home;
> The boat of the fisherman
> Disturbs the lotuses.
> Though the fragrance of spring
> Has passed away,
> There remains much
> To delight the eye
> —Even of a prince.

He willed himself to breathe easier. His heart slowed. How ironic that he who prayed to no god might be spending his last day stuffed, like the holiest of monks, in a cremation jar. He wished he could be amused.

He heard a burst of activity. Were they moving the stove? That wouldn't take long. He checked his matches. At any moment now, the bow-legged vermin would be dropping in on him.

To his surprise the noise stopped. What the devil could the dung beetles be up to? It was unthinkable that they'd uncover an entry and not investigate. Perhaps they'd gone for help, or were enjoying a cigarette. What did it matter? Sooner or later they would come.

Suddenly, there was a sound so unexpected that it took him a moment to recognize the squealing of a spooked pig. Had the Japs gone completely mad? Butchering a pig at a time like this?

No, that couldn't be it . . . they must be trying to stuff the pig into the tunnel. Why? What for? . . . For the same reason he'd ordered the peasants to kill their dogs when he first arrived. With a length of rope, a dog or a pig could be turned into a four-legged canister of gas.

At once he quit the hideaway. He poured the rest of the garlic water over his head. He removed his jacket, tore open the lining. The squealing drew closer, then farther away. Closer again. The pig must have rounded the loop. Yes, the squealing was almost in his ears.

Praying that the creature towing the gas-spewing canister was a piglet and not a sow, he shut his eyes, took a deep breath and held it; then, using his ripped-open jacket like a sack, he pounced. The muffled cries were almost human. Tying the sleeves of the jacket around the squirming mass, he shoved it and the canister inside the hideaway and, with his back, held the hatch closed. He fumbled for his gun, then remembered that a bullet might puncture the canister. Instead of shooting, he jammed the gun into the opening at the base of the hatch to secure it and, still holding his breath, his eyes shut tight against the fumes that seared the lungs and blinded before they killed, he scrambled to get away.

He ran with arms outstretched, careening off the tunnel walls. He felt as if he were about to explode from the lack of oxygen. He must breathe. The gas would be strongest near the tunnel roof. He lay flat and filled his lungs and, with his nose to the ground, he crawled. The Japs wouldn't be coming after him, at least not for a while. Gas was fickle. It worked for him now.

The gas had smoked out the rats, and as he pulled himself along in the dirt, they scurried over and around him; their squeals sounded as if the throng were squalling inside his head. But revulsion was matched by relief; as long as they stirred, so did he. When they were gone, he stood up and tested the air. It was sweet.

He was safe. He grinned. By now it must be close to dusk, when the enemy would begin their retreat to the city. Soon he and the villagers would resume what had become a nightly ritual, substituting wooden bolts for the iron ones on yet another stretch of railroad track.

Plunging through the blackness, he cursed the piglet. Without his quilted jacket he'd freeze tonight; for that matter, every night, since he was unlikely to get another. To delouse that jacket, he'd held it above the stove every morning; and after every rain, he'd done the same, so that its cotton stuffing had become as hard and as lumpy as Ping-Pong balls. Nevertheless, he was attached to it. After all, it was the only jacket he owned. Now, like the militiamen, he'd have to replenish his wardrobe with clothing stripped from the bodies of dead Japs.

Suddenly he stopped. Suddenly the smell of garlic made him ill. Where was he? His stomach heaved. His heart filled his throat. Had he turned right? Left? Had he turned more than once? Had he gone fifty, or a hundred steps?

He raised a foot to take a step, then carefully put it back. A mine might be a step away. He stood absolutely still and willed himself to be calm. To think.

Had he been heading east or west? Which section was this? One that led to safety, or to a trap? Think!

It was hopeless. He couldn't remember how he'd come to this spot. He could only remember that any misstep might be fatal. He had designed the tunnels that way. He wanted to scream: I'm too young, too young to die. A voice within laughed. Both daughters of Wispy Eyebrows had been younger.

Whether to safety or oblivion, he had to move. His head urged him to go, go, go! His feet balked. His hands too. They were braced against the walls.

There was a sound behind him. The rustling of rats? No, the sound was metallic. The fucking dwarfs must've worn gas masks.

He took a step, stopped again. If there were mines ahead, he'd be dead soon enough. Better to wait and lead the bastards on. Take them with him to the grave.

If I live, Summer Wishes . . . If I live, Mountain Pine . . . He smiled, bitterly. He'd never see them again.

In the murk behind him there appeared a faint arc of light. They were coming. He gave himself orders. Don't move. Not a step, not before the light licks your shoes. Come on, you bastards, move those bowlegs, come on!

The arc of light swelled into a cone, creeping across the floor, becoming steadily brighter. It hurt his eyes. He flattened himself against the wall, cutting his back on something sharp. He winced, but uttered no sound.

A blast of thunder and lightning pulverized him.

He found himself on the ground. He breathed dust. It was black as pitch again. Had they set off one of his mines? Had they thrown a grenade? He heard voices yelling in Japanese, then, again, silence.

What was happening? Perhaps the way behind him, and the Japs, was blocked. Perhaps the hour was later than he thought, and the cowards had decided to retreat before dark. But in case he was wrong, he must leave them something to wonder about. Tearing free the gourd that hung from his waist, he set it in the dirt. By now even the dumbest of Japs had learned to fear strange objects planted in the ground.

He waited, listening. Still there was no sound. Just as he'd decided that no one would be coming, he remembered that gas was a silent killer. What was he waiting for? He dashed ahead.

The ceiling was getting lower. He came to a fork. Yes, yes! Suddenly he knew where he was. He veered left, reached a dead end, stepped back four paces, and fumbled in the ground for the lip of a large tray filled with dirt. Lifting it, he squeezed himself down the tapering hole to an even lower level. He crawled. On the maps he had made of the tunnels, this stretch was only a couple of inches long. In reality, it went on for half a li. Creeping on his hands and knees, he found it interminable.

With his first breath of fresh air, he nearly wept. His ordeal was almost over. He shut his eyes against the brightness of the daylight that would blind him, and crawled until the tunnel ended, at an opening hidden in a well, just above the waterline.

Reaching down, he scooped up some water and drank it. He had never tasted so delicious a wine. He put his hands over his eyes before opening them, then spread his fingers slowly to ease in the light. He grinned at the smiling face that floated on the water.

HEEDLESS TRANQUILITY

(1947)

ON THE FINAL night of his stay at the Monastery of Heedless Tranquility, Mountain Pine sat in his cell, feeding the last of his manuscripts into the brazier. He watched a corner of the paper lift, curl, then slowly peel away, as if the flames had the kindness to peruse his poems before destroying them. Such kindness was wasted on fools like him, he thought; for only a fool would have spent nearly two decades writing and rewriting, when all along he knew that nothing would ever come of it.

Writers, after all, were creatures of passion, ready to sacrifice balance in pursuit of some grand conceit; whereas he was, by nature, judicious and, at thirty-three, much too set in his ways to rebel. No wonder everything he scribbled, whatever the subject and whatever the form, lacked that unique voice and authentic power he admired in the works of others. His critical eye alone was true.

He felt a chill. The window was open to let out the smoke; his sweater was already packed. He pulled his chair closer to the fire and, warming his hands, found himself enjoying the bittersweet satisfaction of a man who, after years of carving Buddhas scorned by pilgrims, has sold the wood for a good price.

The enjoyment proved fleeting. Though he was leaving at dawn, he still couldn't make up his mind about the future. He would, of course, go to Chongqing; but should he stay there? Could he bear being so near Summer Wishes? Could he bear not to be near her? Every two weeks, without fail, she had come to see him with bags crammed full of pills and potions, food and clothing and books and, naturally, yet another charm for curing tuberculosis purchased from some charlatan for an inordinate amount. Upon each meeting, she had wept with happiness. Upon each parting, she had wept with sadness. But not once in the two years, four months and sixteen days that he had been at the monastery had she spoken of Steel Hope, even though she was obsessed with informing the invalid of the most trivial details about Cassia and her father—the length of her hair when she married her colonel, who took the name of Tang so that their unborn son would be the family's rightful heir; the wealth that her father, promoted to Minister of Agriculture, was rumored to have accrued speculating in soya beans and rice after the war; and the width of the hat Cassia wore in the photograph printed in all the newspapers six months ago when she and her husband, dressed in identical white double-breasted linen suits, accompanied the recently retired Minister on a holiday trip to Singapore, from which they apparently had yet to return, and which, to Mountain Pine's relief, finally ended Summer Wishes' obsession with the Tangs.

It was the very absence of Steel Hope's name from any of their conversations that revealed to him how time had changed nothing at all.

When his friend was alive, he had balked at being a lamplighter whose presence serves no purpose and destroys the intimacy so desired by lovers; now, when the one whom she yearned for had been a ghost for five years, wouldn't Mountain Pine, by his very presence, eventually offend her, and thus come to despise himself? It would be better to husband their friendship.

But could he look into those lovely, eager eyes and say he wouldn't be staying in Chongqing? He could not, not when the thought had never crossed her mind, not after all she had done for him, sacrificed for him. Without her, he would have died. As it was—according to the four monks who had taken turns feeding him spoonful by spoonful, kneading his flesh inch by inch, doing everything but breathe for him during the six months that he had lain in bed coughing blood—he'd almost died anyway. He wouldn't have cared. But she had cared. If he couldn't leave her when oblivion was preferable to coughing even once more, how could he leave her now? And yet...

After many months of such indecision, he'd been able to rule out only one thing: he wouldn't be a copier of textbooks anymore, not least because, with the end of the war and the closing of campuses, there would be fewer demands for his services, and hence, no telling when he'd be able to pay back the generous amounts Summer Wishes had spent on his behalf. Mercifully, the old fortuneteller had left her ten times more.

But was he prepared to accept the standing offer from the Christian Mission for Orphans in Nanjing? It did include room and board and a nominal sum in foreign currency, which these days was preferable to a cartload of yuan. When he tried to picture himself there, however, he couldn't.

Sweeping up the ashes that had drifted onto the floor, he found some comfort in knowing that, whatever happened, there'd be no more staring at a blank page until the day had mysteriously passed and he was suddenly too hungry or sleepy to stare anymore; no more longing when alone at his desk to be with anyone, anywhere; and no more longing when he was with someone to be alone at his desk.

Pushing the window open wider, he gazed at the sky. It was so clear that the stars seemed within reach. He sighed. He'd miss such luminous nights. And the mountain air. The woods, with trees as dense as the teeth of a comb. The company of men who had no need of company. Even that broth made from goat udder that he had to ingest three times a day and, for some unfathomable reason, had grown fond of.

Perhaps he should stay at the monastery. Here, he led the simple existence of those hermit-scholars who, dynasty after dynasty, had distanced themselves from the turmoil of their times and the wars in their hearts. Perhaps he should shave his head, take vows and devote the rest of his days to copying sutras. He'd even expressed these thoughts aloud some weeks earlier, while gathering wild grasses and roots in the forest with the old monk who preferred communicating his knowledge of healing to communing with the cosmos. "Can you see me as an acolyte?"

"You? You?" The man tittered, pointing like a child who has caught his amah with stains on her new tunic larger and darker than the stains on his own.

He was taken aback. "Why not? Poverty and celibacy are second nature to me."

"You still burn with fever."

"That's not true, hasn't been true for months now."

The monk knelt to study a mushroom growing at the foot of a pine. "Oh, I'm not talking about the fever one measures in degrees," he said. "I'm talking about the fever of earthly desires."

Mountain Pine had blushed then; he blushed now. For even as his poems were turning to cinders, the writer in him was looting the scene for details, hoarding sensations, preying on his own confusion, playing with words. It was no use. What no one else had ever suspected, the old monk had grasped at once. Mountain Pine burned with ambition. And while others settled for mere fortune or fame or power, his ambitions couldn't be so easily satisfied. As for love, he had grown accustomed to confining Summer Wishes to quarters deep within his heart. No, this mortal yearned for a joy even more sublime than the joy of hearing that cry when the city magistrate of the netherworld kicks one's first child into this world. He yearned for a line or two he had written to be remembered by a few yet unborn; he yearned to speak from the grave, to be a speck of sand on the beaches of immortality.

Would he succeed?

In the twinkling of the River of Stars, he imagined nods, and smiled. Hadn't the old monk predicted that he would write a book? So the day would come. But when? A voice within said, When the heavens are overturned, when a bookmate becomes his young master and when China has truly changed.

After eight years of battle and retreat, stalemate and again battle, the war against the Japanese had been won. But victory had not brought peace. Instead, it had ushered in a civil war between the Guomindang and the Communists. Mountain Pine took no sides. He distrusted the glorious promises and scorned the methods of both sides equally. Nor did he join those who advocated a democratic coalition. They were dreamers. All they ever accomplished was to talk themselves into jail. Better to remain neutral and, like most of his countrymen, keep his head low and wait for one of the parties to emerge victorious, knowing that, as always, whoever triumphed would be hailed the emperor, and whoever lost, declared the outlaw. Like most of his countrymen, he didn't care who conquered; he only wished the conquest would take place soon.

Turning to see if the smoke was completely gone from the room, he was drawn to the battered trunk at the foot of his bed, where he kept the letters he'd received from publishers; whether the letter was a single line or several pages long, the message was the same. Also in the trunk were several packages wrapped in brightly colored paper and tied with red ribbons—presents he'd received over seven months ago at Spring Festival. He'd left them unopened, not because he didn't treasure gifts, but because he treasured them more for the feelings of anticipation and suspense, wonderment and surprise that if he opened them would be missing from his life.

Tonight his weary eyes wouldn't grant him even that harmless pretense. As keenly as they had seen through the mountain of words he'd composed, they saw through the fancy wrappings. From the Christians at the mission, there was a calendar with photographs of foreign lands; from Mushroom, a hand-knit sweater in a somber hue; from Summer Wishes, a volume of poetry he had coveted but couldn't afford, perhaps one that she had seen him blow the dust off and finger again and again, before returning the volume to its rightful place on a bookseller's shelf.

Wasn't there anything he could look forward to now?

As the last sparks died in the brazier, he spooned the herbs blended by the old monk into a chipped cup. It was blue and nothing special, part of a set Steel Hope, in one of his fits of generosity, had bought from a roving peddler and then dropped the one time he had deigned to wash the dishes. Like a servant, Mountain Pine had retrieved it from the trash for his own use.

He had been a servant too long. As far as Summer Wishes was concerned, he was still the young master's servant. And yet, when his friend, however cavalier, had been around, Steel Hope had given shape and purpose to his life. He sighed. If loyalty demeaned, it also redeemed.

He poured water from the thermos bottle and downed the tonic in one gulp. It was a bitter brew.

SUMMER WISHES handed her calling card to the gatekeeper at the Residence of No Importance, which, everybody in Chongqing knew, was the home of that notoriously powerful businessman C.C. After examining it, the man, magnificent in blue serge and gold braid, informed her that his master was in Shanghai. Mimicking the authority in his voice, she replied, "Did I say that I was calling on C.C.? I wish to see the matriarch."

The man motioned for the gardener to take over for him, tipped a hat fit for a general and marched off.

She ransacked her purse for a handkerchief without success; then she surreptitiously removed a glove and dabbed her brow, while keeping a watchful eye on the gatekeeper as he made his way up the long cobblestone path toward the mansion of red brick and stained glass. The edifice, which had survived the war unscathed, seemed to sneer, disdainful of airs that impressed hired help, of fake refinement, of her stylish but simple blue coat and beret, of her. Was this queasiness what others complained of on opening night?

To distract her thoughts from the upcoming, dreaded visit, she fixed her attention on two boys squatting by the curb, laughing. One was holding the ends of what looked like a piece of dirty twine, while the other sliced through it with an even dirtier thumbnail. Suddenly, she realized the thing was no cord, but a worm; now two.

She almost screamed, yet even as she stifled the sound, she wondered why the sight should upset her so. What was seeing a worm cut in half compared to watching the expensive foreign exorcist she'd hired the day she bought the theater race up and down the aisles brandishing a headless rooster that spurted lucky blood? No doubt her present squeamishness was a sign. But of what?

She heard a clearing of the throat. It was the gatekeeper. "This way, please," he said. "The matriarch will see you in a few minutes."

The reception room was carpeted with thick Tianjin rugs, and every wall boasted a collection of elaborate clocks. Enchanted, she forgot her foreboding and strolled about, staring at one, then another—at the dancers and the soldiers and the bears on bicycles. A sparrow in a log house looked amazingly alive, and she reached out to touch it. Suddenly, as the dancers twirled and the soldiers marched and the bears bicycled, the bird popped out of its home and screeched and bowed to hail three o'clock. Startled, she jumped back. Her purse fell, scattering coins on the floor. Did she dare pick them up? What if the matriarch came in and saw a stranger groveling on hands and knees? She snatched up the purse and pushed the coins under the sofa with a foot.

How had she ever let Mushroom talk her into coming here? It was a terrible idea. She'd been unable to think of what else to do, however, and so had agreed to beg for help from the only person who could possibly change C.C.'s mind: his mother. But what if the woman were to get angry and throw her out?

Summer Wishes retreated to the fireplace with its ornate marble mantlepiece, above which hung a gilded mirror—and no disquieting clock. On the mantle were photographs of C.C. with other influential, rich or famous people: C.C. and a group of generals, C.C. shaking hands with a foreigner, C.C. toasting a roomful of businessmen, C.C. with his arms around a bride in a Western gown of white lace and a groom in a colonel's uniform. Only upon closer inspection of the small wedding picture did she recognize the smiling profile as Cassia's, and before she could stop herself, its frame was slapped down. "Witch!" she mumbled. "Bad-luck witch!" Though the two women did not meet again after the Jeep accident, Summer Wishes had never stopped blaming Cassia for destroying her life. If it hadn't been for her, the Deputy Minister wouldn't have sent Steel Hope on that trip to Kunming and Summer Wishes would have been an even more beautiful bride, wearing an even prettier gown in the color of happiness, red; not white, the color of mourning. . . .

But there was no time to think of that now.

She must keep busy. She must go on looking at the pictures. C.C. on a horse, C.C. speaking into a microphone, C.C. . . . In the last frame, she recognized herself. It had been taken two years earlier, in 1945, at the opening of her theater. Surrounding her and C.C. were the orphans for whom the benefit had been held. Everyone was smiling. The war had just ended. The balmy day had marked a new beginning for the country and for her.

In the picture, C.C. looked the part of the kindly benefactor he had been to her, and even now, she couldn't blame him for calling in her debts. . . . He'd never pretended to be a gentleman, or anything other than what he was: a man whose past was revealed and concealed by the tangled rumors no one dared sort out; whose displeasure could oust ministers, bankrupt businesses, make men disappear; whose hobby was the opera.

She, not he, was the one at fault. For months after Steel Hope's accident, she had behaved in ways that frightened everyone, and when the wildness had passed, she had forbidden all talk of him. She herself never spoke his name, though every night she would take out his cigarette case and polish it and wonder if it still contained the one gold-tipped 999 that he had vowed to smoke only when it was time for him to cross the Yellow Springs.

She didn't have the courage to open the case. How could she, when she had decided that the presence of the cigarette signaled life? Putting this conviction to the test would risk losing the comfort, however paltry, that hope, devotion and ritual provided her. Still, as months, then years went by, too many sleepless nights of longing had awakened a need to defy the spell Steel Hope had cast when he was near. Where was he now? she asked herself over and over. Why hadn't he come back?

Then the old fortuneteller died and, by bequeathing Summer Wishes his money, fulfilled his own prophecy. The sum was much appreciated, for Mountain Pine was ill and unable to work; but when he began coughing blood she knew it would be far from enough. Out of need and anger, frustration and perversity, she decided to do what Steel Hope had always suspected her of doing, and informed Mushroom that from now on, she would be exchanging her attentions for financial rewards. Without money, how could Mountain Pine get well? And if he couldn't get well, her virtue wouldn't matter at all. Thus, she must be rich: rich enough to buy the finest care for Mountain Pine and a theater for Mushroom to manage; rich enough to produce shows for Summer Wishes to shine in; rich enough to forget how poor she had been.

Mushroom knew better than to argue against this. Instead, she suggested that the actress approach C.C.—a confirmed bachelor with an addiction to squiring beautiful women and an aversion to bedding them, whose invitations she had always turned down. When C.C. enthusiastically agreed to invest her inheritance for her, Summer Wishes broached the subject of a line of credit. "If anything happened to Mountain Pine, I'd . . . " She didn't dare say the unlucky word, but started to explain about their friendship. C.C. stopped her, declaring that he already knew all there was to know about her.

When she asked how, his reply was simple. "There are no secrets from me," he said.

She studied him—his languid eyes and round face, so unnaturally carefree for a man of fifty—and knew that he wasn't boasting.

"My child," he went on, "don't trouble yourself. Leave everything to me."

Now she heard footsteps. Into the room walked a tiny old woman who reminded her of the widows with a coin and a bowl in their outstretched hands who used to wait for the agent boater to pour them an inch of cooking oil. Like them, she was dressed in black, from the tight head-covering that hid her hair to the cloth-soled slippers on her feet; only her tunic was satin and new, not cotton and patched. Could this woman be C.C.'s mother?

Beaming, her hostess said, "Welcome, welcome. You're the singer in the photograph." She took a seat, but left her guest standing. "Is it festival time again so soon?" Before Summer Wishes could reply to this question, she asked another. "But why such a plain costume? The others always came dressed as ladies of the court."

Summer Wishes had no idea what the woman was talking about and wondered if her only hope was too addled to help.

"Oh, don't look so worried," the matriarch said. "I'll give you something just the same, just the same." She popped up and scurried to her knitting basket on the rosewood table, reached into it, then scurried back to her seat, waving a red envelope. She tilted her head expectantly. "This is for you, but first . . ."

At last Summer Wishes understood. The old woman thought she had been sent by her theater boss to solicit contributions. Automatically the actress delivered her lines, though she hadn't said them since her days on the *Pavilion of Fairies* and had always despised saying them: "May your illustrious name be heard throughout the Four Seas and gold surge into your coffers like the headwaters of the mighty Yangzi!"

The matriarch laughed gleefully, then reached out and lifted up one of Summer Wishes' gloved hands, then the other. "What, no endless sleeves? Ai ya, I've lived too long. I liked it so much better the old way . . . no polite little red envelopes, just noisy coins . . . no staircases going up and coming down, just a mu of bottomland all silty and flat. . . ."

Summer Wishes feared the old woman was on the verge of weeping, and to humor her, she tucked the red envelope into her sleeve and resumed her role. Standing tall, she moved her arms in a wide, graceful circle, bringing both hands to rest on her left hip; then, dipping a knee to the floor and bowing her head, she said, "Thank you, Honorable Mistress."

The patroness sighed. "The last time my knees could bend like that was back when Yuan Shi-kai was President, before C.C. moved us to Chongqing, and dampness took up lodging in my bones." Closing her eyes, she began to rock and rub her knees, and, withdrawing into herself, she rocked until gradually her body was still.

O merciful Kwan Yin, prayed Summer Wishes, please, please don't let her go to sleep now.

The matriarch must have heard her prayers, for her eyes opened wide, and she announced, "Your costume isn't as pretty as the outfits of others who've come here, but it wouldn't surprise me a bit if you sang better." Again, she tilted her head in expectation.

Summer Wishes couldn't help but smile: the old woman was determined to get her money's worth. "Shall I sing an aria from your favorite opera or a song from your ancestral home?"

"Singing isn't necessary, isn't necessary at all." The matriarch's voice achieved just the proper tone, between disavowal and surprise.

"But I'd be honored to perform for you," said Summer Wishes.

"Only if you insist."

"I insist. What shall it be?"

"You choose. You choose."

Because it was sung along the shores where the yaolu had sailed, by old women filling matchboxes to earn a few extra fen, Summer Wishes selected a folk song about the Yangzi. From stanza to stanza, the lyrics hardly varied. Repeatedly she sang the river's praises, in summer and winter, spring and fall. While her last note still hovered in the air, the matriarch picked up the tune and, taut with emotion, in a voice as slight as a child's, rendered the tune even more naive, praising the river at sunrise, at sunset. When the song was done, they both sat motionless, as if listening to absent voices sing a last refrain.

Before the song, Summer Wishes had wondered how to broach the subject of C.C. and the money. Now she heard herself telling the story of Firecrackers, who was born the daughter of an agent boater, and how one by one the members of her family had died until, at twelve years of age, she was an orphan, and what had happened next, year by year, until at twenty she had become a celebrated actress, named Summer Wishes.

When the matriarch brushed away a tear, the actress, in the role of supplicant, said, "Old Mistress, I beg you to believe that my father taught me to repay my debts, and if I must, I shall work until my eyes are closed forever to return every penny ever given me. I promise, I swear. But I cannot ... I just cannot ... " She hid her face in her hands.

"What has my son asked of you?"

"He has been most proper, but ..."

"What?"

"It was all my doing. I'm to blame. I should never have asked for favors. It wasn't as if we were related, as if he were obliged to help, as if I didn't know how even the most patient of men would grow impatient."

"And now?"

"C.C. has asked me to quit the stage and marry him. . . ."

From the look on her face, the matriarch was as stunned as Summer Wishes had been by the proposal. Fearing a more violent reaction, the younger woman quickly went on. "I ... I agreed. I was afraid to say no. But it could never work. He has position. I'm just an actress. What's more, I don't know a thing about being a wife. All I know is how to sing, how—"

To her horror, Summer Wishes saw that the old woman was smiling.

"Why, child, there's nothing to being a wife here, not in this house. We've plenty of servants—too many for my taste. I'm not allowed to go to the shops; the shops come to me. I'm not allowed to water my flowers or cut one in the garden or snip off a dead one in any of the vases. I'm not allowed to speak of grandchildren. . . ."

C.C.'s mother had stopped shouting and now whispered instead. "Can you imagine it? My son even hired someone to knit for me! But this time I fooled him, I ... Oh she gets paid, but—don't tell anyone—I myself really knit and purl every stitch." She burst into laughter, the laughter of a child who still sleeps with the muddy doll her elders have thrown away.

Summer Wishes laughed with her, sharing her triumph.

The old woman shook her finger affectionately. "I like you!" she said. "Marry him and you can still sing, sing all you like every day for me."

"It would be a great honor, but . . ." Summer Wishes lowered her gaze, swallowed hard, then worked up the courage to tell this friendly woman she didn't want to marry her son, didn't want to marry anyone.

The matriarch replied kindly but resolutely. "All women must be wives. How else can we be mothers? And without a son, who will sweep your grave?"

"I'm not like other women. I'm an actress."

"But you must want children."

She lied and said no.

"Nonsense!"

"Perhaps the gods have cursed me by making me an actress. But what can anyone do to alter fate?"

This time the matriarch nodded, and Summer Wishes took the woman's knobby hands in hers and pleaded. "Speak to C.C. Tell him that I'm unsuitable—too young, too common, too wanton, anything you wish. Tell him that you forbid him to marry me." Seeing only confusion in the old eyes, she went on desperately. "How can I make you understand? Once I didn't want to be in the theater at all, but now it's my life. Oh, I don't mean that I must own one. But without the stage I have no home, no family, no name. How can I give them up again? Not again."

Suddenly the bird that had startled her before screeched again, springing into action along with all the other animals.

The old woman covered her ears. "Ai ya! How many times have I begged my son to silence that bird? But he's a most stubborn man. . . . Yes, even when he was a boy collecting dung pies, my son never listened to me."

Hearing that C.C. was an unfilial son, Summer Wishes despaired. She used her gloves to wipe her eyes.

"Please don't cry," the matriarch said. "If anyone cries, I cry. Please, I'm too old to cry."

"Help me. I'm afraid of him."

The old woman sighed so deeply that she shuddered. "I'm afraid of him too, so afraid sometimes that I . . ." She paused, covering her face with an elbow. "O Kwan Yin, please forgive me for what I'm about to say, but . . . sometimes I wish my boy and not my girl had gotten cholera and . . ."

What had C.C. done to hurt his mother so? Might he do the same to his wife? "Is there nothing that would change his mind?" she pleaded. "Is there nothing I can do?"

The matriarch asked for her knitting basket.

When Summer Wishes had placed it on her lap, she took out a photograph of a young girl with a big smile and showed it to her. "My daughter."

"Is she ... ?"

The matriarch nodded, then, speaking as if to herself, went on to describe her son as a man who couldn't bear anything used. "He even throws his socks away after a single wearing. Do you understand what I'm saying?"

Summer Wishes didn't understand at all and shook her head.

"A man like that would never marry another man's wife."

"But I've never been married."

"Marry someone quickly before C.C. returns from Shanghai, someone who doesn't care if you don't give him children, if you sing and dance for strangers. Do you know such a man?"

Yes, she did. Someone who had loved her for years and would love her always, though he had never once alluded to his feelings, perhaps because he was unwilling to evoke even a single one of her tears. "But won't marrying him only make C.C. angry?" she asked. "Angry enough to take revenge on both of us?"

"My son hates not getting his way, but he won't go after you. He'll leave you alone."

"How can you be sure? I've heard that he's had people assassin ... hurt."

For a long time, the matriarch sat staring at the photograph of her daughter, and when she spoke again, there was a hardness in her voice. "A mother knows her son better than he knows himself. I promise you, my son would rather swallow his tongue than let it be known that an actress refused him. No matter how much he might want to, he won't bother you. If he did, there'd be rumors. Even the great C.C. can't stop people from tittering behind his back. How could he risk that? So get married, pay him back the money and go far away from here. He'll let you go."

Summer Wishes shook her head and for once regretted her spend-thrift ways. "Even if I sold the theater and everything I have, the money wouldn't be enough."

"Pay what you can. I'll give you the rest."

Summer Wishes couldn't believe the words, but there was no mistaking the look of determination on the woman's face. "Why?" she asked. "Why should you want to do that for a stranger?"

C.C.'s mother squinted, and for the first time Summer Wishes saw a resemblance between mother and son. "I've got reasons. I've got money too. Besides, it won't be lost—just going from one pocket to another under the same roof. And you're not a stranger. We sing the same songs."

Summer Wishes fell to her knees.

The good-hearted woman pulled at her. "Oh, you mustn't do that. Get up, get up. Times have changed. I remember when honoring an old woman with a kowtow was done every year at Spring Festival ... when an elder was an elder, a son, a son. But that was long ago ... long ago, when a barefoot boy named Padlock fetched straw for the stove and no one in the world had heard of a man called C.C."

AFTER LEAVING the Residence of No Importance, Summer Wishes didn't go to the theater, where Mushroom waited for news of the visit, but instead returned to their house. Sending the servant away on an errand, she locked the door, then removed the telephone from its stand. For a moment her eyes swept the place, looking for Treasure, a stray cat she'd befriended after Steel Hope had gone; then she remembered that it had disappeared some time during the move from the attic to this house, which C.C. provided. And yet, she could feel a pair of eyes following her into the bedroom, where she took the silver cigarette case from the bureau drawer. It was cold to her touch, colder still to her lips.

She held it next to her heart, whispering as a mother whispers to her baby who only moments earlier has cried to be nursed but is now asleep at her breast. Why didn't you wear my talisman over your shoulders? Wasn't it good enough? Pretty enough? New enough? Or did you, in your hurry to be somewhere else, forget? How could you? It was the most precious of talismans. Perhaps I shouldn't have given it to you; perhaps its magic was never meant to be shared. But I did give it to you, and now it's gone, has been gone for five years, and there will never be another. What can I do but forget?

As darkness fell she sat by the window, polishing the case with the hem of her dress. Over and over, her fingers worked on one side, then the other, again and again, as if they belonged to someone else. When finally they had grown too cramped to rub anymore, she looked up to see her reflection in the windowpane. It was more substantial than Summer Wishes.

She released the catch and opened the case.

The Winning Hand

Early the next morning Mountain Pine and Summer Wishes registered their marriage in the dingy office of a nondescript clerk who mumbled. Then, leaving Mushroom behind to settle their affairs in Chongqing and send off a telegram to the House of Li announcing their marriage and immediate return, they boarded the next boat going downriver.

The only available cabin was far below the main deck, and the single porthole was so streaked with mud that it hardly let in enough light for them to make out the color of its iron-gray walls. Unpacking was impossible; there was no storage space, no place even to sit except the lower bunk, held off the floor by rusted chains. Like strangers, they sat side by side staring in silence at the door that, upon closing, had shut the world out and them in.

The longer the silence, the more Mountain Pine realized that their marriage was a fatal mistake. He should never have agreed to it. But it had happened so fast . . .

Weary from the bus trip, he had checked into a cheap hotel, unpacked, left word at the theater that he was going to bed and would be seeing the women tomorrow. But once in bed, he had stared at the cracks in the ceiling as if they were the cracks in an ancient oracle bone, searching for clues to the future. Hours later, still awake, he'd found himself reciting a poem by Yuan Mei.

> The same illness has been with me for years
> but I did not weed it out.
> Like a bird in the air,
> I have risen to sink again:
> Like the fish in the pool,
> I come only to go.
> I seem to be in port, only to be at sea:
> The chariot moves,
> but at once the steeds are unyoked.
> God's children indeed!
> It is He who is the child,
> and we mortals the toys with which He plays.

At dawn, he'd answered an insistent knock.

Mushroom dashed in panting and, after several tries, announced that Summer Wishes had at long last accepted Steel Hope's death. Then, while she all but dressed him and threw his clothes into a suitcase, she described the crisis and the matriarch's plan. The news of his impending marriage to Summer Wishes, the fulfillment of a dream that he'd never dared to dream, had made Mountain Pine angry, and throughout the mad rush to be married and get aboard the *Lotus* before C.C. returned to Chongqing, he had said almost nothing; but if the women noticed, they didn't say.

Still, even if he'd had more time, what choice was there but to agree? The woman he'd loved from the moment he'd seen her gliding across the opera house stage some seven years before was in trouble. And in large part, his illness had been responsible. What was more natural than for her to ask him for help? He didn't blame her, he blamed himself. He should have walked out of their lives the day after their reunion. He'd known then, as the young master and the actress whirled in and out of the halo of light, spinning in a world of their own, that he'd be forever haunted by the vision of a graceful couple dancing.

Now, sitting in the gloom of their honeymoon cabin, he ached as he had ached when he pretended sleep so as not to intrude upon the dancers; pretended ease so as not to disturb the lovers; pretended normality so as not to behold the ghost she lived with. Can't you see, Summer Wishes? he wanted to cry out to her now. Can't you see that no matter how long or how hard we try, your husband will never be able to waltz?

He glanced at her profile, willing her to say something, anything, but she didn't speak or move. Her spirit was somewhere else. Surely she was thinking of Steel Hope and wishing he were here in Mountain Pine's place. Though she had kept her thoughts of Steel Hope to herself since the accident, she had shared all others with him. Now, she shared only silence. He wanted to plead with her: Speak, don't shut me out. Don't you realize that silence is the most hurtful of all lies? His head, however, told him that Mountain Pine must be wise, wise enough for both of them. He said nothing.

For the first time since his recovery, he felt as though the coughing would return. I must leave this prison cell of a room, he thought. But he didn't.

Through all the years she had kept the dead man alive, he had learned to live within limits others would find intolerable. So had she. But if the walls of their self-made prisons had confined, they had protected as well. Without them, had she already begun to despise the man she had married? Without them, would their friendship become so poisoned that it would end, and he be left with nothing at all?

"Summer Wishes?"

She turned.

To spare her the pain of looking at him, he stared straight ahead. "Nowadays, people don't always stay married. People can be divorced and marry again. It is done more often than you might think. . . ."

"Don't you want me for a wife?"

"Of course, but . . ."

"Then why talk of divorce, Mountain Pine?"

"Because you would never have married me if . . ."

"If what?"

". . . if Steel Hope had lived."

"But he is gone. . . ." Shutting her eyes, she breathed as she did when, standing in the wings, she banished the woman she was, to become the woman who would walk on stage. "Steel Hope is dead," she said at last.

Hearing that word from her lips for the first time didn't fill him with relief, as he would have expected, but with an overwhelming sadness. He liked her better when she didn't speak the young master's name, when she didn't lie. "But if there were no C.C., Steel Hope would still be very much alive for you," he said.

"How do you know?"

He didn't reply. He couldn't put the obvious into words without breaking the last slender thread of what had been his habit of pride.

"How do you know something I don't?" she asked. "Mountain Pine, do you think you were the only man in all of Chongqing who was willing to marry me?"

"No, I don't think that."

"Then what's wrong?"

What could he say? Everything was wrong. He didn't know whom he pitied more, himself or her.

"Look at me," she said.

He obeyed, and saw that her eyes were dark pools of kindness. But kindness wasn't what he had missed in his life, and when she went on, her voice was so gentle that the very sound of it made him ache even more.

"After my brother crossed the Yellow Springs, I was as sure as Kwan Yin is merciful that my mother wished that he had stayed and I had gone. Even now I know that this was true. But on that night of the fullest moon, when she ran about calling my name, I learned something truly important about her, about myself, and about love.

"If only I'd had the chance to tell her ... that it didn't matter how much more she loved my brother, that it was enough to know that she loved me as well."

AFTER THE steamer moored at the wharf where the bride and groom had first met, they lingered at the rail, aloof from the clamor of gongs, whistles and bells and of the other passengers, who, in their haste to collect their parties and possessions and disembark, battled and shouted like the fearful depositors who were daily assaulting the banks.

Basking in the warm sun and the friendly breeze, filling his lungs, Mountain Pine felt so expansive that the whole of the world seemed within the reach of his hands. A flotilla of junks caught his eye and, pointing, he asked Summer Wishes if she could see that the sails, so neatly arrayed and deceptively still, were no longer sails, but the winning hand displayed by the Mighty Ruler of the Deep.

Nodding solemnly, she replied that the sails had indeed changed.

But you, he thought, must always be Summer Wishes.

Playing the game they had played throughout their week aboard ship, she pointed in turn. "To the right, what does my husband see?"

At first he didn't spot the bamboo rafts, roped together and heaped with casks and baskets, bales and earthenware jars, that floated in mid-channel, because he couldn't persuade his eyes to stop gazing at his wife.

Dressed in a plain qi-pao of pale yellow silk, with her long hair pulled back in a single braid, she wore no adornments other than those with which nature had endowed her.

Tugging at his sweater, she prompted, "Well?"

He thought for a moment. "How about ... a caravan of camels reclining upon dunes of golden sand?"

"And that?" She pointed to a swarm of sampans bobbing in the waters directly below.

"That's easy. They're your devoted fans."

She stretched to lean over the rail for a better look, a long look, then, puzzled, turned back to him. "But what could sampans have to do with my fans? Is it something from a poem or book?"

"No."

"I give up," she said. Regarding him with furrowed brows, she added, "Promise to read to me every day so that I'll learn to see what my husband sees, and someday"—she paused, blushing—"what our children will see."

He resisted the disgraceful urge to embrace her in public.

Without warning, the temperamental star commanded, "Meanwhile, just answer me. Why are those filthy, broken-down sampans like my noble fans?"

He couldn't resist anymore and pulled her close. "It's just one of my feeble attempts at a joke. I only meant that the sampans were at your feet."

She considered his words, then shook her head. "But they're not. They're in the water."

"Yes, that's literally true, but figuratively the phrase, quote, 'at your feet,' unquote ... "

Everything was a blur before he realized what had happened. She had snatched his glasses and declared that she had flung the damn things into the river. Unable to see the expression on her face, he didn't know quite what to make of this gambit. Had his impromptu lecture offended her?

Suddenly, she was laughing. "I'm jealous—jealous of anything, besides me, that you need," she said.

Even before she had replaced the glasses, the world was in focus again, and he laughed, the laughter of the happiest of men.

Arm in arm, they strolled toward the bow, then stopped to take in the scene on the wharf. Though fifteen years had passed since the spring of the Middle Heart, little had changed, except that there were fewer rickshaws and long gowns and more cars and tattered beggars; and the bride and groom reminisced for a while, chatting effortlessly about Steel Hope, as if she had never forbidden the subject at all.

"If our young master hadn't raced to catch a boy named Firecrackers that afternoon, who knows where we'd be today?"

"We'd be here," she said simply. "You and I are each other's destiny."

He nodded, thrilling to her words, but when a bunch of dead roses floated by, he experienced a pang of melancholy. How long could happiness such as his—stolen from the gods, if not another man—last?

Another tug. "Everyone's gone ashore. Shouldn't we go too?"

"Let's wait a few minutes." Recalling the lines of Yuan Mei's poem, he was suddenly afraid to step ashore. *I seem to be in port, only to be at sea . . .*

"What's wrong?" Edging nearer to him, she averted her eyes and whispered as if the words had to be forced out. "Are there . . . questions you want to ask me? I don't mind. Ask. You can, you know."

He had questions about the future, not about her past; but before he could say anything, she bowed her head and began to speak haltingly about the day the four of them had gone to the market fair and eaten ice cream and laughed at a little woman pulling a big man by the ear.

"You remember, I heard drums and thought—" She stopped in mid-sentence, trying to summon the courage to tell him what had happened after she and Steel Hope dashed away to catch the bridal procession.

"Hush." He put a hand to her lips. "It's not important. You don't have to say any more."

She glanced up at him, her eyes glistening with gratitude. She swallowed hard. "After I came home from the Residence of No Importance, I opened it. I finally opened it."

"What?"

"His cigarette case."

"If you thought there might be a note inside, why didn't you look when I first gave it to you? Why did you wait five years?"

"Can't you see that I had to be absolutely, positively sure that he wasn't still alive?"

"I don't understand."

Shaking her head, she said, "I couldn't. I just couldn't. I was afraid. You must understand. . . ."

Of course he did, and asked gently, "Was there a note?"

"There was no note. But there was a sign. . . ."

Unlike Steel Hope, he had always humored her superstitions; they were for the large part harmless and a source of indispensable comfort, and he would never deprive anyone, least of all her, of that. But the sudden realization that something as arbitrary as one of her signs stood between his new life and the old caused him to falter. Holding fast to the railing, he asked, "What was that?"

"A gold-tipped 999. Steel Hope promised to keep it always. If it was there, it meant that he hadn't left me. But the case was empty, and I knew what for some time I had already felt in my heart—that my first love was gone."

Silently, he thanked the stranger who had collected what was left of Steel Hope's belongings from the wreck, for surely the man must have looked inside the case and, never thinking it would be missed, helped himself to the cigarette.

"My husband, can we go now?"

Following his wife down the gangplank, he noted with pride the many admiring stares Summer Wishes attracted and took no offense when the porters on the dock hovered about her, hawking their services, while dismissing him as a retainer no better than they. How could they act otherwise?

Summer Wishes, ignoring their pleas like an empress, signaled her uncouth subjects to make way, then stepped past them as if jade flutes were playing and the entire court kneeling, waiting to obey her slightest whim. But it was what happened next that truly took him by surprise, for she proceeded to shed the very decorum she'd worked so long and so diligently to cultivate and stunned the crowd by taking his arm. "Take a good look, you dimwits," she said. "This man is my husband, and in our family he's the big boss."

The dust swirling around the open mule cart forbade conversation, and the bride and groom rode in silence. The town was shabbier and somehow smaller than it had been when fate brought them together, as if the occupation that had diminished pride had diminished architecture as well. But except for this, and the pillboxes the Japanese had erected and the whitewashed rectangles on the walls where the enemy had painted rising suns, the place was as Mountain Pine remembered. Barely wider than the span between the wheels of their cart, the side streets were still lined with dingy shops, where craftsmen made everything from pots to coffins exactly as their forebears had done. Pedestrians still pretended not to see the beggars with their outstretched hands and tales of woe. Old women still drew water from the wells. Coolies still did the work of beasts. Only the children at play were carefree.

Apparently nothing had changed—that is, until, as the cart turned the corner onto the Avenue of Endless Nobility, he glimpsed the House of Li. The lane to the front gate was now shaded by a row of mulberry trees, the crumbling garden wall had been rebuilt and behind it were new roofs of shimmering green tiles. How had this come about? The letters from Amber Willows had offered no clues to the changes in their lives. Every month, some retired clerk, sitting at an outdoor table, had penned almost the same sentences as those written for Jade to her son. He started to question the driver, then thought better of it, remembering suddenly that Grand Hope had had something to do with the Japanese. Steel Hope had known more, but while he had always cursed his brother, he had been too ashamed to talk of it. In any case, it was certain that, at a time when rampant inflation was robbing all, the Lis could not possibly have accumulated such wealth by honorable means.

When they stood between the stone lions, the gatekeeper, to Mountain Pine's chagrin, refused to announce their arrival. "I don't go nowhere. You wait here. Somebody's bound to come out." From his unusual height and his accent, Mountain Pine assumed that the man was a native of Shandong; from his tough demeanor, that he was another ex-soldier turned paid bully.

Through the gates, he saw that the elegant lane and rebuilt walls and new roofs had lied. The courts, besieged by unruly trees and shrubs and weeds, appeared deserted. Could something have happened to the mistress? Could the clan have left the place? Could they have sold what hadn't been sold already to Watermelon Wu or some other collaborator, who had then been hounded out of town after the Japanese lost the war?

But someone was calling his name. Amber Willows, who had obviously been waiting by a window, hurried toward them.

She embraced him with abandon, weeping openly, as if he were not a man but still her baby brother. He didn't know where to put his arms or what to say. He'd never seen his sister cry before, not even on the day when he and Steel Hope left for the interior. The years had etched lines on her face, but if they detracted from her loveliness, he couldn't judge. In his eyes, that would never change.

Now, suddenly, she was laughing as she reached to take Summer Wishes by the hand, her eyes darting from the groom to the bride and back, again and again, as they proceeded into the courtyard. "Why, Sister-in-law is the most beautiful woman I've ever seen! And you, my brother, are blushing."

Summer Wishes came to his rescue. "And you, Elder Sister, are as kind and warmhearted as your brother and Steel Hope have told me." At the mention of the young master's name, there was a pause when no one spoke, for it was most natural and appropriate that each take a moment to recall the one who would never be coming home. Mountain Pine's thoughts turned to the great iron lock on the open gate, which had prevented the boy Steel Hope from carrying out his many threats to run away. How strong it had seemed once; how useless it must have been during the occupation.

Oddly, a neighbor's boy—or was it a spirit?—chose that moment to throw a pebble over the wall. It landed at his feet. He pocketed it, along with his memories.

Amber Willows broke the silence. "Come quickly," she said. "Mistress is waiting. But you mustn't mention anything about the death of Steel Hope."

He readily agreed. Were there any words to comfort a mother who had lost her only son? Even if there were, how could he say them? He was the one who had kowtowed before Kwan Yin and vowed upon his life to care for Steel Hope.

As they hurried toward the Patriarch's court, he noticed that all the shutters and doors of the adjoining courts were not only shut but barred with wooden slats. The receiving hall, though still furnished as it had been, no longer had a bevy of relatives and servants in attendance. Jade, in her rosewood chair, was alone. Seeing her, he quickly lowered his gaze to hide his thoughts. Yes, grief and the years had aged Amber Willows. But how cruelly they had marked the mistress! Her hair was gray and untidy. Her hands, more like talons, gripped a cane. Her pocked face, without rouge or powder, repelled.

Returning his deep bow, she nodded slightly and asked with little interest if they'd had a smooth voyage.

"Very smooth, Mistress."

"You mean to tell me nothing unfortunate happened?" Her tone revealed disappointment.

"No, nothing."

"How can that be? All the talk these days is about how the Communists are causing trouble everywhere," she said.

"Farther north or south, I believe."

She went on as if he hadn't spoken. "Sharing wives, seizing property, slaughtering gentry, violating everything sacred. They're worse than bandits . . . worse even than the Japanese, and since you were nice and safe upriver, let me tell you a thing or two about those smelly bowlegged turds, those barbaric shits, those . . ."

He winced at her choice of words. That was different too.

Obviously, she had many more epithets in her current repertory, but as she paused to catch her breath, his sister deftly seized the moment and stepped forward to present Summer Wishes. The eyes of the mistress narrowed. This time, she didn't even nod to acknowledge her guest's deep bow, and suddenly he remembered that, except for Amber Willows, Jade had never been able to abide a comely presence.

"Welcome to the House of Li," she said, her voice as flat as a cracked bell.

No matter how spacious the courts, he thought, they mustn't stay long. Summer Wishes, however, seemed oblivious of the perilous envy she'd roused. Stammering with heartfelt emotion and sincerity, she said, "Oh, Mistress, I'm sure everyone has told you . . . so many times you must be tired of hearing it, but now that we've met . . . oh, please forgive me . . . it's just that I can't help myself . . . I must tell you how much of you I saw in your son, especially your wonderfully expressive eyes."

The effect was miraculous. His wife had totally disarmed the mistress, for Jade couldn't have been more gracious after that. She herself poured the tea. She asked Summer Wishes endless questions about the theater. Now and then, she even smiled.

She said nothing, however, about what had happened to the House of Li during the past ten years, or the situation now. It was as if the other ladies were seated alongside and servants were hovering about, so that discretion was called for.

"The theater was yours?" she asked for the third time. "You mean that you, an actress, actually owned it? So much has changed."

He must have tapped his fingers nervously to express his frustration, for Amber Willows put her hand over them and whispered, "You don't know how good it is for the mistress to have company again. It's been too long."

He nodded, though her words alarmed him even more.

After Jade left for her nap, he didn't want to spoil Summer Wishes' triumph by questioning his sister then and there. Instead, he asked her to show them to their room.

She took them not to the servants' quarters, but to Stone Guardian's study, which was only a few short steps from the reception hall. He was unprepared to see only a rickety bed and a primitive wardrobe. Had all the other rooms been emptied too?

When Summer Wishes yawned, he saw his opportunity and said, "My wife, you must be tired. Rest, while my sister and I take a stroll."

As they walked away from the gates, in the shade of the mulberry trees, Amber Willows whispered, sketching only the barest essentials. Clearly she'd been commanded to say so much and no more. He didn't dare probe.

After Steel Hope and Mountain Pine left for the interior, Grand Hope and Jade had no longer even pretended civility. Worse, the new Patriarch never addressed her by her rightful name, referring to his stepmother only as "that woman." And without a rightful name, she had no rightful place. She became the object of every Li's contempt.

Jade took revenge. She demanded that her father fire Grand Hope. At first the merchant refused; after years of watching his protégé ruin their competitors, he knew the terrible risks of making the young man an enemy. But when his daughter vowed to commit suicide and shame the House of Li herself if he didn't acquiesce, he also knew that Jade would make good her threat. He did as he was told.

Grand Hope took revenge. He convinced the merchant's Japanese backers to call in their loans and put him in charge instead. Soon the new owner was the number-one puppet in the county, hated and feared by all true Chinese. He ordered the Peace Preservation troops to arrest and execute his former patron. They did as they were told.

Overnight the merchant became a patriotic martyr, and Jade seized the moment to protest publicly against the villainy of China's enemies by quitting the infamous House of Li for a miserable rented room. There, with only Amber Willows to attend her, she waited for the occupation to end, waited for the return of Steel Hope, waited for the day when together they would take revenge by being the ones who would restore honor to the House of Li. Meanwhile she sacrificed every comfort—even the cosmetics she used to hide her pockmarks and prized above all else—and led the life of a sainted victim. Safe in the knowledge that no one would bother with the insane, she sat night and day by her window, regaling passersby with a litany of insults and grievances against her nemesis, Grand Hope.

To Amber Willows, Jade claimed she had never been happier. She even reveled in the hardships, declaring that they would add to the ecstasy of her ultimate revenge. She talked of little else. She was so certain that nothing could spoil her plans.

Of course, something did—that fateful letter from Mountain Pine.

Without a tear, Jade had burned the letter on the spot. Bribing the letter reader with her last gold bracelet, she convinced the man to move forthwith to Shanghai. Then, turning to Amber Willows, she swore to choke her blue if she didn't stop crying. "Bury my son and you bury my only claim on the House of Li. Nothing happened today or any other day."

Had news of her son's death made Jade's feigned insanity real? Or had her desire for revenge consumed even her grief? Amber Willows still couldn't decide. But so strong had been Jade's will and so convincing her demeanor that at times Amber Willows wondered if Mountain Pine's letter had ever existed.

The day the occupation ended, Grand Hope had been executed for treason. The frightened clansmen had dispersed, who knew where, leaving Jade, the only unsullied member of the House of Li, as its sole mistress. Assuming her rightful place in the courts at last, she had taken every precaution. She continued to live simply, seeing no one except Amber Willows and the gatekeeper; and by selling what the clansmen hadn't carted off, she had held on to the remaining courts.

Amber Willows wouldn't say more, and when Mountain Pine told the story to Summer Wishes, he advised her to ask no questions. "Now that we know this much, and the mistress knows that we know, it's best not to delve further."

ONE MORNING, after they had been Jade's guests for some weeks, Mountain Pine paid a call on the mistress to beg permission to accept pupils and hold classes at the compound. "Of course, I shall pay rent."

Jade's curt promise to give it some thought couldn't hide her enthusiasm.

At first there were only three students—the butcher's teenage son, a neighbor's child, and a woman of leisure who talked more than she listened. Thus he had little choice but to tutor them singly. His earnings didn't cover the cost of food, much less rent. Nevertheless Summer Wishes continually postponed her return to the theater. "Let me wait until Mushroom arrives," she said. "Without her as my go-between, the theater people will treat me no better than a coolie."

While Jade fretted continually about the lack of students, she didn't press them for more money. Summer Wishes sensed the reason for her generosity—that while the changes in attitudes and society wrought by the upheaval of such an extended war couldn't be reversed, the mistress still wasn't anxious for the townsfolk to ogle a guest of the House of Li whose profession was to display herself on stage.

By the time Mushroom arrived, it was winter and Summer Wishes was expecting a child.

Mushroom's unique skills were nevertheless gainfully employed. Canvassing the town as tirelessly as she had once canvassed villages up and down the river for ticket buyers, the honey-tongued woman talked the most unlikely people into enrolling at the school. She promised everything except heaven: a higher salary, lower taxes, no more fees to letter writers, medicine men or fortunetellers, a wealthy husband, a beautiful wife, obedient children, new respect from all associates, especially mothers-in-law, and glory of glories, a career as an official. In return, the students paid their tuition not in worthless yuan but in goods and services.

And so, while the civil war raged on elsewhere, within the House of Li there was harmony. Summer Wishes presented her husband with a healthy son and, proudly, Mountain Pine presented Jade with respectability, for she was no longer the ugly second wife of the Patriarch, but the local patroness of scholarship.

THE READER OF HEARTS AND MINDS
(1948)

FOR LI after li, along an empty moonlit road, Carter Zhou prattled in his loud, raspy voice, while Steel Hope hinted that he preferred silence by burrowing deeper into his greatcoat and feigning sleep. To no avail. Whether the cadre liked it or not, the fool was intent on ingratiating himself with the Party by parroting every last tract.

". . . But thanks to the wisdom of Chairman Mao, the courage of the Eighth Route Army, and the leadership of the Party, the masses are disgorging bitterness and turning over . . ."

Of course, Steel Hope could shut him up with a word. But how could he say it? The poor soul would have been snoring in his warm kang if he hadn't postponed his return home by offering the cadre a ride to the village where Steel Hope had lived, off and on, throughout the years of mop-ups, and which was the subject of his next report.

". . . Gone are the blood debts. Gone are the local despots. And soon Bandit Chiang Kai-shek, that running dog of imperialists, will be roundly defeated. . . ."

Steel Hope flexed his weary shoulders and sighed, succumbing to a rare bout of nostalgia for the years of hiding by day and setting traps by night, when his adversaries wore uniforms, and overcoming them could be as simple and as satisfying as digging shallow pools near tunnel entrances that let two-legged waders pass but would drown any four-legged canister of gas.

Memories of a time before this belonged to a stranger whom Mountain Pine and Summer Wishes would have mourned when the Jeep, not its driver, had been lost, but who had since died after all. He couldn't be certain of the exact date of that young engineer's death. Perhaps it had happened when the girl ran from the reeds. Perhaps when the blacksmith bared his chest to the bayonet, or when the women crossing the pumpkin field removed their shoes, or when the war had been won and he decided not to contact Jade or Amber Willows, Summer Wishes or Mountain Pine. Still, there was no doubt that the revolutionary who had been born during those three years of working behind enemy lines had been conceived and cradled, nurtured and taught by the very peasants whom he had come to protect; and it was to them that the new Steel Hope dreamed of returning the gift of life, a new life, a better life.

He grinned, remembering the triumph he'd felt upon seeing his reflection in the well water after that mop-up in East Village when the Japs had found the entrance to the tunnels behind the stove, and the relief later that day when he learned that all the villagers had crawled out of them safe and sound. Of course such feelings couldn't last, for they inevitably brought to mind the enormity of the price paid. Before the Japanese began retreating in 1944, finally leaving Hebei the year after, there would be more mop-ups and hostages killed in his district; and though by some miracle all his villages were spared and his tunnels lasted until the peasants removed the wooden struts for rebuilding, these losses, tragic as they were, had only steeled his will and validated his dream. Never again had he succumbed to weeping.

When the war was over, and the Japanese were back on the islands where they belonged, he had felt that same urgent need to talk to Lincoln Chen; this time, about how best he might serve the cause. This time, the professor had said that Steel Hope was ready to be his reader.

"Go back to Hebei and read for me the minds and hearts of the people in the unfolding story of the revolution. Need I say that this is no mission for a hero? Need I remind you that you will be my eyes? And if you become an accomplished reader, be prepared for recurring nightmares."

And so, throughout the three years since the Allied victory, while the continuing civil war with the Guomindang was fought in areas of more strategic importance, he had traveled alone from one liberated village to another and back, in an ever widening circle. At each stop, the meetings often lasted for weeks. Throughout, he would sit stiffly behind a table, questioning every leader and every family in the village, listening to their reports on local conditions and developments: births and deaths; the building of a school; the opening of a workshop; the success or failure of the planting season, or the harvest; the visit of a drama troupe; and, of course, what had happened prior to, during and as a result of land reform. Throughout, as the activists wore him down with slogans and accusations, and others colored their opinions to please him, while most nodded meekly in agreement with whatever the new village leaders proclaimed and proposed, he, as Lincoln Chen's reader, disciplined himself not to intervene or adjudicate, but to remember and recount every facet of this historic transition in his confidential reports.

Always, there were hints of favoritism on the part of the locals in charge, and questions about the arbitrariness of the rules by which the lands and goods had been divided. Always, some feared that they would be named as objects of the struggle meetings, when villagers were urged by their cadres to vent their anger and exact vengeance for wrongs, past and present; and more than likely, some of those fearful ones were right. Always, there was the unspoken fear of a Guomindang victory, however slight the odds of that were now, and the reprisals that would surely follow. And always, since the land reform, there was the unspoken fear of the middle peasants that they might be reclassified as rich, and their belongings appropriated and distributed to the peasants classified as poor.

The years had passed in a blur, for his days were so alike and he so alone. To maintain an air of authority and fairness, he'd discouraged familiarity from his former comrades in arms and those he'd once been responsible for, without exception. Even Lincoln Chen's letters were never more than instructions; he understood that his old professor must maintain authority and fairness as well. He also understood how much easier it was to build bridges that would stand triumphant over time than to build a road of hope. Others in the Party would no doubt have explained that he had successfully rid himself of his bourgeois need to restore one family's honor by embracing the welfare of all the people. He didn't feel any urge to explain. He saw for himself how revolution was changing the Chinese people, battling the cancer of fatalism.

Still, time after time, the loneliness of standing on the threshold of some empty temple, watching dusk fall and the villagers strolling home, was like dying again.

When could he go home? And home, where was that?

Others might look to the vaulted sky for an answer hidden in the pathways of stars. Steel Hope, of course, knew better. How could the heavens possibly be mindful of a curl of dust scudding across the desolate plains of Hebei?

"... Then with all China united under communism, everyone will have an upstairs and a downstairs, electric lights and telephones...."

He cursed silently. The devil was parroting every word a second time.

"... Generation after generation, we peasants suffered oppression and—"

To Steel Hope's astonishment, Carter Zhou stopped in mid-sentence. Peering over his collar, he saw that they were approaching the graveyard, the same graveyard where the people of East Village used to exit the tunnels during mop-ups. Now, the trees that had once distinguished it, and had hidden the secret egress, had been chopped down for firewood. Now it was no different from all the other places in the district where landlords had been buried, and from which their clansmen had fled. Some had left even before the Japanese appeared; others had gone more recently, because of land reform. The few who remained would have chosen, as he had chosen, to forsake family ties. With no one to tend them, the bare mounds looked as forbidding as they were forlorn.

The silence, though, was delightful. How ironic, he thought: saved from another round of revolutionary zeal by the old-fashioned fear of ghosts.

The carter's whip cracked faster and faster, but always in the air, never brushing a hair on the hide of his precious mule. Perhaps that was the trouble, Steel Hope thought, as after a halfhearted attempt at trotting the beast slowed to a shuffle and then, smack in front of the entrance to the footpath that wound among the graves, stopped altogether. Now Carter Zhou cowered with the whip clasped to his breast, quivering like the uplifted leg of a puppy caught marking the bed of a huge black cat. His eyes darted frantically, searching for the ghosts that must have stopped the cart, and no doubt envisioning his welcome at the Ninth Level of Hell.

Steel Hope was tempted to sit back and enjoy the farce, but it was late and, relenting, he jumped out of the cart to lead the animal past the danger zone. Gently he coaxed, then he pulled on the bridle, pulled harder. Still the mule balked, refusing to budge a hoof until it had done what it had obviously intended to do all along.

As the steam rose from the pool of piss, and they were once more under way, the carter's embarrassed giggles gave way to revolutionary songs.

The voice, no longer raspy, possessed a fervor as unstudied as it was poignant; and listening to the singer even without his megaphone, Steel Hope marveled at the transformation. For as he contorted his wrinkled, mobile face and gestured awkwardly to the moon, Carter Zhou seemed to shed the inhibitions that a lifetime of obliging others had instilled in him and, reveling in the sound of his own voice, to perceive for a rare moment that he had been set upon the earth to please only one man, himself.

As sometimes happened at even the most distressing of meetings, or unexpectedly, as now, Steel Hope was filled with the certainty that he and Carter Zhou weren't merely a curl of dust scudding across the desolate plains, but travelers on the road of hope. Once again, a peasant had touched something at the core of the cadre that was sincere and strong, however indescribable and at times indefensible—his faith in the revolution.

Steel Hope didn't realize that he'd joined in the singing until the carter leaned over to put his shoulder to the cadre's and started the two of them swaying from side to side.

"We march, never to return, until our rivers and hills are again home. We march, never to return . . ."

They turned off the thoroughfare where the twin good-luck poplars still stood. The pumpkin fields that flanked the dirt road were brown and sere in the wintry cold. The trellises were bare. The ditch was empty. The villagers, whom he hadn't seen since the start of their land reform last spring, were all safe in their own beds.

As soon as the cart had pulled up at the temple, which now, as in most other villages in Communist-held territory, served as the Party office, the carter grabbed his bucket and ran to fetch water for his mule, abandoning the cadre without a word. Steel Hope grinned. So much for revolutionary zeal. He reached up to get his bedroll, then, realizing that he too was thirsty, headed for the well himself.

So startled was Carter Zhou to find Steel Hope alongside him that he dropped the bucket and, cowering again, said, "Honest, I was coming back to give you a hand. It's just that"—he paused to offer the cadre a silly smile—"all my life I wanted to own just one leg of a mule, and never even got close enough to sniff a fart. Then, the great Communist Party distributed the fruits of land reform, and I got so happy I lost my head. Now I'd rather sleep with that mangy animal than my wife. Go ahead and kick my butt, Master, I won't mind." He offered the cadre a patched target.

Steel Hope didn't know who was to be pitied more—the submissive slave or the reluctant lord. "Don't be an ass, Comrade," he said. "I came for a drink, that's all."

IT WAS almost dawn when Steel Hope finished eating his breakfast of man tou and dried turnip. The bread was several days old, hard to chew and even harder to swallow, but the turnip, crisp and salty, was delicious. As usual, what he missed most was a cup of tea. Until stoves were lit later in the morning and he could start buying hot water and meals from the villagers, well water would have to do.

He rolled up his bedroll, washed and dressed, then began his ritual: sitting stiffly and reading old newspapers at a table placed in front of what had been the altar. The pose discouraged lengthy welcomes, chatter and effusive offers of hospitality. There was never a need to notify the people of the cadre's presence in their village. Somehow they always knew.

He didn't read for long. The local leaders arrived, followed by non-party members; and though, throughout the day, he mostly listened, saving his questions until everybody had his turn to speak, the meeting exhausted him. The tension of acting as if he'd never met any of them before, neither when he lived among them nor on his several visits since, was like wearing an unwieldy, expressionless mask from dawn to dusk.

Alone again, he paced, then organized his notes and wrote a report on what had been said thus far about their land reform. When his duties were done, he didn't want to eat or sleep. He craved fresh air, and went for a stroll.

A half-moon lazed in the cloudless sky and the byways were blissfully empty. Only smoke escaping from the chimneys affirmed that the village hadn't been abandoned. At the well, he stopped to sit on its rim just as he used to do when he was their new cadre waiting for the villagers to fill their water gourds, before setting out to sabotage the railroad tracks. Then, he'd ask and they'd answer:

"How can China win?"

"By cutting their communications."

"Am I your teacher?"

"No, you're our comrade."

Now he smiled at the memory. More than once, upon returning, their laughter would shake the poplar trees as they ambled home while he—too proud to ask for a sip, too proud to bring an extra gourd—

sprinted toward this well and nearly fell in. He hoped that in the privacy of their homes tonight, the villagers were still laughing at that thirsty cadre.

Though the land had been parceled out to the tillers and life was very different now, by the look of the place in winter, little had changed, and for him, memories were engraved everywhere. On mud walls pocked with bullet holes. In the near fields and the distant bamboo grove. At doorsteps.

Gazing at the tallest thatched roof, he hummed the song that Carter Zhou used to sing from his post as singer. From that roof, as well, the cadre had set off the firecrackers to welcome Spring Festival the year the Japs pulled out.

Again he smiled. Perhaps his home was here.

Suddenly he made up his mind. For once he'd break his own rule and visit with Wispy Eyebrows.

When the door opened, the elder welcomed him inside, insisting that an old peasant didn't deserve such an honor as he scrambled to show the cadre to a seat on the kang. The brick platform heated by the stove quickly took the chill out of Steel Hope's bones. It was the same bed where he'd slept as the new cadre; the same stove that had hidden the entrance to the tunnels.

The room seemed larger than he remembered, or perhaps it was only that Wispy Eyebrows' mother and wife had died, leaving the man who had no sons to live out his days alone. Its whitewashed walls were tearstained from the rain that filtered through the roof. Its earthen floor was so worn that it looked wrinkled. Yet there was an aura of dignity about the sparsely furnished room that befitted the man who had led the village throughout the war.

Wispy Eyebrows began the ritual welcome. "Have you eaten today?"

"I'm well, thank you. And what about yourself?"

"I am well."

The old man hurried to the niche in the wall where he kept his pipe and, with a burning straw from the stove, lit it on the first try. He puffed to make sure it was drawing nicely before offering it to his guest. As the old comrades in arms passed it back and forth, the elder, whom Steel Hope remembered as a silent man, was surprisingly talkative. So had the others been who'd sat facing him all day. Wispy Eyebrows spoke mostly about the weather and the crops and what the two men had accomplished together during the war, though he avoided mentioning the pumpkin fields. As Steel Hope listened to the familiar voice, he heard another voice, even more familiar—his bookmate reciting a poem he had taught the young master as a child, the poem Steel Hope had favored above all:

> You ride a horse, I wear out my sandals
> Upon meeting, we smile and bow low.
> On your back a sheaf of hay, on my back a mantle of silk
> Upon meeting, we smile and bow low.

Finally Steel Hope broached the subject that had brought him there. "Why did you refuse the land that everyone agreed you deserve?"

The question was answered with another. "And what would you have an old man do with it?"

"Others have sold their shares."

"Ah, but what a shame to trade a mu of land for paper or, for that matter, silver."

This was true. "What about the other fruits of land reform confiscated from the runaway landlords?" he asked. "You could certainly use a chair or a cupboard."

"I've lived all these years without them. New things would only be in my way."

"What about a pair of pants or a padded jacket or a quilt?"

With perfect timing, the old man flashed his eyes at him like an eager spinster and asked, "Comrade, are you trying to marry this old man off?"

They laughed together and the laughter warmed his heart, but when it finally ended Steel Hope resumed his probing. "Then a wheelbarrow. A peddler of bean curd could always use a newer one."

"You aren't wrong."

Steel Hope slapped the kang. "Then it's settled. You'll accept a wheelbarrow."

"Did I ever tell you about my wheelbarrow?"

What was the old devil up to? He'd never even told Steel Hope about his eldest daughter. "You taught me everything I needed to know, Wispy Eyebrows; but you never spared a word on any story."

Scratching his neck, the old peasant replied, "That's true. . . . Well, long ago my father planted a seed and watered it faithfully, and when the sapling was grown, he chopped down the only tree we ever had, and made a wheelbarrow for me. How could I use another? It would be unfilial."

For a long time Steel Hope was unable to speak. He looked at the peasant who sat beside him—his face little more than cheekbones and jaw, his hands gnarled from a lifetime of grinding beans, his patched clothes—and envied him.

It was the elder who finally broke the silence. "Comrade, please don't misunderstand. I know that you wish better for me, but I'm set in my ways, too old and too slow to change."

"There must be something you want, something you can use."

"I can only wear one suit of clothes at a time, and I'm wearing it. I can only sit in one place at a time, and my bottom is most comfortable here on this kang. I can only eat one bowl of food at a time, and I have one of my own, and my wife's and my mother's for guests. I can only smoke one pipe at a time, and it warms my heart when a friend shares it with me. What else do I need?"

"Grain! Your jar is almost empty."

This time the man didn't have a ready reply, and Steel Hope grinned, thinking that he'd won a point at last.

But finally, once again, the elder shook his head. "Do you remember the four militiamen in the ditch with us that day?"

"Indeed, three are now Party members, and I've just spent the entire day with them."

"Did they talk about the fourth?"

"They might have. I don't recall."

"It doesn't matter. He no longer lives in this village. When his rich cousin ran away this spring, he gave a few mus of land to each of his poor relations, including the militiaman. So our comrade became a landlord. It's his grain you'd be putting in my bin. How could I swallow a bite? Our daughters died together before our eyes."

*

STEEL HOPE continued to travel from village to village reporting on the local situation while Communists won the great battles in the north and more and more Guomindang troops defected. At the end of the following January, the city of Beijing surrendered without a fight.

Orders came from Lincoln Chen, who by declining any official role was able to wield even greater influence over the ambitious cast of political players in Beijing from off stage: "The time has come to build a new China. Start at the beginning." And so, in the wake of the triumphant People's Liberation Army, the cadre, now a political officer, began his journey south toward the Yangzi, to the place where he was born.

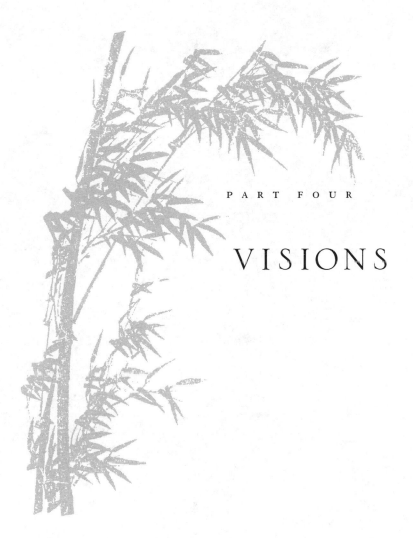

PART FOUR

VISIONS

TURNINGS

(1949)

OVERNIGHT Wen Shui was festooned with red flags. Those who feared the new ways had fled. Those who stayed were desperate for peace and order. All knew that China couldn't continue as it was, with shoppers wheeling carts piled high with bank notes that beggars used for kindling.

Now change had come in the guise of an army of shy peasant boys, dressed in homespun cotton uniforms, singing as they marched through the streets. Loud cheers greeted them and waves of relief followed in their wake. They were so unlike the fierce mercenaries many had expected. Whenever a schoolgirl thrust flowers at a soldier, he blushed redder than the blossoms, lost stride and, as though attempting to divine the secret of putting one straw sandal forward at a time, diligently studied his feet. It was this innocence that invested the townspeople—jaded by the cynical government and virulent corruption—with laughter and hope.

Mountain Pine hoisted Little Panda on his shoulders so that his son could see the lion dance, the stilt walker, the musicians. Snatching fistfuls of his hair, the baby bounced with delight. Smarting, Mountain Pine let out a yelp of surprise.

Mushroom scolded. "Let go of your father's hair this minute."

"Sit still, Little Panda!" said Summer Wishes.

Mountain Pine laughed. "I don't mind. He can't really hurt me."

The baby gurgled and tugged harder.

"What a grip!" exclaimed Mountain Pine. "This son of ours could ride a dragon."

Summer Wishes feigned a look of displeasure. "You mustn't spoil him, you really mustn't."

As he gazed helplessly into Summer Wishes' eyes, she tried and failed to tame the corners of her lips. She turned away to hide her smile.

Mountain Pine tilted his head upwards. "Believe it or not, Little Panda, there are people who claim that your mother is a great actress."

The stilt walker bent down to give the baby a friendly pat, eliciting crows of delight, then went on his way, broadcasting his message: "See? We Communists mean no harm. Don't listen to rumors. Chiang and his running dogs will never be back. Reopen your shops. Workers, return to your jobs. Students, return to your classes. Everything will be fine. Peace is here."

More soldiers passed, chanting the promise they had made all along their march from the northern provinces:

Never, never will we steal!
Not an old needle!
Not a used thread!
Not a sip of water!
We soldiers will sweep!
We will sweep, sweep all the dirt away!

Their voices boomed. Their faces beamed. The gladness was infectious, and Mountain Pine, standing tall, thought, Remember this day, my son.

Following the men came boys beating drums—the towels wrapped around their heads were like those worn by men of Yenan, the revolutionary stronghold—and girls in braids, waving red ribbons and dancing as they sang "The Rice-Sprout Song." Suddenly, they broke formation to push and pull at the astonished spectators, exhorting them to discard their inhibitions and join the parade. While children hid behind their parents, Mushroom needed no more invitation, and, snatching a ribbon, she sallied forth, wiggling and waggling with an abandon worthy of the Drunken Maiden. Onlookers burst into applause. Then a grandma with bound feet caught the urge.

Summer Wishes tugged at Mountain Pine's sleeve. "Would you mind?"

"Mind? I'd be proud."

She hesitated.

"Go! Dance for both of us."

Beaming, she joined the joyful cavalcade and, with every wave of her hand casting a spell as sure as the wave of a fairy fan, children, like the children at the nearby orphanage the actress used to visit as a favor to the monks of the Monastery of Heedless Tranquility, skipped merrily out of hiding to follow in her wake.

Now more soldiers came marching, carrying giant portraits of the Chairman; as they passed they sang, "The East is Red, the sun has risen, China has produced a Mao Zedong. . . ."

Row after row of gaunt, sun-browned faces filed by, one almost indistinguishable from another. Had the soldier in the rear not marched alone, Mountain Pine never would have noticed him, for his dress wasn't different from the others', and his shoes were also of straw. Only the red tassels tied to the holster on his hip signaled rank. Once Mountain Pine had noticed him, however, he couldn't take his eyes from him. There was something about the man. His walk, while graceful, was almost a swagger. His face, though shadowed beneath his cap, seemed refined.

As he marched past, Mountain Pine sidled through the crowd, doing his best to keep abreast of him, increasingly puzzled by a vague feeling that the man wasn't a stranger, but someone he knew. He shouted greetings but, even as he did, knew they couldn't be heard above the din of the crowd. The gap widened, and the soldier disappeared from view.

Only then did Mountain Pine realize that Little Panda had fallen asleep. Gently he lowered the boy from his shoulder and, cradling him cheek to cheek, returned home.

There were a couple of soldiers by the gate, but the lazy Shandong bully was nowhere in sight. Why Jade didn't fire the man was more than he could comprehend.

Since the advance party of Red soldiers had moved into the school a few days before, Mountain Pine had often stopped to chat with the men whose lives would have been the mirror image of his had he never been a bookmate, but this time he was in no mood to explore another way of life and merely waved; then, pointing to his sleeping son to explain his haste, went straight into the house.

That night he lay awake, unable to fathom why, in the midst of new hope for the future, the old melancholy, dispelled by marriage and fatherhood, had returned. When Summer Wishes asked what was the matter, he folded her into his arms and whispered, "Nothing is wrong. Everything will be fine, just fine," but the words sounded to his own ears like a prayer.

In the morning, while Summer Wishes soothed Jade, who was afraid the Reds wouldn't leave her school after the promised few nights, but would appropriate the House of Li before she could have the satisfaction of seeing her in-laws slink back into town begging for forgiveness and favors, Mountain Pine went to check on the soldiers. He found everything in order: even the doors that had been taken down and laid across pairs of desks and chairs to serve as beds were back on their hinges; the bedrolls were packed. No one was about except a single soldier with a bandage wound around his head, who was peeling turnips in the alley.

Somehow the thought of going back into the house and saying "Nothing's been disturbed, the soldiers will be leaving today" made him walk to the alley instead.

"Good morning, Comrade. Did you sleep well?"

The man jumped to his feet. "Like a rock."

To keep the conversation going, Mountain Pine said the first thing that came to mind. "I suppose you're used to sleeping just about anywhere."

"Probably the only place I can't sleep now is home."

And the second thing. "How long have you been away?"

"Seven years."

"No leaves?"

The man burst out laughing. "We're soldiers, not schoolboys."

"Are you married?"

"Since I was sixteen, and I've got a son, too."

Mountain Pine tried to imagine what it would be like to be gone so long from Summer Wishes and Little Panda. He couldn't.

"Don't look so worried, Teacher! You're safe. We've got all the volunteers we need now! Who wouldn't join up for a mu of land?" Lowering his voice, the soldier confided, "But don't think that's what we veterans did. We joined to kill Japs. Take our political officer. He's right here in his hometown, but has he gone running off to see his family? No, he sets an example. He's a Party man, through and through."

"What's his name?"

The soldier shrugged.

"What does he look like?"

"Never was close enough to see. But he's no different from the rest of us. Families've got to wait till the rest of China's liberated. We've still got the People's work to do."

When he returned to the main house, Mountain Pine started to tell the women about this conversation, then refrained. Somehow the vague sense of unease had returned; he was certain that the political officer was the man in the parade who had caught his eye. "I'm going to check on what's happening in town," he said. "Don't hold lunch for me."

He walked for hours, ostensibly to see if businesses had returned to normal and what orders were being issued. But he neither stopped to ask anyone nor read the notices posted everywhere. Instead he looked for red tassels on the holsters of soldiers. Finally he found himself near the wharf, which was crowded with troops waiting to board ferries. With Guomindang soldiers deserting like startled tadpoles and so many towns won without firing a shot, it wouldn't be long now before all of China was liberated. The word had an odd ring.

He bought some scallion cakes from a peddler and ate them as he strolled slowly toward the water's edge. A breeze lifted his hair. There was always something mysterious—no, magical—about the river, and now, with each step, he had the unmistakable feeling that he was literally walking into the past. Watching the boats sail for the opposite bank, he was a bookmate again, sitting with his young master on the levee. He searched the sky, half expecting to see a flight of birds with reed whistles tied to their tails and to hear the sounds made by a boyish hero imitating gunfire.

A stone fell into the water, making ripples. Another. He turned. Off to his right, a man stood silhouetted on the embankment. Mountain Pine shielded his eyes against the sun. It was a soldier. The resemblance was uncanny. No, it couldn't be. His mind played tricks. He blinked. The phantom was still there. Backing away, he waved his hand to dismiss it. But another stone flew—no, floated—through the air, and another and another, and he felt his throat tightening and his lungs collapsing with the fear of suffocation that he hadn't felt for years. He scrambled to get away. He fell. He didn't dare move, look up. How could the man be Steel Hope and not his ghost?

"Comrade, are you hurt?"

At the sound of the familiar voice, he bolted upright.

Face to face, Steel Hope burst into laughter, embracing him.

As if anesthetized, he couldn't move. His jaw was slack. His arms dangled. But his mind, compensating for this sudden loss, sent him speeding away from his confusion to his wife, and allowed him to feel how she would feel being in Steel Hope's arms again.

"Bookmate, you're not seeing things. I haven't returned from the dead. I'm alive."

Mountain Pine told himself that this wasn't happening, that everything would be fine, just fine, in a minute.

"Have I changed that much? Don't you know me anymore?"

He couldn't stop staring.

"How are you? What have you been up to for these past seven years? When did you leave Chongqing? Did you come right back here? Tell me everything!"

Mountain Pine managed to say, "You first."

Steel Hope pulled him to his feet. "Come, let's go and sit where we sat as boys, and I'll explain." Again, he laughed. "It's an amazing story. You're just the one to write it. You're still writing, aren't you?"

He shook his head.

Steel Hope slapped his back affectionately. "Well, my story will get you started again."

He almost shouted, I don't want to start again. I don't give a damn about your story. Why didn't you stay away? Why have you come back?

Steel Hope began with his journey to Kunming.

Listening to him, Mountain Pine watched a lone gull wheeling in the sky, and heard a poem by Li Po:

> Hard is the journey,
> hard is the journey,
> so many turnings,
> and now where might I be?

There were no more soldiers waiting on the wharf when Steel Hope finished telling about the years they had been apart. Throughout, Mountain Pine had barely said anything, had understood only some of what he was told—wondering, always wondering, when the moment would come that he would be doing the telling and what that would bring.

"... After I saw the last of the soldiers going south safely aboard the boats, I was going to call on my mother and your sister, but I never thought I'd find you back in town too. I can't get over such good luck. Damn! It's great to see you. It's great to be alive. Honestly, after all the years I never dreamed I'd feel the same. It's been so long since I had someone to talk to that I—"

The joy in his voice was unbearable, and suddenly Mountain Pine was pleading, much too loudly, for him to stop. "You must listen, you must let me speak."

Steel Hope laughed. "At last, you've found your tongue. I was beginning to think you'd never recover from the shock."

"Steel Hope, I didn't ..." The words jammed his throat like a fist.

"Didn't what?

" . . . return alone. She returned with me."

"Summer Wishes! She's here too? Why didn't you say so right away? What a homecoming this is!" He bounded to his feet, pulling Mountain Pine up with him. "Take me to her this minute—take me to her now!"

"No, not yet." With a strength he didn't realize he had, Mountain Pine forced Steel Hope to sit down again. "First, you must listen to another story."

"Later, later. You've got plenty of time to tell me later."

Mountain Pine almost wept, seeing the boy in the man, and spoke sternly, as he would have to the young master. "Steel Hope, you simply cannot have forgotten that we all thought you were dead. She . . . she . . ."

"What about her?"

"She refused to believe you were truly gone for months—no, years. But no one, not even she, could mourn forever. You must've known that eventually she'd . . . she'd have to . . ."

"You mean . . . she's married?"

He nodded. Recognizing the sadness that suddenly dulled Steel Hope's eyes as kin to his own melancholy, Mountain Pine put an arm around the soldier and said, "You must also know that if, by the strength of his desires, anyone could prevent the leaves falling from the trees or the snow melting in the sun, she would have prevented the seasons turning and waited for you. But spring must pass. And what was is no more. . . ."

He heard himself addressing not only Steel Hope, but himself as well; and, losing courage, he cried, "Why didn't you try even once to let us know?"

Steel Hope shook off his friend's embrace and, skipping a pebble across the water, said bitterly, "Weren't you listening? How could I?" He fired another stone. Another. Another.

The sun sank silently behind the far hills.

Here and there the clouds near the horizon still glowed faintly, like the last cinders of a fire.

When, finally, Steel Hope spoke again, there was no urgency in his voice, no anger, not even regret. There was only the weariness of an old soldier who, having outlived his young recruits, must trudge on. "My friend, in the beginning I furnished the emptiness in my soul with remnants from the past, coloring my memories with each recall. I left a cigarette . . ." He paused, as if he were seeing the gold-tipped 999. Blinking, he went on. "But when I was fighting behind enemy lines everything changed. I had to change and I did. Always I had to pretend to be more than I was.

"And then, having buried the past, I thought that it didn't matter anymore. I was wrong. A moment ago, just knowing that Summer Wishes was near, I felt her spring to life, as if those seven years hadn't passed, as if she were a part of me, as if we still belonged to each other. How ridiculous of me. But you, my friend, know better than anyone what a dunce I can be. I . . . I simply forgot. . . ."

The breeze stiffened. The night had swallowed the world on the opposite shore. For a long time, they sat in silence. Mountain Pine was grateful that the sun was gone and the moon nowhere to be seen. Yet he could see that there were tears standing in the soldier's eyes. Were they tears of anger or release, of love or self-love, of loyalty or betrayal? He didn't want to know.

Finally, Steel Hope asked him to describe the man she had married. "Is he worthy of her? Is he kind and good?"

"He's a pale shadow of the first man she loved, but has more substance than his ghost."

"Who is he?"

Mountain Pine reached out to cover Steel Hope's hand with his and found it cold. The rancor he had felt before was no longer there; compassion for hapless mortals like themselves had taken its place.

"Who is he?"

"He was and will always be your faithful friend."

No sooner had Mountain Pine stepped inside the gate of the House of Li than the four women scurried out to buzz around him like agitated bees, all speaking at once.

"Where have you been?"

"Are you all right?"

"We've been worried sick."

"Why didn't you send word?"

He apologized and smiled weakly when Summer Wishes put her palm to his forehead. "I'm fine. Just a little tired from walking."

Jade tapped her cane. "Well, don't keep us in suspense. How many executions did you see?"

Just one, he thought.

Mistaking his hesitation for reluctance, Jade arched an eyebrow. "That many?"

"Sorry to disappoint you, Mistress, but nothing of that sort happened." He offered her his arm. "Let's go inside first, and over a cup of tea I promise I'll give you a full report."

While Mushroom and Amber Willows hurried ahead, Summer Wishes walked around to offer Jade a second arm and, by recounting some feat their Little Panda had performed that day, to divert her. As they made their way through the darkened compound to the house, he could feel the old melancholy seeping back into his bones; with each step, his leg grew lamer.

The next thing Mountain Pine became aware of was the cup slipping through his fingers. It couldn't have been more than a second or two before he reached into his pocket for a handkerchief to blot the spill, but it seemed much longer; the stain forming on the prized rug, which Jade had said she'd rather starve than sell, transfixed him. Wasn't this the very spot on which he had stood during the Grasping Ceremony when, without warning, the birthday boy had grabbed his ankle? He was certain that it was.

Mushroom pushed him away, took up the task. He turned to Jade. He must have said something, because she snapped, "Never mind that. Sit down and tell." He turned to Summer Wishes. She pushed her cup toward him with an encouraging smile.

He took a sip.

There was a thumping. It was Jade's cane. "Well, well, well . . . ?"

He cleared his throat. His mouth tasted of ash. He couldn't remember how the town had changed; the morning belonged to another lifetime. He rubbed his palms nervously. They felt unclean, gritty from his fall at the riverbank. He couldn't think. "Where was I?" he asked.

Mushroom rolled her eyes. "That, my friend, is what we want to know."

He couldn't keep them waiting any longer. He had to say something. He decided to tell them what they were hoping to hear: how festive the town looked, how the soldiers behaved like scholars, how the residents ran out of their homes offering the strangers bowls of noodles for long life. "All in all . . . I think that . . . yes, the stories we've heard about what's happened in other cities weren't lies. Yes, everything is exactly like that. Or perhaps better. . . ."

"Don't stop. Tell us more."

Their enthusiasm forced him to go on. "Well, there was a peasant from Hebei who saved an entire village by . . .

"Oh, yes, there was a teacher from Yenan who was trapped in the swamps. . . ."

It was almost midnight before they allowed him to retire. He didn't stop to kiss Little Panda goodnight. Somehow he undressed. He had never been as tired, not even after those weeks of lugging books on an empty stomach up and down the mountains on the way to Chongqing.

Closing his eyes, he thought that keeping his promise not to say a word about Steel Hope's return had proved much less difficult than he had feared. It was easy, surprisingly easy, to hide the truth, to tell lies.

AFTER LUNCH the next day, while Little Panda was napping and Amber Willows shopped, the others lingered at the table. Like a child who wants to hear her favorite tale retold, Jade kept commanding Mountain Pine to tell the same stories, which by now all knew by heart.

He was relating for the third time the tale of the pumpkin fields when there was a knock. He swallowed hard. Damn that bandit! What good was a gatekeeper who refused to announce guests? Another knock. Still summoning his courage to go to the door, he saw that Mushroom had already crossed the room. As she opened it, she let out a gasp, then stumbled backwards, speechless.

Steel Hope stepped inside. Bowing formally, he said, "Mother, it is so good to see you."

Anticipating this moment, Mountain Pine had imagined Jade swooning, and for a breathless moment an expression of utter shock like one drawn in cartoons was affixed to her face. But then, to his amazement, she jumped to her feet and, without the aid of her cane, ran toward her son, shouting, "I knew you'd be coming back to me!"

While Steel Hope was submitting to her frenzied cries and embraces, Mountain Pine kept his eyes on them to postpone looking at Summer Wishes. He needed more time, much more time, though he'd lain awake for hours before dawn trying desperately to imagine what might happen, and thereby prepare himself for this fateful homecoming. Over and over he had imagined his wife brushing away tears of happiness; heard her calling out Steel Hope's name; felt the air stir as she dashed past her husband to go to him. And still he couldn't trust himself not to lash out, not to howl like some crazed beast at the inevitable moment when the shock would pass and she would realize that the man she loved above all had returned to her.

Now that moment was here. How much longer could he resist the truth? How much longer could he stare at mother and son, at the motes in the air? How much longer could he keep from seeing in her eyes the love that came first and only once? He turned.

Her chair was empty. For a second he thought she might have fainted, and glanced at the floor. There was only the shadow of a tea stain on the rug. He looked about. Summer Wishes was nowhere to be seen. But hadn't she been sitting beside him when the knock came? He had anticipated her tears, her joy, but not this.

He stared at the seat cushion on the chair where she'd been sitting. It was embroidered with a profusion of flowers, but he saw only the butterfly. He felt as perplexed as the philosopher Zhuang Ze, who didn't know whether he was a man dreaming of being a butterfly or a butterfly dreaming of being a man. He reached out to touch it. The warmth of her was still there. No, she hadn't been a dream. His wife was real.

She had fled. He wouldn't go after her. What comfort could he afford her? She would resent, no, despise his words, his touch, his very presence. He was her jailor now.

He would do as he had planned: wait, pretending shock, until Jade and Mushroom stepped aside, and then offer his hand to the ghost.

Steel Hope shook it as if they were strangers, and though he smiled, the words he spoke were resolutely correct—so unlike the old friend who, the day before, had embraced him with fervor on the riverbank. Suddenly Mountain Pine realized that throughout the women's emotional outpouring Steel Hope hadn't acted like a long lost son. Instead he had displayed the same compassionate but impersonal forbearance that a general would exhibit upon delivering sad news to the family of a foot soldier serving in his command. Who was this man? This stranger?

Now Steel Hope was edging toward the door. Once again he regretted the pain they had suffered because of him, then quickly went on to state that he couldn't stay, that urgent duties demanded his attention, that explanations beyond the fact that he had spent the last seven years serving the Communist cause would have to wait until a more convenient time.

"You can't go," cried Mushroom. "You haven't even sat down."

"Duties await."

Mushroom tried to ease Jade toward her son. "You must stop him. You must order him to stay."

Jade slapped the offending hand. "Are you blind? Can't you see that my son has changed? Can't you see that he's become a most important official, in charge of the most important business? I've waited this long, I can wait some more. What matters is that he's back. The rightful heir of the House of Li has returned."

Steel Hope bowed again. "Thank you, Mother, for being so understanding."

Mushroom pushed him aside to block the door. "I don't understand. You haven't said a word to Summer Wishes yet."

"But how can I?" the soldier said. "She's not here."

Mountain Pine felt paralyzed. When he didn't move and Steel Hope did, again in the direction of the door, Mushroom began shouting, "Summer Wishes! Summer Wishes!"

"I'm coming." There was the sound of running footsteps.

Summer Wishes appeared. In her arms, she carried their sleepy son. She thrust the child into Steel Hope's arms, then quickly stepped away as if withdrawing from a precipice, and without offering a greeting or saying his name, asked, "Doesn't my baby look just like Mountain Pine?"

With his eyes firmly focused on the boy, Steel Hope nodded solemnly. "Though it's been years and I've forgotten many things, how could I not recognize the features of my oldest friend?" Then, hugging the child to him, tight, he bestowed a long, tender kiss on his forehead and said, not in the voice of the stranger, but in the voice that had once echoed through these courtyards, "May you never have to leave those you love and go off to war."

REQUESTS AND REPRISALS

(1956)

STEEL HOPE smoked cigarette after cigarette, staring at the blank page on his desk until the glare of the pristine paper seemed as unforgiving as the sun. His head began to throb. In all his seven years as Party Secretary of Wen Shui County he had never missed a deadline, and now, late by a week, he still didn't know what to say about collectivization. Working in teams and pooling resources to boost harvests made eminent sense to everybody except the peasants. And instead of yielding, they had deliberately and systematically destroyed their implements and stock and, worst of all, their grain. Without grain, how long before the people starved?

Clearly, the policy had backfired. But was the policy at fault? Or did the fault lie with the cadres on the scene? He had his opinions, but how many blueprints for transforming a country as vast and as backward, as populous and poor, as China had he himself designed?

Out of desperation, he jotted down the questions to which he had no answers, hoping that the physical act of writing would somehow trigger an acceptable first sentence. Why couldn't peasants ever see beyond the earth underfoot? Why didn't they trust the Party enough to give the new policy a chance? Why had they cut off their arms to spite the tailor?

He underlined the word "trust"; then absently, like a schoolboy practicing his calligraphy, he drew the same character in a hundred different ways, from the styles found on ancient bronze vessels to that of the latest in neon signs, and after each "trust" he added a bold exclamation mark. When the page was full, he turned it over to start again.

The door banged open. An aide with his shirtfront wet stormed in, wringing out a piece of sudsy laundry. Steel Hope slid the page of doodles into a folder and started to upbraid him, then shrugged. Knocking politely could only seem a vain and useless nicety to Comrade Kuo, who, before Liberation, had lived with three generations of his family in a room shared by a flock of chickens.

Presenting his back, Kuo announced with the formality of a bailiff, "A letter for the honorable Party Secretary of Wen Shui County." Then, forgetting himself, he added, "From the feel of it, I'd guess three pages."

Steel Hope stretched to remove it from the man's pants pocket, and was about to tear open the envelope when he realized that Kuo was waiting to see if he'd guessed right.

"That'll be all," he said. As an afterthought, he snapped, "And don't let me catch you doing the wash in the toilet again, you hear!"

Steel Hope had trouble reading the reply to his request for another posting. The childish sentences were peppered with unintentional homonyms. He smiled sadly. The arbiter of his fate was yet another peasant who, by fortitude in battle or long loyalty to the cause, had earned the boon of spending his days out of the hot sun, shoveling papers rather than night soil. He skipped to the last paragraph, where the inky ideograms had obviously been redrawn more than once. It began with a quote from Chairman Mao extolling duty and ended with "Request denied."

He crushed the letter. What the devil was going on? It wasn't as if he'd asked to cut short his tour, as he had when volunteering to fight in the Korean War. But in 1950, less than a year after Liberation, the Party had decided that Wen Shui needed him more, and in retrospect, he was grateful to have had more time to rectify the harm Grand Hope had done and to get started on rebuilding the levees and redeeming honor for the House of Li.

But now . . . he shied the crumpled letter at the wall clock. It wasn't as if he'd asked for a promotion or to be posted to Beijing; all he wanted was a simple transfer to somewhere else, anyplace else.

His files had encroached so far into the spacious room that they barred pacing, and he was forced to circle his desk. Perhaps he'd been too flexible, and should have named a specific job. Perhaps he should have swallowed his pride and used his connections. It would have been easy, and nothing so crass as sneaking with gift in hand through the back door of some higher-up; just a casual expression of wanderlust slipped into a letter to Lincoln Chen. His old professor would have immediately picked up the phone and he'd be riding a train to the capital now.

He cursed. The hell with openness, flexibility and pride! Next time he'd know better. But next time wouldn't come for at least another year.

He kicked a drawer and succeeded in denting the solid brass handle that he prized for its singularity. He groaned. His life was spent in buildings that had risen like yeasty dough, without any concession to tradition or taste and, within a few short months of occupancy, had settled into grayish heaps indistinguishable from all the other grayish heaps that now dotted the county. He worked in one. He slept in another.

Fingering the scarred metal, he knew that henceforth the small depression would draw his attention with an irresistible attraction, the way a jagged tooth draws the tongue. Damn it to hell, was there nothing within his control?

Hearing hoots of laughter, the kind that belonged in a soccer stadium, he shot a glance at the door. It was closed. As the sound faded, he began to wonder if there was a hidden reason for the denial of his request. The most obvious was also the most benign: the peasant had learned the secret of being a bureaucrat—to do nothing, to leave well enough alone. But what if someone whom he had disciplined or neglected or overworked had decided to make it his business to spoil the County Secretary's plans? It wouldn't be the first time, nor would it be hard to do. There were ample opportunities at the criticism sessions for a disgruntled comrade to let drop an ambiguous remark. That was exactly why Steel Hope found those weekly meetings so distasteful. They bred suspicions the way a grubby quilt bred lice.

Yet how else, when others for centuries had failed to modernize China, could China modernize unless there were Chinese willing to destroy the old to institute the new by whatever means, however flawed and fierce?

But it was a hell of a way to build trust!

At that thought, he cautioned himself against lodging an appeal. No loyal cadre questioned orders; therefore those who did must be disloyal. He must take care or, before he knew it, the two-legged maggots with nothing better to do than lurk in hallways would be dining on rumors about him.

He lit another cigarette. It tasted like offal. He stubbed it out.

Suddenly, he recalled a seemingly innocent remark some comrade had interjected when he had been holding forth at a recent meeting just down the corridor. Though it had evoked a burst of laughter, he hadn't given it a thought until now. "You chose to be a revolutionary out of the goodness of your bourgeois heart. We wretched peasants are revolutionaries by birth, by blood." In other words, Steel Hope wasn't truly one of them. People of his class were notoriously unreliable. They changed their minds as often as what they wore and ate. They changed their hearts as often as the phases of the moon.

How much easier his life if his heart *were* so easily changed.

He picked up the unsmoked cigarette and relit it, and suddenly, without any reason or warning, that gesture, so ordinary and so often repeated, evoked a long-forgotten memory of Summer Wishes. She had made a face after a puff and he had apologized for the cheap cigarette that tasted like sawdust. She had thrown it away and he had retrieved it.

How could he stay in the same town as she? There was no avoiding her: his duties included improving the cultural scene, and Summer Wishes, who, upon Liberation, had returned to the stage in a show of support for the new China, now *was* the arts to the people of the lower Yangzi. Also, the cadres at the theater had just nominated her for Party membership, and when she was accepted, as she almost certainly would be, they would be thrown together even more. Surprisingly, even Mountain Pine seemed to favor her joining, and had brought up the subject at the recent opening of *White-Haired Girl*.

"Do what you can for her, will you?"

"I already have."

"The honor means so much to her."

And to me, Steel Hope thought. Her unshakable faith in the Revolution could only help ensure his.

Mountain Pine must have read his mind, for he quickly added, "After she's admitted, watch out for her, will you? We both know her limitations. Don't let her become embroiled in matters she can't possibly understand."

Of course, he'd agreed to this as well. Her popularity with the people would be a great asset to the Party. But seeing her three or four times a month, instead of three or four times a year—how could he hope to keep up the charade of being a model cadre with nothing except Party work on his mind?

He couldn't. Even now he couldn't. He had tried, tried hard. In fact, that letter from provincial headquarters was the second rejection he had received this month. On the first of November, he had asked Comrade

Ying to marry him. True, he didn't love her. But still they had much in common: distinguished ancestors, college degrees, responsible positions and, what appealed to him most, her frequent avowal that Party work, and not irrational sentiments, was the key to her personal happiness. He had argued that these shared attributes, and the fact that they were both lonely, should guarantee the success of their marriage. Love, after all, was a bourgeois idea. She, however, had wept. She wanted more. So had he at her age. In the end, and despite the way the Party, not to speak of Jade, would have applauded his marriage, he'd been relieved to see Comrade Ying close the door behind her.

He went to get a glass from the top of the bookcase, then picked up the crumpled letter that had landed alongside it. Rereading the three pages more carefully, he found not a hint of censure and much praise for the work of County Secretaries in ending inflation, building morale and support, increasing yield and production, maintaining order, establishing schools, training cadres and more. The list took up most of the letter and, with a few exceptions, applied to the job that he himself had done. He wondered if he was being as wrongheaded as the peasants. To put his needs above those of the Party would be unworthy at any time, but inexcusable in the midst of a crisis.

Heaving a sigh, he resolved to regard the matter closed. He would stay in Wen Shui, without rancor or regret, for another year.

He unscrewed the thermos set on the windowsill. The tea tin beside it was empty, had been for weeks, but he hardly missed it; he rather enjoyed drinking plain hot water. It brought back the days when he had lived in huts among peasants, who couldn't afford tea and whose women sometimes had to trek lis before dipping their buckets into a lake or river. For these people a bowl of hot water represented a gesture of hospitality grander than any gold goblet filled to overflowing with the finest mao tai.

Peasants. How he admired them. And despised them.

Once everything had depended on the peasant comrades. Without them, the war against the Japanese could never have been waged, much less won. Without them, China would still be at the mercy of people like the Tangs. Hadn't peasants earned their right to lead, then? Why should others, who'd never believed, battled or bled, take their place? Just because they could read and write better, add and subtract? Were these reasons enough?

Of course not. But such veterans nesting throughout the system nearly drove him mad: queen bees that didn't lay eggs, worker bees that didn't tend to business; even the drones were impotent. If they weren't playing cards or chatting, they were leading idiotic pep rallies that went on for days, boring even themselves to sleep. When pressed for decisions, they assumed an air of thoughtful deliberation and spouted a reply perfected by endless repetition. "It's difficult to say which is the correct choice. All are being studied, and eventually will be sorted out. Already I've consulted with Comrade So-and-So, and as a result he's talked to Party Secretary Such-and-Such."

On and on, ever upward, once again the matter would be passed. Meanwhile, nothing got done and the situation at the factory or office or store had totally changed. What was the answer? Was there an answer? Why should it be that those who were able weren't trusted while those who were trusted weren't able?

Sipping his glass of hot water, he gazed out the window. Below, the streets were tidy, swept clean of refuse and cleared of the beggars that had once cluttered the walks. Passersby stepped gingerly around the laborers patching the roads. His eyes came to rest on the gardener, rooting a sapling that was little more than a leafless twig across the street. He imagined it in bloom.

On the other side of the half-finished compound wall, little faces popped up and down like springs, as a group of grade-schoolers jumped for glimpses of a soldier struggling with his high-spirited horse in the yard. Alternately the man cajoled and chided, one hand tugging the animal's halter, the other stroking its neck. The horse skittered and neighed, puffing white plumes that vanished into the frosty fall air. Steel Hope nodded, feeling more kinship with the beast than with his comrades.

Again Kuo banged the door open. "Comrade, it's Saturday and almost twelve o'clock."

"So?"

"Your honorable old mother asked me to make sure you left for lunch on time. She'll be waiting."

Jade was always waiting, waiting for him to come to lunch, waiting for him to give her grandchildren. "Make yourself useful," he said. "Run over with my apologies."

"Take pity, Comrade. Not again. My legs are worn out. My tongue too. You must go this Saturday. It's your mother's birthday."

All the more reason not to go, he thought. His presence would only spoil the celebration. It was awkward enough seeing Summer Wishes, the actress, at official functions; impossible seeing the wife of his oldest friend privately.

Comrade Kuo heaved a long, pitiful sigh; then, shaking his head, proceeded to trail the cadre step by step around the desk, with sad imploring eyes.

"Look!" Steel Hope shouted, rifling the papers piled high on his desk. "Speeches at factories, schools, work units. Meetings with peasant associations, women's groups and resident committees. Decisions to be made on personnel. Reports due on everything from price controls to the availability of fertilizer, from thought reform to public security. Not to mention—"

He made the mistake of stopping to take a breath. Seizing the opening, Comrade Kuo backed him between two file cabinets and let his skinny body go as limp as a dead squid. "Oh, have pity. Please go, or your honorable old mother will chase me down and holler at me and she won't care where."

He couldn't say the man exaggerated.

"She'll call me a lazy good-for-nothing and a lot worse and everyone around will laugh at me." Kuo spoke with such bathos that the droplets leaking from his soaking wet hair might have been tears.

It was no use. He could never outwit a peasant. Snatching his padded jacket from the back of his chair, he slammed the door behind him. As he marched down the crowded, noisy corridors, he cursed the comrades who ate not at tables but on their haunches.

The fresh air cleared his lungs of the stink of pickled cabbage that clung as tenaciously as paint to the halls, and at the gate he stopped to take a closer look at the spirited horse. He chuckled ruefully. The creature was circling the yard like a docile donkey. On its back perched a young girl in pigtails, wide-eyed and tittering. She waved shyly; somehow that courtesy eased past the pain to graze his heart.

I N   N O   H U R R Y to get to lunch, Steel Hope took neither the official car nor his bicycle, but walked across town to the House of Li, and when he was almost there, lingered outside Widow Xu's shop. It had been a favorite haunt when he was a boy, and he could still see the pages torn from foreign magazines that had kept loose plaster from falling into the burlap sacks of beans, rice and flour below—the colorful pictures of sleek automobiles, fiery cauldrons of molten steel, skyscrapers, and strange modern gadgets whose uses were beyond his imagining. How proud he had been when the widow asked him to pen labels for her; how red-faced when he was forced to consult his bookmate on the proper strokes for "mushrooms" and "cinnamon bark." It was there that he had tried unsuccessfully to buy his first cigarette, choosing among brands not by price but by name: Red Wheel, Brave Soldier, Flying Machine, Iron Horse. . . .

Opening the familiar black door, he found several middle-aged men behind the counter finishing up their bowls of noodles but, of course, not Widow Xu, who had retired several years ago, when the county began converting privately owned stores into cooperatives. The ceiling was still papered, now with the black-and-white newsprint of *The People's Daily*. He flipped through some magazines, and would have flipped through more; but the sound of the nearest clerk tossing an orange, while waiting for his customer to make up his mind, unnerved him. He bought a bottle of Jade's favorite herbal tonic, a pack of cigarettes and five lollipops, one of each color, and left.

Only when he caught his first glimpse of the graceful, arching roofs of his ancestors' halls did he realize what else in the shop had changed. The smell of incense was gone. Widow Xu had always kept several sticks burning before a miniature altar placed next to the box of lead weights, each with a single loop of green cord threaded through the handle, and the bronze scales, which had been passed from generation to generation. Recalling the day when she had awarded Mountain Pine the honor of using it to demonstrate the principle of the lever to his charge, he was glad she had taken her treasure home.

He quickened his pace when he saw Amber Willows waiting at the gate. How long had she been standing out in the cold? He tried to apologize. Laughing, she grabbed him by the hand as if he were still her naughty boy, and, suddenly, pleasure surged through him as she pulled him eagerly along to see the rock from Wuxi Lake take the shape of a monkey in honor of Jade's birthday.

As suddenly, when the door shut behind them, pleasure was gone.

He stiffened, feeling himself turning into a caricature of himself as Party Secretary. How could he not?

Always, upon seeing her son, Jade would blubber and mewl.

Upon seeing his wife's first love, Mountain Pine would appear to shrivel up. Indeed, the poor fellow, ever discreet, had turned into a mute outside his home and the classes he taught, so as not to call any attention, especially political attention, to himself, since more and more of the writers he admired were being accused of anti-Party sentiments. A while ago, Steel Hope had even caught his old bookmate backing away from a stranger who'd stopped him to ask directions. The man was harmless, just another student in saddle shoes returning from abroad to support the new China.

Upon seeing the dissembler all Party Secretaries must be, Mushroom would focus a professional eye on him as if to correct the way he looked, breathed, stood, walked and said his lines.

Upon seeing the stranger he had become, Summer Wishes would reach for Little Panda, though he was too old to sit on her lap, and wrap him around her like the threadbare talisman she couldn't do without but had given to him. Did she think he needed to be reminded of her marriage and motherhood? How could she misjudge him so?

As on previous visits, he almost addressed them as he would address a Party meeting at which he had arrived to find everyone else already seated: "Comrades, please begin." All he could think to do instead was bow.

To his relief, Amber Willows, at least, did something normal. Smiling, she took his overcoat, clucking over a small tear in one sleeve, then straightened his shirt collar as if sending him off to school. But even his beloved amah was at a loss for words to span the sea of awkwardness that his aloofness and absences had created, and as soon as they were seated, set herself to mending the coat.

Feeling like a condemned man, Steel Hope inquired after their health as he joined them at the table, pulling up a chair to squeeze in between his mother and Mountain Pine. Then, while Mushroom shuttled to and fro, carrying one steaming dish after another from the kitchen before finally sitting down, Jade, breathless with excitement, launched into a recital of her latest accomplishments as a member of the local neighborhood committee.

What a dreadful mistake he'd made encouraging her to join! A year or so ago it had seemed harmless, a way to divert her energies from the constant matchmaking, which had begun the day of his return and nearly drove him mad. Who would have guessed that overnight, she would transform herself into such a thorny zealot, or that she would presume to make herself into the eyes and ears of the Party, bringing the failings and foibles of every comrade who served with her to the attention of her son, until one member after another, claiming high blood pressure, had resigned. The fact that the Party Secretary had never acted on any of his mother's complaints mattered less than the possibility, however remote, that one day he might.

"Please, Mother, no reports on your birthday."

"But what I have to say is important. It's official business. You must—"

"Later. Later."

When she persisted, he ignored her by whipping out the lollipops to wave aloft—a diversion that had become a ritual; that is, if the infrequency of his visits would permit anything he did to qualify as ritual. In the beginning, Little Panda would plop down on all fours before crawling toward the prize, and then, scooping up the baby, Steel Hope would hold him until he fell asleep.

Today the boy who jumped and snatched at the candy seemed to defy gravity. Steel Hope gave him a friendly pat. There was no embracing

Little Panda now. Noticing paint stains on the boy's cuffs, he smiled, and was about to ask whether the mural he and Mushroom had started to paint on the wall of her quarters was finished, when a neighbor's boy knocked; too shy to come in, he waited for his friend by the door. Little Panda said, "Uncle, I'm sorry. I've got to go. Defender of Country and I are partners in a Ping-Pong tournament."

"Where? Is it far?"

"At our own School Number Three. It's just the first round."

Steel Hope almost asked to go with them, then thought better of it. But as Summer Wishes hastened to fetch the paddle to give to her son, he dared not follow her with his eyes or take note of her return. How he missed the scent of her baby's cheeks.

As soon as the boys left, Mountain Pine boasted that Little Panda's excellence at Ping-Pong was second only to his excellence in friendship, for no one else had wanted the lead-footed boy as a partner. "But it was Summer Wishes who actually convinced Defender of Country that without his steadying presence, which was how she so nicely described his virtual immobility, the team didn't have a chance. All it takes is a word from her and any child thinks he's invincible."

A blushing Summer Wishes returned the compliment by asking Steel Hope if he'd like to see the kite in the form of a school of fish that Mountain Pine had helped the boys make, but before he could say yes, Jade started in again.

". . . And I was forced to suggest holding another meeting to discuss the vaccination program. . . ."

She hadn't missed a beat. Losing patience, he said grimly, "Not now, Mother! Are you deaf? I told you, not now."

When Jade flinched, withdrawing into a wounded silence that had become as natural to her as a carapace to a turtle, he began piling his plate high. No one else made a move. His chewing seemed to grind louder and louder as their silence, sodden with disapproval, dragged on.

Even Steel Hope himself didn't know whether it was to save his mother's face or his own when he finally laid down his chopsticks and explained politely that such an important report deserved his undivided attention, and therefore he'd thought it best to wait until the table was cleared, when he could use notebook and pen to record her observations properly.

Taking his explanation for a license to do exactly what he had just asked her not to do, Jade sat up straight and nodded with the hauteur of a member of the Politburo. "No need to take notes now. I'll be happy to repeat my report after lunch, but in the meantime, let me get started. All the residents in my neighborhood are depending on me to . . ."

For the rest of the meal Jade jabbered happily, while the others nodded encouragement and occasionally asked a leading question, like a proud chorus supporting an internationally acclaimed but aging guest star, and he resisted the temptation to ask how, despite rationing, such plenty had found its way to their table. Actually, the answer was obvious. The lamb and pork, chicken and eggs could only be gifts to the most tireless member of the neighborhood committee, who, coincidentally, also happened to be the mother of the Party Secretary. It was best not to know who paid these circuitous bribes. It was imperative that he put a stop to them. He couldn't acquire a new mother, but by removing Jade from the committee he could at least take away the bribers' transparent excuse.

". . . My son, how else would the Party know about those wicked landlords who have snuck into town, about the children who haven't been vaccinated, about the articles lost or stolen—"

He interrupted. "Mother, you work much too hard."

Jade bowed her head with feigned humility. "Yes," she said. "But ask anyone and he'll tell you that no matter how badly I feel or how cold the weather, I make my rounds. I knock on every door and stay for hours. You're not the only one who gives his all to the People!"

"Naturally the Party is most grateful. But speaking as your son, I think you've done more than your share, and besides, you're not so young or strong anymore. Mother, perhaps you should consider retiring."

Jade recoiled, her face turning pale. Only now did he see how the pockmarks and wrinkles had melded together to score her skin like mottled rattan; still, he refused to be moved, and went on praising her good works and affecting filial concern. It would only be a matter of time, he thought, until she resigned of her own accord. The proof of a Party Secretary's skills was in his powers of persuasion.

"The comrades would sympathize. They know of your extraordinary dedication. Weren't you the first to set an example of sacrifice by surrendering the deed to the House of Li to the People? And if not for you, there'd be no School Number Three for boys like Little Panda to attend. Surely you've done enough. Surely—"

Fighting back tears, Jade groped for her cane and, refusing help with a pained shake of her head, used it to push herself to her feet; then, without a word, she slowly made her way from the room.

Long after she had disappeared, he could hear her cane tapping.

He turned to the others. They averted their eyes.

When he stood, only Amber Willows had the courage to speak. "Don't. You mustn't make things worse by leaving in anger. Oh, Steel Hope, you don't understand, you don't understand...."

The words, the tone of her voice, sounded strangely in his ear, as if they had traveled a long distance. He was almost at the door when he remembered. He had heard the same plea the night he had burst into a darkened room to find Stone Guardian and his amah in bed.

He turned to stare at the woman who'd betrayed her mistress. What right had she to rebuke him? "Of course I understand," he said coldly. "I understand very well."

Amber Willows would not be rebuffed, and approached him. "What is it you understand?"

"The food."

"What about it?"

"Mother didn't pay a fen for the chicken or the beef or the lamb or anything else that was put on her table, did she? Did she?"

To his surprise, it was Summer Wishes who answered. "They were gifts."

Had it not been she, he would have shouted, "They're not gifts, they're bribes!" But the sound of Summer Wishes' voice always disarmed him. "Well," he said lamely, "Mother shouldn't have accepted them. She could get along without all that rich food."

"Of course she could," said Amber Willows. "Oh, Steel Hope, haven't you noticed that she barely ate a thing? Old Mistress has had no appetite for years, not since you disappeared. She cares nothing about food. The gifts are unimportant."

"They are to me. So much uneaten when supplies are short."

At this, Mushroom joined the fray. "I've never wasted food. I've never thrown away a single grain of rice!" she snarled. "I serve the same dishes meal after meal until each plate is as clean as if a tomcat had licked it."

Why Mountain Pine, who had barely said a word since his arrival, decided at this moment to speak up mystified him, but if his bookmate thought to diffuse the tension, he utterly failed. "I can attest to Mushroom's claims. Just look at what happened today—the same meal was served for your mother's birthday party *and* her surprise retirement party."

Ignoring him, Steel Hope looked to Mushroom and snarled back, "How many times you serve the same meal entirely misses the point!

The point is, why should all the other people restrict their diets to simple fare when I, who urge sacrifice, have a family that will not?"

Amber Willows tugged at his sleeve. "Please, don't fight. Steel Hope, from now on, I'll return the gifts secretly. But . . ." With her hands placed together as if in prayer, she pleaded, "Oh, Steel Hope, let Old Mistress keep her position on the committee. For once, she has been able to hold her head high. For once . . ."

"Well, if it's recognition she wants, I'll have a ceremony and present her with a certificate stamped with a host of official seals and a red paper flower to wear on her chest so enormous that even in the thickest fog no one could miss it. I'll do it right away. Tomorrow! But after that I'll not stand for even the appearance of impropriety. After that, Mother is retired."

He looked around, expecting someone to take his side; finding only disaffection, he was offended—at them, at himself—and mystified as well. Out of habit, however long curtailed, he turned to his bookmate for an explanation. "Mountain Pine, be brave, tell me what's really going on here."

Out of habit, Mountain Pine coaxed his charge to find the answer himself. "What filial son would need to be told?"

Taken aback, he nevertheless decided to make light of the remark "Please, don't act as if I were a schoolboy, just tell me what I don't know."

Mountain Pine didn't bother to hide the disdain in his voice. "Can't you get it through your swollen skull that your mother is afraid? Afraid to serve you anything less than a feast and thereby give you an excuse *not* to show up next Saturday, or any other Saturday after that, since it was blatantly obvious that our esteemed Party Secretary barely made it here this Saturday for his own mother's birthday? Afraid that you care for 'all the other people' more than you care for her? Afraid that if she retires and has no more reports to make on 'all the other people,' you'll never come to see her?"

Rooted to the spot, Steel Hope tried to remember the last time someone had dared to reprimand him to his face. Perhaps if it had happened more often, he would not feel so humiliated now.

Amber Willows and Mushroom cleared the table. The only sound was the clatter of dishes.

Finally Summer Wishes spoke his name and, with her head bowed, gently reminded him that not all the people were seventy years old and not all the people had devoted a lifetime to the House of Li. As always, her kindness wounded him in ways no enemy could.

Then, gazing directly into his eyes for the first time that day, she flashed a smile. "Before Liberation, when I was still superstitious, I would have also reminded you that it's bad luck to lose your temper on your mother's birthday."

He couldn't recall the last time he had heard laughter in this room. He returned to his seat and stole a glance at Summer Wishes. My mother is right, he thought. Her son would seize any excuse to avoid coming home.

After tea had been served, Amber Willows and Mushroom slipped away, leaving the three old friends at the table. Steel Hope, choking with loneliness, thought, as he had thought every time he'd entered this house since marching into Wen Shui, that it would have been better if he'd never returned from the dead; better if he'd stayed in the north, where he could sleep without dreaming, where temptation didn't sit across the width of a table.

Summer Wishes asked if he cared to smoke. Without waiting for a reply, she left the table and returned with the silver cigarette case, filled with gold-tipped 999s. Only when he was certain that his hand wouldn't shake did he take one. She struck a match and held it for him. He couldn't take his eyes from her graceful fingers, so soft and so warm to the touch. He leaned toward her. She lit his cigarette. He blew out the flame.

He searched for something ordinary to say, but whatever came to mind, once spoken, would no longer be ordinary. Every sentence would yield up secrets he had vowed not to reveal. If only his request for a transfer—or his proposal—hadn't been denied; if only the aide hadn't reminded him of Jade's birthday; if only he hadn't made such a fuss. If only . . .

Again it was Summer Wishes who broke the silence. Her words, at first, were a bit too rushed, her voice a bit too high, but soon she was speaking as naturally as in Chongqing, when she had amused them with tales about her latest performance.

". . . With every seat taken at our People's Theater, we had no choice but to dress the drunkard and wheel him on stage in a big chariot with Mushroom stuffed inside it to turn his head, wave his arms and say his lines. Heaven knows how we ever managed to get through the entire play, but we did. No, no! Don't laugh yet. That's not the end of the story."

Mountain Pine said, "It's not?"

Steel Hope said, "There's more?"

Summer Wishes nodded so eagerly that one of her hairpins would have fallen had her husband not reached over and pushed it back into place. "For weeks, the man refused to speak to Mushroom. For weeks, he went about denouncing her. . ." She paused dramatically.

"Why?" the two men responded on cue.

Her eyes shone as brightly as the moon.

"Why?"

"He accused her of spiking his tea to steal his part."

"He must have wind for brains!"

"Don't you know, Steel Hope, that actors are madmen?"

"What about actresses?"

"That is for Young Master to decide."

Their laughter was so inviting that Amber Willows and Mushroom returned to the table. Then, finally, Jade as well. And as lunch extended into dinner Steel Hope forgot the time, his work and his discontent, and luxuriated in the familiarity of a friendship so rare, so deep and so mellow that he would forever recall this occasion as the day he finally came home.

AFTER MIDNIGHT, he lay in bed and wondered how it was possible that the one who seemed most lost had found a way to lead them through overgrown thickets and perilous traps back to the place where a young master, his bookmate and the gravekeeper's daughter first met—to loyalty, to the Middle Heart.

Again he prayed, as he'd prayed through all the years since his homecoming: Let affections be strong enough to tame love.

U ND E R A moonless sky, Steel Hope stood on a fallow field lit with torches and disfigured by haphazard heaps of earth and hollows; were it not for the cold night air that frosted his breath, an errant owl might have mistaken him for a disabled scarecrow.

It had been a long day. In yesterday's post, he'd received a letter from provincial headquarters reprimanding him for his neglect of duty, noting in particular the undeniable fact that his report on collectivization was long overdue; and that morning he'd arrived at his desk determined to complete it even before the custodians fired up the furnace and the workday started. Again, he'd stared at the pristine page until, fingers stiff with cold, and too restless to sit a moment longer, he had marched off to the maintenance shop, jumped into the nearest car and, without any idea what he meant to do, driven into the countryside. He'd had to get away. Away from the report he didn't know how to write, away from the House of Li, away from the prospect that emotions, unleashed by the rejection letter and Ying's refusal and now this reprimand, and embold- ened by his visit home last week, might explode.

Shoulders hunched, straining forward, he'd clutched the wheel as if the effort would keep the car's old engine from expiring, as if he were a fugitive and the few inches that separated him from the back of the seat would make all the difference between getting away and getting caught. As he drove past one indistinguishable field after another for god knew how long, his thoughts had shuttled back and forth between the blank pages on his desk and the prospect of disaster in the years ahead until, impulsively, he had decided to do something about them both. He'd surprise some peasants, make them dig until their arms fell off, and then perhaps they'd "find" some of the grain they'd supposedly destroyed, and he could put a stop to their resistance and folly. He'd slammed on the brakes and accelerated backwards, swerved off the main road and sped toward the nearest meeting hall.

Now, hours into darkness, the fields already pocked with craters like the moon, he was still standing watch over the recalcitrant diggers. Thus far they hadn't unearthed a kernel. It had been a very, very long day. He felt lightheaded and his limbs stung like frostbitten flesh thrust into boiling water, but he couldn't even summon a flush of anger, for there was no one but himself to blame. He had declined their food. He had also spurned every offer from the local cadres to take his place standing guard. He still refused to sit in the overstuffed red chair that four of them, puffing and perspiring, had ferreted from the inner recesses of the hall and carried as painstakingly as if it were a giant tray of gold dust past the chaos of hoes and sawhorses, buckets and fishnets awaiting repairs, clear across the field for the comfort of their visitor from higher up.

Leering like lecherous simpletons, they had boasted of its comforts, exclaiming that the cut-velvet covering was softer than a virgin's breast and more commodious than a prostitute's snatch. Indeed, curlicue by curlicue it had been copied on the orders of Landlord Wang from the chair in a picture of a bearded English king with twice the girth of a buffalo. What a pity, they clucked, that the oppressor of the masses, that son of generations of depraved landlords, had never had a chance to enjoy it. Arriving at the start of land reform, the work of art had come too late. The man's brains had already been kicked free.

Suddenly, as he watched over the lone cluster of diggers yet to be discharged, Steel Hope wondered if he might have misjudged the relentless solicitude of the cadres. Had he paid too much attention to their antics and patter, too little to their intent? Eyeing the ridiculous chair, he began to see it differently: not as a sorry attempt by underlings to curry favor but as an object less benign ... even menacing.

He scowled. Would those comics dare to threaten him? Of course not. How absurd! He was just cold and bored and feeble after a day spent watching peasants shovel, spade and scoop to no avail. Besides, why on earth would they want to intimidate him? They'd never even met before.

He banished the idea, but it kept drifting back into his thoughts like an infuriating mote that one cannot control.... Wasn't it the Party that had told them how to be champions of the People by taking land from the rich to give to the poor? Wasn't it also the Party that had later told them to take the land back from the poor to give to the collective? But the Party hadn't told them that when they announced the latter directive their clansmen and neighbors would spit on the champions of the People. And who spoke for the Party? It could only be the Party Secretary. It could only be Steel Hope.

He shut his eyes to control a shiver. When he opened them again he couldn't help imagining the dead man's chair awash with blood. He quickly turned away, fixing his gaze on the laggards. They were working slowly but steadily, like insomniacs forced to do t'ai chi before dawn. He pitied them. He pitied himself. How could a good policy have gone so wrong?

He didn't want to think about that. He wanted the digging to go faster, but the longer he watched, the more it seemed that he was cursed to relive this one moment over and over again, for no matter how many shovelfuls of soil were dug and heaped, the pile refused to grow. He inched closer, but the smoky torches, twisting with the wind, cast a swath of fitful shadows that made it hard even to distinguish the women from the men. Perhaps the late hour and his eagerness to be done with this treasure hunt, which seemed increasingly pointless, had made him exaggerate the length of time the peasants had actually worked on this side of the field, where a spindly, leafless willow stood. But no, that wasn't it. The diggers moved oddly. And even if they belonged to the same family, could all eight be cursed with a stiff leg? They might play him for a fool who didn't know enough to eat when food was offered or come in out of the cold, but he'd go to hell before he'd let them play him for a blind fool.

He tucked his hands under his arms and let his head droop, pretending to fight sleep.... And as they became less careful, he realized what was happening. The sneaks were pushing dirt back into the hollow with their feet. At last! This must be the place where they'd buried the grain.

He smiled a slow, crooked smile and shouted "Hey!" But as he started to rebuke them, he beheld a panoply of eyes arraigning him, eyes

that shone with dewy sadness, like those of an old dog, and he changed
his mind. He wasn't interested in naming the culprits or punishing them,
but only in teaching them and their fellows a lesson. "That's enough
digging," he said. "You can go now."

They didn't move. They didn't even blink.

Damn them. "Go!" he shouted, waving them away. "Go, go, go!"
They stood fast.

"What's the matter with you? Get going!"

They must suspect a trick. To allay their fears, he growled for them
to take their shovels with them, explaining, "It's late. I'm tired."

Darting like field mice, they disappeared into the darkness.

He yelled after them. "Hey! Don't even think about not returning
those shovels to the collective tomorrow!"

Feeling rather pleased with himself, he started to whistle an old
tune. What harm could there be in letting the poor bastards go? The
grain was what mattered.

He went searching amid the other mounds. Just as he thought, a
neglectful son of a bitch from an earlier shift had left his shovel behind.
He raced back to the spot by the willow, and, digging, he was no longer
tired but energized. Surely this would turn out to be his lucky day. And
about time. He deserved it.

Hardly a foot into the earth his shovel hit an object, and after more
digging he confirmed that its shape was rectangular. With the back of
the shovel he tapped along the length of its surface. The sound was dull, too
dull for whatever it was to be the wooden hatch cover of an underground
chamber. Much more likely, it was a quilt wrapped and sewn around—
what? He tugged, trying to drag it out of the hollow. He threw off his
coat, used his sleeve to wipe away the sweat, tried again. It was no use.
The damn thing was much too awkward and heavy to dislodge.

Kneeling, he patted it up and down; and when he was almost positive
that there was something other than grain inside, his imagination raced
ahead. But where would they get guns? And what were they going to
use them for?

He took out his pocketknife and was cutting an opening when, out
of nowhere, a dog pounced on his back. He shook it off. The mangy cur
wasn't very big, quite skinny in fact, and after an obligatory round of
snarls and barks lost interest in the man and began sniffing at the opening
he'd made. He shoved it out of his way and returned to work. When
the dog circled back, he hurled it out of the hollow. Panting, it slunk
away into the shadows.

He tried ripping the sack apart, but he had little leverage kneeling, and his elbows were confined by the sides of the hole he had dug. Whatever the material was, it wasn't strong. Taking up the knife again, he began sawing through it, only to discover a second layer.

Just as his knife pierced this last barrier, the dog pounced again. This time it knocked him flat, shoving his face into the opening he'd made. Only then did he realize what he'd unearthed. His stomach revolted. Heaving as if he were about to disgorge boulders, he somehow managed to struggle out of the hole before succumbing to a prolonged frenzy of spitting and hacking, scraping and scouring as he nearly tore his face open, so intense was his disgust, his anguish, his need to purge himself of every last trace of the putrefying corpse.

Afterwards, he lay exhausted. Damn those peasants, damn them to hell! You gave them orders. They smiled and nodded. You turned your back and they disobeyed. Cremate, you'd said. The land is precious. It must be for the living, not the dead. . . . They'd smiled and nodded and gone right on burying their departed family members. When would they ever change?

Suddenly he felt something warm and wet trickling down his cheeks, like blood draining, and all he could think was that, in his hysterical effort to rid himself of rotting flesh, he must have gouged out an eye. He yowled. He yowled until the fearsome sound he made was finally swallowed up by the night. In the eerie silence that followed, he felt as if this place was no longer of this earth, and he, no longer a man.

It took him a long time and every ounce of his strength to collect himself, to refashion Steel Hope from the quivering mass he'd become. He wondered if he'd gone temporarily mad, for the thing that had incited his primeval terror had been nothing, nothing at all. Tears.

He tried to move, but his body was as recalcitrant as lead. Forcing his lids open, he saw that most of the torches had burned to extinction, and as he lay there, looking up at the heaps of dirt in the shadows, they gradually assumed the shape of a hillside. And though it wasn't the Day of Pure Brightness, nor were there willows in bud or members of the House of Li kneeling to perform the ancient rites, he could hear Stone Guardian intoning: "O Spirits of our Noble Ancestors, we, your children, have traveled from near and far to attend your needs in the afterlife, to venerate your memory, to enshrine forever your legacy of honor and attainments in our hearts.

"We who still dwell in the earthly realm beseech you who abide in the netherworld to intercede on our behalf. . . ."

He had never gone to visit his father's grave. Now it was too late. The hillside had been repossessed from the dead and returned to the living.

For a moment he wasn't certain that he had heard another sound, and as his eyes swept the scene, he saw that the field looked the same, only now the sky was a cauldron of churning black clouds, though there was no sign yet of lightning or rain. He heard it again . . . barely audible, but not out of the ordinary, indeed familiar. Nevertheless, in his torment, he couldn't place where he had heard it last or what word was used to name it.

Then, suddenly, he knew. He bolted upright.

Though the sound came from the hole he had dug, all he could see of the grave was a white tail wagging.

Steel hope had fled from the fields, chased by the specters of calamity and chaos that the digging had unearthed, dashing and stumbling and falling until, breathless and still half-crazed, he'd scrambled into the safe haven of his car as the storm broke.

Now, he found himself parked at the entrance of School Number Three, which had been the back gate of the House of Li. He didn't know how he'd gotten there from the countryside, except that he must have driven through a terrible downpour like a man bent on suicide. His watch said nine-twenty. The streets were still flooded, though now it was only drizzling. He was certain of only one thing: Even if it meant breaking Party rules and risking censure, he had to talk to someone tonight. Still, as confused as he was, he understood that airing forbidden thoughts was best done with someone trusted without reservation, and that, sadly, only Mountain Pine, the perennial pessimist and a non-believer, qualified. If talking with him sullied honor and pride—to hell with them.

Opening the glove compartment, he found his cigarettes, then got out of the car and, with his coat over his head, ran past the deserted compound that had been the Li servants' quarters toward the original storeroom, which Mushroom had turned into a space for sewing costumes and living quarters for herself. At the door, he checked to see if anyone was about, then knocked softly.

Mushroom answered. "Amber Willows?"

He flinched at the woman's booming voice, then knocked again.

"What does the mistress want of me at this hour?"

Still he said nothing, and when at last the door opened, he quickly squeezed inside and closed it. Before him was the mural that Little Panda and Mushroom had painted on the windowless back wall—a moongate leading to sunlit vistas.

"You! Why are you here?" asked Mushroom, eyeing him from head to toe. "And what the devil happened? You look like you've fallen in a grave!"

He recoiled: how did she know? For a moment, he wondered if she was too prescient and too apolitical to be trusted, but, giving in to his desperation, he ordered her to go to the house. "Make up some excuse for you to stay there, and for Mountain Pine to come here."

Shrugging, she headed for the wardrobe. "First let me get you something else to wear."

He grabbed her by the arm. "Just do as I say. I've got to see him right now."

"What's wrong?"

"That doesn't concern you." His tone was the one he used to dismiss Comrade Kuo.

Regarding him with wary eyes, she shrugged again, then slipped off her shoes, rolled up her pants, grabbed an umbrella and went out.

Suddenly he was exhausted. He yanked the quilt off the bed and sank into a chair, and, despite himself, his lids were closing when an unfinished costume on the sewing table caught his eye. It was yellow, the color of a flowering shrub he could see clearly—tiny petals that grew in sprays, supple and tall, blooming even before it greened. Now he remembered its name. Forsythia.

Summer Wishes had worn a dress of that same hue at the opening of the People's Theater a month or two after Liberation. Even then, he had envied her childlike faith in the Party. No believer could have been more innocent, more sincere. Even now, when others read, dozed or knitted throughout the day of political speeches that inaugurated this or that mass campaign, be it for the propagation of newspaper-reading groups or against vice, Summer Wishes would sit, eyes fixed on the stage, as attentive as an urchin who, having finally been permitted to join her betters at school, has discovered, to her delight, that she is the teacher's pet. "China has stood up. I have stood up." When she spoke truths such as this, they didn't sound trite or contrived.

At the sound of the door, he started.

"Mushroom didn't exaggerate. You're a fright!" said Mountain Pine.

"I slipped and fell." Steel Hope smiled weakly.

"Well, my esteemed Party Secretary ..." His umbrella was stuck and Mountain Pine struggled unsuccessfully to furl it. "I hope you got me out in this weather to tell me the good news that Comrade Ying has changed her mind. Nothing would make me happier than to drink a toast at your wedding."

Not that hoary subject again. Steel Hope threw off the quilt, snatched the umbrella away and snapped it shut.

The movement brought him nearer to the lightbulb overhead, and for the first time Mountain Pine had a good look at the Party Secretary. He was distressed not by the welts on his face, the bloodshot eyes or the matted hair, but by the unholy mix of panic and ferocity that he emitted like sweat and heat. Before Mountain Pine could even react, he was being shoved, then practically flung into a chair.

"I've got to tell somebody or explode! Explode, you hear...!"

Suddenly Mountain Pine knew terror. It was one thing to be bookmate to the young master, or even to be known as a friend of Steel Hope's—though that relationship was one reason he'd taken such care never to be conspicuous or to say anything in the least controversial. But to be confidant to the Party Secretary? He might as well ride through town on the back of a tiger. "Have mercy," he wanted to shout. "If you must explode, do it elsewhere, not in front of me. You'll survive. I won't." But he could only summon the presence of mind to ask, "Are you sure you'll not regret saying what you're about to say?"

Steel Hope was the one doing the shouting. "I had them digging all day and all day they came up with nothing—not a damn kernel! And that's what the people will have to eat. Nothing!"

Mountain Pine was only half listening. With no way to stop the tirade except to walk out—and that he couldn't do, not to the young master who had chosen him for a brother; not to Steel Hope, who had saved him from being buried alive—he remained in his seat, feeling, moment by moment, the miracle that had been his life since Summer Wishes and he sailed down the Yangzi slipping through his hands like water. The Party Secretary would have his way, and he would be left trying to hold on to past happiness, which he could no more do than he could hold on to late afternoons, when classes were over, and he would watch the goldfish nibbling at the shadow he cast while he waited for his son to join him in the garden, and his wife's singing drifted from the house to stir the boughs of the cypress with delight.

"Mountain Pine, listen to me," the young master implored. "You must listen to me!"

He looked away, down at his hands. They were fists. "No, for once you listen to me," he said through clenched teeth. "That day you returned from the dead, came back into our lives, we made a tacit agreement that there are things better left unsaid. We knew then, and we know now, that nothing good, only incalculable harm, could come from voicing them. . . ."

Hearing his own misgivings expressed aloud, Steel Hope felt even more keenly the need to speak his mind and, jumping to his feet, started to object.

"You sit and let me finish!" Mountain Pine shouted in a voice even angrier than he had intended.

Stunned by his friend's fury, Steel Hope found himself seated again.

Mountain Pine swallowed hard, then, regaining partial control, spoke as he would to a distraught student, slowly, emphasizing the critical words. "Why should we amend that agreement? It's worked very well so far."

"Very well for you, perhaps, but—"

"No, not just for me. Very well for everyone concerned. And I do mean everyone."

Steel Hope shook his head violently. Not for me, he thought. Not for the one who wakes and sleeps and lives alone.

"Now more than ever, there are things better left unsaid. You have responsibilities. You alone know best what they are. I, too, have responsibilities. And we both know what they are. I'm not your bookmate anymore. I'm a husband. I'm a father. Let's go on the way we are. Let's say no more. If our friendship means anything at all to you, do as I ask. Please, I beg of you."

He was trembling, and Steel Hope thought, Can it be that my bookmate is afraid of me? But why, when I've never done anything to deserve such a response? Had Summer Wishes told him that she still loved Steel Hope? If that were only so.

"Please, I beg you."

"All right, all right. You needn't say a word. I'll do all the talking. Would merely hearing me out be asking too much of my oldest friend?"

"Only you can judge."

By the way Mountain Pine said "you," Steel Hope knew he was referring to the Party Secretary; yet in theory, the official and the man were one. It was Party policy to call upon every citizen to examine himself, to urge stragglers forward, to remold society according to socialist ideals. But never had he minimized the travail, especially when a friend was pressed to report a friend. Nor could he dismiss as laggards those who barred intimacy to avoid confidences. But surely his bookmate need not fear him.

"Mountain Pine, we are alone, no one but Mushroom knows I'm here, and I swear I'll never do anything to compromise you, no matter what." Though, even as he said those words, Steel Hope knew that no member of the Party had a right to make such a promise to anyone.

Mountain Pine sighed, and Steel Hope took this to be an assent.

Again he paced. "I can't sleep. I'm haunted by the sound of crickets. The summer before last the crickets screeched so loudly, it was as if they nested in my head. You remember, that summer, on my orders, the land was cleared of thousands of graves. A farmer dug between rows of cabbages for his father's coffin. With each spadeful, he shed a tear. His wife, keening like a crazed animal, groveled in the dirt, shoving new earth back into the old grave. Over and over, the filial son struck the filial daughter-in-law. And there was nothing I could do but submit to those hellish crickets.

"Remember the prized cricket that Father kept in his antique gourd? Well, I held my hand over the air holes and . . ."

While the Party Secretary's sodden shoes squeaked, shedding footprints on the earthen floor, Mountain Pine merely sat slumped in his chair, like an old retainer weary from being embroiled in the affairs of a family that assumed it was still the center of his life. Again he recalled those afternoons in the garden with Little Panda, this time a particular day when a sparrow, now very rare, as were all birds and insects, had alighted, jittering charily on the porcelain cistern whose broken rim had saved it from the pawnbroker, and which doubled as a fishbowl. He'd stood still as the wary visitor darted glances right and left, then jabbed the water and tossed a droplet down and, edging closer, cocked its head quizzically as if to ask, "When did we become enemies? What was the war about?"

And then, suddenly, Little Panda had started slamming the door again and again, harder and harder, and laughed with giddy menace at the tiny creature blindly seeking an escape through the thick garden walls. . . .

Steel Hope stopped to light a cigarette, then went on. "Can it be that what my critics say is true? That I'm tainted by the fatal disease dubbed 'bourgeois sentimentality,' that I contracted it in my mother's womb and from my father's genes? I can't even defend myself. What good can be served by sympathy alone when the needs of the People are beyond measure? What good when . . ."

What good indeed? Mountain Pine's head throbbed. He locked his jaws. He must say no more now than he had then, during the Campaign Against the Four Pests, when children banged on cooking pots, shook pebble-filled cans and shouted along the towpaths and sidewalks, from housetops and treetops, keeping the little grain robbers in flight until, utterly spent, they swooned to earth, carpeting the land with feathered corpses and blood. What pride the children had taken in each downing! What wicked glee! Over and over, he'd told himself that they were innocent, they were only obeying their elders, performing their civic duty, shedding personal sensibilities for the greater good, aspiring to revolutionary ideals, belonging in a way that had never been open to him, the orphan, the servant boy.

The sparrow in the garden had flitted ever higher, faltered, and then, in a desperate spurt for survival, darted over the garden wall. "It's gone, Little Panda," he had said. "You can stop now."

And Little Panda had pouted for only a moment, then dashed for the cistern, laughing as he greeted each of the fish by name. "How're you doing, One? Two? Three? Four?"

Originally the pets had been a teaching tool, but the species his son had chosen—with pendulous eyes that looked like raw eggs and long, graceful fins—had become a source of continual delight for Mountain Pine too. Was it because as a child he couldn't have pets? Or did their grotesque beauty touch the failed poet in him? . . .

Steel Hope was stamping out a butt. There were five others on the nearby floor.

". . . I joined knowing full well that what Mao said is true—that revolution isn't a dinner party, that it can't be so refined, so unhurried, so elegant, so gentle, polite and modest. I joined to accomplish what only the Party has in fact accomplished, is accomplishing, will accomplish.

"Without the Party, the House of Li would be home to traitors, not schoolchildren, and China would still be overrun by foreigners, who once shat on my countrymen; by corrupt gentry with their clannish ways, who once preyed on the masses like vultures, with impunity.

"Without discipline, the Party would falter, splinter into factions, disintegrate into that proverbial pile of sand of no fucking use to anybody. And what would become of China then? Chaos! Once again, all over again. If I know anything at all, I know that should chaos return, this time the cancer would be fatal and our country doomed. . . ."

Mountain Pine thought bitterly, There is nothing I can do to save China, Steel Hope. All I want to do is save my family, save those afternoons with Little Panda; but you and your Party . . .

Though the room was choking with smoke, Steel Hope was still puffing away, as if without the cigarette to occupy his hands, they would strike out at everything in his way. "And so, faithfully, I keep discipline, carry out my orders, beautify the ugly, simplify the complex, silence and sound out the populace on command, sacrifice the present as I did the past for a future I may never live to see, a future that will prove all that we do in the name of communism is ultimately worthwhile. But I can't sleep. I'm haunted by crickets. . . ."

And I'm haunted by the dream that I live, Mountain Pine thought. A dream that I'd do anything not to lose. If only there were an island where there were no capitalists or Communists, revolutionaries or counterrevolutionaries, Leftists or Rightists, oppressors or oppressed; or peasants—rich, middle or poor. If only, between heaven and earth, there were only he and his wife and his son. They would pick mushrooms and herbs, fish and hunt, go bathing in the sea. . . . Why, then, did he feel ashamed that the husband and father had consumed the man?

He refused to think about this. He fixed his gaze on the mural and heard Little Panda say, "Papa, Papa, it's your day to choose."

Choosing the role Summer Wishes would sing to open her throat for that night's audience was an indispensable part of their family ritual.

"Who shall I be?"

He didn't have to think. Of late, she had invaded his dreams. "Mu Guiying."

Summer Wishes walked to the far corner of the room and, facing the wall, waited for him to set the scene for their son.

"When the town of Hangzhou is seized by the State of Liao during the Sung Dynasty, its commander sends for the woman general and asks her to bring reinforcements. Though with child, she obeys, but her husband ignores military discipline and refuses to leave for battle, thinking his wife will choose love above duty and forgive his cowardice. He is wrong. She orders his execution. . . ."

Once again, it was Papa's day to choose. And Papa, Mountain Pine decided, chose to leave the room as soon as possible.

Now the floor was littered with ashes and butts, and Steel Hope had just shied the empty pack against the window. Its panes shook from the wind, and for a long while the two friends stared out into the night, monitoring the storm. Steel Hope unconsciously lit and extinguished match after match, until the acrid smell of sulphur permeated the air. Like a sudden whiff of ammonia, it roused Steel Hope from his stupor and he became vaguely aware of the rude stranger who had somehow taken possession of his speech, his faculties, and was only now yielding them once more to the Party Secretary.

He shot an angry glance at Mountain Pine. How could anyone be so indecent as to witness such a spectacle? What kind of a friend would let him pour out his heart and never once do anything to comfort him? Narrowing his eyes, he dared him to speak.

Mountain Pine was mumbling something under his breath.

"Speak up, you lame coward! Speak up!"

To his amazement Mountain Pine didn't shout back, but calmly made his way to the sewing table, where, fingering the hem of the unfinished gown, he recited in a voice filled with tenderness a poem by Tu Fu.

> In the city of Brocade
> lutes and pipes make riot all day:
> Half of the music is lost
> in the river breezes,
> and half in the clouds.
> For this song belongs only to heaven:
> Among mortals how seldom can it be heard.

Repeating the last line, Mountain Pine unfurled the umbrella and walked out the door, slamming it behind him.

Paralyzed with anger, Steel Hope shut his eyes.

For what seemed a lifetime the only sound he heard was the persistent drumming of the rain. It drummed on the floorboards of the ferry, punctuated by the blistering blows of his father's hand. It drummed louder and louder until abruptly it stopped.

In the eerie silence that followed, his eyes were drawn to the mural, and the longer he gazed at the moongate the clearer he saw what lay beyond it: a forest studded with eucalyptus and pine and overgrown weeds trampled flat, and a path which, rounding a massive boulder, led to a small, deserted temple. Only tonight it would not be deserted. The person to whom he should have gone for understanding was there.

WHITE-HAIRED GIRL

THAT SAME NIGHT, at the People's Theater, Summer Wishes sat staring into a mirror. It was framed with vivid scenes, carved in ivory, of the House of Li at the summit of the clan's glory. To everyone's astonishment, Jade had presented the heirloom to her when Little Panda was born. After Steel Hope's return, however, she had demanded to have it back. "Things aren't the same anymore," she said. "Rightfully, it belongs to my son's wife."

Instead of yielding this time, Summer Wishes had lied. "Of course," she said. "Did I forget to tell you that I have already given it to Steel Hope?" The cadre had no use for sentiment; no reason to give her away.

As usual, the evening's performance had left her drained but wakeful. She was in no hurry to remove her makeup or to walk in the rain, stirring dead leaves on her way home. The hall was empty. The others had taken advantage of a lull in the rain and had departed almost as soon as the curtain closed, and she welcomed the solitude. As always, the lamp cast a glow of intimacy that contrasted with the earlier clamor, transforming the narrow dressing room into a sanctuary where she might permit herself to think forbidden thoughts. Hanging from hooks, the array of colorful costumes evoked the finery once worn expressly for journeys into the world of shadows. Strewn about were pearls like those inserted into the mouths of the dead, gold coins like the ones that closed unseeing eyes, and papier-mâché props like the implements burned for the convenience of loved ones in the afterlife. These familiar objects, even in their morbid duality, were comforting. They belonged to the heroines she acted with such abandon.

This evening had been no exception. Her interpretation of the white-haired girl driven to apparent madness by a cruel, carnal landlord had been a triumph. On stage, she never faltered. Lines were fixed, characters drawn. At will, she could summon a laugh, a tear. Always, she knew what she must do, what was expected of her, what would happen next and, most important, how it would end.

Pretending to be the Summer Wishes that Mountain Pine had married was much, much harder.

As she had done whenever she was alone since Steel Hope returned, she set herself to remembering, as if reliving that fateful day over and over would somehow inoculate her against the ache that would never cease. Seeing her former love hauled out of a coffin before her eyes couldn't have been any more shocking than seeing him alive, there in the House of Li. In the excitement no one had noticed when, to keep from running to him, she had run out of the room to fetch Little Panda. He was fast asleep, wedged in by pillows on their bed. Shoving them away, she scooped him up and squeezed him so hard that he woke instantly. The baby didn't cry. He only looked up at her with rounded, unblinking eyes, as if he somehow understood that his mother was the more fragile of the two, and that the slightest sound or movement on his part would shatter her. Her knees gave way. She sat on the bed. The baby smiled, and she drew strength from that smile.

She must have changed him, for the next thing she knew he was wearing his new red suit and tiger shoes and hat when Mushroom called and she had no choice but to go on stage.

The room rocked like the *Pavilion of Fairies* buffeted by wind and waves. But she must act as if nothing were happening at all, and she had seized her cues from the aloof stranger no less gratefully than in a maelstrom she would have seized a tree. Otherwise she would have been possessed by the wildness that charged her to strike him, to embrace him, to will him dead, to wish her son had never been born, to curse the gods for banishing her in one swift, unexpected stroke from the heights of contentment to unrelenting loneliness. She had returned unfeeling with unfeeling. It had been the most difficult performance of her career.

How much longer must she, could she, go on acting in this play without an end? And how much harder it had been since last week, when she had taken out his silver case and lit his cigarette.

Absently she straightened the snapshot of her family tacked to the wall, then dipped her hand into the jar and smoothed a dab of cold cream across her forehead, while out of the past came the faint sound of drums ... then a couple, young and merry, darting past barrels of crabs and eels, past the herbalist, the locksmith and the weaver of baskets, racing to catch up with the brightly painted sedan chair bearing the bride. As they drew near, the drumming became louder. Louder. Only after the sudden screeching of tires did she realize that the sound hadn't been made by kettledrums, but by the coughing of an engine as a car maneuvered to park outside. Her thoughts flew from the temple to that fork in the road, two days later. She wondered what had become of the bride, if she still served her mother-in-law or had adopted a son, if she still embraced her husband in her dreams, or had grown to despise the wooden tablet....

When her face was completely smeared with cream, Summer Wishes had vanished and in the mirror hovered a pale apparition. She leaned closer, sighing. The glass clouded over. If only she could disappear as easily; vanish by passing beyond the Yellow Springs. But even if she had the courage to sever the tangled threads that bound her, what of Steel Hope and Mountain Pine? They were equally caught. There was no other way but to go on as they did, each trapped in a prison of loyalty and loss.

With a sleeve, she polished the mirror until its surface shone, then wet her washcloth in the basin and began removing the layers of cream and makeup. She splashed her face with water, then toweled it dry. She studied her features. Her skin glistened and her eyes shone. How was it possible that the pain wasn't revealed? No mask fashioned by the most gifted of craftsmen could have created so perfect an illusion.

She opened a drawer and reached in it for the yellow silk sash, which she then proceeded to wrap around the mirror as tightly as the bindings that were once wound to shape feet into golden lilies. If only, upon waking, Mountain Pine didn't smile, she thought. If only, at meals, he didn't select the choicest morsels for her bowl. If only he didn't cherish their child. If only he were stronger ... like Steel Hope.

She stared at the threshold reflected in the window glass and willed Steel Hope there, but he would not come for Summer Wishes. Closing her eyes she pictured Firecrackers—in one outstretched hand a scrap of old newspaper, in the other a burnt piece of kindling. But she couldn't see the kindhearted boy, only the man he was now whenever they happened to meet on official occasions. So austere, so cold.

She posed him the question that was lodged like embers in her throat: "Do you ever remember the temple in the woods? Do you ever . . . ?"

But he replied as if addressing a crowd at one of the political meetings held with increasing frequency at the school, between rehearsals at the theater, at neighborhood gatherings since the People's Republic was established. "Remember that China has stood up. Remember that we Chinese are no longer the pawns of the imperialists, the slaves of the landlords and capitalists."

She wanted to banish the Party Secretary from her thoughts. She couldn't. "Just once, don't keep your distance," she said. "Confess your love, Steel Hope, confess."

He nodded. But he spoke the lines everyone had committed to memory. "Confess and the Party will treat you with leniency. To refuse is pointless. Ample evidence already exists of the wrongs you've committed in the past. Don't make it harder on yourself. Do what you must!"

"Oh, tell me what I must do!"

"You must give your heart to the Party . . . give your heart to the Party."

"Why even in my dreams do you refuse to speak to me? Is this your revenge?"

He smiled. For a fleeting moment, it was his old smile. Then it froze, set in falseness. "Revenge is not, as it was in the old China, the purpose of punishment—reform is. Reform, Summer Wishes, so that you may be returned to society and start anew."

Start anew. How was that possible?

With both hands she carefully returned the mirror to its proper place, hidden, along with the threadbare shoes that she had never worn, between the folds of a blanket—an unworthy talisman that had taken the place of the one she had given to her beloved. Sliding the drawer shut, she heard the rasp of wood on wood and confused the tautness she felt with the closing of the doors to her heart. Suddenly she was no longer wakeful, but weary, so weary that she had to cradle her head on the table and rest.

She didn't know how long she had slept; it could have been an hour or a minute or two. But when she woke, she had the unmistakable sensation that someone was there, watching her. Looking up, she saw no one in the window, only the miniature faces of her husband and child smiling for the camera. She stretched out a hand to cover their eyes.

*

HAD STEEL HOPE not been watching at that precise moment from the shadows just outside the door—so near that he could fill his lungs with her perfume, hear the rustling of her gown and almost touch the scarlet ribbon entwined in her hair—he would have happily, wantonly crossed the few short steps to take Summer Wishes in his arms, to insist, to tell her what he had never told her or anyone else before, and together they would have stepped into the abyss—or was it oasis?—from which there was no returning. But he had been watching. And he saw the wife of his oldest friend stretch out a hand to caress the photograph of her husband holding their child in his arms.

TIN BUDDHAS

(1957)

MOUNTAIN PINE shuffled amid the invited crowd jostling to squeeze inside the theater. Despite huge signs proclaiming the performances canceled, he recognized the expectant excitement of a special opening. Like privileged ticket holders, everyone surged forward cheerfully, turning to gawk at notables or glower at upstarts, to greet friends and, above all, to congratulate themselves on being representative members of the various neighborhoods, schools and work units of Wen Shui.

He smiled sardonically. There must have been a mistake. Why else would he have been summoned here? Pushed from the back, he apologized to the cadres ahead. Stalled, he apologized to the model workers behind him. Elbowed from all sides, he wished he could simply let everyone by. But straggling into an important meeting such as this would be noticed. It would reflect the disaffection he'd worked so assiduously never to reveal. He pressed on.

Across the stage hung a red banner with characters five feet high: "Let a hundred flowers bloom! Let a hundred schools of thought contend!"

He slid into a seat near the back as the workers from the silk factory stood and burst into a song praising socialism. After several choruses, the students took up the challenge, singing another even louder, and the competition was on, as one work unit after another, up and down the aisles, tried to outdo the rest. At last Summer Wishes led the opera company, seated toward the front, and the entire audience in a final song.

> South of the river, harvests of plump rice
> East of the river, granaries bursting with millet
> Red sorghum and white cotton
> Sky-high mountains
> grazed by herds of buffalos and flocks of sheep
> A river ever wide
> Two shores perfumed by a breeze
> There precisely stands my home . . .
> Behold the grandeur of our ancestral land!
> Behold the grand era of socialism!

The loudspeakers called the meeting to order. A dozen men, wearing identical suits of dark blue gabardine, filed in from the wings to sit in their assigned seats at a long narrow table draped with a spotless white cloth, upon which teacups and shallow clay pots of spring lilies were set at precise intervals. Last to enter was the Party Secretary for the County, who took the chair at center stage.

Mountain Pine was struck by Steel Hope's appearance. There was no trace of distress. He embodied confidence, if not downright conceit. His voice resonated as he began to address the audience.

"Comrades, two months ago Chairman Mao Zedong made a major address to the Supreme State Council entitled 'On the Correct Handling of Contradictions Among the People.' Its contents, until now, have been closely held. Today, I have the honor and privilege of informing you of important developments. . . ."

A murmur swept through the hall.

The Chairman's message was unprecedented. In a secret speech, Mao had denounced those Party members who presumed to pass judgment on what ideas, and whose ideas, were acceptable. That right belonged to the masses. He admitted that all too many innocents had been branded counter-revolutionaries. He proclaimed that they should never have been arrested, sent away to be reformed through labor or punished by force. Constructive criticism must never be put down, "not by the wooden rod, not by dunce caps." The People should always be encouraged to speak out, to air their thoughts. In doing so, all would be guided. In doing so, injustices would be addressed.

Mountain Pine sensed how the crowd was at first cynical, then wary and then increasingly confused, but without a doubt, by the end of the long speech, totally disarmed.

When finally Steel Hope stopped reading, everyone burst into loud applause. Could this beaming Party Secretary be the same man who had bared his soul to his old friend that stormy night? Of course he was. And of course he was the one who had summoned Mountain Pine here. He needed him to witness this dramatic reaffirmation of the Party's righteousness, and of his own faith in its cause.

Well, he had come, and heard, and his palms smarted. How could they not? The rest of the audience was still clapping.

His thoughts drifted to a secluded stretch of an ancient canal, beside a dwelling no more substantial than a watchman's hut thrown up at harvest time, where his sworn brothers had tied socks filled with stones around his ankles, promising that a lame youth would become brave and strong. "Trust us! Trust us!"

Poor Young Master, Mountain Pine thought. Once again he has been seduced by hope.

AFTER THE UNPRECEDENTED rally, people inside and outside the Party "bloomed." Their criticisms, no matter how severe, how trenchant, were printed. The Party Secretary of the *China Youth Daily* bemoaned China's plight and lashed out at cynics who pretended faith, acolytes who toadied, incompetents who blundered. The Forestry Minister demanded amends for those unjustly sentenced. A vice-chairman of the National Defense Council denounced China's Elder Brother, the Soviet Union, for plundering the industries of the Northeast after the Second World War and for maneuvering China into expending blood and treasure in the Korean War. Rectors and priests declared that the Party had become an instrument of oppression. Students called for democracy. Workers charged cadres with gross favoritism and arrogance. Farmers pressed for the immediate dissolution of the collectives.

Only some intellectuals refrained. How could they be sure that tomorrow the Party wouldn't punish them for deeds the Party encouraged today?

Among these cautious ones were Mountain Pine and his colleagues at School Number Three, where by mutual agreement the School Party Secretary and the teachers had thus far confined their political discussions to reading the published accounts of this latest movement aloud. All realized that such uneventful sessions could not last.

Now it was the last week of May, and Mountain Pine scrambled for the seat behind the only table in the meeting room. It was reserved for the note taker, who would normally be last to speak. By then, everyone, including Secretary Hua, would be thinking of going home for dinner, and he could get away with repeating some innocuous remark. This strategy had yet to fail him. As always, he was worried nonetheless.

Glancing at his fellow teachers, who chatted in groups of two or three, he wondered if he'd slighted any of them in the past. Did he imagine a look of disapproval from Chen? True, yesterday, when she'd asked him for ideas about a lesson plan, he'd had to excuse himself. At the time, she'd smiled and cooed, "Of course you can't be late to take Little Panda to buy a paint set." Still, what had she meant by adding that hobbies were what boys "like him" needed? Please, Comrade Chen, he pleaded with his eyes, I never meant to be unfriendly.

What was the matter with him? These weekly sessions were usually more tedious than threatening. The confessions about giving too much or too little homework, and the accusations about being late for this or that class, were trifles. Hadn't he seen how friends had even conspired to fabricate lapses for each other so that both would have something to say? Perhaps he should have made one of them his friend. But who? Wang was affable enough but spent his spare time courting the ladies. Gu was too smart for his own good. There was always Fang, the only one besides himself who had taught at the school when Jade was its patroness, but a friendship between a close-mouthed woman like her and a close-mouthed man like him might cause others to wonder whether, behind their reticence, there were secrets. As for the rest—they were all talkers.

While his fellow teachers milled about, he busied himself sharpening pencils with a penknife. Perhaps he should make an effort to join their conversation. Perhaps he should eat his lunch at school like the others. . . . The knife slipped and cut a finger. The wound was slight, but when a drop of blood stained the blank white paper, he had to stifle a cry. He cursed himself. Why must he see a hurricane in every shower.

When he spotted School Secretary Hua by the door, counting heads, he immediately lowered his gaze. The portly veteran of the Long March disdained his charges as a hardworking buffalo would disdain monkeys; for all their cunning and nimbleness, teachers were weak, unappreciative creatures bent on making a fool of him. That had been his attitude when he first arrived at the newly opened School Number Three, and nothing in his five years as its Party Secretary had changed his mind. But there was no avoiding the man, and so from the start Mountain Pine had diligently flattered his superior and covered up his mistakes. It had done no good. He'd been naive to think it would. To the insecure, every hand extended was a threat. Hua despised the sight of him.

Glancing up again, Mountain Pine saw that Hua hadn't moved. What was he up to? Their eyes met. Instead of his usual scowl, Hua smiled, but the physical effort, unsustained as it was by goodwill, vanished before Mountain Pine could return it.

Now satisfied that the staff were all assembled, the Party Secretary strode into the room with his hands clasped behind his back, like the general in an opera about to disclose his battle plan. His monkeys hustled to their seats, which were arranged in a circle. Instead of going straight to the chair with arms opposite the table, Hua took out a pack of cigarettes and offered them around, smiling again that smile. Everyone was shocked; dubbed "Fat Pack Rat" by a student whose father had marched even longer than Hua, the man hoarded everything from peach pits to broken rubber bands. So shocked were they, in fact, that all, smokers and non-smokers, took one. Seeing an opportunity to be friendly, Mountain Pine scrambled to light as many as he could before lighting his own, and though he gagged and coughed, he was determined to smoke it to a butt.

Finally, amid smoke and grim geniality, Hua called the meeting to order. He dispensed, however, with the reading of the editorials from *The People's Daily*.

"Comrades, our great Chairman Mao has explained that there are two kinds of contradictions."

His voice sounded odd, strained. Mountain Pine wondered if the Party Secretary, whose normal speaking voice would be audible above the sounds of furious combat, was suffering from a sore throat. Or was it a fever? Hua's face, round and flat and brown, like an earthen plate, glistened.

"The first kind are mali . . . maliciously . . . insti . . . gated by evil outside sources. These contradictions must be put down by force. These threaten the People.

"The second kind of contradictions happen among the People. These are sort of, like, misunderstandings. These don't have to be put down by force. But some cadres didn't understand . . . they didn't know . . ." Hua paused to wipe his brow with a sleeve.

"And instead of using persuasion, they carried things too far. They made mistakes. They didn't listen to the masses. They made people not want to tell them things, things to help us work better. Because of this, work is not as good as it could be.

"So . . . the Party wants you to tell about these things. So . . . tell me the things you didn't want to tell me before. . . ."

His voice trailed off. The monkeys cleared their throats and shifted nervously in their chairs. Gradually, like sand drifting to the ocean floor, a silence settled over the room. It grew thicker and thicker. All seemed to be waiting for another, less patient, to break it, but no one did. Mountain Pine escaped in his mind to where his son waited for him. A book lay across his lap, but Little Panda's eyes were fixed on the door.

Suddenly Hua repeated his invitation, so loudly that everyone was visibly startled. When again no one responded, he waved his arms and urged, "Come, come, be free in your talk, be free! It is the wish of our great Chairman Mao. Speak up!" He looked at Liang, an activist who always had something to say. The man turned his attention to scraping dirt off a shoe. He tried smiling encouragingly first at Wang, the bachelor, then at Bald Liu, who taught sixth grade, and then at Young Liu, who substituted for anyone indisposed. They quickly bowed their heads. Hua suggested that perhaps he hadn't made himself clear and repeated his entire speech from the beginning, stumbling over the very same words.

Still no one volunteered, and Mountain Pine almost pitied the martinet who pleaded for a scolding from his despised charges. Almost, but not quite. Let Hua sweat to fulfill his quota of criticism, as at all previous meetings they had had to sweat to fulfill theirs.

Desperate, Hua finally called Liang by name—who then claimed that he'd always felt free to say anything and everything, closing with, "Besides, I nurse no criticisms against you."

The next one called on was Fang, who said that she, too, had no criticisms, "none whatsoever!"

Exchanging quick, knowing smiles, others took up the phrase. "None whatsoever!"

Hua ground his teeth, then spat. The phlegm, thick and yellow-green, landed on Mountain Pine's shoe.

Their eyes met.

Mountain Pine refused to utter a sound. Calmly he took out his handkerchief and wiped off the stain; then he folded it neatly before putting it away, thinking, He's nothing to me. Nothing at all.

Jabbing an accusing finger at him, eyes bulging, Hua shouted, "Don't tell me you don't have anything against me, Teacher. You have plenty.

You do!" Then, making the same violent gesture to each of the others, he shouted louder and louder, "You do too! And you! And you! . . ."

After this ludicrous outburst, the atmosphere cleared. Perhaps, mused Mountain Pine, it was because no one was smoking anymore. Perhaps not.

Though none had dared to so much as snicker, now the teachers, like inattentive students, folded their arms, sucked their teeth, slouched, twisted their hair. Hua seethed, his nostrils flaring. Mountain Pine wondered if he'd ever been as riled by enemy fire as he was by their passivity, and decided it wasn't likely. In battle, he could act. Here, he was bound by Party discipline to undergo this ordeal—an ordeal that refused to start but must take place. And for what? For doing his utmost in the service of the Party.

Mountain Pine took no delight in this ironic twist. Whatever his failings as a cadre, the man had been courageous once, which was more than he could claim for himself. Hua hadn't misjudged them. They were like monkeys, all too eager to mimic one another, all too willing to settle for the comforts of conformity. Why? The answer was obvious. Fear. No doubt fear was paramount, as in his own case.

Yet, studying the silent circle, he pondered another, less apparent, more complex answer. For thousands of years, Confucianism had taught Chinese to prize family above individuals, hierarchy above equity, harmony above conflict. Thus generation after generation had learned to yield to authority, to withhold subjective opinions and to withstand hardship in all its manifestations. And now if they didn't, the Communist Party made them pay dearly. No wonder they—

Mountain Pine felt a tug on his right sleeve. Alerted, he looked at Hua. The Party Secretary's demeanor had completely changed. He was grinning as if he'd just single-handedly captured enemy headquarters. Mountain Pine tugged Fang's sleeve, on his left, passing along the warning.

"Comrades," shouted Hua, "Our great Chairman Mao also said that those who don't speak out aren't our friends. So far nobody here's said a thing. So far nobody here is a friend. If you aren't friends, what are you?"

Pointing to Liang, he asked, "Are you a friend?"

"I am."

"Prove it!"

Trapped, the activist sputtered, citing complaints printed in the newspapers as examples of what some people thought.

"Do you agree?"

"Well, they're very important people and should know what they're talking about."

"Do you agree?"

"Not always."

"When, then?"

"I agree that there have been a few instances when teachers were a better judge of their students."

"Better than who? Speak up!"

"You."

Hua asked another if he agreed.

"Yes."

The answer was barely audible. Mountain Pine glanced up quickly to see who had given it, then continued transcribing.

"What else?"

"Sometimes teachers know better how to teach."

"What else?"

On and on it went, Hua grubbing perversely to bring to light the forbidden thoughts, the shams, the unsettled scores buried deep beneath layers of prudent civility. He delighted in the digging, forgetting that the ore he mined was being forged into bullets aimed at him. The teachers' remarks, at first mild, became barbed and, at last, brazen.

Suddenly, after years of yielding, withholding and withstanding, the teachers snapped. They clamored wildly for the floor. They spewed attacks until they were breathless, reviling the Party Secretary with a shrill vehemence no one, not even they, could have suspected lay dormant within their hearts. They accused him of arrogance and subjectivism, slander and stupidity, authoritarianism and bureaucratism. They harried him with lurid accounts of his misdeeds, of how they and their families had suffered, of how the students and the school, the Party and the country had suffered. They heaped abuse upon abuse, until Hua was cowed into sullen silence.

Scheduled to last for an hour or two, the meeting had gone on for much longer. Now there was barely enough light for Mountain Pine to write. His hand ached. His spirits reeled. A part of him reveled in the release of his fellows' pent-up fury. A part of him recoiled from their folly.

Hua struggled to his feet. Misery distorted his features. With eyes fixed on a spot in the center of the circle, he announced in a quivering voice, "All complaints will be forwarded to the proper authori—"

"Sit down!" Liang interrupted him. "We're not through. Mountain Pine hasn't had a chance to speak."

"Yes, sit down!" the others cried.

Hua stumbled backwards into his chair. Resigned, trembling, Mountain Pine handed the pencil to Fang. It fell and rolled across the floor. Chasing it, he prayed the point had broken. Sharpening it would permit him a moment to think.

"Don't bother, I have my own," said Fang.

He returned to his seat, painfully aware that all eyes were riveted on him. He started to speak, then stole a glance at the Party Secretary and refrained. At once the mood changed, from boisterous expectancy to sober suspicion. At once the outsider was no longer Hua, but Mountain Pine.

He smelled the stink of panic and disgust. He smarted from the silent shrieks of "Traitor! Traitor!" He shrank, shriveling until nothing was left of him but a knot of shame. Staring out the window in the direction of the cypress, he spoke in a voice as weak as the whine of a mosquito that has outlived summer. He spoke at length, recalling the grand achievements of the Revolution in which all took pride, the leadership of the Party, without which there wouldn't be a new China, the sacrifices made by those whose faith had never wavered throughout decades when the future was bleak.

All this, Mountain Pine knew, wasn't at issue. Still, he elaborated. Only Hua listened to the obvious.

"To those of us who didn't sacrifice, who never fought, I ask, are we so confident of what must be done, of how else to do it? Are we so good as to be beyond reform? Are we so wise as to spurn advice? I, for one, am not so confident, so good or so wise."

Or honest, Mountain Pine heard them thinking, and plowed on. "Besides, if there is a tin Buddha strutting about the school, haven't we acted like superstitious old women who feared the mere mortal as though he were a true god? Haven't we kowtowed before him? Haven't we bathed his feet?"

At that, someone clucked. Bitter laughter followed. "Tin Buddha!" cried one. "That's good."

"Hey, Tin Buddha!" shouted another.

Hua looked confused. His eyes darted around the room as if to search out the deity in question.

"Tin Buddha!"

He glanced at the door. He jerked around to look behind him and held for one perplexing moment that stiff, awkward pose. Then slowly, wearily he turned back to face his pitiless captors.

"Tin Buddha!"

"Yes?" Hua said.

"Call this meeting closed!"

T HE SEASON for blooming ended as abruptly as it had begun. Criticisms, once praised as flowers, were now exposed as poisonous weeds. Critics, once honored as patriots, were now hounded as Rightists. A quota was set. Five percent of the people employed by all work units were to be arraigned at meetings throughout the country.

Comrade Hua accused the coward who had dubbed him a tin Buddha of being a Rightist. And when it became clear that the Party Secretary's vengeance was directed solely at Mountain Pine, the rest of the staff, smarting from acute relief and guilty gratitude, joined in Hua's vendetta. No one objected to the torrent of accusations—not even the accused.

Take care! Mountain Pine cautioned himself. Forced to sit on a child's stool with his knees drawn up to his chin, facing a row of his former colleagues, he dared not budge. He hung his head to avoid looking into the eyes of these hostile strangers, who saw before them not a human being as vulnerable as themselves, but a dog. Admittedly, the creature had been docile once. But not anymore. Now it was a rabid cur that would bite them and everyone dear to them if it could. Thus, for the sake of the community, respectable citizens must strike first, strike with the utmost speed and force.

Only an abject confession had the slightest chance of lessening his punishment. And so, with his head bowed, the husband of Summer Wishes and the father of Little Panda elaborated on how he deserved to be disciplined for concealing insolent, disloyal and unrevolutionary thoughts, how necessary his indictment was, how just the cause of his accusers. By the time his monologue ended, even Hua's implacable eyes were averted from the hideous sight of Mountain Pine, who had, layer by layer, peeled away every vestige of honor and pride.

While waiting for sentence to be pronounced, he was expected to keep to routine. He went to class, but no students came. He walked the streets, but no one greeted him. Summer passed, and fall.

*

IT WAS the morning of December 22. Summer Wishes sat at the bedside of her son, holding his hand. Little Panda's eyes were shut, but as so many times before, she suspected that the truant was neither asleep nor ill. Summoning her strength, she managed to pull the quilt around his shoulders. If only, she thought, if only I could crawl beneath the covers and . . . But how could she? She wasn't a child. She was . . . what was she? To the Party, she was a member who had been granted one last chance to draw a clear line between herself and the Rightist. To her work unit at the theater, she was an actress who made the others feel at once envious and superior. To Jade, Amber Willows and Mushroom, she was a mother who alone could save her son from a life without prospects or hope. To her husband, she was a wife who must, out of mercy, divorce him. To her son, she was a mother who had lost all her magical gifts.

She stared at Little Panda's hand. It was the size of her twin brother's hand when she held it for the last time; only his had been neither warm nor supple nor soft. She studied her own, the hands that Mushroom boasted could summon moonbeams or dismiss thunder with a gesture. What good were they now? They couldn't move a single heart. They couldn't change a single mind. They were useless. Making fists, she dug her long nails into her flesh, deeper and deeper, until the welcome pain became intolerable and the fingers sprang open of their own accord, revealing tender palms stitched with welts. She smiled a bitter smile. This hurt, at least, was allowed to show.

Slowly the redness disappeared, leaving only the lines that fate had inscribed—lines as fixed as the pathways of stars, as faint as cobwebs.

Her thoughts strayed. They drifted from snippet to snippet of memory, each marked by impending doom, until her attention was arrested by an image of those giant steely-eyed warriors that guarded temple gates, their unforgiving hands raised in anger. Without bidding, her hand floated upwards to assume that pose; but holding it, as if she held a saber above her head, must have proved much too difficult and too unnatural, because she was suddenly aware that her hands had mysteriously come to rest, folded just so, across the bodice of her dress. One wrist lay on top of the other. The hands were slightly cupped; the fingers closed. She could hold this pose easily. She could hold it forever.

Her thoughts drifted again, this time to visit scenes that might have preceded such a peaceful ending. It wasn't difficult to know where to find them. She needed only to peruse her own repertoire. Hadn't she mastered flinging a rope across a rafter, mixing potions from opium or poisonous mushrooms or roots, falling on a sword? How simple, really quite simple, it was to die. . . .

She heard a child's voice. "Mother?"

Looking about, she saw that the chamber was as before.

And the voice of a woman. "How can we celebrate the bond of all bonds when one among us is missing? I must go after her. . . ."

"No, let me! This time let me!" It was Firecrackers who should have sunk to the bottom of the river. It was Firecrackers who should have hit her head on the stone.

"I must go after her. . . ."

"Mother, don't!"

This time, how familiar the voice. Was it her own or that of her son? It didn't matter. Only the urgency was real, as real as the tightness in her throat. She mustn't fold her hands like a corpse. She mustn't think forbidden thoughts. But what if the gods already knew her thoughts about the rope, the potion and the sword? What if they exacted further retribution? . . . Terrified, she bent down to listen for the sound of Little Panda's heart. Hearing only the drumming of her own, she was about to throw off the quilt when the child stirred, folding his limbs to his chest, making himself small.

She fell to her knees. O merciful Kwan Yin, all-seeing Buddha, holy Jesus, Allah the compassionate and all who wield power over mortals, oh hear me, please hear me. Save my husband. Save us. Tell me what to say. Tell me what to do. Please, oh please grant me a sign. . . .

She started to kowtow, then caught herself before she committed another wrong. The Party taught that the gods didn't exist, that religion was mere superstition, a corrupting legacy left by feudalism, a tool wielded by evil tyrants to oppress the masses.

She scrambled to her feet and, fumbling to brace herself on the nearest object, knocked the portrait of the Chairman off the desk onto the floor. His eyes never left hers as she picked it up in both hands and set it reverently back where it belonged. As she did, the corners of his mouth lifted ever so slightly, bestowing upon her a beneficent smile.

Was this the sign she'd been praying for? Perhaps she should send a letter to the Chairman after all. Perhaps he could . . . Then she recalled Steel Hope's warning: that the letter would never reach Beijing, and even if it did, Beijing would only send it back—not to her, but to Hua.

She slipped into the bed beside her son.

LATER that evening, Summer Wishes and Mountain Pine sat huddled by the brazier. No matter how many times he added new coals or stirred the old ones, she shivered. He coaxed her to drink the tea he had prepared. He pulled off her shoes, wrapped his sweater around her feet and rubbed them.

Suddenly, he burst out laughing.

This was so unexpected and so inappropriate that the sound, far from being infectious, only triggered her alarm.

"No, no, no . . ." He was obviously trying to say something to reassure her, but laughter kept getting in the way of words, until finally he succeeded in engineering a lull by holding his cheeks. "I haven't gone mad. It's just . . . it's that the answer just popped into my mind."

"The answer?"

"To the question I've been asking for months. Why has all this happened to Mountain Pine? It's so obvious. I don't understand why I didn't think of it before. . . ."

How could he sound so carefree, more carefree than he ever had? Since his confession, everything about her husband had baffled her. He didn't curse those who harassed him. He didn't protest or falter. Instead, he seemed content, as though all was well.

"Summer Wishes, pay attention. How many people are there in my work unit?"

Why was he asking her this?

"How many, my good wife?"

She had no choice but to humor him. "Ten."

"What's five percent of ten?"

She could only shake her head.

Snapping his fingers, he shouted gleefully, "A half! A half! Ladies and gentlemen . . . oh, sorry, wrong era. Comrades, I hit the lucky number. A half!"

He's gone mad, she thought. My husband's gone mad.

"Don't you see? With one short leg, I'm the closest thing School Secretary Hua has to a half."

He was laughing again as he gently stroked her hair. "A bad joke. Please forgive me. I know how hard these months have been for you."

"Why haven't they been harder for you?" Summer Wishes asked, searching in his eyes for an answer that she could comprehend.

He gathered her into his arms and held her for a long moment, then, still holding her, spoke in a faraway voice that sounded like an echo. She listened intently, afraid of losing a syllable.

"Perhaps because you hurt enough for both of us. Perhaps because I knew that sooner or later this was bound to happen, and when it finally did, the melancholy that had tormented me suddenly vanished along with the waiting. Perhaps because . . ."

The echo faded into silence.

"Because?" She prompted him. She must understand.

He nodded. "Perhaps because I needed a starring role that only I could play."

What did he mean? She could recall all the words, and each word was one she knew. But what did he mean? "I don't understand," she said.

"Oh my dearest, I don't know if I understand it myself." Cradling her, rocking her, he spoke as if he were reciting an allegory to a sleepy child—slowly and softly. "When the flood came, I could have died, but I lived. When my leg wouldn't grow, I could have become a beggar, but my sister found us a home where we were clothed and fed, where the master's son treated me like a brother. Even so, I could have grown up ignorant. Instead, the mistress sent me to school. When the House of Li no longer needed me, I found a Christian mission where I was needed. When the war came, I escaped harm. When my health failed, I could have wasted away, but you and the monks made me whole. When love was only a word, you taught me how to feel every nuance of its meaning. When we thought our oldest friend was dead, he came back to us."

She pushed him away. "Steel Hope is no friend!"

"You don't mean that."

"I do. I do. He's no different from the rest. He never comes to see
you anymore."

"You mustn't hold that, or anything else, against him. However far
apart Steel Hope and I had been, in the end, when it was most meaningful,
we both returned to the Middle Heart. You should know that he did
come. But when he did, I made him promise not to come again."

Kicking off the sweater, she bolted for another chair. "How could
Steel Hope promise such a thing! He's not my friend. And if you say he
is, you're not my friend. I have no friends, not one, not one. . . ."

"You don't mean that."

"Jade, Amber Willows, even Mushroom. They're all against me.
They never stop urging me to draw a clear line, to . . ." Even in anger,
she couldn't bring herself to say the word "divorce."

He stretched out his hand. Ignoring it, she glared at the shutters
across the room as if they, too, were foes; and except for the faint stirring
of embers, the silence was complete.

She could never abide stillness—especially not now when the ardor,
more practiced than true, that she had somehow rallied for this outburst
was fast deserting her. Sighing, she wondered how many promises had
been sought, and how many promises fulfilled out of kindness, because
of her . . . because of her . . .

"My wife . . . my wife . . ."

He is calling me, she thought.

"I didn't mean to keep secrets. I had always planned to tell you,
but postponing that moment seemed harmless enough . . . until now."

Why now? No, don't tell me, she meant to cry out. I don't mind
secrets. I'm not ready. Not now!

Solemnly he brushed away her tears. "Steel Hope came to see me
as soon as he heard about the accusations. One minute he was mute; the
next, he raged. But from the start, we both knew that no matter how he
objected, nothing could be undone, nothing could be changed. I begged
him not to try. Any intervention risked an even worse outcome—not
only for me, but for him. He said he didn't care. I told him I did. I
needed him. You needed him. Little Panda, too.

"He asked why life had suddenly turned so cruel. I told him that
life has always been beginnings and endings."

No more, she wanted to say. Please. No more.

"Eventually, Steel Hope promised. He would not endanger his standing in the Party. He would never see me again unless I sent for him. He
would forget the Rightist Mountain Pine. . . . You must promise too."

"I can't."

"Think of our son. Would you have him spend the rest of his life in bed? Once I'm sent away, no one must ever speak of me again, so that Little Panda will learn not to talk about his father. Since my existence can only harm him, I must cease to exist. You must see to this."

She couldn't stop the trembling. "But . . . I don't know how."

"Pretend that you're in a play. . . ." He paused, then spoke the words a second time, as if he were addressing someone else. "Pretend that you're in a play. Afterwards, you must marry. . . ." Again he paused, nodding almost imperceptibly. "In a year or so, when our son has forgotten me . . ."

"How can Little Panda forget his own father?"

"You must help him, as you once helped him to walk—patiently and watchfully and constantly, knowing that the inevitable falls will hurt you more, knowing that it is for the best. He must draw a clear line. He must call someone else Papa. . . ."

"You ask too much."

"I ask what only you and my son can give me. If not the happiness I have known"—his voice was stronger now—"the peace of mind I will need to endure what I must."

"What about me? How shall I endure?"

"Someone will always be at your side to help you."

"Little Panda is only a child."

"I don't mean our son. I mean . . ."

Their eyes met. She looked away, staring at the sweater she had discarded. It was old. The colors were fading. There were holes that should have been attended to long ago, but he had never mentioned them and she didn't know how to mend anything. Now it was too late. Her husband meant to give her away as once her father had meant to do. Only this time it was to someone she knew, and not to a baby but to a man. . . . She was weeping openly now.

"Don't. It's all right, really it is. Remember the lesson you learned and wished you'd had a chance to tell your mother before she disappeared? That it didn't matter how much more she loved your brother, that it was enough to know that she loved you as well? Well, that lesson still holds . . . except that I'm luckier than you were. I have the chance you never had. You couldn't tell your mother, but I can tell you. My wife, in your own words and from my own heart—it is enough to know that you loved me as well."

She clung to him, hiding her shame with sobs that racked her until there were no more tears, and she felt as thin as the shadow Summer Wishes cast on the wall.

Cupping her face, he smiled a long, tender smile. "He'll be a good husband for you and a good father for our son. And . . . yes, you must bear him children, though at our last meeting he foolishly vowed to have no other son but Little Panda. Our friend deserves more.

"And you, my dearest wife, will sing for him and for them and for the people who love you. You will dance. You will lighten their hearts as only you can."

"What about my heart? Doesn't my heart matter at all?"

"Of course it matters. That's why you must do as I ask, and know that henceforth whatever happens to me will be but a very small payment on the debts I've incurred while we were husband and wife. How could it be otherwise? This beggar has lived the life of a king. No one—not now, not ever—can rob me of my memories. Remember this, remember this above all. Whatever happens, I shall know happiness."

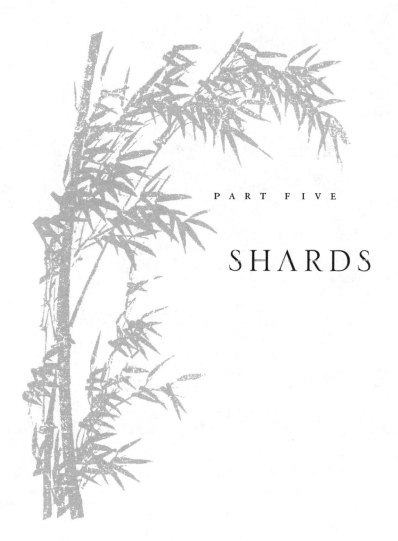

PART FIVE

SHARDS

INCARNATION

(1966)

THE TWENTY MEN, lying on the kang head to heel like a row of efficiently packed shoes, wager a turn at sleeping next to the wall on the temperature outside. Mountain Pine bets it's only thirty below. Recalling that the last time they were allowed to spend a day indoors was when the mercury dipped to forty below, the rest say forty below, at least forty below. Not a gambling man or a dreamer, Mountain Pine knows better. Another day, another win. He smiles.

Smiling—that bequest of marriage and fatherhood, not of nature—is almost a reflex in his present incarnation. If anyone bothers to ask "How can you?" he smiles and shrugs. It's simpler that way. Trying to explain how smiling is proof of his membership in the human race, blunts pain and soothes the soul would only confound them, if not himself.

Since his arrival here two thousand nine hundred and sixty-five days ago, he has refused all letters and packages and expressed gladness at the most inappropriate moments. Within a week, the guards decided that the new prisoner was on the verge of lunacy. Perhaps they were right. Then again, perhaps he'd never been saner. When reality transcended hallucination, by what standard could anybody judge? It was the time of the Great Leap Forward, when Mao exhorted the masses to do twenty years of work in a day so that China would be as industrialized as England within the decade;

when an entire nation slaved around the clock at backyard furnaces, melting down anything metal to make steel that turned out to be worthless until there was hardly a pot left to boil water in; when seedlings were planted as densely as hair in soil shunned by the most undiscriminating weeds and aerated by giant fans and lit by floodlights pulling scarce and costly electricity; when flourishing orchards on rocky slopes were razed to sow wheat that any village idiot knew would never sprout; when record harvests were tallied daily, and daily peasants feasted on bark.

Still, lunacy would have explained why when the guards ordered Number 5799 to work an extra hour, he'd smile and work an extra two; why when commanded to rise two hours earlier, he'd smile and rise three hours earlier; why when required to go hungry for a day, he'd smile and refuse food until the guards, fearing a hunger strike, ordered him to eat.

Certainly he'd never planned on perpetrating anything, much less mischief. At least, not in the beginning. It just ensued. Perhaps he was only following the example of others—collaborators who, out of cowardice or cynicism, would curry favors and favor; disciples of communism who, out of guilt and guilelessness, sought to expiate the crimes they hadn't knowingly committed against the Party, which they held to be infallible. Or perhaps he was too dim-witted to note the obvious—that the crucible of prison life transforms men indiscriminately, the extraordinary as well as those like himself who never merited a second glance.

Only later, much later, when even the cruelest jailers refrained from abusing the "crazy cripple," did he belatedly grasp the appeal of mischief. Nor was he aware that his fellow inmates were cheered by his ways until one day they literally cheered Number 5799. This happened at roll call after the guard dubbed X-Ray Eyes ordered him to unwrap the head scarf that everyone wore around his face against frostbite—the same guard who, the day before, had detected his sorry attempt to cultivate an illegal moustache. "You can't trick me!" he screamed. "Don't just stand there. Show me your fucking face!"

Number 5799 obeyed. Pandemonium, as forbidden as moustaches, greeted the scrupulously clean-shaven Rightist, who now also had no eyebrows.

How ironic that such foolishness, along with his old repertoire of stories, should win him what he'd never enjoyed before—a large circle of friends, albeit unsavory ones. Now, not even the vilest thugs, thieves, rapists and murderers would think of knocking his bowl to the floor when their own was licked clean and he was still eating like some heedless gourmet who has only to nod to obtain more. Other slow eaters were not so accident-proof, for while the soup would be irretrievably lost, the bits of cabbage lying in the dirt were fair game.

Yes, yes! The temperature is thirty below and not a degree lower. He sighs. To be honest, it was no contest. Number 5799 has lived in the wilderness longer than the others and knows the score. . . .

Why, then, are they the ones snoring in sweet sleep while he stares like a wide-eyed corpse? And corpse he'll be if he doesn't get some sleep. In the eight years since he arrived here, he's seldom been bothered by insomnia, but tonight, for some inexplicable reason, banalities like a neighbor's breath on his feet hardening into ice, unscratchable itches and a barking belly are keeping him awake. He shuts his lids. He strains to shut down his brain. He pretends to sleep.

He fails. His thoughts race ahead to tomorrow, to the terrible trek they must make to reach the work site, to how exhausted he'll feel, how far behind the others he'll trail, how cutting the wind will be, how brittle his ears, how red the eyes of the wolves that prowl these wastelands near the Soviet border. . . .

He mustn't think of what will happen to him if he doesn't sleep. He diverts his thoughts to an event in the past, to the words he's chosen to describe it and committed to memory, words that—if ever fate were to grant him another chance to write—he would put on paper. . . .

Here, one day in winter is like another. The skies, an unbearable helmet of lead. The earth, bare. In every direction flatness, unrelieved except for the long, gaping wound that dynamite has gouged in the frozen ground. And though the wind howls and the noise of shovels and rakes at work never ceases, the sounds only serve to deepen the primordial silence.

There are no guards at the work site. They've already planted the red flags that mark the boundaries beyond which even a strong, healthy, well-fed youth cannot live, and none has strayed. What's more, prisoners, if they hope to survive the cold, must work nonstop. Thus, why should any guard stand watch? They are superfluous.

One contingent of prisoners toils at the bottom of what in summer will be a waterway, heaving frozen clumps of dirt topside, where another contingent toils to rake it smooth. Strangers to these camps would not see any difference between those who shovel and those who rake—they all look

equally emaciated and grim, with their heads cocooned
in vapor. To the prisoners, who know why some and not
others are given the easier job, there is all the difference
in the world.

A shout shatters the silence, but it goes unheeded: the
men think that the wind must be playing tricks, for who
among them would waste the energy? Every scintilla must
be meted out as judiciously as ladles of cabbage soup to
keep lungs pumping and limbs moving.

"Hey, you lucky son of a bitch!"

It isn't the wind after all.

"For god's sake, rake faster. Pitching this damn crud
out of the hole is bad enough without having to pitch it
higher and higher." It's the new inmate, who has yet to realize
that only dumb beasts of burden survive. Now he is yelling
continually, louder and louder. "Hey, how about giving me
a turn on top? . . . Hey, what does it take to get a cushy
job around here? . . . Hey, you lucky . . ."

The raker immediately above him ignores this clamor
for justice until he is so moved by the irony that he can't
help but speak. "Ah, who would have thought there is a man
in this world who envies me?"

"And why the hell not? You get to stand on dry land
and fool about. I get to break my back mucking around
in this freezing shit. When do I get my turn? When?"

"Soon, my good fellow. Soon."

"When?"

"When you're only a step away from the grave, like
me."

Still sleepless, Mountain Pine wonders what ever happened to the new
prisoner. Was the man dead or with a group transferred long ago to a camp
even closer to the border? Or was he among those released when prisoners
were being discharged early because the Great Leap Forward had produced
one of the worst famines in history and there wasn't enough to feed the
guards, much less so many inmates? While his fellow prisoners had prayed
to be among the lucky ones, he had thought, What good my homecoming?
No good at all. For even if the authorities did reissue his old residence permit,
reassign him to teach at his former school and certify him rehabilitated, he'd

still be a leper in the People's eyes. Worse, his presence would inflict unending pain and misfortune on his family and friends.

At the camp, he knew how to get by. At home? By that time Summer Wishes and Steel Hope would have married and had a child, or at least one on the way, and he, who had blessed their union, would be honor-bound to stay within the confines of friendship, and thus consigned for life to being both his own prisoner and his keeper. What could he hold on to, then? Not the solace of having returned happiness for happiness, friendship for friendship, loyalty for loyalty. Not the knowledge that he had given Little Panda the only gift of value that a Rightist could give a son—his absence. Not the prospect of living out his days at peace with himself.

He looked back at his life not as husband or father or friend, but as if his feet were planted on the far side of the Yellow Springs. From this vantage point he could see the paths that led nowhere, the rivers that twisted and turned, but inevitably flowed into the ocean, the landscape of destiny. Consequently, when his name failed to appear on any lucky list, he wasn't disappointed. Not disappointed at all. . . .

Now he remembers: the disgruntled inmate was released early. Had he been able to change places with him then, he'd be at home today. . . .

Home? The camp is his home.

How absurd that must sound to those on the outside—like the drivel of a starving simpleton who slaps his own face until it swells to twice its normal size so others will envy him for being rich enough to eat and eat, and grow fat. Is he turning into that character Lu Xun created to mock the tortuous mind-set of his countrymen? Is he another Ah Q? Is he a self-deluding fool?

No! Ah Q tortured facts. Ah Q would proclaim Labor Camp #5 a worker's paradise. Mountain Pine could never mistake it for anything other than what it is—a freezing hell. Only here would a man too feeble to work fear, above all, less work. Only here would a condemned man be grateful for the monstrous practice of exacting twenty-eight fen from the loved ones he has left behind to pay for the bullet his executioner will shoot him with because at long last they will know his whereabouts. Only here would a man sleep with his filthy half-frozen shoes clasped to his bare bosom like some treasured memento because shoes not warmed by human flesh will freeze, and once frozen be impossible to wear for work, and without work . . .

Still sleepless, he wonders if there's anything in the world that he'd be good for now—besides serving himself up as an endless banquet for bedbugs and lice. . . .

A textbook illustration of nature's food chain pops into his mind, slightly altered, and Number 5799 smiles. He and his fellow convicts are not disposable after all. In the ultimate scheme of things they're indispensable. In the revolutionary scheme of things as well. Without Enemies of the People like him to blame, who would be accountable?

His neighbor's heel taps his nose. He dutifully passes the signal along. In a few moments every man on the kang is poised to about-face, for unless they move in perfect unison they don't move at all: the kang barely leaves space enough for a fart, much less for a man to shift his position at will. When the flip is achieved without a curse or a groan, and everyone has landed safely on his other side, Mountain Pine finds another reason to smile.

DURING THE REIGN of Emperor Qian Long, the tenth Patriarch of the House of Li ordered a vault dug to preserve the New Year's gift he prized most among the scores his admirers sent to his ancestral home—a wagonload of pears, as fragrant as opulent wine, as crisp as icicles. Its value to him was far beyond silver or gold, for each bite recalled the growers of the fruit, and the lessons he, as a young magistrate, had learned from their example.

Serving in a district not far from the birthplace of Confucius, he had seen how the lowly farmers nursed every bud that flowered in their small family orchards with a devotion equal to that of the Sage's disciples, even shedding their ragged coats to clothe the trees in years when winter lingered into spring. And he had seen, when time came to reap the harvest, how the trees rewarded their caretakers. Henceforth, he tended the people as they tended their trees, and taxed them only on the pears sold.

Thus, he enjoyed a long and brilliant career; and to honor his teachers, he commanded a master artisan to craft the subterranean chamber, where the fruit of their labors would not spoil, as though it were to house all the wealth of the land, concealing its entrance beneath the tiles of the floor the way a cabinetmaker conceals the secret compartment of a dowager's jewel box. No wonder, then, that with the passage of time and disuse, later generations forgot that it ever existed.

One day, some months after Mushroom moved into the storeroom, a tub overturned, and when, astonishingly, the flood disappeared in a moment, leaving only a trace of dampness on the floor, she recalled a trick that the magicians at the fairs where she performed as a child had taught her and, pushing each corner of every brick above easy reach, discovered the mechanism that opened the vault.

When a peek revealed the depository was home only to scorpions and spiders, worms and rats, she dismissed the find, recalling its existence during the ensuing twenty years only when the walls of the storeroom needed to be painted or patched, until the day after Jade's stroke. For around that time the Chairman had launched the Cultural Revolution by dispatching the young on a crusade to save the nation from its enemies old and new—enemies who were everywhere, from the highest councils in the land to everyone's own home—so that the People's Republic, purged of evildoers and of the Four Olds—old customs, old habits, old culture and old thinking—might be reborn according to egalitarian ideals. Since then the vault had served as Jade's quarters.

*

NOW JADE is dying, and Steel Hope is keeping vigil. He doesn't know how long he's been there. Perhaps a few minutes, perhaps hours. He sits on a low stool with his back against the mound of rotting cabbages that repels intruders and hides the bed crafted of wooden crates upon which his mother lies. Too weary to push back a sleeve and glance at his watch, he fixes his gaze on the invalid, who sleeps. The illumination shed by the rapeseed-oil lamp, with its three-sided mirror to enhance the light, intensifies Jade's pallor, so that her face looks more like a waxen mask than a face, its features nearly dissolved. If it weren't for the pockmarks, he could claim that the woman was a stranger to him. If that were so, they'd both be better off.

The thought of disavowing his own mother doesn't shock him. Nothing shocks him now. Now that the personal ties that were life's moorings have become wide leather belts with which one is flogged. Now that the world has careened out of orbit.

He wills his lids not to close, but after so many days and nights of interrogation, of wakefulness imposed by the Red Guards, who have seized Party Headquarters, the effort lasts no longer than one of Jade's labored breaths. . . .

The sun is so bright over Tiananmen Square that, attending the chain of goldfish soaring overhead, his bride squints, but somehow she has never looked lovelier. The long kite darts higher and higher. It skims the ermine hem of an unseen god, who undoubtedly is smiling upon the black-haired people on this wondrous day.

He forgets himself and cinches her waist from behind, and like heedless children, they romp, circling the Monument of the Martyrs in tandem. Laughter trails gossamer fins heavenward.

Heads turn. Strangers gape.

He waves. "Take a good look, Comrades," he shouts. "You'll not see another such happy bastard ever again."

Suddenly she stops. The spool is empty. She strains to reel in the runaway fish and fails, then sprints ahead to let the tether slacken. The northeast wind is strong. It hoists the kite higher, pulling her arms up and taut. She falters. Her toes skid and skip over the ground.

He races after her. Her skirt is a fingertip . . . an arm's length . . . away.

She loses a shoe, then the other as she leaves the earth, ascending higher and higher. Desperate, she looks down at him.

"Let go, Summer Wishes, you must let go."

"How can I?" she cries. "How can I let go of Mountain Pine?"

"Let go, my wife, you must let go."

The capricious wind swallows his words.

"Who's there?"

What . . . ?

"Do you think you can trick me? I demand to know who's there!"

At the sight of the lamp flame standing almost upright, Steel Hope remembers where he is—in an airless tomb. He lowers the ear flaps on his hat, and secures it to hide his half-shaved head, before hoisting himself up and dragging the stool the step or two across the narrow space to her side. "It's Steel Hope, Mother."

"O merciful Kwan Yin, I've waited so long, so long," Jade says. "I've waited so long. Oh my beloved son, you can't imagine . . ."

Passionate outbursts, especially heartfelt ones, have become such an anathema to him since young zealots began shouting the praises of the Great Helmsman of the ship of state during their incessant interrogations of the Party Secretary of Wen Shui, that he automatically retreats into numbness.

He waits for her cries to subside before speaking again, and then the words are ill chosen, made hollow by overuse. "I came as soon as I could, really I did. You do believe me, don't you?"

"I believe you, my son...."

How can she?

She strokes his arm. "I understand. I understand."

As for him, he understands nothing.

"Don't think I don't know what happens to high officials like you...."

He freezes. Can it be that she knows the truth?

"You're always traveling on the Party's business," she says. "Staying on and on. I know. I know from my years . . . on the neighborhood committee. The Party's business is never done."

The combination of relief and disbelief almost makes him laugh out loud.

"Was it a Red Flag?" she asks suddenly.

Until she repeats the question, he thinks he has heard wrong. What does a flag have to do with anything?

Her hands grope the air, then tug at his collar. "Oh, say it was a Red Flag, a huge Red Flag."

Instinctively, to keep her from disturbing his hat and exposing the unmistakable sign of his downfall—no, worse, much worse, of his utter humiliation—he twists away, and sees staring at him in the lamp's mirror three aspects of the same unshaven face, so wan and gaunt that for a moment, he doesn't recognize himself. The eyes accuse the County Party Secretary of Wen Shui: It's you who have lost your senses, not she. How could you forget that the stroke blinded her?

Jade is calling out his name and he turns to take her hands in his. "Was it a Red Flag, just like the Chairman's?" she prompts.

What an idiot he is. She isn't talking about a banner but about a Red Flag limousine. This time, he does laugh, an uncontrollable wheeze of a laugh that goes on and on and on, until it shakes him out of his daze, and eventually becomes a rueful smile. Stroke or no stroke, Jade is still Jade. He embraces her, wondering why the constancy of her regard for the accoutrements of high office, which proved such an embarrassment to him before, should endear his mother to him now. Now that he's powerless to grant the smallest wish. Now that it's too late.

Seizing the chance to please her, to reward her constancy, he boasts, "How right you are, Mother. It was a Red Flag, no different from the one that conveys the Great Helmsman himself."

Only now, when she tries to clap, extending her hands toward him, does her fragility become real: her long, tapered fingers, the sole attribute of Jade that the women of the House of Li conceded might compare favorably with those of her husband's first wife, resemble mottled shoots of bamboo, withered in the absence of air and light. At any moment she might crumble into nothingness as easily as a parched leaf underfoot.

"Tell me more—more."

He stops to think . . . the only time he ever rode in one of the big Soviet-style limousines was in the capital, where they went to celebrate their marriage. It arrived at the Beijing Hotel to whisk Summer Wishes to a command performance at the Great Hall of the People. To impress the white-gloved chauffeur, she sat very straight, with her eyes trained on the man's cap, pretending not to notice the bright flags that fluttered from the lampposts along the Avenue of Eternal Peace, as if they were as ordinary as towels hung out to dry. Only the squeezes she surreptitiously gave his hand hinted at her exultation. He exulted too.

Now, he swallows hard and tastes bile. How could he have foreseen where that ride would lead? He must stop searching for signs along the route they have traveled. None exists. Neither that occasion nor any other makes any difference at all.

"Well?" Jade prompts him again. "Well? Well?"

He thinks, My mother is like a child, and goes on with his make-believe story. "Confidentially," he says, "my Red Flag was the very same model as the Chairman's, down to the lace curtains, the jeweled knobs, the gold dials and buttons and the number of handmade knots in the priceless rug."

Again she tries to clap. "Oh yes . . . and even from behind the curtains, you could see how, everywhere you passed and everywhere you stopped, people envied you, couldn't you?"

"Yes, I could. And"—he pauses dramatically—"how people also envied my mother."

"Ai ya! The wish I've wished for all my life has come true. With such an honored official for a son, I can hold my head high as I cross the Yellow Springs. I need no longer fear . . ." She stops to blow her nose and dry her eyes, then goes on. "The members of the House of Li will all be there to greet me. Never again will they treat me like a stranger as they did in this life. Oh, Steel Hope, you've made this mother so very, very proud."

For as long as he can remember, making Jade proud has been, in her eyes, the reason he was born, and for as long as he can remember, he has recoiled from the very idea. But now that she has pronounced the deed done and he is liberated, he aches, as if a fistful of regrets were lodged in his heart. Before he knows it, he is crying out to her like a filial son before the altar of ancestors—on his knees.

She gropes for him. "Don't," she says. "It's forbidden for cadres to kowtow."

WHILE Steel Hope attends his mother, Summer Wishes sits, toying with her food, in the private dining room of the Shanghai Hotel. Its plush velvet drapes, crystal chandeliers and intricately worked brass fixtures are a legacy from the era when foreigners ruled and the city built upon swamps was known as the Paris of the Orient. Since Liberation it has catered to high Party officials. Once, being the guest of honor in such an exclusive setting would have thrilled her. But after spending every few months of the past seven years on national tours, she is accustomed to being feted, and has come to regard dining with strangers as part of the price exacted for her success.

So famous is she now that whenever she is in town, local officials and their many friends use her presence as an excuse to wine and dine at the state's expense, and thus, tonight's invitation was more or less expected. She is taken aback, however, to find herself sitting at a small square table with only the host, Comrade Wang (or did he say "Huang"?), and a younger man, who was simply introduced as his aide. No doubt they mean to be considerate. After all, she has just spent the last three weeks in the hospital.

Wishing that she had never come to Shanghai, never heard of Hospital #27, never urged the charwoman on her floor to tell her stories, she arranges the chili peppers on her plate.

"Don't you share our Chairman's love of hot foods?" asks Comrade Wang, a balding man dressed in a white shirt so expertly tailored that it takes no more than a glance to see the difference between it and the shirts worn by lesser men.

"Oh, but I do." She immediately picks up a tiny green pepper, which Mushroom would use to flavor an entire dish of spicy beef, dips it in red pepper paste and, without shedding a tear, eats it. She eats another. And another.

Comrade Wang nods appreciatively. "Ah," he says, "if only an iron stomach were proof of loyalty, then you'd rank right up there with Auntie Jiang."

For a moment she doesn't understand, then realizes that, of course, he's referring to Jiang Qing, the Chairman's wife. She also realizes that she's expected to say something. What? Steel Hope has forbidden her to utter an opinion, even in the privacy of their home, on the woman whose tastes are now sacrosanct in the realm of the arts. She stalls for time by excusing herself and bending down to retrieve her "lost" napkin. The ruse never fails her. Either the worrisome conversation is ended by the commotion, or she comes up with an idea during the search.

She decides to cull a green pepper from the chicken dish and challenge her host. Smiling her most charming smile, the actress offers it to him. "Care to put your guts to the test, Comrade?" she asks.

Instead of being amused, as she expected, he ignores the question, and summons the waiter to order more wine. When the aide bends his head to devote his undivided attention to excavating the last of the meat from a lobster claw, she begins to wonder if the dinner is more than the usual courtesy. Might they have chosen this grand place for conducting sensitive Party business? A special assignment perhaps? A tour overseas? A role in one of Madame Mao's new revolutionary operas or movies?

She has been a cadre long enough to know that she must heed discipline and wait until the superiors are ready to inform her, and so she compliments her host on the wine, and he appears pleased.

As the men exchange news on who among their ranks is or isn't being promoted, she feigns interest, while letting her thoughts drift. She wonders how late the hotel store stays open. Such an exclusive shop is sure to have items not sold elsewhere, and she wants to surprise everyone at home with gifts. Perhaps she'll get something for herself as well, to celebrate her recovery—though, in truth, there was nothing seriously wrong with her, and if Steel Hope hadn't gone to the trouble of making all the arrangements, she would never have given her lingering cold another thought. But he'd been adamant. Her voice was a gift to the masses and deserved the best of care. Never had she seen such loving concern in anyone's eyes, and to please him, she packed. By the time they reached the station he had, as always, converted her entirely to his way of thinking, and she'd been giddy at the prospect of exercising yet another privilege granted to celebrated cadres alone. Even members of the Politburo, he whispered in strictest confidence, escape from their bickering aides and onerous duties, from newspapers and telephones, by checking into Hospital #27 year after year for a pampered month of well-deserved tranquility.

After one day of hospital routine, she'd been ready to flee home. But how could she? Steel Hope despises officials who traffic in favors. "Have they no principles?" he says furiously. "Have they no pride?" Yet to obtain a room for her at this famous place, on such short notice, and for so extended a stay, he must have done the unthinkable and betrayed his principles. What's more, it was he, not she, who needed a rest.

Night after night during the month before they parted, when in her sleep she fumbled for him, his absence would tease her awake and she would spot the tip of his lighted cigarette in the dark. But if she turned on the lights and asked what was wrong, he merely shrugged and, keeping his silence, tucked her in as gently as he would have done the baby that fate hadn't meant them to have.

These bouts of insomnia aged him as all the years before hadn't; overnight his shoulders slumped, his temples became gray. How then could she have gone against his wishes and added to his burdens, burdens she knows nothing about and can't even imagine, burdens he's always taken on himself? How then could—

Her host is asking her something.

"Yes?"

"Comrade, surely you've met him."

"Who?"

"Lincoln Chen."

When she replies that she's never had the pleasure, but the name does sound vaguely familiar, Comrade Wang looks annoyed; then he breaks out laughing. "Only a great actress could make the unbelievable so nearly believable. The fact is that all of China has heard of Lincoln Chen since the man—" He stops in mid-sentence to cough, then turns to his aide and adds, "Indeed, we'll remember her performance, won't we? Especially remarkable when Chen is known to have been a patron of her husband for ages."

At the mention of Steel Hope, she stiffens. Cadres don't go about dragging relatives into their conversation for no reason at all. Such breezy behavior is left to those outside the Party. Should she show her displeasure? But before she can make up her mind, Comrade Huang (or is it Wang?) lets the subject drop to engage his underling in what can only be a face-saving discourse on how best to peel an onion without weeping, and she congratulates herself on observing more discipline than he. . . .

Hospital #27, she decided after a few days, was filled with clandestine lovers. Though the food cart stopped at each door, the occupants might as well have been in traction for all she ever saw of them. On the rare occasion when she did spy a pajama-clad soul shuffling aimlessly in the halls, the prominent personage obviously considered her much too junior to warrant a nod. The staff, however, was always popping in on her— to forbid this and that and to caution her against aggravating her condition by opening the windows, which, in any case, looked out on nothing but a wall. What was wrong with everybody? No carrier of deadly microbes could have felt as abandoned and isolated as she.

Only an elderly charwoman on the midnight shift deigned or dared to chat with her, and she, her voice a feathery whisper, spoke only of ghosts. Did the cadre know that, in the years before Liberation, when this was a maternity hospital, stillborn babies suckled throughout the night, and their mothers woke to find their breasts dry and marked with tiny pink hands? Did she know that one ghost picked locks, searching for his legs, which had been severed by a streetcar . . . that another dripped puddles on the stairs every Saturday evening, the day of the week she had drowned . . . that another opened the same third-story window through which he had plunged, while his grandmother, dead from shock, rang bells to alert the nurses of patients contemplating suicide? Did she . . . ?

Again Summer Wishes' host interrupts her revery, asking where she stays when performing in Beijing. "With friends?" he wonders.

"No. I prefer the Beijing Hotel."

"I understand many foreigners stay there as well. By now you must know a lot of foreigners."

Summer Wishes shakes her head. "I don't speak any foreign language."

"Is that so? I'm almost certain that more than one person has told me he's heard you sing in English."

She informs him that she can sing in other languages but not speak them. "Whenever I'm invited to perform for important foreign guests of our government, I learn to sing one of their native songs."

The cadre smiles weakly and turns again to his aide. This time she doesn't even feign interest.

A diner sporting five ballpoint pens clipped to a shirt pocket—the customary badge of high office—parades past their table on his way to the lobby with a bucketful of live crabs, and she sighs. Steel Hope loves the delicacy. Oh well, even if the chef were inclined to impress the actress, the costly tribute would never survive the journey home.

For the hundredth time she curses herself for ever having spoken with the old charwoman, and most of all for asking her, "Aren't you afraid of these ghosts?"

"They don't bother me. It's the screamers who give me the shivers. Or worse, those who wail without making a sound or shedding a tear."

"Tell me who!"

"Oh, there've been plenty, but the girl who gave birth the first day I worked here—not mopping floors, but taking care of newborns—is the one I'll never forget. I can still see her face...." The old woman paused, bringing her hands up to the light like a photographer framing a portrait. "It's as clear as yours. No, better ... my eyes were good then...."

"Go on!"

"Her newborn was the first one I held. Unlike some others, she had no reason to be sad. Her husband was rich and couldn't take his eyes off her even when his baby was in the room, and his baby wasn't a good for-nothing girl or damaged in any way ... unless you counted that tiny birthmark. To me it was just a dash of gravy on the belly, but others swore that it looked exactly like a kingfisher."

Certain that there couldn't be two such birthmarks, Summer Wishes seized the old woman's hand and, pressing its knobby knuckles to her cheek, gushed of her astonishment at meeting the good woman who had caught her husband on the day the city magistrate of the nether lands kicked him into this world.

Though as amazed as she by the fateful coincidence, the woman had expressed no interest in the son, only in the mother. But the more they talked, the less they agreed. No, she was young, just a girl. Yes, her baby was born in the spring of 1919. No, her complexion was smooth. Yes, she was pretty, very pretty, but sadder than a woman with ten daughters who has just given birth to a stillborn son. No, she couldn't be mistaken—her name was Jade and she hadn't a single pock.

Again and again the same questions and the same answers, until the charwoman suddenly recalled another face from the past ... the person who had always accompanied the husband to the hospital. "What a witch that one was, complaining about the way I held the baby, the way I washed the baby, the way I burped the baby, anything and everything, as if I were a moron and she the lucky mother. Hah! Not a chance! Not if she never crossed her legs and paid gold for an army of peasants, and each one as horny as a camel that's traveled the length of the Old Silk Road to hump its mate."

The old woman laughed, a surprisingly robust laugh, then, casting a guilty glance at her mop, started to rise from her seat. "I tell you, one look at that one and I knew she was drier than a bone, but . . ." There was a sound in the corridor. In mid-sentence the woman stopped, grabbed her mop and, mumbling about dirty floors, swiftly withdrew, leaving Summer Wishes alone to piece together the secret of Steel Hope's birth. When she had done so, she implored the gods to grant her the diligence and strength never to reveal what she had learned. Exposing secrets buried in the heart would be like exposing the dead buried in the ground. . . .

"Comrade, the meal is over and you've said so little. Now we must ask you to think harder and report all that you know about that traitor Lincoln Chen, who jumped from the roof of the Revolutionary Museum to escape the People's justice. The Party is fully aware of every last detail of his dealings and his Revisionist clique, but we're going to give you a chance to tell us in your own words. Start with Chongqing during the war. . . ."

The aide takes out a notebook.

"And be sure to include your husband's other close friends, the Rightist Mountain Pine and overseas Chinese like the Tangs."

The interrogation begins.

As STEEL HOPE pours rapeseed oil to keep the lamp burning, Jade drifts off to sleep. Her breathing is shallow, but less labored than before. He eases himself back down on the stool to doze as well, but seeing (or is he imagining?) the barest hint of a smile on her lips, he recalls that when the House of Li was "cleansed" two weeks before, everything the Red Guards didn't cart off was ripped to shreds, burned, smashed or flushed away. Now he fights sleep. He is determined to etch in his memory the likeness of the woman who gave him life and whom he will never see again, for once she is gone no other likeness will exist to show him or anyone else what Jade looked like.

A memory of his mother on the morning he left home for Nanjing subverts his concentration, and again he is racked by regrets, feeling the fist in his heart open and close, again and again. . . .

She had chattered as she fussed about his room, picking up balls of crumpled paper, plumping a pillow as she might on any other day— seemingly a different woman from the one who earlier in the week had screamed at the top of her lungs, threatening to hang herself if he left her side, until he lied to her about how the highest officials had all graduated from schools in Nanjing. Still chattering, she'd paused to look in the mirror, and, licking a finger, used it to smooth the long bangs that concealed her pitted forehead. The gesture, so familiar, had suddenly seemed unbearably intimate, and as he lowered his gaze from her puffy red eyes, he'd experienced, perhaps for the first time, a flicker of empathy. Jade was being very brave. It was more, much more, than he had thought her capable of. . . .

Suddenly the idea that at any moment now there will be no one left in the world to call him son fills him with infinite sadness, as only an idea so unexpected, and so unworthy when compared to his mother's dying, could. He sees himself at his Grasping Ceremony, searching the circle of faces, desperately trying to locate his father. He sees his father on his deathbed, desperately trying to locate him. He sobs for a watch that never worked and that after years of constant wearing he finally threw away. It was the only gift his father ever gave him directly—if something tossed like a coin to a leprous beggar could be a gift—and it had been his most precious possession during his first two years at school. Following a lecture on the virtues of being on time, Stone Guardian had fished the watch out of the bottom drawer of his desk, where the rejects from a factory the clan once owned were kept. His son had worn it after the stem was lost and after the glass was cracked; only when the band was beyond repair had he removed it from his wrist.

Realizing that his thoughts, even now, aren't of the dying Jade but of Stone Guardian, he bows his head. Innocent of the crimes they accuse him of, he is guilty just the same. He remembers the silver pin he stole. He remembers his oldest friend, who is no longer at his side, and who pleaded to be buried in the past as if he were dead, so that he wouldn't have to die again and again. He remembers what is happening in the world above.

He cannot bear to remember Summer Wishes, and tries to find some solace in knowing that they are at least spared the agony of standing by with a bucket of water between them to save their small son or daughter from the prairie fire that is consuming China.

Until Summer Wishes changed his mind, Steel Hope, tortured by the sufferings of Mountain Pine and the inexplicable contrast between Stone Guardian's love for one son and his loathing for the other, believed that he must not father a child, but be a father to Loyalty—the name he gave Little Panda when the boy reached the age to have a youth name. Not long after that, however, her doctor had discovered tumors in her womb and it was removed. From that day forward, when gazing at Loyalty she would whisper, "If only I could have given you a son." And he would say, "But you have, a son who is tall and trim and as handsome as his mother is beautiful." What he kept to himself was how much Loyalty reminded him of Mountain Pine. Both carried books in their pockets the way others carried change. Both craved order. Neither went out of his way to make friends, though no one privileged with their friendship would ever be able to find another to take his place.

He thinks: If you, my bookmate, ever felt indebted to Steel Hope because he happened to be the one who dug you out of the rubble in Chongqing, well, my friend, your good son has repaid that debt a hundred-fold today. If Loyalty hadn't lied about the vault and talked Defender of Country and their fellow Red Guards into punishing the County Secretary by locking him in the same dungeon where the Lis used to punish their slaves, I wouldn't have had this chance to say goodbye to my mother.

His lids are closing. Weariness as implacable as grief overpowers him and he sleeps. . . .

The moon is high but the courts are dressed in shadows. He marvels at the graceful arching roofs in silhouette and the lanterns hanging like giant drops of rain clinging to spouts. Gone are the peeling paint and the buckling wood, the cracked tiles and broken stones. A breeze carries the distant playing of lutes and pipes, a song that is seldom heard.

He walks through the puddles. His shoes are small, no bigger than a boy's. His hands as well.

Looking up, he sees his father and says, "I came as soon as I could, really I did. You do believe me, don't you?"

"I believe you, my son. . . ." On Stone Guardian's face is a big smile.

Hand in hand they stroll toward the Hall of the Ancestors.

"Was it a Red Flag, my son?"

He doesn't know the answer at first. Then he remembers. "No, Father, it was the Flag of the Rising Sun."

His father weeps and weeps, and shrinks until he is the size of a child.

Hand in hand they stroll toward the Hall of the Ancestors.

He walks through the puddles. His shoes are big. A man's shoes. His hands are a man's hands.

Looking down, he sees Little Panda and asks, "Why are you crying?"

"I have no father. I have no name."

"Mountain Pine is your father. Loyalty is your name."

The boy asks, "Where is my father? Why doesn't he live with Mother and me? Did you send him away so you could take his place?"

He weeps and weeps, and shrinks. . . .

"Are you still there?"

"Yes, Mother."

Jade's hands close over his, and she prays. "O merciful Kwan Yin, thank you for sending Steel Hope to me one last time. Now you may lead me across at your convenience. Your faithful servant is ready."

He slides his hands from hers and objects with an outpouring of assurances, but even as he does so, he cannot conjure any brightness at the end of the long, dark corridor that stretches into the years ahead—unless, he hears the weary voice within interject, it is the headlight of an oncoming train.

Jade gives a sigh, more like a shudder. "Don't be sad for me," she says. "Dying in pieces is no blessing. I'm happy to go."

He doesn't know what to say . . . but neither can he endure her stoicism, all the more disturbing because it is new. He has to do something. He kneads his hands. He fiddles with the ear flaps of his hat, then almost yanks the damn thing off. He paces.

Suddenly—to distract her restless child, he supposes—Jade initiates a tantrum of her own. "Damn those demons to hell! They think that because I'm blind and bedridden, I can be fooled. Well, I see them for what they are. They're nothing but ingrates and impostors, traitors and thieves!"

He stops in his tracks. She does know! She must have known all along. Has he allowed wishful thinking to addle him? Who has been acting out a charade for whom?

"To think that I took those two sneaks into my home. . . ."

Two? Only two? There had been hundreds when they stormed Party Headquarters, at least eight, Loyalty and Defender of Country and six others, when they brought him here and threw him into the "dungeon." She can only mean Amber Willows and Mushroom, who by concealing Jade from the Red Guards have been risking their own lives to comfort their dying mistress.

"Why, I'd be better off if I'd opened my door to the plague!"

Afraid of saying something that might give the two faithful servants away, he cradles her in his arms and rocks her; but his silence, his refusal to engage her, stokes her frustration, until there is no stopping her from expending her last breath to expose Amber Willows and Mushroom.

She says that after the stroke she fell into a coma and woke up in this place unable to see or walk. The two women described her new quarters as ideal for her convalescence. They claimed that she had been carried up the sacred mountain like an empress in a beautifully decorated sedan chair to a sanatorium, where nuns vowing silence gathered wild herbs, cultivated exotic animals and restored health to all who drank their potions, followed their unorthodox rituals and obeyed their rules.

He has no choice but to listen. Once again, he is a silent witness. Once again, he wonders how a good deed can go so wrong.

She suspected their account from the start: If they were in the mountains, why was there never a whiff or crackle of pine cones burning in the brazier? Even so, she has allowed herself to be lulled, for they wait on her and she is dying. Every morning, Amber Willows devotes hours to styling her hair and painting her face, until the results never fail to elicit the compliments of her visitors . . . but why is it that the paste never smells of honey and every change of clothing has the feel of coarse cotton? And why are the visitors who come to entertain her with their adventures never people she knows, and why do they all sound as though they come from Mushroom's village? At mealtime, they prepare her favorite delicacies, but each mouthful tastes like another version of cheap bean curd. . . .

She pauses to catch her breath.

"Mother, you've talked long enough. You must rest."

She shakes her head. "I'll have all eternity to rest." Her voice is stronger, as if she is energized by the act of unburdening herself.

She says that she wanted to believe them and so, for the longest time, she did, but then one night young voices shouting woke her. Snatches of angry words filtered down from above. They were reviling her. And Amber Willows and Mushroom were leading the chorus! She is almost certain she heard them shout, "We spit on Jade's grave!"

The next day, when she demanded an explanation, the two servants were at first speechless. Then, twittering like conspirators, they answered her question with another, asking if anyone in his right mind would permit children to play at war on rooftops. Of course not! She must have been dreaming.

But the nightmare turned out to be a recurring one, and the third night she made sure she stayed awake throughout the ruckus, by pulling out a hair, winding it around a button and knotting it, then another and another, until all her buttons were marked—a task beyond any dreamer.

In the morning she fingered the buttons and found the strands of hair—the proof that she had been awake all along. She almost suffered another stroke.

Her voice is a spiteful hiss as she rages. How dare the two women stage such an elaborate hoax? How dare they accuse her of revolutionary crimes? How dare they speak of her as if she were dead? The answers are obvious: They dare because she is alone and helpless and their secret prisoner.

Why do they do it? Why? Only one explanation makes any sense. They are no better than her greedy in-laws, who never came back to Wen Shui after Liberation to pay their respects or their debts. They plot to part her from her money and her home.

"But what can I do about their lies and tricks? Nothing. If everyone thinks I'm already dead, what difference if they poison me? None. So I play along, like the dupe they think I am, and the deceivers rob and rob.

"I ask for my fur-lined jacket. Sold. I ask for my jewels. Sold. I ask to be moved to another room farther from the kitchen, because this one reeks of cabbage. All taken. I ask to go outside. Not allowed."

He has been afraid that it might come to this—that somehow Jade would ferret out the facts. But if ever there was a time when facts had nothing to do with the truth, that time is now. Of course, he can reveal the truth. But not without sacrificing the good, and the good, however paltry and inconsequential and fleeting, is the only straw people with conscience have to cling to in the whirlwind.

"... The traitors must be punished. Oh, how I prayed! Oh, how I hung on! Swear you'll avenge me, my son!"

How can he object?

"Swear—you must swear!"

How can he refuse?

"Mother, I swear ... I swear to you that justice will be done."

Within the hour Jade is dead. On her face, a look of pride.

*

LOYALTY is strong and has no trouble overpowering Steel Hope when he emerges from the storeroom. With one arm clutching his father's throat, he rips off the offending hat.

He and his companions harangue the Party Secretary of Wen Shui. They shove him onto the floor of the truck and climb in to take their seats. As soon as the engine starts, the young men, exhausted from making revolution, sleep.

Steel Hope waits for the right moment, then tucks the torn piece of newspaper he has been carrying inside his shoe into Loyalty's shoe. On one side are doodles of triangles which, only to someone with a wild imagination, resemble mountains, and printed on the other side is a map of northeastern China on which there is a doodle of a pine tree, rooted near the Russian border.

At Party Headquarters the Red Guards shove him out of the truck. They revile the Capitalist Roader.

Without a struggle Steel Hope allows himself to be propelled down the familiar corridor, now plastered inches thick with layers of Big Character Posters denouncing high cadres, past knots of youths trading Mao buttons, and bathrooms where some of his top deputies scrub urinals, past bands of youths running off to conduct raids on schools and hospitals and offices, where they will attack the Stinking Nines and Cow Demons and Snake Spirits—anyone more expert than Red. He wonders how long he must go on bowing to boys whose voices have barely changed, to girls whose braids have only recently been shorn.

Loyalty grabs what hair is left on Steel Hope's half-shaved scalp and yanks his head forward. "Bow your head! Lower!"

He is thrust inside his office. There are more commands. "Keep your trap shut."

"Filthy Revisionists must never be heard from again."

"Where's your sign?"

He gets down on his knees and gropes for the placard in the darkness, then threads his neck through the wire from which hangs the wooden rectangle painted with a giant black X over the characters of his name written upside down.

"The cap!"

With difficulty he reaches around the unwieldy placard to place the tall dunce cap on his head.

"Don't let us catch you without them on!" The door slams shut. The lock turns.

He waits for the footsteps to fade, then drags himself across the room, now emptied of his desk and chair and files, to peer through a crack in one of the boarded-up windows. He sees Loyalty, a tall and trim silhouette, dashing toward a battalion of Red Guards throwing objects into a huge bonfire.

He grins. Damned if that boy of hers wouldn't make one hell of an actor too! As always, however, the pride he takes in Loyalty makes him feel like a thief. For though it was Mountain Pine himself who made them all promise to act as if Little Panda's father never existed, Steel Hope alone had profited. He had gained a filial son.

An hour passes. The door bangs open.

The Red Guards curse the Party Secretary of Wen Shui. They shove him down the corridor....

AMBER WILLOWS and Mushroom dig. The digging goes slowly. The earthen floor beneath the vault is hard. By the time the hole is deep enough, and wide enough, they can barely move. And yet, lifting Jade in their arms, they feel that somehow the mistress has forgiven them. Somehow, she understands that their charade was never meant to deceive a blind old woman, but to shield the daughter of a traitorous merchant and second wife of the Patriarch of the House of Li from a fate worse than death. For Jade has had the kindness to weigh nothing at all.

*

AMBER WILLOWS and Mushroom walk along a deserted stretch of the riverbank. Every now and then they stop, look about. Again, Mushroom whispers, "Must we?" Again, Amber Willows nods. Mushroom reaches under her jacket and removes the blanket with the antique mirror and the threadbare shoes hidden among its folds and flings these Four Olds into the water.

*

SUMMER WISHES steps off the train from Shanghai into a strange land, where Big Character Posters written on used newsprint blanket every wall and flutter overhead, accusing family and friends, colleagues and neighbors, even complete strangers, of crimes committed in this and other lifetimes; where red lights mean go and green lights mean stop; where youths are elders and elders are chastened tots; where good people like Steel Hope stand accused and bad people like Cassia and her father have long since escaped to Taiwan; where hate is extolled and love is reserved for a portly, half-bald Middle Peasant named Mao.

*

MUSHROOM cuts holes in Summer Wishes' dark blue pants and jacket. She sews patches over the holes.

Summer Wishes checks her work, then scolds Mushroom. "How do you expect me to wear this outfit in the street? Try again. It's not ugly enough."

*

SUMMER WISHES finds her drawer empty and says nothing. A cat, entangled in the curtain ropes, is dead. Who will they accuse of this heinous crime?

*

LOYALTY and Defender of Country, along with their fellow Red Guards, round up all those accused of espousing expertise above ideology at the People's Fertilizer Plant. They push one into the broom closet and paste strips of paper marked with a giant X on the door to seal it closed. They shove another into the utility closet, a third into the furnace room, a fourth into the coat closet, until all these Stinking Nines, Cow Demons and Snake Spirits are shut up.

They proceed to do the same at the People's Electrical Plant, the People's Hospital, the People's Research Center, the People's Theater....

*

AMBER WILLOWS shivers along with the other neighborhood women seated on benches in the schoolyard. Staring at the Little Red Book gripped tightly in their hands, they listen to a ten-year-old girl reading from her own copy.

Yesterday, when Mushroom laid her Little Red Book down in her lap to blow on her icy fingers, it slipped off, and *The Sayings of Chairman Mao* landed in the slush. Now Mushroom is gone.

*

SUMMER WISHES trembles. One of the spears in the prop room is broken. Who will they accuse of this heinous crime?

*

MUSHROOM is back. Her head is bowed over the Little Red Book. To keep from grinning, she bites her lips. Silently she crows. The Little Red Terrors will not "teach her a lesson" again. As an old trouper, she knows her lines better than those neophytes. She can recite the Little Red Book from cover to cover. She has beaten them at their own game.

*

SUMMER WISHES hears whimpering. It comes from inside a wardrobe closet taped shut with white paper marked with a big black X. She bolts into the lobby, where she hears whimpering. It comes from the broom closet, taped shut with white paper marked with a big black X. She bolts into her dressing room. It is empty. She still hears whimpering.

*

THE CADRE behind the spectacles demands, "Tell us about the Tangs and how you have been in secret alliance with them since Chongqing." Steel Hope responds for the hundredth time.

*

LOYALTY, along with the East Is Red Branch of the Red Guards, ransacks the cluttered home of School Party Secretary Hua. Everything they toss from drawers and shelves is old, but nothing can be classified as a Four Old until, axing the floorboards, they discover a sword with chrysanthemums etched on the scabbard, several bayonets and a collection of knives. At once Loyalty accuses the former soldier of being a saboteur. The others unbuckle their belts to punish him for his crimes. Hua stabs himself through the heart.

*

THE CADRE behind the spectacles demands, "Tell us about the Tangs and how you plotted together to sabotage the rebuilding of the dikes in Wen Shui."

Steel Hope almost bursts out laughing.

*

SUMMER WISHES asks, "What else sounds like the characters for 'spear' and 'cat'?"

Amber Willows demurs. "I'm terrible at games."

"Think! Please think!"

"Well, I can't think of anything except perhaps . . . But that can't be it." Anybody using the name of the Chairman in a game is asking to be shot.

*

SUMMER WISHES sits in the front row of the People's Stadium, near the spot where, the year before, Steel Hope officiated at the opening ceremonies of the soccer championship. To her right is Loyalty. To her left are Mushroom and Amber Willows. The stands are packed with youths dressed in the discarded uniforms of People's Liberation Army soldiers, wide leather belts and red armbands, shouting, "Chairman Mao, Ten thousand years! Chairman Mao! Ten thousand years!"

How many of these mass meetings will they attend? Fifty? A hundred? Can she play the role everyone in and out of the Party—the masses, her enemies and friends, her son and husband—has cast her to play? She mustn't think or feel or be herself. That would spoil the performance, and the performance must not disappoint.

Now, the last of the warm-up acts is over. Mushroom nudges her. Oh, yes. The herbal pellet to moisten her throat and open her voice.

From stage left, enter three guards pushing and pulling the manacled villain. In the uproar that shakes the stands, like wave after wave of earth tremors, she grips her seat and monitors their progress, lamenting Steel Hope's hair and his socks. Why couldn't he have shaved himself totally bald before the Red Guards arrived to ransack their house? If he had, then that burly one wouldn't be able to pull him along by the hair. Why couldn't he have worn his thickest pair of woolen socks the night he was taken away? If he had, then his ankles wouldn't be raw. My husband, she tells him silently, you were wrong to say that nothing you did or didn't do would have made the slightest difference. Don't you see, there were things, many things, that could have made a big difference.

Waiting for her cue, she dons her mask and escapes. . . .

It is night and the moon is haloed. She wears the silk that he bought for her, that Amber Willows and Mushroom cut and stitched for her—a long, flowing tunic much too elegant to wear in bed. It is more delicate than the wings of dragonflies, the color of forsythia in bloom.

She hears a song and wonders who is singing, then blushes when she discovers that the unfamiliar tune, so gay and girlish, rises from within. She smiles at the face in the looking glass, which is framed in ivory and decorated with scenes of the House of Li at the summit of the clan's glory. She gazes at the portrait that Loyalty has painted to commemorate their wedding day. It is more than a likeness; it is a map of his heart.

There is a knock on the door. Her husband calls gently. His voice thrills her as it always has, ever since she was an urchin the age of her boy, and it calls not "Firecrackers" or "Summer Wishes" but her rightful name—"my wife."

She looks at the door and whispers, "Enter, my husband" . . . and as soon as that last word is spoken she hears the clamor of gongs, whistles and bells. She sees the Mighty Ruler of the Deep hold up his winning hand, and is flooded with bittersweet memories as abiding as the yaolus that sail the Yangzi. Suddenly she fears there will be a ghost in her bed.

The door opens. The northeast wind stings her eyes.

He cups her face in his hands and smiles. A tear escapes and he kisses it away, another and another. She falters. He lifts her in his arms and carries her across the room.

They embrace.

There are no ghosts hiding beneath the quilt to haunt her after all. There are only his lips, his hands, his tenderness, his desire, his love. . . .

". . . Chairman Mao, ten thousand years! Ten thousand years! Ten thousand years! . . ."

Another nudge. She scrambles out of her seat and onto the stage. Someone presses a bullhorn into her hands. She mustn't weep, not yet, not yet. Shaking a fist at the villain, who stands bent at the waist with his arms stretched backwards in the "airplane" position, she starts her tirade, and soon the crowd is hushed and listening.

"Yes, I know this filthy Revisionist better than anyone. I'm his wife and have known him since he was a child. His clansmen have been oppressive landlords for too many generations to count. His father owned factories where hundreds were worked to death. His mother was the daughter of a hateful capitalist who was an eager collaborator of the Japanese. Even as a boy, he . . ."

For almost an hour she is able to divert the audience, but then the actress senses that the youths are tiring of her solo, are eager to bolt from their seats and take matters into their own hands. She beckons Amber Willows, Mushroom and Loyalty to join her on stage and tell of the crimes the villain has committed against them.

But the audience is still restless.

The actress spits on the villain. The others spit too.

The audience expects more.

She strikes the first blow. The others jostle one another to get their hands on him. They slap him, in turn and together. They kick him and punch him.

The audience screams for blood.

She removes her shoe.

Mushroom circles the victim and for a moment blocks the view from the stands. Steel Hope lifts his head and steals a glance at Summer Wishes. His eyes implore her to go on. She smacks him on the ear with the soft sole of the shoe, and he is stunned. But it isn't enough. Head bowed, he addresses the heroine of the play. "Please, I beg you," he says hoarsely.

She turns the shoe to expose the heel. She holds it high. She hesitates.

"Please. You're my wife. Please."

She strikes him. This time the blow works. He bleeds. The crowd cheers.

Now she can weep, the loud, sorry tears of a woman long deceived and betrayed, at last victorious. Hot and wet, they flow easily as she picks up the bullhorn and leads the audience in a triumphant chorus.

". . . Ten thousand years . . . ten thousand years . . ."

At long last the guards remove the villain from the stage, out of the reach of the crowd. This performance is ended and she is free to go. Free, until the next performance.

*

A M B E R   W I L L O W S attends a neighborhood celebration to honor a Hero of the People, the late School Party Secretary Hua.

*

S U M M E R   W I S H E S sits in the front row of the People's Theater. It is packed with youths dressed in the discarded uniforms of People's Liberation Army soldiers, wide leather belts and red armbands. . . .

*

M U S H R O O M walks past the hospital and sees the head surgeon, the man who saved Summer Wishes' life. He wears a dunce cap and a wooden placard. He is sweeping the sidewalk. She doesn't turn away from him, nor does she lower her gaze and pretend not to see him. Instead, she nods slightly. Tears of gratitude spill from the doctor's eyes.

*

S U M M E R   W I S H E S sits in the front row of the auditorium at School Number Three. It is packed with youths. . . .

*

L O Y A L T Y marches off with a contingent of the East Is Red Branch of the Red Guards; the rest remain in the school compound to debate what to name their splinter group.

*

S U M M E R   W I S H E S sits in the front row of the People's Agricultural Commune. . . .

*

S U M M E R   W I S H E S wakes Amber Willows in the middle of the night and asks, "Is there nothing we can do to save him?"

By now Amber Willows is used to being disturbed at strange hours and, alert, scrambles to her feet. "Why are you asking me this now?"

"If only they knew. . . . If only Steel Hope wasn't Jade's son. . . ."

Amber Willows feels faint: How and what does Summer Wishes know? Jade and Stone Guardian are dead, and she's never uttered their secret to a soul. Sitting down, she manages to say, "But . . . but he is her son."

"What if I can prove that Steel Hope doesn't have a single drop of blood from that traitor of a grandfather of his or from his daughter? Wouldn't that prove he's not a traitor to the Revolution? Wouldn't they let him go?"

Amber Willows shakes her head.

"They would. I'm sure they would."

"Summer Wishes, listen to me. You mustn't say these things. You mustn't. . . ."

"Why not? They're true. They can make a difference."

Amber Willows shakes off her confusion. She must be calm. She thinks: Poor Summer Wishes, for someone who's a star and has traveled everywhere, when it comes to real life, you're like an infant who doesn't even know how to suckle. She says: "Dearest, if they were true, don't you think his wet nurse would have suspected Jade? Dearest, if they would make a difference, don't you think I'd be the first to tell?"

Summer Wishes nods. "But . . ."

"And besides, isn't Steel Hope's blood the same as that of Stone Guardian?"

She bites her lower lip to stop it from quivering and mutters, "Oh, I forgot."

*

THE CELL DOOR bangs shut. Steel Hope staggers to the cot and falls instantly asleep.

A husky voice shouts, "Sit up. Sit where we can see you."

He sits up, edges toward the foot of the bed to face the narrow slot in the door and a pair of eyes.

*

LOYALTY is stripped of his armband by Defender of Country and is thrown out of the East Is Red Branch of the Red Guards for returning home to recuperate from exhaustion instead of taking part in another roundup at the People's Theater.

*

SUMMER WISHES tosses and turns in bed. Who are these monsters who devour their own kind?

Who are they, if not people like herself?

*

LOYALTY circles the cistern where the goldfish used to swim before they were condemned as a Four Old. He punches his palm again and again out of frustration. Not one of the ten Red Guard battalions in Wen Shui will accept him.

*

STEEL HOPE sits in his gray cubicle, holding his head in his hands.

A husky voice shouts, "Are you sick?"

He shakes his head.

"Are you sure?"

"If I wanted to die, I'd have died long before today," he says, and thinks: The truth is, I don't have the courage to join my old teacher Lincoln Chen on the glorious roster of China's heroes whose death by suicide shamed an unjust Emperor.

A few minutes later, the cell door opens. It is the prison doctor. Steel Hope unbuttons his shirt.

*

THROUGHOUT THE DAY, day after day, Loyalty lies in his bed staring at the empty shelf that used to be filled with his diaries and scrapbooks, which Mushroom has burned.

*

STEEL HOPE sits in his gray cubicle and tries to name everyone who lived in East Village when he lived there. It doesn't take him long. Most people were related. He spends the rest of the week mapping out their plots of land, which were strewn about the village like the pieces of a puzzle in a box.

*

STEEL HOPE sits in his gray cubicle. He coughs.

A husky voice shouts, "Are you sick?"

He shakes his head.

"Are you sure?"

He nods.

A few minutes later, the cell door opens. It is the prison doctor. Steel Hope unbuttons his shirt.

*

SUMMER WISHES sits alone on the stairs at the People's Theater between the second- and third-floor landings. Her job is to make sure the men branded "Stinking Nines" sleeping in the rehearsal room above don't escape, but remain isolated until dawn, when they'll be trucked to Labor Reform somewhere in the countryside.

She hears a faint creaking from below. She looks down the dim stairwell and catches a glimpse of snow-white hair. She blinks and looks again. The stairs are empty, but she is certain that Han, the ticket taker, is still there. Summer Wishes covers her mouth with both hands. Suddenly her heart is racing so hard that she feels faint. She prays, Go away, please go away.

She hears the creaking again.

She can't make up her mind whether to cough or not. A cough would surely be enough to send the woman fleeing.

But what if it were her husband instead of Han's sleeping above?

But what if she shuts her lids and another Stinking Nine wakes and, seeing Han in the room, reports Summer Wishes for neglecting her revolutionary duties or, worse, for being an antirevolutionary herself?

But what if she keeps her eyes open and after tomorrow, Han's husband never comes back? What if this were her own last chance to say goodbye to Steel Hope?

She pretends to be the bravest woman in the world and, squeezing her eyes shut, snores lightly. O merciful Kwan Yin, she prays, let Han be as silent as moonlight, let her hurry in and out, and please, oh please, let everyone else be dead to the world.

*

Steel hope sits in his gray cubicle. He sighs.

A husky voice shouts, "Are you sick?"

"Don't bother with the doctor. Don't worry about me."

"Who's worried about you? Die for all I care, but not on my shift. Nobody accuses me of helping a dung worm like you escape the People's justice."

A few minutes later . . .

*

Loyalty succeeds in squeezing through the press of youths on the jam-packed train to stick his head out the window and wave.

Summer Wishes waves back. He looks so happy, the way Little Panda looked when feeding crumbs to the goldfish after school. He shouts something that is lost in the clashing cymbals and drums of the send-off band, and points to the huge red flower pinned to her blouse. It's made of paper and is awarded to mothers who have urged their children to volunteer to go and populate the borderlands.

But it was Loyalty who begged her to let him go. He said he must have this last chance to prove and improve himself. How could he do so in Wen Shui, where everyone knows his father is a Rightist and his stepfather, a Revisionist? She couldn't refuse him. He spoke the truth. She had to let him go.

*

Steel hope saunters on a narrow walk between high gray walls. He turns the corner and strains to hear the footsteps of his fellow prisoners, his fellow human beings, around the corner ahead and around the corner behind. He wonders, but will never know, if they are strangers or people he once saw every day. He gazes upward and sees a narrow strip of sky. It is gray as well.

*

LOYALTY peers out the window as the train slows to a halt. It's the last stop before the northeast frontier. The station is stacked with wooden crates resting on the frozen ground and, here and there, clusters of people with frosted features and heads cocooned by vapor. Beyond that is emptiness without a horizon. Never has he seen such a beautiful sight. Here, he can start a new life.

*

DURING THE DAY Summer Wishes pushes a wheelbarrow filled with soil at a May Seventh School in the countryside fifty lis from Wen Shui.

At night, she sits in political meetings, fighting sleep. Day and night, she is surrounded by strangers who eye her and one another, looking and probing for antirevolutionary thoughts.

In bed she's afraid to close her eyes, afraid she might talk in her sleep, afraid she might say something wrong, afraid someone in the room will hear and tomorrow accuse her of antirevolutionary dreams.

*

YEAR AFTER YEAR Steel Hope sits in the interrogation room, refusing to confess. Only once does the expression on his stone face crack, when in his fatigue he sees all his accusers at the table somehow transformed into Mountain Pine. Silently they count on their fingers as his bookmate used to do in the distant past, allowing his charge ample time to examine his actions and ample dignity to enumerate whatever wrongs he had done in the privacy of his conscience.

He hears a small voice within name the political campaigns that the Party has launched and he has furthered since Liberation: Land Reform, Suppression of Counterrevolutionaries, Three Antis, Five Antis, Elimination of Counterrevolutionaries, Collectivization, Anti-Rightist, The Great Leap Forward . . . and note the numbers condemned to imprisonment, labor camps or worse as a result—one million . . . two million . . .

*

STEEL HOPE saunters on a narrow walk between high gray walls and sees a single blade of grass pushing through the concrete. Its greenness fills him with indescribable joy. He lowers himself to his knees. He waters it with his saliva and prays for its life.

Thinking of his wife, son and friends who, by assaulting him again and again themselves, had saved Steel Hope from the mob's wrath, and worse, bestial humiliation, he lifts his gaze heavenward and silently beseeches, Bless them, bless the keepers of our humanity.

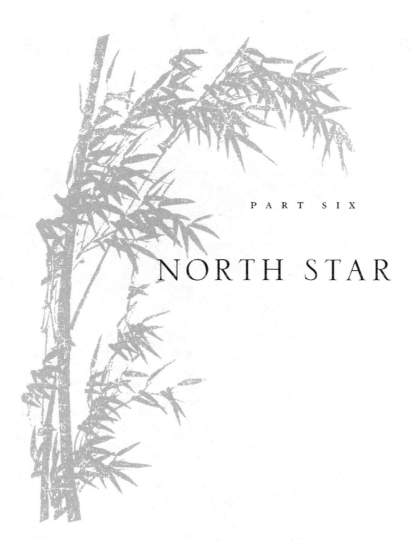

PART SIX

NORTH STAR

Spring Festival

(1971)

T H E O N L Y true happiness that Loyalty had ever known was when Papa and he lived under the same roof, but the memories from those childhood years were the ones he had worked so hard to erase. At the age of nine, the effort had made him ill. The sickness had begun as a ruse for avoiding school the morning after Mountain Pine was forced to contemplate his crimes, seated on a stool at its gate while students and teachers came and went, whispering and glaring or spitting at him. When he finally returned home, he held Little Panda and dried his tears, but never explained, and silently placed a finger against the boy's lips whenever he was about to speak. Thus Little Panda learned what he must do.

The ruse became real when, one morning, several weeks later, he saw two toothbrushes on the bathroom shelf instead of three. Papa and everything that belonged to him were gone. Having learned his lesson, Little Panda didn't ask, and no one explained.

The doctors promised to cure him if he would only tell them why he picked at his food. He never told. They would have laughed at him. How could he say that it was because a blue toothbrush was missing? By the time he finally had the strength to face returning to school, over a year had passed. The photograph of Papa that he had hidden behind the mirror in his room was flushed away; he was no longer Little Panda and the man he called Father was Steel Hope.

To despise the Enemies of the People, no matter who, was a cardinal virtue. Was this not taught at school, in the newspapers and on the radio every day? Loyalty wanted above all to be good. He was an excellent pupil and learned his lessons well—though long after hate ruled, the mere sight of a goldfish floating pale and motionless on the water could cause him to weep uncontrollably. Unable to fathom why, he redoubled his efforts; determined never to make any mistakes that would cause Loyalty to vanish too, leaving not even the sound of his name, only silence behind, he studiously examined his actions by writing them down in a diary. He also filled scrapbooks with photographs and clippings of the rising career of the actress and the activities of the County Party Secretary, because both worked late and were often out of town, but above all because he feared that a boy who could forget his father, a woman who could forget her husband, a man who could forget his oldest friend might not be able to stop themselves from forgetting others as well.

Though Mushroom was always at home to care for him, she spoke so openly about every subject but the subject of Rightists that he feared her candor might be infectious and avoided engaging her. In the same way he avoided everyone at school—the few who still acted as if he had measles and the many who offered the son of the highest Party official in Wen Shui the pick of their lunch. Defender of Country was the sole exception; his father had also disappeared, so he knew how to behave. Out of friendship, Loyalty continued to compete in Ping-Pong, because his partner would otherwise have been thrown off the team. To the extent possible, he hid behind books, but only after locking himself in the bathroom and shaking out the pages: What if some Rightist had left a note inside?

On those rare occasions when the family sat through an entire meal together, his mother would recount one happy episode after another from her latest tour, using all the magic at her command, pausing at the most improbable moments to plant a kiss on her son's cheek, or to bestow on her husband a smile that lingered so long it elicited a blush and a crooked grin, until both man and boy, bubbling over with laughter and pride, fell madly in love with Summer Wishes again. She would barely touch her plate. "I've saved so many words to tell you that they've filled me up," she would say, and regale them with another of her adventures.

When he and Steel Hope ate alone, their conversations were usually confined to Summer Wishes or her tales, a drawing he had finished or a book he was reading or what had happened at school or Ping-Pong—nothing memorable. But somehow just being with his father made Loyalty feel more at ease with the world than he felt at any other time.

Years passed, but for him nothing really changed until the outset of the Cultural Revolution, when Steel Hope, advising Loyalty, as always, to have faith in the Party, encouraged him to answer the Chairman's call by joining his classmates and becoming a Red Guard. The Great Helmsman was right. Something had gone very wrong. Society was unjust. People were unequal. So many cadres were hypocrites, urging others to serve the country selflessly while accruing privileges and power for their own ends. Only China's youth, uncorrupted and unjaded, embodied true revolutionary ideals.

Later, when the world was turning upside down, his affection and admiration for Steel Hope gave Loyalty the courage to risk all to give the County Party Secretary a chance to bid his mother farewell, but beyond that, he didn't know what to think, what to do. Were love and friendship only a prelude to betrayal? Must so many and so much be sacrificed for the greater good? What was the greater good? Whose son was he, Mother's or Mao's? Why did Steel Hope give him the map—so that he should seek Mountain Pine or stay away from him? Why did Defender of Country never answer the letter he had slipped under his door—had his offer to renew their friendship come too early or too late? Not knowing where to stand or where he stood, he decided to flee from confusion and chaos by volunteering to live among the poor peasants in the borderlands and be reborn.

Once again, his father had disappeared and he must forget.

N O W I T was the fourth Spring Festival in a row that he had pledged to stay at the Ever Bright Commune for the week-long holidays. This time, however, all his fellow volunteers had chosen to get away from any reminders of their frustrating life as farmers and reclaimers of swampland and return to their old homes in the cities. But with his mother away undergoing reform and his father jailed, how could he, even with Mushroom and Amber Willows, bear to celebrate the New Year in Wen Shui?

Alone, surrounded by the inhospitable fields that would never yield enough wheat even to feed the two hundred volunteers living in the dreary mud-brick dormitories they had built, much less produce a surplus, he took on the task of fixing the broken cultivator, without much hope. When his Spring Festival card to Defender of Country was returned unopened, he decided to push the cultivator northward in hopes of encountering someone who could take him to Small Brother, the master mechanic at the labor camps whom the peasants claimed could repair the machine. Any task, however long, hard, and futile, was better than having to spend another minute dwelling on his dark thoughts; for the effort to erase memories had grown harder and harder in the vast emptiness of the Great Northern Wilderness where Mountain Pine also lived, and more and more he wondered if death might not be preferable to a life of self-imposed forgetfulness.

He left at once to take advantage of the unseasonably mild weather. With only one road, he couldn't get lost, and along the route he would stop to draw. Food was no problem. While most comrades relied on family allowances and some stole from the peasants farming more fertile fields, who had never had any use for the volunteers and now despised them for their laziness, incompetence and immoral city ways, he was among the lucky ones who had something to trade for their needs. In exchange for his New Year's paintings of chubby boy babies and lucky carps, he had acquired enough biscuits, candies, dried fruits and boiled eggs to last the week. He packed the food in a bundle, roped it to the cultivator on top of his bedding and drawing materials and set off.

When, near dusk on the second day of his trek, he saw tacked on a tree just off the road the sign identifying Reclamation Site #9, he didn't trust his eyes. The boundless, murky-green swamp, which had swallowed three new volunteers last year, had frozen into a magnificent snow-white expanse. He decided to camp beside it for the night. Tomorrow, he would sketch the strangely shaped trees, half dead and half alive, that contrasted with the virgin snow to give the scene a poignancy that echoed the stirrings of his memory.

HE THOUGHT the sound he heard was the sound of birds at the coming of dawn, and closed his eyes. When it woke him again, he wondered if he'd been dreaming, because this time it recalled his mother's laughter. Something caused him to look toward the frozen bog, but though he could make out two people pulling a makeshift sled on which stood a third, he wasn't immediately startled by the sight, for caught between sleep and waking, his imagination was at its most vivid.

Had he not been wrapped in bedding, however, the sudden screech of wild delight he heard next would have jolted him upright. The three figures were real! Instinctively he flattened himself on the ground to avoid discovery as he waited to see what would happen next.

At first he thought the rider brandishing an imaginary whip must be a child ... then drunk or mad, for as he watched she tossed her hat high in the air and let her hair fly. It was extremely long, as long as the triple-eyed peacock feathers that only the imperial prince and the mightiest general wore on stage; as long as Summer Wishes' hair when Papa and he, standing side by side, would comb it dry. Who was this woman who dared flaunt her vanity? All other women had chopped off their hair and, since the start of the Cultural Revolution, wore it plain, at most an inch or two below the ears.

"Faster, faster!" she shouted. "I want to go faster!"

The pullers, one tall and one short, spurted ahead, but before long slowed, then stopped, doubling over.

"You can't be as tired as that already," the rider complained.

"We are ... Young Mistress," gasped a male voice. "We are."

"Then you ride and I'll pull," she cried, and, laughing and twirling with arms outstretched, as if such movements were as natural to her as honking and flapping were to a flock of geese flying south, she whirled her way toward the others. Loyalty, spellbound by such spontaneity, didn't realize until she had stopped to pick up the reins that the short man had called her "Young Mistress," a form of address that no one ever used except at Struggle Meetings, when angry citizens vented their outrage at an antirevolutionary.

Shaking their heads and waving their palms furiously, both pullers declined a ride. Only when the tall one giggled did it occur to Loyalty that this puller might be a woman, for even from a distance he was certain that she was taller even than Mushroom. As she went on to say, in a most dignified manner, "Young Mistress, be reasonable. How can we allow you to pull us? That just isn't done. Not done ...," he also realized from her accent that she was originally from the south. How in heaven's name had she ended up here?

"Well, you could take turns," the rider suggested. "First Tall Sister, and then Small Brother."

Everything about the three was so alien, so fantastic, that Loyalty didn't find it at all implausible that the short man would turn out to be the master mechanic he had come looking for; the coincidence was merely another twist to this mystifying encounter, so like those in the fateful tales Mountain Pine used to tell and Summer Wishes performed.

Suddenly the two pullers were running away from the young mistress; like children playing tag, they hooted and howled as she scrambled after one, then the other, to her left, to her right, around and around. One against two was hard work.

His stomach groaned, but he made no move to satisfy it, for now Young Mistress, flushed by her exertions, began to undress as she darted this way and that, flinging one layer of bulky outer garments after another into the air with such abandon that for a moment he thought she would strip herself naked. Some modicum of modesty, however, prevented her from shedding the layer colored scandalously red, which could only be long underwear; or was it merely exhaustion, for she collapsed on the ice just as the tall one tiptoed behind the short one, who was half her height, to hide? Loyalty almost joined their laughter. When he had to hold his shoulders to stop them from shaking with glee, he realized that it had been years since he had experienced such sensations.

The sun now sat on the horizon, and Small Brother and Tall Sister climbed to the top of a rise, from which they waved and shouted, telling Young Mistress that breakfast would be ready soon and she should put on her clothes and not be long.

For a moment, Loyalty considered trailing Small Brother home, but dismissed the idea when Young Mistress picked up the reins and pulled the sled in his direction. She also sang. Her singing hurt his ears. She danced. Her dancing was, at best, untutored. Embarrassed for her—or was it protective of her?—he peered up and down the road, though on this stretch there were probably never more than a bus or three or four trucks and a dozen carts a day, and surely during the New Year's holiday peasants on foot would be loath to leave their kangs. Even so, he sighed with relief when he saw no one else about.

In the pale gold light of early morning, the energetic sprite, unencumbered by quilted outerwear and dressed all in red, was like a leaping flame; and the longer he watched, the more he felt the warmth of its glow. Now he could see that she was about his age, and though her face wasn't what others would consider pretty, Loyalty wished that he were as bold as even the shyest of his comrades, who would have coughed or rolled up his bedding in hopes that she might take note of him. But the habit of never attracting attention to himself was too deeply ingrained, and he continued to hug the ground.

Still pulling the sled, she began to run in earnest, faster and faster. As if she weren't a stranger, but someone dear, he thrilled to see that there was nothing awkward about her movements now. If only he had unpacked his sketchbook. If only he could capture the ecstasy of a carefree soul.

Visibly panting, she stumbled several times, but continued to press ahead with the ardor of a racer running against the clock, until the sled flipped over and twisted the reins, forcing her to a standstill. After several hard yanks, the sled landed back on its runners, but then proceeded to shoot off on its own, taking the reins with it.

His heart raced: The sled was heading straight toward him.

"Come back here!" she shouted. "Come back here, this minute."

There was such authority in her voice that he half expected the sled to obey, instead of merely slowing to a stop. Even before it had done so, he could discern how beautifully someone had painted sprigs of plum blossoms on the wood; and the sight of those delicate petals, which bloomed in winter after all other flowers had died, filled him with such an overwhelming yearning and tenderness that he failed to notice how perilously close the sled was to him until a snowball aimed at the runaway splattered even closer by. Having missed her mark, the girl pouted—and won his heart.

How was it possible that he should know what had happened to his heart when he had never been tempted to befriend even one female among the seventy or so living at the commune? He had always believed that keeping one's distance from women until the age of twenty-seven, when men could legally marry, was not only what the Party vigorously taught but, despite the contrary conduct of many volunteers, natural. How was it possible . . . ?

The answer emerged in the flash of yet another memory: Little Panda had often overheard Papa whisper to Mama, as they stood beside his bed in the dark, "I loved you the instant I saw you."

Suddenly Young Mistress made a dismissive gesture, then simply turned her back and walked away from the sled. As his eyes followed her until she disappeared over the rise, he couldn't decide whether he was glad or sorry to have escaped discovery.

His stomach growled again and this time he got up. He was certain that she would be back after breakfast for her things and he would be able to watch her again and remember joy.

HE WAS wrong. Small Brother returned alone. Perhaps that was just as well, because in the absence of the spell she cast, he was able to speak and ask the master mechanic for help. Together, they pushed the broken cultivator to the workshop just outside one of the labor camps, where Small Brother fixed the machine and Loyalty made detailed drawings of the process. From beginning to end, neither uttered an unnecessary word, and yet the silence conveyed mutual respect.

It was twilight when they returned to Reclamation Site #9. In gratitude, Loyalty offered Small Brother all the candies and dried fruit he had.

Small Brother declined, as he had declined a ride on the sled, shaking his head and waving his palms furiously. "Keep the food for yourself. Instead of a gift, will you let me ask a question? You don't have to answer if you don't want to. I'll understand. . . ."

Loyalty didn't have to wait to hear the question before giving the reply. "I am the son of Mountain Pine, a Rightist," he said simply.

Small Brother nodded, then walked away across the glistening surface of the swamp.

Loyalty thought that they would never meet again. Again, he was wrong. When everyone had returned from the cities, Small Brother visited the Ever Bright Commune to choose an apprentice from among its members. The cadres in charge of the labor camps had granted the master mechanic the extraordinary privilege of selecting whom to train and how. Though everyone at the commune hoped for such an honor, and even more for the chance to quit farming and reclaiming swampland, Small Brother warned them of his stringent requirements. The apprentice must be both exceedingly quiet and a meticulous draftsman. Only Loyalty qualified.

T
HE STRANGE GIRL on the sled was called Cinders. She had
been so named by her father, a Guomindang general whose features
varied according to the latest portrait she drew of a soldier wearing a
uniform with shiny buttons. Only his expression remained the same—a
smile from the heart. With no memory of her father or a single photograph
of him, she gave the man characteristics to suit herself. Though she didn't
know whether he lived, she was nevertheless certain that with his last
breath, hers would be the name he called. She was also certain that she
knew him far better than those daughters who lived all their lives with
their fathers ever could.

During the late 1920s, he had served as a young military aide at the
Chinese Embassy in America, and it was on this tour abroad that he had
improved his English by reciting a children's tale nightly to President
Abraham Lincoln, who, seated in his massive marble chair, always listened attentively. Years later, when his daughter was born, he almost
named her Glass Slipper, after the article of apparel that led to the story's
happy ending, but his bookish wife, who normally deferred to him in all
matters, objected. "My husband," she said. "To call our daughter a shoe
is undignified." And so the baby had been named after the story's heroine
instead.

Cinders also had no memory or photograph of her mother, but a look in the mirror revealed the woman exactly. Small Brother and Tall Sister, who never addressed Cinders by name, only by the title "Young Mistress," had repeatedly told her so.

Small Brother had been her father's chauffeur, though when seated behind the wheel he could barely see over the dashboard. Less of a target that way, the general bragged. Tall Sister had been her mother's handmaiden, though from the back she looked like a man. More of a shield that way, the general boasted. Side by side, the two servants sparked peals of laughter everywhere they went, but the general—an inveterate matchmaker with all the proclivities of that hopeful profession—saw diamonds in every lump of coal and pronounced the pairing otherwise ideal. Both were capable, fearless and loyal; they had been born in the same village, each to a poor family who farmed other people's land; and each was the eighth of eight children, though he was three years older than she.

The general officiated at the wedding. He also hosted a sumptuous banquet on the occasion for everyone in their hometown, hiring scores of acrobats and magicians and a magnificent band led by an exceedingly handsome bugler to supply the music. And the merry matchmaker danced every dance.

To honor servants in such a way was unheard of. In time, however, the general's grand gesture would be repaid ten-thousandfold. For one day, in the summer of 1949, with the victorious Communist army marching south to take Shanghai, the chauffeur and the maidservant edged along the crowded platform, bobbing and weaving, to catch a glimpse of the general, his wife and baby as they made their way toward their seats on the last train heading south to Fuzhou, where there were boats sailing to safe haven and kinsmen in Taiwan. When they finally emerged at a window, the general opened it and offered Cinders to her amah for a last, farewell kiss. The two-year-old, determined to play her favorite game, thrashed and threw her arms around Small Brother's neck instead. "Horsey!" she demanded. "Horsey!"

Suddenly the locomotive lurched forward. In seconds the multitude turned into a crazed mob battling to clamber aboard through any aperture and to remain there, by any means, fair or foul. The train sped away, separating friends, lovers and families.

When weeks went by without word from the general, Small Brother traded most of his master's parting gift of a gold bar the size of a brick for fuel and a dilapidated truck, packed it full of the books the general's wife had had to abandon, and then, with the child bouncing gleefully on Tall Sister's lap, drove toward the remotest region of the Great Northern Wilderness, where a family of poor peasant origins might settle without many questions being asked.

To the few who, in the ensuing years, stumbled across the secluded three-room house in the hollow, with books stacked to the ceiling against every wall, this family of three was unlike any other. They were hospitable enough, but said barely a word except to explain that the books—their share of what had been confiscated from their landlord during land reform—were good for keeping down drafts and dust, for keeping in the cooler, night air in summer and for keeping out the winter's icy cold. The parents treated their daughter as though she were the man of the house, while the man of the house was the only one of them ever seen at market, and then rarely. The girl ate the choicest morsels, however plain the meal, wore no patches on her clothing, however coarse the material; and was never permitted to do any chores, however many there were to be done.

Small Brother landed the job fixing machines at the labor camps, after muttering a confession and making a claim. He confessed that his shy brain could only think if he was left alone. He claimed that his smart hands could repair any machine, no matter how old or modern, how neglected or abused. When his boast proved true, the cadres in charge accepted him as he was, and gave the indispensable worker, as blameless as he was small, no further thought. Thereafter, during the most intense of the political campaigns, when even those like himself, who had been born into the Reddest Classes, had to display the fierceness of their faith in the Party, inevitably an essential piece of equipment would break down and require Small Brother's undivided attention.

Never seen at market, Tall Sister was never missed. Never seen at school, Cinders was likewise never missed. From the lessons the general's wife had once taught her servant, the child learned to read and, with books to liberate her from the confines of experience, she never stopped educating herself. Out of those pages marched an endless parade of personages, from Emperors to embalmers, each with a story, which she illustrated and recounted again and again to populate their isolated realm.

While shunning the world, the small family didn't dare shut themselves off from its news, for its news signaled political campaigns. Small Brother built a radio, collected discarded newspapers and reported everything he saw or heard. The accounts didn't entice Cinders, as she grew older, to quit her seclusion, however. What did society have to offer the daughter of a Guomindang general besides its implacable hatred and scorn? And so she determined to enjoy her life and never to be lonely or bored. Didn't she have books to read and pictures to draw and Small Brother and Tall Sister to keep her company? Besides, there was no limit to her imagination, and it always served her well. She needed a father who was good, and a good father she had. But what she had never had, she wouldn't miss. For her to yearn for more would be as foolish as a fish yearning to live on land.

The first time Cinders ever saw the sketch pad, it was slipping off Small Brother's lap as he dozed in his chair, waiting for the young mistress to retire. On the cover, in fine calligraphy, was the name of the apprentice that the aging model worker had at long last chosen from among the educated youths living in the surrounding hinterlands. Inside there were diagrams of motors, but, to Cinders' surprise, nonmechanical drawings as well.

She thought the sketches admirable—gnarled pines threaded with mist, the sun easing itself down between western hills, streams meandering through the woods, goldfish swimming in a cistern, sprays of plum blossoms that looked vaguely familiar. She couldn't see a single fault. Nor could she detect any trace of erasures—any evidence of a wayward impulse, a second thought or an aspiration unfulfilled. This flawlessness troubled her. Everything she had read had taught her: a true artist dared to fail. She suspected that the apprentice didn't trust his intuition or his feelings, especially not his feelings, and therefore reflected overly long on what to do.

Still, she was intrigued, and having flipped to a drawing of the setting sun, within its borders she dashed off the back of a small figure gazing at the sky.

A week later, she spotted the pad in Small Brother's toolbox, and found that the same small figure had been transported to every drawing, except for one she hadn't seen. It pictured a plum tree in bloom and an empty bench and, cast upon the snow, a seated shadow belonging to someone who had yet to be drawn.

Cinders laughed out loud, glanced at her feet, and this time, with the utmost care, drew her scruffy black shoe; as she was about to close the pad, she decided to throw in a second seated shadow.

When, aspect by aspect, their self-portraits were completed, months had passed and they had still to meet. Nevertheless she felt a quickening that couldn't be subdued whenever she gazed at the handsome young man with furrowed brow and the sincerest eyes who sat next to her on the page, and knew this feeling was love. That she knew this did not seem strange for someone who heard the sound of the ocean that she had never been near, who smelled the perfumes that she had never worn, who felt beloved by parents who had gone away and could not be recalled. To her, art and life were all the more alluring for the mysteries that could not be explained.

The first time she saw Loyalty, he was walking beside Small Brother, who was explaining the uses for an object cupped in his hand to the first person he had ever invited home. They passed by the house on their way to the shed, where the truck that had brought the family to the wilderness rusted, and odd lengths of hemp and wire, scraps of metal and sundry other discards were kept for future use. He didn't glance up. He didn't speak. She sensed, however, that he knew that the woman pictured in their joint effort was watching him from behind the opened door.

She listened until Small Brother's voice grew faint and the hinges of the shed door creaked, then resumed reading the book she had held clutched against her heart.

At dusk, Tall Sister took a quilt and food out to the shed and Small Brother returned to the house alone. Cinders didn't ask him about the apprentice. Nor had she done so before. A young mistress didn't notice, much less inquire about, strange young men—especially one as splendid-looking as Loyalty, especially when, by his failure to acknowledge her presence behind the opened door, he had shown that he must have found the features of her self-portrait lacking. What other reason could there be? But disappointed though she was by his apparent reaction, she still loved him; indeed, being Cinders, who prized the flaw in art, she loved him even more. And since she was assured of always getting her way at home, she never doubted that someday, somehow, his love would follow.

Thus, throughout the months the apprentice learned by fixing the truck, only a stone's throw away, she read book after book, and the contents of each page were enhanced by the murmur of voices emanating from Small Brother's radio in the shed, signaling that Loyalty was near. Only once could she decipher what was being said—when he turned up the volume during the shocking announcement that the first officials from America since Liberation had visited Beijing. She wondered if this meant that other implacable enemies of the Party, like Guomindang generals, would also be visiting the capital.

She read as the apprentice and Small Brother pushed the old rusted truck out of the shed and toward the raised meadow near the swamp where, when it was frozen, she went sledding, and as it disappeared from view, she experienced a feeling of loss.

Once the vehicle was gone, and the apprentice too, she couldn't sit still—not to read or eat or speak. She felt as if everything within her was being constantly rearranged, as if she had been put together wrong. What had happened to the woman she was? The one who did as she pleased and hadn't a care in the world? But that world, she now realized, could no more last than could the snow-white surface of the swamp when winter passed. Loyalty had given her no sign and she was lost.

She walked. Day after day, she walked. She walked everywhere except in the direction of the tire tracks.

Then, one night, the full moon beckoned, and as if dragged by her defiant shadow she walked until she came upon the truck standing in the meadow, its wheels straddling a newly dug pit. It was cloaked in unearthly light and cold to the touch. She pressed herself against its frame, hoping that her feverishness would subside.

When she saw the sketch pad on the dashboard, her breathing almost stopped. Had Loyalty left it for her to find? Was it the sign? Was someday here? She prayed that it was so, and this time she would sketch herself differently—prettier, much prettier. Hoping that she had guessed correctly, she crawled into the truck. When she looked, she found the page on which she had drawn her portrait gone . . . but in its place there was a sketch of a runner pulling a sled with her long hair flying, and before she knew it, she was letting out a screech of wild delight. It was more than a sign. It radiated such joy that she, as subject and as viewer, felt it too. Clutching it to her chest, she curled up behind the wheel to keep that feeling only for herself, grateful for the itinerant cloud that now dimmed the light of the moon.

She dreamed that the inveterate matchmaker removed his coat with the shiny buttons and bestowed it upon Loyalty and then, to the music of a magnificent band led by an exceedingly handsome bugler, he and she and her mother and father and Small Brother and Tall Sister and all the people, from emperors to embalmers, who populated her world danced every dance.

When Cinders awoke, he sat alongside, gazing at her.

Her impression of him, formed when she saw his drawings for the first time, turned out to be true. Loyalty didn't trust his intuition or his feelings, especially not feelings. It didn't matter that they had already been bared by a sketch of a runner and a sled; he sat in silence and apart, reflecting overly long on what to do, and in the end, it was Cinders who reached out to him.

Hand in hand they sat dangling their feet off the back of the truck, which that day Small Brother had inspected and judged to need only fuel to run. They communed in silence—not the silence of a wall or a void, but one as lush and as alluring as a garden tended by the gods. Silence deepened the enchantment of a love that had been evoked in him by a glimpse of spontancity on the ice and in her by a drawing that took months to complete, while they both sensed that words between a man and a woman from two different worlds might turn them into strangers again.

Cupping her face, he compared its features to the ones that had haunted him since the day he wakened to the sound of laughter. They were identical, only now he could see himself in her eyes.

Until that moment she had never seen him smile, however briefly. Now he smiled from the heart. She embraced him. Then, lifting her gaze to the sky, Cinders wished that she might recall this moment in its entirety when, white-haired, she closed her eyes for the last time. She wished to remember the placement of every star that shone then in the heavens, to smell the hint of autumn in the air, to hear the grass bending with the breeze, to feel his hand in hers and the callus on the tip of his third finger that came from holding pencil and pen. . . .

Someone whispered "I love you," and for a breathless span she didn't recognize her own voice.

"Even before you knew I existed," he whispered, "I loved you. And even after I no longer exist, I shall still love you."

And for the first time, they kissed . . . each for the first time.

When the kiss finally ended, he drew from the shadows her scruffy black shoe, and once again they revealed themselves to one another, aspect by aspect.

THE LAST TIME

THE NEXT evening the lovers met again on the meadow, and after rapture was shared, they lay in the back of the truck in each other's arms. Cinders must have fallen asleep, for when she woke, Loyalty was no longer at her side but walking in circles around the vehicle. She went to join him.

Without speaking but hand in hand, they continued to circle, until after a while he stopped and peered into the distance. The silence was different now. It didn't include her. He seemed to be addressing his thoughts to the world he had come from and she had never seen, to a horde of ghosts massed there.

She let go of his hand.

He snatched her up in his arms and held on to her as tightly as if he were a drowning swimmer surfacing at last and she were the only thing keeping him from being towed to his watery grave.

She could barely breathe.

Without asking her, he announced his intention to beg her father's permission tomorrow to marry her in four years' time, when he would be twenty-seven and their marriage would be allowed, and then, before she could react, he declared his misery ended. He would join her and her parents in their isolated hollow and live in harmony. He would be done with a world that had no use for him. He laughed, a bitter, desperate laugh without mirth, then proclaimed that his prayers had been answered—he would marry her, he would marry into the Reddest Class.

Cinders stiffened. She was no peasant.

"How else can I escape?" he whispered, thinking of his father, the Rightist; his mother, undergoing re-education; his stepfather, the Revisionist. "How else can I be reborn?"

She didn't hear these words, and freeing herself at last from his embrace, she informed the brazen stranger that she hadn't agreed to marry him.

He tried to explain. She put her hands over her ears. He tried to take her in his arms again. She struggled. He held her tighter. She announced that she was the daughter of a Guomindang general.

He let go. "How can Small Brother be a Guomindang general?"

She slapped him. "He's not my father!"

She didn't see the hopelessness in his eyes as he turned away. "What kind of man are you?" she cried. And even after he had long disappeared into the darkness, she still shouted, "What kind of man are you? What kind of man is Loyalty?"

*

SMALL BROTHER TOLD the authorities that the accident must have happened when, pouring gasoline into the tank, the apprentice dropped his cigarette.

After the cadres and the police had gone, he took the sketchbook from his toolbox and, with both hands and a formal bow, offered it to Cinders. She couldn't recall seeing Small Brother and Tall Sister embrace or cry before.

The woman who had raised her said that they had meant well.

The man who had sheltered her said that it was all his doing, all his fault.

Cinders asked, "What?"

Small Brother replied, "Choosing such a careless apprentice and teaching him how to strike a match."

Cinders clutched the sketchbook against her heart and didn't open it until long after she had reached the charred clearing. Twisted steel strewn about the field in clumps was all that remained of their haven. In the July heat, the smell of burnt earth was overpowering. It made her faint. It made her sob.

Inside the sketchbook was a letter.

Cinders,

You asked, What kind of a man is Loyalty? I am a weary
runner who realizes that he can never outrun his shadow.

I was nine years old when my father suddenly
disappeared and ever since I have renounced even the
memory of the man. To you, I confess that for a long time
I did keep a photograph of him hidden behind my mirror,
and every day without fail, I would snap awake before others
stirred and study it. Without fail, I would shiver and
sweat and clutch my stomach while summoning up the
courage to look. At the picture. At my reflection. Again
and again, until I had finished comparing each and every one
of our features.

What if overnight, I had changed? What if today
people saw his nose stamped on my face? Then,
neighbors would say, Like father, like son. The teacher
would demand my red scarf back. The masses would
torment me as they had my father. The children would
shun me as they would a rabid dog. Then, for the
good of the country the Party would have no choice but
to do to me what it did to him—one day without
warning I too would disappear, and no one who had cared
for me would speak of me or mention my name, just
as they never spoke of my father or mentioned his name,
Mountain Pine.

Shhhh . . . I mustn't either.

Never could I recall which morning it was—whether
the skies were burnished or dull, whether the trees were green
or bare, whether the walkways were dry or wet with shiny
patches of rain—but I was certain that it was morning,
for once again I stood gazing into the mirror, once again
the fear gnawed at my belly. Then suddenly, between
one heartbeat and the next, a love that once flowed through
me as effortlessly as blood hardened into a loathing as
pitiless as stone, as brackish as tar.

To my relief, I grew up to look like myself.

I also grew up to believe that forgetfulness and hate

and loneliness were natural. Then I saw you sledding
and remembered joy. Then I studied your drawings and
remembered love. Then I held you and was reborn.

But where in this life can two people as different as
you and I sit side by side under a plum tree in bloom?

LOYALTY

The page with the plum tree blooming in the snow had been restored
to its original place in the book. But the man and woman seated on a bench
looked so distant that she couldn't be certain it was the couple they had
drawn. Like strangers, they stared at her blankly in the tradition of an
ancestral portrait painted by strangers to recall the features of elders whom
younger generations have never glimpsed, to remind mourners of whom
they mourn.

In fine calligraphy, beneath their shadows on the snow, was written,
"If only my father were here to call me by my rightful name."

Cinders removed her blouse and wrapped the pad in it and pinned
the packet to the ground with stones to keep it safe against a wind growing
angrier and angrier. She removed her pants and tied the cuffs and, dragging
them along, crawled in ever widening circles, searching every inch of the
charred clearing to look for him, gathering up his bones.

Throughout the night she knelt, unaware that her hands and knees
were bleeding, hugging the two bundles tight.

At dawn, she buried Loyalty in the pit in which he had stood to repair
the underbelly of the truck, and prove himself a worthy apprentice the
pit he had dug. She buried his sketchbook and his letter, to remind him of
her.

FOR WEEKS afterwards, awake or asleep, she would sit staring at the
seated shadow lying on the dirt floor, mumbling over and over the words
she had never said to him and begging his forgiveness. Had he kept
silence and never spoken, she would have remained mad forever. But he
did speak.

Three months after his death, the shadow rose from the dirt floor
and stood and gradually, aspect by aspect, emerged into a splendid Loyalty
wearing her father's coat with the shiny buttons. He whispered her name
and urged her to get well. Our child needs a mother, he said. A mother
who is strong.

She knew then that he had forgiven her and loved her as before. A father didn't entrust his children to someone whose heart was lacking. But before she could swallow her tears and reply, he knelt to touch her shoes and, smiling a smile from the heart, his likeness withdrew from this world. She knew then that the mother of his child would get well and be strong. For whatever might happen and wherever she might go, walking alongside her would always be Loyalty's shadow.

*

SMALL BROTHER and Tall Sister didn't speak of the apprentice or of her condition, but when the time came Tall Sister delivered the baby and Small Brother told her about a former prisoner from Wen Shui named Mountain Pine, who now lived in the shed by the tall birches. Small Brother didn't explain why the young mistress should have this information, or how he had ascertained it. Perhaps he had overheard the prisoners or the warden talk about the lame Rightist from the Yangzi, or had stolen into a locked file at camp to read all that was true and untrue about a prisoner named Mountain Pine. Perhaps he had spent so many months choosing an apprentice because the man he sought had to meet his exacting needs—had to be another misfit who would gladly devote himself to Cinders as they had done. Perhaps Loyalty had spent his last hours writing a note for the model worker to destroy, since such an antirevolutionary act as suicide could only be grounds for compounding the man's guilt and, had he had a son or daughter, bequeathing that guilt to the child along with his other attributes. Or perhaps, even in the wilderness, there was no escaping the cycles of history.

Wᴴᴇɴ Mountain Pine had completed his fifteen years of hard labor in the Great Northern Wilderness, he was assigned to man a first-aid station not far from his old prison camp. The warden rejoiced. He had dreaded the day when the inmate from the Yangzi, who had served as the prisoners' doctor for the past three years, wouldn't be around to ease the pain in his joints, and thanked his good fortune—though fortune had less to do with the posting than hints dropped by his wife into the proper ears.

The station stood at the edge of several agricultural communes to which educated youths from the cities, once hailed as Red Guards for their revolutionary zeal but now regarded as troublesome idlers, had been banished to "learn from the peasants" and eke out a living in the hinterlands. It had one room, partitioned by a chimney and stove. Though it was encircled by a windscreen of tall birch trees that was visible from all directions and for many lis, the site was isolated. Mountain Pine welcomed the solitude after so many years of sleeping twenty bodies to a kang.

True, he would have preferred to teach. But armed with what the monks at the Monastery of Heedless Tranquility had taught him and what he remembered of the medical books he had copied, along with the experience gained from caring for the ill and injured at the labor camp, he felt at least as qualified as the previous barefoot doctor, with his grammar-school education and six months of training.

Unlike others denied permission to return to live in their hometown, he didn't mourn his fate, for he had never changed the decision made fifteen years ago, that Mountain Pine would stay far from the Yangzi and keep harmony. In this wilderness he was free from the abiding lures and fresh sorrows of the life he had left behind, and from that torment of torments, hope. Here he would still be a servant, but one whose stern master was of his own choosing—himself. Here he would live among others irrevocably fallen from grace, with nothing to win and nothing to lose; comrades with whom he could share the moment and history and air irreverent views; brothers who had spared him a spoonful of cabbage soup when they would have strangled another for trying to steal the same from their bowl. Here he would never be short of money, for a trio of thieves at the camp, in return for his doctoring, had awarded him a map and half of their loot. Here he would be able to start writing again; nothing ambitious, perhaps a diary.

ONE LATE AFTERNOON, a month after he had shuffled out the prison gate, he and two of his old kangmates, Baldy and Maestro, lounged on the steps of the first-aid station, shelling peanuts and passing a crock of brandy. Breezes relayed the scent of stagnant pools and ripening grain. A pale moon, as slender as a filament, drifted near the horizon.

"Professor wrote another letter," Mountain Pine announced, referring to another kangmate who, unlike the three of them, could legally return to live in his hometown.

At that, all burst out laughing. A letter had landed the man in the camp and another had doubled his sentence. There was no need to mention that he had given his second epistle, advising the Premier of the inhumanity of the security forces, to the wrong mailman, a sex offender they called Gigolo who was about to be released. Unbeknownst to the obliging Gigolo, his illiterate wife never failed to ferret out his letters and have them read aloud by her cousin the Chief of Police.

They could laugh about this now. Countless tellings had recast tragedy into farce. Still, the laughter lasted too long.

"Well, go on, what did he say?" asked Maestro.

"That the moment he set foot in his hometown, he hotfooted it to the bathhouse."

"I can understand that," Baldy said. "What I *can't* understand is why the moment *you* got out, you hotfooted it here...." He paused to rap the stairs. "Now me? I hotfooted it straight to a bowl of noodles, and I can still taste those scallions and peppers and the sesame oil...."

"Oh, please..." Maestro held up a palm, ready to conduct. "Haven't we talked enough about food to last us several lifetimes—this and that dish, who made it, who ate it, how it was made, how it could be made, when and where we ate it first and last and all the times in between, what other dishes went with it, might go better with it, over and over, year after year after year? I must eat, but I absolutely refuse to say or hear another word on this subject. No more, for my sake, no more."

For a while after this tirade, each kept his own thoughts. In this company, outbursts, Mountain Pine supposed, occurred about as often as they would among brothers. It wasn't their frequency that struck him—but what triggered them. Recently he'd alarmed a patient who after swallowing a pill was about to toss out the water that remained in the glass. Before Mountain Pine knew it, he was screaming at the boy to stop, terrifying every patient in the hut and shocking himself with the urgency of his cries. Of course, he apologized immediately. Only later did he realize what had caused the fit—too many seasons of toiling under a ruthless sun without a sip.

Maestro broke the silence. "Get back to the letter."

"What?" Mountain Pine looked about. He needed brandy.

Baldy handed him the crock, but before Mountain Pine had drunk his fill, gently retrieved it. "Take it easy, my friend," he said.

Nodding, Mountain Pine returned the smile. The drink had warmed his spirits, and he recited the verse Professor had written in honor of his bath.

> Bathing is a blessed dispensation
> till that portly pope catechizes
> how sinful a capital crime
> is shucking good old plebeian grime.

Even Maestro found this barb worthy of a chuckle; that was, until Baldy stated the obvious. "How about that! Not even home yet and he shoots one arrow and hits two bull's-eyes—the Chairman *and* the envelope steamers at the post office, who, fortunately for him and you, Mountain Pine, are semiliterate and bound to miss the point. Remember—"

"Oh, please ..." Again Maestro held up a palm to put a stop to an impending diversion and again Baldy swatted it down, which, of course, again set the kangmates quarreling—safe in the knowledge that affection allowed them to indulge in bickering without consequence.

Mountain Pine cursed. "Want to hear what happened or not?"

"I'll quit when Maestro quits. Who does he think I am? The kettle-drummer he banned from his famous recording of the *1812*?"

"That man was no drummer," replied Maestro. "Even with an array of jeweled watches crawling up his arm he couldn't grasp the concept of keeping time. To him, a note, a rest or a stop were nothing but gravy stains on waste paper. Besides, he's the last person you should pity. While we were digging ditches, that shameless, sloganeering stooge managed to—"

Baldy finished the sentence for him: "—catch a helicopter ride with Madame Mao's crew straight to the top."

"Who told you?"

"No one had to tell me. It's the same everywhere. Those who could, go to jail. Those who might, get a one-way ticket to May Seventh School. Those who can't, run the country."

Maestro heaved a tremulous sigh, wistful as an arpeggio plucked on a harp, then went on to curse the bespectacled and bucktoothed Madame Mao for outlawing the music of Beethoven.

"Oh, please," mimicked Baldy, waving a palm, "let's not start that. . . ."

Mountain Pine grabbed his hand and held it down. "Professor found the noisy bathers all right, but when he removed his towel and was about to step into the water, the people froze. Every eye looked his way. He about-faced, expecting to see that some voluptuous maiden had wandered into the men's bath. There was no one, female or male. He turned back to the crowd. They were still speechless. Still staring. He wondered if they knew him. But how could they all be acquaintances? He wondered if they took him for an escapee. But their stares weren't trained at his shaved head. They were gawking at his nakedness. But why should they? All were equally naked.

"For the longest moment, he just stood—until he noticed a mirror across the way. Suddenly he was gaping too. The reflection was of no one he knew. Two eyeballs on top of a shaky pillar of bones . . ."

Wordlessly Maestro shook his head, then in one swig finished off the brandy. Baldy shrugged, opened another crock and took a long gulp before passing it on to Mountain Pine, who raised it in a silent toast to the moon, then drank and drank.

There was no reason to put into words what each knew the others were thinking. All had assumed that mirrors were forbidden in camp because glass was so fragile, so easily broken; now they realized how wrong they had been. Mirrors were hard, hard enough to shatter, with one glance, a man's image of himself.

When the second crock was empty, Maestro rose and, eyes shut, began to conduct the birches, humming the *1812* Overture, waving his arms, tossing his head, urging on the winds, leaning farther and farther forward to shush the string section until he tumbled down the steps. "Who . . . who moved my podium?" he mumbled from the mud.

It was Baldy who stumbled to the rescue, trying to push and pull the awkward heap into some semblance of a man and get him back up the stairs only to discover that he had completed the journey alone with just a shoe to show for his exertions. He blinked. He peered down at his extremities, tottered, thought better of bending over, picked up the right foot and then the left. Assured that both were shod, he grinned. "Who belongs to this? Who's got no shoe? Who?"

Until then Mountain Pine hadn't followed these proceedings. Instead he'd been attending another reunion, one that had taken place on a night when the moon was bright, and three friends, so unknowing, had stood at the entrance of a cave dug into one of the cliffs of Chongqing. "We cannot undo our separate births, but on the same day we mean to die. We cannot undo . . . undo . . ."

"Dammit, who in hell does this belong to?" Baldy hollered.

Suddenly Mountain Pine lunged for the shoe. "Give me that. It's Firecracker's." Clasping the trophy to his chest, he explained, "Amber Willows sewed it. And Young Master . . . he . . . no, no, we did . . . we, he and I, we gave it to her . . . the day she went away. . . ."

Before the befuddled others could respond, he staggered away, holding the shoe aloft and crying out like an abandoned nomad mired in sand, "Wait . . . wait for me. . . ."

MOUNTAIN PINE lay sprawled on his back, unable to remember how he had landed in a bed of tall grass until, reaching up to brush away a blade that was tickling him, his hand scattered the stars. I'm dreaming, he thought. In a blink the luminaries returned even brighter, even more numerous, to bless the evening with mystical solemnity.

Playfully he did the backstroke and marveled at how a mortal as unathletic as he might swim in an ocean of stars.

He extended his left leg into the air, then let it fall like a meteor to earth, sweeping an arc of the heavens clean. He laughed. How auspicious! What next? Up went his right hand. It was holding a shoe.

Shoe? He winced. He'd been awake, in a stupor all along. For what seemed like hours he sat immobile with his head in his hands, cursing himself for downing such an inordinate amount of brandy, fearful that even the slightest movement of an eye would transform those shimmering sparks into a firebrand and touch off the arsenal of cannons the cheap liquor had loaded and primed in his empty head.

He blinked. Miraculously no explosions followed. His skull remained intact. Eyes again closed, but on the mend at last, he removed his glasses and, with a corner of his shirt, wiped away the film. Slowly, very slowly, he tried moving his head. He felt no pain. He felt fine. Indeed, remarkably refreshed, if not positively young . . . as he had felt upon awakening after the lapping of the Yangzi against an ancient wall, the caress of balmy breezes and the warmth of the sun had conspired together to lull both the exuberant young master and the exhausted bookmate to sleep.

Glasses back in place, he saw true, and the lover of poetry rejoiced. Before him, above him, all around him billowed an ocean of fireflies. He had seen them, the singular glory of this wilderness, every spring for fifteen years, but only now as a free man, and suddenly he was an innocent again, viewing the world for the first time. If ever he had doubted, he would never doubt again that nature, and not any man, was the most ingenious, most sublime poet of all.

When, however, he finally stood to search for the birches and his way back to the aid station, the trees refused to appear. The twinkling ocean of fireflies obscured the horizon. And yet . . . he didn't believe himself lost.

From a distance came the robust cries of a baby. Oddly, he wasn't startled. Somehow the phenomenon befitted the fullness of that night. It drew him toward the source of the sound, slowly at first; then, before realizing why, he was hastening as he used to hasten when, his heart quickening with prayers and pride, barefoot, stumbling in the dark, he scrambled out of bed to offer a shoulder and promises to his son.

The cries faded into silence, but he didn't turn back. He continued to make his way through the grasslands, now increasingly marshy, until he came to the edge of a small, charred clearing with what looked like a tree stump at its center.

No, not a stump. Whatever it was, rocked. He was sure it rocked.

And it was human. He could see now, a girl with a baby. Was it a stranger or one of his patients?

He squatted. He must be still or he might frighten her. No doubt she was a desperate mother who had snuck out in the gloom to find a desolate site where—unheard and unseen and against every instinct of womanhood—she would leave her newborn in the lap of the gods. It wouldn't be the first time a luckless girl had done so. Nor would it be the last, for inevitably women not yet twenty-five and men not yet twenty-seven, working side by side, would break the law by falling in love.

And there had been rapes. . . .

The fireflies had gone.

Suddenly there was a flash. Of steel? "No!" he shouted. "Don't! Please don't . . ." He scrambled to his feet and headed toward the girl as fast as he could. But halfway across the clearing, he slowed to a hobble, no longer confident that he wasn't approaching a tree stump after all. The figure had made no move or sound.

But now, again, he heard an infant cry. Moving closer, he could make out the mother and child clearly.

"You woke her up." The voice belonged to one very assured and very young. She motioned for him to sit beside her. A silver bracelet flashed.

Speechless, he obeyed.

"Here, hold her for a while," she said, thrusting the bundled baby into his arms. Then, with effort, she stood up and began to pace awkwardly, favoring one leg. In her blue pants and jacket, she seemed for a moment like a miniature Mountain Pine.

A dream, he thought. This must be a dream.

Recalling skills that, once mastered, are never lost, he patted the baby, whispering in her tiny ear a poem by Meng Haoran, the tones and rhythms of which another armful, who also blew bubbles and clasped Mountain Pine's thumb tight, had enjoyed a quarter-century ago.

> In my bed among the woods, grieving that spring must end,
> I lifted up the curtain on a pathway of flowers,
> And a kingfisher bade me come
> To the dwelling-place of the Red Pine Genie.
> . . . What a flame for his golden crucible—
> Peach trees magical with buds!—
> And for holding boyhood in his face,
> The rosy-flowing wine of clouds!

When the infant had been still enough, long enough, for him to count each tiny lash, he looked up to find the girl dancing, her limp gone.

"I hate it when a leg goes to sleep, don't you?" she said, pointing to his.

"My leg wasn't asleep."

"Oh . . ." She leaned over and touched his graying temples, as if their chopsticks had always been set at the same table. "At your venerable age, the freezing wind often gets trapped in the bones."

"That too. But I was born with a limp."

Accepting this news in the same way he had accepted his imperfect leg, without fuss, she settled down opposite him, within easy reach, but shook her head when he offered her the child. "You're doing fine," she said.

With the glow preceding dawn, the shadows faded, allowing him to confirm that none of the girl's features warranted admiration: the eyes were too far apart; the nose had a definition that forbade indulgences, whether in her favor or not; the mouth was generous to a fault. But like the artless in a work of art, collectively they captivated. Suppressing an urge to pat her head, to assure himself that this sprite was real, he cleared his throat and asked what she was doing there.

"I come often."

He looked about; there was nothing but burnt stubble. "Why?"

She smiled a slow, bittersweet smile that pinched his heart. "It's a secret," she said, putting a finger to her lips.

HOURS LATER, upon his return, he found the aid station empty and his old kangmates gone. He smiled; almost smirked, yielding with relief to mankind's ignoble habit of husbanding what's his. There would be no questions asked about where he had spent the night.

If required, however, he could have accounted for his absence in a sentence—that he'd happened upon a girl, holding a child, with whom he had talked briefly; then, in silence, they had kept watch until the first rays of the sun opened the sky, whereupon she took the infant and left. The end.

The words were factual. Their meaning, lost. For he was certain— as certain as he was of having spent the last fifteen of his fifty-nine years in the wilderness—that somehow, from this morning on, through all the seasons to follow, the nameless girl would center his life.

CHARRED CLEARING

D<small>URING THAT SUMMER</small> and fall, Cinders came often to the station, though always late in the evening and only if Mountain Pine was alone. She never knocked or otherwise announced her arrival, preferring to sit silently with the baby in her arms until he noticed them on the steps. She never had to wait long. He looked often. They read books she brought with her, and on occasion recited poetry, but mostly they would gaze at Baby, whom she neglected to name but nurtured like an offering from the mercurial gods.

It took him over a dozen visits to piece together who she was, many more to learn about the baby. Like her, he preferred to wait; waiting wasn't hard, especially now, when he was closer to the end of life than to the beginning—that time when one's eyes glisten with fondness at memories, pleasurable or not; when fervor is foreign.

A HAUNTING SYMMETRY existed between them that was more, much more, than their love of books and their ease with solitude. He didn't know how—in a land where seasonally, according to Chairman Mao's calendar, citizens were thrown to the cadres, and cadres were thrown to the citizens; where suspicions ruled, and sundered the bond of all bonds, family—a trust like theirs, denying time and defying reason, could exist. He only knew that it did.

One evening as they were reading, Cinders, for no apparent reason, giggled. When Mountain Pine asked what amused her, she shook her head, giggling all the more. He nodded knowingly. For a young woman some words, printable and readable, weren't repeatable.

She blushed. "No, no, I'm laughing at Baby."

He nodded again. The child was a source of merriment.

"Look at her eyebrows."

"Eyebrows?"

"Don't you see, Baby hasn't any."

What's gotten into the girl? he wondered. Giddiness didn't become her. To avoid her eyes, he fixed his gaze on the tiny face peeking out from layers of flowered bunting and placed like a bouquet at the exact center of the table between them, rose-cheeked and captivating even in slumber, and saw another tiny dreamer whose dreams had yet to outgrow the powers of those who cherished her to make dreams come true, and for many a long moment he was lost . . . lost somewhere in the distant past, now formless and silent, that had been—except for the meaning with which it endowed his life—almost forgotten.

By the time he returned to the present, Cinders was once again absorbed in her book, and he was mercifully spared the further vagaries of youth.

Later that week, he opened his monthly letter from Professor to find it addressed to "The Right Honorable Hairless One," and a ditty commemorating the day he had exasperated the guard and cheered the inmates by exhibiting a countenance without eyebrows. Only then did he wonder if Cinders had giggled for a reason; if she had heard of him before that night of the fireflies. But from whom? It could only have been someone at the camp.

On her next visit, Cinders set a roll of paper on the table and announced, "For you."

"Drawings?"

She nodded.

He had started to untie the string when, in the confident voice of a young mistress, she admonished him, "Gifts are never opened in the presence of the giver."

"I'm sure that rule needn't apply to artists and their works."

Obviously pleased to be counted among artists, she nevertheless closed the subject by asking for tea.

That night, when they reached the charred field where they had met, as always he asked permission to carry the baby the rest of the way home. As always she replied, "Not yet." But walking away, he thought he heard her add, "Soon."

He posted the drawings on the wall opposite his bed and fell asleep gazing at the three portraits of Baby—alone, with Cinders and with a young man who was unknown to him. In a few bold strokes of ink, the artist had caught the innocent, the irrepressible and the melancholy likenesses of their souls.

The next day winter struck, and stayed in force, and Cinders didn't appear again until one afternoon when the snow and ice were just beginning to thaw. This time she knocked frantically. She shouted. "Come quick! Bring your box."

"The baby?"

"Yes! She's alone. Small Brother and Tall Sister went back to their village for Pure Brightness." She raced off before he could ask what had happened.

Grabbing the medical kit he kept by the door, he went after her. He did his best to keep up, but the uninterrupted days and nights of writing at his desk had stiffened his gait even more, and all the while he had to be mindful of negotiating the fog and the slush; not to hurt himself falling, not to lose sight of the runner.

At last she paused to warn him of a slick patch. At last he could shift the heavy wooden box from one shoulder to the other, and at last, having forced himself to stop panting, to swallow and take a deep breath, he could speak; but before he could ask how much farther, she was racing across the charred clearing, crying, "Hurry! Oh, please hurry!"

Then, suddenly, she was gone. Ahead he could just make out a roof.

When he finally saw the house, he nearly wept. For some unfathomable reason the dwelling had been built at the bottom of a hollow, as if to obscure it from view and, unfortunately, from the sun's rays as well. He fell again and again trudging through the deep drifts of snow before he reached it.

Somehow he managed to climb the steps. He propped himself against the jamb of the opened door, to ease the exhaustion that was blinding him. He heard a frantic fluttering, so frantic that he feared it might be his lungs and heart giving out. His legs were collapsing under him, but he mustn't stop. He must go to the baby.

Recovering somewhat, he realized that he wasn't responsible for the alarming sound. It was the wind riffling the pages of a pile of books.

He got to his feet and pushed the door shut.

"Here! In here!"

He dragged the medicine box into the next room and found Cinders crouched in a corner, shaking uncontrollably.

"I can't . . . I'm afraid to look." She pointed to a large basket hung from pulleys in the rafters, high off the floor, where wolves couldn't reach. "You bring her down."

He untied the rope from its hook and lowered the basket, but even before it had reached the ground he saw a tiny fist move and immediately assured Cinders that the baby was alive. Cinders started toward them. He stepped in front of the basket. He didn't want the mother to see how swelling and red welts had disfigured the baby's face, though, from her breathing, he could tell that any real danger had passed.

"Baby will be fine . . ." he said, holding Cinders by the shoulders. "I promise you."

Every emotion from elation to dejection was suddenly stamped on her face. "Are you sure? How can you be sure?"

"As sure as you and I are standing here."

"Let me see for myself," she said, and tried unsuccessfully to go around him.

"No, not yet."

"Can't I hold her just for a minute?"

He walked her to the door. "The baby will be fine, but I've got work to do."

"Let me help."

"In a little while. Stay in the other room until I call."

She started to object, then nodded.

As he prepared the salve for what were spider bites, Cinders' voice filtered through the closed door. She must be praying, he thought.

It wasn't until he'd finished dressing the wounds that he realized for the first time how much Baby had grown, and truly heard Cinders' words: "Make her well. She's all that I have. Make her well. She's all that you have. . . ."

For months after that night, Mountain Pine wrote only a few lines in his diary.

*

Cinders was here again. The baby too. I let them sit.

•

I mourn. The blackness I feel I've never felt before. Like a
huge sullen beast it crouches at the outer portal of my
consciousness to maul me the instant I wake.
    I sit. I stare. I reek of black bile.
    I pray for unending sleep.

•

I am locked in a lead box only I can see. It is home.

•

If only she would read, instead of jabbering on and on about
the same old events.

•

To get away from them, I spent the week at the camp. This
time the warden hadn't sent for me.

•

I went looking for Maestro. He has gone off somewhere.

•

Cinders never meant to tell me as she did, in one emotional
outpouring. She intended to scatter allusions bit by bit,
now and then, here and there; and so ease the blow and allow
enough time to pass for the baby to appropriate my heart.
Only someone whose namesake lives in a foreign fairy tale
could think that all I would need was time.

•

My son is dead. He died in a charred clearing, leaving his
mother; Steel Hope, who loved him like a father; Cinders
and an unborn child.
    How can I explain that I mourn myself?

GRACE

(1979)

THROUGHOUT the night the dogs whined, signaling the advent of a severe snowstorm. But when at first light the skies were clear, Steel Hope and Summer Wishes dismissed warnings and hollow offers of help from their hosts and left commune headquarters on foot, alone. The locals wondered why the rush—there was no grave to sweep. Perhaps they had come to see the plum tree, which peasants claimed had been planted in the charred meadow by the ghost of the dead apprentice, and the meadow itself, which, once burned, had never greened again. But would people who had waited this long to see these wonders risk being caught in a storm?

The answer lay in an envelope addressed to the Vice-Minister of Administration, the Ministry of Culture, Beijing. When Steel Hope opened it, he had found no letter; only a homemade map of the area with, at its center, a drawing of a plum tree marked by the word "Loyalty." One look at the calligraphy told him who had sent it. As for where Mountain Pine could be found—there would have been no other reason to include the first-aid station. The only question was why, after more than two decades, he and Summer Wishes were being summoned.

They walked east toward the charred meadow, and didn't head for the birches until it was lunchtime and even the most outrageous snoops would have turned back. Now the flurries came, and gusts soon followed. When the trees had faded into the vast whiteness, Summer Wishes— who seldom left the apartment anymore, yet had voiced no misgivings about making such a long journey—became alarmed. "Are you sure we're going in the right direction?"

"After the tunnels, I could find due north sleepwalking."

"But that was . . ." She frowned in concentration, then sighed. "Numbers buzz like hornets in my head. Tell me how long ago."

"Thirty-five years."

She groaned. "Ai ya, we're lost."

"We're not," he said, patting the arm that she had threaded through his as tightly as a sailor ties a knot. "I went over every inch of those tunnels in my head more times than I can count while I was in—Oow! That hurts."

She relaxed her fingers so her nails stopped digging into his hand, but he could feel the tension in her body. "Must you talk about . . . that?" she hissed. At nearly sixty, she was more superstitious than ever, and he, who had spent ten years in solitary because of ideological crimes defined by words alone, could do little to disabuse her of the notion that certain words, if uttered, possessed the power to inflict their substance on the careless. He knew that Summer Wishes was continually adding words to her list but couldn't possibly name them since fear forbade her to speak them. He also knew that these subjects, by their absence from their conversations, stood between them like a vacuum, slowly sucking the vitals out of their marriage. Though love as an emotion was not at risk, it was no longer spontaneous and unalloyed, but fused with impatience and pity on his part, and on hers, desperation and need.

When they first moved to Beijing, he couldn't understand why she refused absolutely to ride in the official car or take the bus, why he had to spend the next year putting up with and constantly apologizing for her tardiness. It was only after she suddenly sold her bicycle and left the apartment less and less often that he and Mushroom determined the source of Summer Wishes' fears. They heard neighbors talk of seeing a cyclist crash into the gates of their compound around the time she sold the bike. Comrade Xu even remarked that Summer Wishes had fled the fatal scene. Yet she had never mentioned the incident, and when they asked her why, upon hearing the word "accident," she immediately left the room. At last they understood her bizarre behavior. The gods, who had never meant Summer Wishes to enjoy her stolen life, had arranged for the Jeep accident, and then, when Steel Hope didn't die, Loyalty's accident. In her mind, the gods were forever watching, waiting to catch her or her loved ones unaware, waiting to exact their revenge, waiting to instigate an accident.

Now he felt her nails again. This time she was gently brushing the snow from his face.

"Steel Hope, what's wrong? Are you sure we're not lost?"

"No, dearest. We can't go wrong heading north."

She nodded, and as they continued on their way, he thought how much harder his decade of solitary confinement had been for her. In fact, in the two years since his release, he had sometimes found himself longing for his old cell, where there were never any choices, and thus no decisions to be made. Vice-Minister of Administration indeed. More like Vice-Minister of Frustration, serving at once both heaven and hell. After the death of Mao and the subsequent jailing of Madame Mao and her Gang, policies were hopelessly muddled as factions within the Party competed for power and the succession problem remained unresolved.

She stopped in her tracks. "Someone's out there," she whispered. "Someone's watching us."

This time it wasn't her imagination. Through the swirling curtain of snow he could make out something in the distance, but not what or whom or whether it was coming toward them or moving away, until a female voice called out. Summer Wishes stiffened, then scooted behind him and, in a quivering voice, said, "Beijing has sent someone to spy on us. All the locals we've met were men."

He started to say this was impossible, then had second thoughts. For ten years he had been able to identify his opponents by the way their shoes echoed in the concrete corridors. Since then, they had come wearing masks as changeable and confounding as the political weather.

Summer Wishes whimpered. "This can't be happening now. We're almost there and we have to turn back."

The hell we do! he thought, suddenly disgusted with the infectious timidity that he had been able to bar from his cell but that now permeated the country. "Let's go and find out who's there," he said.

She pulled him back. In her eyes, fear. It was always there, though usually no more than a faint glimmer. Now it flashed wildly. He tried to calm her, describing once more all the steps he had taken to request permission and obtain the letter, complete with official stamps, stating that he might leave Beijing for the Great Northern Wilderness to visit the place where their son had lost his life. "No one can find fault. I've done nothing wrong."

"What wrong did you do before?" She was trembling.

He told her what he had told himself. "Before is before. Everything's different now. The Party's admitted its mistakes. The entire Politburo was at the Great Hall of the People when Lincoln Chen was memorialized last month. I've been reinstated. And not only that, transferred to Beijing and promoted." What he didn't tell her was how often he wondered whether in conferring these honors, the Party had done him a favor.

She smiled wanly, then, cupping her hands to his ear, whispered, "Liu Shaoqi and Lin Biao got promoted too. Both were second only to you-know-who"—she paused, pointing to her chin to indicate the spot where the late Chairman Mao had had a mole—"and both are"—again she paused—"no longer with us."

For a second he didn't know which irritated him more—the way his wife talked or the way his Party worked. Neither irritation, he decided, was as great as his irritation at himself for being irritated with Summer Wishes. Who didn't shrink from contemplating what could happen to him if Liu, second only to Mao in power before the Cultural Revolution, could choke to death on his own vomit in jail and Lin, second only to Mao in power during the Cultural Revolution, could be shot down with his plane—and in both instances few had known what happened until years later?

"It'll be all right," he said, embracing her. "We're together."

Out of nowhere appeared a stranger, a woman. As if surprised by a big dog, they stared at her—not moving, not making a sound, alert, wary. It was Steel Hope who recovered first, asking if the comrade could point them toward the plum tree in the barren meadow.

The woman bowed slightly. "Please follow me. The storm is going to get worse." When Summer Wishes refused to budge, she added, "We've been expecting you—we've been expecting his mother." Before they could react, she had turned her back to lead the way. Her pace was swift. Arm in arm, they hurried after her.

By the time the windscreen of birches emerged from the whiteness, they were less than fifty steps from the first-aid station. Summer Wishes, panting hard, released her hold on Steel Hope for the first time since they had started out. "You go ahead."

"Catch your breath. I'll wait."

She shook her head. "What can I say in front of that woman? Please go and send him out to me."

He hesitated. "Will you be all right?"

In a proud voice, she declared, "I'm not afraid of the weather."

She removed her plastic cape and scarf. She dusted off the snow from her clothes and scraped the mud from her shoes. She smoothed her hair. It was short. Mushroom had wept while cutting it to conform to the accepted style, straight across the nape, barely below the ears; but at the start of the Cultural Revolution, Summer Wishes hadn't cared. Now she tugged at the ends, coarsened and white, harder and harder; welcoming the hurt, for she couldn't bear the thought that Mountain Pine wouldn't be seeing the wife he remembered, just another old woman in a dark blue padded jacket and pants, no different from anyone else.

It was true what people said, that the sun ages. Unlike Steel Hope, she had spent most of the years of their separation outdoors, filling, pushing and emptying wheelbarrows of dirt, afraid of wearing a hat or washing herself clean and being branded a political laggard who clings to vain, decadent ideas. Though Steel Hope had claimed upon homecoming that he had nearly forgotten how to speak, she knew the real reason for his silences was the shock of seeing her so changed by the years. She felt the difference all the more keenly because, except for white hair and a leanness that was new, he looked much the same. Tricking his eyes with dye, powder and rouge would have been easy, but how could she face the neighbors, who would accuse her of spreading bourgeois pollution?

Darkness must have fallen within the span of time it took Steel Hope and the woman to reach the house, for the light that shone as the door opened and closed hurt her eyes. Waiting for it to open again, for Mountain Pine to appear, she stood as still as she could in the storm and, with the customary slow and evenly timed deep breaths, tried to summon the actress. But the actress, long retired, refused to obey, while over and over the merciless wind seemed to wail, "Just another old woman, no different . . ."

How could she bear to see that look of shock again, this time on Mountain Pine's face? The pelting snow stung like sand. She couldn't stop shivering. Again she tugged at her hair.

Then, suddenly, Mountain Pine was hurrying toward her, one hand holding a lantern high. As he came closer, she saw that on his face there was a huge smile. She prayed that it wouldn't vanish when her own was revealed.

"Oh, Summer Wishes," he said. "You're as beautiful as ever."

Her knees gave way and she kowtowed.

*

NEITHER COULD recall what happened after that or what was said or even if they spoke at all, but Mountain Pine did eventually write that by the time they entered the house, Loyalty's parents had discovered that only together could a father and mother ever properly mourn the death of their child, only together could a husband and wife somehow find the grace to forgive themselves for not holding tighter to their son, for living on.

I N   H I S   C E L L , with only *The People's Daily* and the collected works of Mao to read, Steel Hope had staged the reunion of the sworn brothers of the Middle Heart, however unlikely, countless times. And in as many ways he had varied the scene. But never once had he dreamed that they would be spending that initial hour as if it were any hour—cheerfully chatting about the vagaries of the train trip, their health and the weather.

Unthinkable too—for even now, more than two years after the Cultural Revolution had officially ended, for reasons noble and ignoble, the closest of relatives still took the precaution of dodging one another—that the presence of strangers didn't inhibit them. As it happened, the woman who had led them to the birches, and her young daughter, who had gazed at Summer Wishes with the awe of one seeing at last the moon that others had nightly described, hadn't been introduced, but had busied themselves in the kitchen just as Amber Willows used to do for welcomed guests at his father's house. At their apartment in Beijing, only a few lis from the political epicenter, hospitality, like most of life's pleasures, had been another fatality of mass campaigns.

Perhaps it was the storm that made the difference. He had never pictured a backdrop of snowdrifts, or winds howling incessantly, or, for that matter, a setting where books rose to the rafters like brick walls. But even if he had, nothing would have given him the audacity to imbue the players with the extravagant feeling which no word could describe but which they so obviously shared. It recalled those lazy summer afternoons when a young master, his bookmate and a gravekeeper's son, with folded arms pillowing their heads, reclined on the banks of the Yangzi gazing at the gulls in the sky; only now the three friends were the ones defying the powerful forces arrayed against them—wheeling and idling, wings spread wide.

Even as they sat shoeless around a brazier warming fingers and toes, sipping beer, he wondered how it was possible. How was it possible for them to feel so utterly indifferent to the world, when it was the world that had conspired to part them and keep them apart? There were no bashful silences, only artless familiarity. They didn't invoke the past. They didn't address the future. As carefree as motes loitering in the rays of a clement sun, they luxuriated in the moment, certain that everything would be revealed—but leisurely. Time, for them, stopped.

"To reunion!"

"To this day!"

"To us!"

Mountain Pine was about to open another bottle when the woman peered around the corner and shouted, even more boisterously than the toasters, "To the table!"

Following her directive, they created giddy havoc—colliding with one another moving chairs, clearing the table, fetching the chopsticks and spoons and bowls and cups and the myriad fixings for a holiday hot pot.

When, at last, all four were ensconced in their chairs eating, mixing condiments, selecting paper-thin slices of raw lamb or dunking them in the bubbling soup simmering on the charcoal burner set in the middle of the table, Mountain Pine said, "I think there couldn't be a more propitious moment than this to present to you Cinders, my wife. Tomorrow, you'll meet our daughter, who's gone to bed."

Steel Hope was stunned speechless, but a smiling Summer Wishes reached out a hand to caress the woman's cheek. "The minute I stepped into the house I knew that you three were a family," she said.

He didn't believe her. Suspecting collusion, he shot a glance at Mountain Pine, who immediately threw up his hands in mock surrender. "Don't look at me. I told her when I told you, no sooner."

Turning to Summer Wishes, Steel Hope asked, "How did you know?"

She shrugged. "Oh, I can't explain it. I just did."

He didn't know why he was upset or with whom. "That's irrational. Think!" As soon as the words were out, he regretted them, and the irritation in his voice.

Accustomed to his ways, Summer Wishes nodded absently, then, cupping her chin, peered upwards as if the answer were secreted in the fragrant vapors rising from the soup. "Well, let's see . . . yes, I suppose it was because Mountain Pine didn't introduce us."

"And what's unusual about that when saying 'thank you' and 'please' are considered hypocritical nonsense from the feudal past?"

"But *he* wouldn't think that." She looked at Mountain Pine. "You were just waiting for the right moment, weren't you?"

When he rewarded her with a slow smile, Steel Hope saw an intimacy that could only be between a man and a woman whose absence each felt when they were not yet parted and whose presence each felt whenever they were apart. Now, for the first time in a long time, he saw the Summer Wishes whom he had visited in solitary, the exquisite apparition whose mere entrance had once banished all others from the stage. He felt like an intruder.

To occupy himself, he focused his attention on extracting morsels lost in the bottom of the pot, while complimenting Cinders on the delicious meal.

Cinders laughed, an irreverent, appealing laugh. "That's because you're famished!"

"No, no, I mean it. Sincerely."

"Aha!" Cinders asserted, wagging a finger. "Then *you* must be the one sporting the immaculate sash."

He hesitated, searching for a riposte equal to her allusion to what the Sage had once said of a honey-tongued man. "So my reputation, I see, has preceded me."

"It has?"

"It must have. Otherwise, how would you know what I do at the Ministry?" He paused, enjoying her puzzlement. " 'Not one damn thing but talk, talk, talk, talk—' "

" '—to guests and visitors at court.' "

When Cinders jumped in to finish the quote, he laughed, feeling a surge of happiness for his old friend. Not only was his wife amusing and assured, young and comely, she was lettered as well.

Tapping his chopsticks against a bowl, Mountain Pine asked, "What's the laughter all about?" and Summer Wishes chimed in, "Please, *don't* leave me out."

Even in private, much less in company, Steel Hope despaired of explaining anything remotely literary to Summer Wishes, and, with hopes of closing the subject, he declared, "Under the influence of my esteemed bookmate, Cinders and I decided to brush up on the *Analects* by swapping quotes from Book Five."

Again Cinders jumped in. "But we stumbled so badly that we had to laugh. And, come to think of it, the most appropriate saying for this occasion is from Book One. Therefore I'll begin again with another quote. . . ." She paused to raise her glass to her husband's former wife. "And this time, Summer Wishes will complete it."

Summer Wishes tugged at her hair, pleading, "No, no. I've changed my mind. I can't, really."

Cinders ignored these protestations. "Get ready. Here I go—'Friends from far quarters—' "

Without missing a beat and with jubilant conceit, Summer Wishes crowed, " '—is that not a delight?' "

Steel Hope looked at Mountain Pine and shook his head in wonderment, thinking, Your Cinders is a diplomat from heaven. Only someone of that caliber would have chosen a quote everyone would know.

Mountain Pine, responding to his silent comment, shook his head too, then said, "This calls for a toast. To the two luckiest husbands in all of China."

As the men reached for their beer, Summer Wishes unfurled her napkin and deployed it to execute the intricate movements of the long, flowing sleeves that proper maidens of bygone days once used to hide their smiling lips, even as they highlighted the joy in their eyes. "Oh, Mountain Pine," she said, "you've taught your new pupil so very, very well."

Again he threw up his hands. "I wouldn't presume to teach Cinders. All those weighty volumes belong to her, not me."

Suddenly the actress was out of her chair and, with a graceful flourish, dipped a knee in obeisance before the lady scholar, igniting laughter and applause.

When finally the merriment had subsided, Steel Hope thought the moment for unraveling the past had arrived, and to begin, he asked Cinders to recount the story of her library and her life.

WHILE CINDERS was describing how Small Brother had always managed to be absent for Struggle Meetings at his work unit, Mountain

Pine cleared the table. He had to avoid sitting across from Summer Wishes for the remainder of Cinders' tale. What if she were to catch a look of apprehension on his face? A jiggling of his foot? A breath held too long? Any such sign would alert her to something amiss.

Over and over he washed the same bowl, ignoring the numbness from soaking his hands in the bucket of half-melted snow. He couldn't stop worrying about Summer Wishes' leaps of intuition. He and Cinders must be careful not to reveal what she mustn't know. How vulnerable she had looked in the snow, as vulnerable as a kite in a gale tethered by the slenderest of strings.

Steel Hope didn't worry him. He'd know better than to voice any misgivings about Cinders' story in front of Summer Wishes. He'd realize that whatever the deception, Mountain Pine's sole motive had been to spare her. Besides, when it truly mattered—indeed, when an occasion called for the impossible—Steel Hope had always been able to master his emotions in front of her. What better proof than the way, upon his return from the "dead," he had disguised his yearning and his pain so completely that she believed he no longer cared? And through all the years Summer Wishes had been married by default to his best friend, Steel Hope had never once removed that intolerable stone mask.

Mountain Pine had no such skills. Earlier, if he hadn't tapped his chopsticks and she had looked into his eyes a second longer, she would have learned the truth: that Mountain Pine had never loved any woman but Summer Wishes; that the bond between him and Cinders, however strong, was one of elder and child, and they were married only in name.

Innocently she'd have asked why, and all would have been lost.

He was stacking the dishes when Cinders reached the topic of how she and Mountain Pine had met, and he stopped to flatten himself against the dividing wall and listen.

". . . Small Brother didn't trust the young men who were sent to settle the wilderness to stay in the wilderness. He claimed that the minute it was allowed, every one of them, even the most idealistic, would drop everything and fly back to the cities. They would have seen how unyielding the land is and how unsuited they were to be peasants.

"As for the locals, Small Brother didn't think them suitable. They could barely read or write. Mountain Pine was much older, of course, but Small Brother had faith in Rightists. They appreciate the benefits of solitude and can be counted upon."

Good girl, Mountain Pine thought. You're doing beautifully.

"... The first time Mountain Pine came to call, he practically did a dragon dance at the sight of all those books. Tall Sister saw a man more than twice my age with a bad leg. I saw a kindred soul who'd be a good husband to me. I wasn't wrong."

Steel Hope asked when they had married.

"Right away."

"Just like that?"

Cinders' laugh came on cue, but it didn't sound practiced, and she added with just the proper pinch of irony, "You high-ups in the Party should know that neither of us enjoyed a plethora of choices, at least not in this life. Seriously, I wanted a child badly and—"

Take care, Mountain Pine urged her silently. The minefields are ahead.

" —at his age it was best not to wait. He had missed seeing Little Panda grow into a man. He wanted a second chance.

"Of course no one had any idea then that the apprentice Small Brother had chosen, and I had never met, was, in fact, his Little Panda. And by the time Small Brother had somehow pieced together the connection, Loyalty was already ... it was too late."

There was silence.

Cinders, keep talking, Mountain Pine wanted to beg. Don't give her a moment to think or wonder. Go on! Go on!

But she said no more, and he was about to risk returning to the table when Steel Hope asked, "What happened to Small Brother and Tall Sister?" His voice sounded strained.

This time Cinders told the truth.

"When our baby turned two, Small Brother informed me that his work was done. I thought he was talking about his latest apprentice, whose training was almost completed. I didn't realize he was talking about me. That night, after eating his favorite meal of pork and steamed buns, he died in his sleep.

"Not long afterwards, Tall Sister became ill. When Mountain Pine couldn't find anything wrong, she pointed to her spleen, saying it was angry at those in the other world who laughed and measured her husband's worth by his size.

"She told me not to cry ... I had someone to care for me and I had someone to care for ... and Small Brother was waiting for her spirit to join him in the nether lands so that their wrists might be tied together with a red string. Only if they were tied would they be assured of finding each other again in the next incarnation. United, she said, they could withstand every trial and hold their heads high no matter what, no matter how others might sneer.

"Then Tall Sister smoothed my hair and tucked it behind my ears just as she used to do when I was small and she taught me to read, and when every strand was in place she went to join her husband. . . ."

As Cinders' voice trailed off, Mountain Pine stole into the back room that grateful patients, his old kangmates and Small Brother had helped him build, the room where Loyalty's daughter slept and the women would all sleep that night. He had to avoid the inevitable. Inevitably Steel Hope would ask Cinders what she knew about the accident. And inevitably tears would flow.

"The accident? I wasn't there . . ." said Cinders, pausing to drink some tea.

O merciful Kwan Yin, prayed Summer Wishes, don't let me hear a word about the accident. It was the same prayer she had prayed ever since she learned that her son was gone. What good were details? They wouldn't bring him back. They would only fuel her raging nightmares.

FROM THE MOMENT Summer Wishes learned that her son was gone, she thought, Once again the gods have exacted retribution. She grew thinner and thinner. What if her heavenly accounts were still not settled? What if every day she lived still belonged rightfully to someone else, someone to whom she belonged—Steel Hope? What if, like her mother, she also went mad?

To hold on to sanity, she could only think to pretend. But there was no Firecrackers to put on *her* son's clothing and take his place. She was alone, pushing wheelbarrows far from the Yangzi, living among strangers who reported her every move. If she pretended Loyalty was beside her, they would lock her away as they had locked away her husband.

What else, then, could she pretend? Summer Wishes could pretend that she knew for a fact that her son hadn't suffered, but had crossed instantly to where her father and mother and twin brother waited to make him a home. What other solace was there for a mother who had lost her only child? She clung to her ignorance of the facts. She refused to visit the commune where her son had worked. What if someone who had been present when the accident occurred told a different story?

But she owed Mountain Pine debts she could never repay, and so, when his map came, she had had no choice but to travel to this vast, empty land where Loyalty had labored, perhaps, like his mother, alone.

And now that Steel Hope and she were here, sitting in the secluded aid station, protected by the storm from the intrusion of strangers, how could he not ask about the accident? How could Cinders not think a mother would want to know? She knew of no way to stop them from talking. . . .

"No, I wasn't there," Cinders said again. "No one was. But Small Brother told me that, from what he saw at the site and his knowledge of machinery, it could only have happened instantaneously, and therefore the apprentice did not suffer at all."

Summer Wishes almost cried out, O Kwan Yin, you are merciful. Suddenly she felt weightless; all the years and burdens, the strictures and the pretenses, had vanished like magic. Her spirits lifted as effortlessly as a kite on a day when breezes off the Yangzi collude with children at play.

Soaring above the clouds, she barely heard Steel Hope ask if the authorities had held an investigation.

"They came. They said accidents happen. That's all."

"That's all?"

Summer Wishes put a palm over his lips. "Please, no more questions," she begged. "My son is gone. Nothing will bring him back."

When Cinders made a move to leave the table, Summer Wishes stopped her by taking her hand and holding it to her heart. "How can I ever thank you for your gift? No one has ever given me anything as precious. I'll always be grateful. From this day on, you'll be in my prayers."

Cinders' eyes shifted between Steel Hope and her. "I don't understand. I've given you no gift. I've done nothing to deserve such gratitude."

"But you have. You've answered the one question that I have desperately avoided asking, the same question whose answer I desperately needed to know; but you must . . ." She stopped in mid-sentence, sifting for the thought she had somehow lost, and then, when she had found it again, the words to express it were scattered—swept away by others from long ago.

"But only if . . . no, not if . . . I can't . . . I would go mad. . . . And then, don't you see, they'd cage me up like the performing bear in the act that followed ours, and then . . . and then I'd be even worse than the lowest of the low."

She was choking. She couldn't stop the tears. She started to tremble.

She remembered the perversity of the gods, who relished toying with mere mortals. She recalled women she knew who had survived the Cultural Revolution intact, only to break when it was over and they heard good news. One who had shouldered all the responsibilities for six nieces and nephews while their parents were undergoing rehabilitation, and when they finally returned began snatching children off the streets and shouting slogans at them from the Little Red Book, the same slogans she had ceaselessly drilled into her charges like incantations, to save their souls. One who had kept her son's room exactly as it was on the night he was taken away, with his glasses still in the open book and the left shoe that he hadn't had time to put on under the bed; and when the son returned as suddenly without his sight and without a left foot because his diabetes had gone untreated by physicians fearing political contamination, she had hurled everything in the room out the window, including herself. One who had pretended . . .

When Cinders tried to ease her hand away, Summer Wishes gripped it harder, so hard that she knew she was causing Cinders pain, but there was nothing she could do except stare at her own fingers, which before her eyes were growing fur and claws.

"Stop that! Stop it now!"

The urgency in Steel Hope's voice made her hand reappear, and when she looked up to see tears in his eyes she was moved to reassure him. "My husband, you mustn't be alarmed. I'm fine. Really, I'm fine. I just have to tell Cinders something more. . . ."

Suddenly Cinders' hand burned like coals and Summer Wishes let go and crouched in a corner of her seat. She tugged at the ends of her hair. She stared into the mid-distance, then turned to fix her gaze once more on Cinders, but when she spoke again it was in the softest of whispers, as if she were addressing herself.

"No! Mustn't be stupid. How could I expect you to understand? That would be impossible. You've never seen him smile. You've never held him in your arms. You've never heard him tell you that he needed and loved you.

"Only someone who prayed day after day, night after night that she be haunted by him forever rather than be forever without him could understand how much it means to learn that Loyalty never suffered . . . never suffered. . . . Only someone like that could understand."

She stopped speaking, and the silence around the table was so thronged with unspoken thoughts—hers and Steel Hope's and Cinders'— that it lasted an endless while.

Suddenly Summer Wishes collapsed to the floor and, seizing Cinders by her feet, wailed, "O Kwan Yin, you are merciful, you have answered all my prayers. My son did not suffer the worst agony of all—the agony of knowing that he would be leaving everyone and everything and all he was, with his memories of happiness and unhappiness, forever. O Kwan Yin . . . thank you for sparing my son the worst agony of all, the agony of knowing that he would soon, so very soon, be leaving the whole of the world behind and never ever coming back."

I T WAS NOT yet five when Steel Hope awoke, thinking of
the two women. Summer Wishes had recovered momentarily from her
delirium and, except for asking Mountain Pine to prepare the same herbal
brew that used to help her sleep after performances, had chatted as if
nothing untoward had happened or was happening. Cinders, on the other
hand, had sat silent and taut, staring at her shoes like someone who
feared that, unattended, they would disappear. Steel Hope had followed
Mountain Pine's lead, leaving Cinders undisturbed, while contributing
his share to the appearance of normalcy.

He couldn't remember what was said, but it had crossed his mind
that the determination fixed on everyone's face was the same; and that
it was the same as the expression on the face of Stone Guardian in his
recurring nightmares; on the faces of peasant women tiptoeing across a
field of pumpkins; on the face of Loyalty berating the County Party
Secretary; on his own face, he was sure, as he affixed his thumbprint next
to every sentence on every page of every one of the countless statements
he had written for the prison authorities about every facet of his life since
before he was born.

Finally, Cinders had stirred when Summer Wishes announced that
she was ready for bed. Waiting until the door to the back room was

closed, he had asked Mountain Pine if Cinders was all right. Mountain Pine nodded; then, in turn, asked the same question about Summer Wishes.

He, too, had nodded. Then, feeling the need to reassure himself, he had gone on to explain how she was just tired from the trip and the long walk in the snow, and how, under the circumstances, getting a bit overexcited must be expected. "She'll be fine after a good night's rest."

"Yes," said Mountain Pine. "Let's all get a good night's rest."

When Mountain Pine began removing books from the wall to erect a makeshift sleeping platform, Steel Hope had done the same.

Now, waiting in the dark for Mountain Pine to wake, he was impatient for the truth. A timely whisper made him wonder if his old bookmate still had the knack of reading his mind, or was it that former prison inmates, however long since their release, still regulated their lives by prison clocks?

"Steel Hope, are you awake?"

"Yes. But I feel as if I've never gone to sleep."

"I'm sorry."

"Whatever for?"

"For sending you that letter. Can you forgive me? Perhaps I should have left the past in the past. Her confusion is my fault."

Steel Hope sat up to light a cigarette. "I wish I could blame it on you or anyone else, but I'm to blame. In any case, it was bound to happen. She's been on the verge of hysteria since my release, and if you must know, I was relieved when she lost control here and not elsewhere."

He filled his lungs with smoke. It made him wheeze, but he inhaled again, deeper, mustering the will to express thoughts he hadn't confided to anyone. Until now, pride had kept him from adding his voice to what had become a deafening chorus of the wounded, heaping blame for all of China's sorrows on the so-called Gang of Four. Such thinking was ludicrous! One might as well blame an earthquake on a few sticks of dynamite. Pride had also kept him from joining the ranks of those who compulsively stripped themselves naked to compare scars while conveniently forgetting that they had spilt, as well as shed, blood during the Cultural Revolution. How he pitied and despised them. He stubbed out the cigarette, asking himself what made the Vice-Minister think that his stubborn pride made him any better than they.

"Steel Hope, are you all right?" asked Mountain Pine. "Let me make you some tea."

To hell with tea. He needed to talk. Grabbing Mountain Pine's arm, he pulled him down hard on the pile of books that had been their bed. "I've got something to say, and not in front of them...." His voice sounded as shrill as that of the spoiled young master and, running a hand through his hair, he was perplexed by how effortlessly he and Mountain Pine, who forthwith asked him to keep his voice down, had slipped into behaving as they did in childhood.

He lit another cigarette, wondering aloud where to start.

"Start anywhere. It doesn't matter."

Once started, he couldn't stop. The need to confess his cruelty to Summer Wishes was suddenly overwhelming, and just as suddenly he dismissed all rationalizations of his conduct. So what if the Cultural Revolution was an endless orgy of hate? So what if the crowds, given the slightest excuse, would have torn him apart as heedlessly as a curious child would tear the legs off a cockroach? How could he have assigned her the hardest role—a role he, in every aspect the stronger, had declined, out of stubborn pride, to play? She had given performance after performance. Fifty, a hundred times she had attacked him on stage. "Each time she completed the task, there was a moment when I was certain that she would recoil and ruin the spectacle. Each time, again and again, I urged her to revile and beat me so the crowds could see my blood oozing. She never failed me. But each time, time after time, I could see how she teetered ever more wildly at the edge of an abyss from which there would be no coming back. And yet, I urged her on and on and on.... When they finally decided to end the circus and lock me in solitary, I almost ..."

"I'd assumed that you were attacked, even viciously, but for some reason never considered solitary.... How long?"

"Ten years."

Mountain Pine mumbled something like "That long?" Nothing about the Cultural Revolution could surprise him anymore; his bookish mind had learned how to deflect the hardest blow. This time, it did some quick calculations and came up with an interesting statistic: both the servant and the young master had spent more years away from Summer Wishes than at the side of their wife.

Steel Hope threw off the quilt and paced—four steps forward, four steps back; out of habit, no less, no more, recalling how slowly each second in his cell had passed, and how fast the years. "Ah, but what a hero I was. I battled every step of the way. I used to sit on that stump of a stool, looking up at the interrogators, daring them to lose their composure and leave their comfortable chairs and come out from behind the table to exert themselves, to abuse me. I never said a word. I never signed a confession. I never named names. I was a hero to the end."

He spat. "Hero! A hero who let his wife do all the dirty work. She talked, she signed, she lied and lied and lied until she had forfeited every ounce of her spirit, her soul. And she did it because I told her to. I, her loving husband! I was the cadre who said she must never question policy. I made her promise that she'd always believe in the Party and carry out orders regardless of who was hurt—whatever the consequences. She always kept her promises to me."

He couldn't go on, couldn't say that he had been able to direct her every move even from solitary, for no longer was she a person with a will and mind of her own, but a puppet. Only Summer Wishes wasn't made of wood.

"Do you wonder that she's half-crazed?

"To be a hero, I willingly, knowingly, intentionally condemned the woman who loved me, who could never say no to me, who had believed from the age of twelve that nothing she was, or could be, was as honorable and admirable and unassailable as being my wife, to a hell crowded with demons where there was no one she could turn to, not even herself. And to this day, she thinks that her troubles had nothing to do with me and only with her.

"Can you imagine anyone else in all of China as foolish as that?" He swallowed hard, grateful that it was still too dark to see a hero's tears.

"She claims that I wasn't responsible, that it was her fate. It seems that before she started out for Chongqing some old hag foretold just such a fate in an insipid rhyme about flashes and ashes. What a joke! I, the second son of the House of Li, Vice-Minister of Administration in the Ministry of Culture, former Party Secretary of Wen Shui—hero!—saved from defeat and shame and oblivion by a faker's mumbling. And she, too naive and blind and trusting to comprehend what I've done to her."

"But you're wrong."

"What do you mean, I'm wrong?"

"I mean you're wrong to blame yourself. Remember, she went free and you went to jail."

He laughed, a contemptuous laugh. "My dear fellow, you've been stuck in the wilderness too long. You have no idea what a sanctuary solitary can be."

Remembering the years of sleeping twenty to a kang, Mountain Pine thought he did, but didn't say so. "Be that as it may," he said, "what could you have done to change anything?"

Steel Hope laughed again. "I could have changed everything at any moment of any day."

"I don't believe you. But for the sake of argument, say you could—why then didn't you?"

"Why didn't I? At first I convinced myself that suicide would harm her more. But that was an excuse, not the reason. It took me a good decade of keeping company with a colony of ants to figure out the reason. The sad fact is I didn't have the courage to leave this world without knowing what would happen to it. I had to stay around to see the look on their faces when I was ultimately declared innocent. How could I die a traitor like my accursed brother? How could I die like my wretched father—tormented, guilty of impotence and best forgotten? I had to prove myself pure and just and true of heart. I had to win. To win, I had to live.

"And when the accident took Loyalty from us, I couldn't die and let there be no one left to restore some modicum of honor to the House of Li. . . ."

There was nothing more either of them could say. Mountain Pine got up to boil water and Steel Hope lit another cigarette. By the time they were drinking the tea, he already regretted his confession—not because Mountain Pine had heard it, but because he had unburdened himself.

Dawn had turned the room from black to gray. Now his eyes could make out, on the floor where she had dropped it, the napkin that Summer Wishes had transformed into long flowing sleeves. Without her magic it was just a rag.

Finally Mountain Pine spoke up. "While the women are still asleep, let me tell you why I sent for you. Though Cinders and I are married, we've never lived as husband and wife. . . ."

"Then whose child is she?"

"Her name is North Star and she belongs to all of us. . . ."

The Sword of Heaven

WHEN MOUNTAIN PINE finished whispering the true story of Cinders, he dared not look up to meet Steel Hope's eyes, certain that any intimacy so soon after learning of Loyalty's suicide would unleash emotions neither could risk or, once expressed, rein in. As it was, he could almost smell the huge, sullen beast that had once lurked in the outer portals of his consciousness and that the pleasures of family routine had caged. He quit the room to fetch more tea.

Returning, he was stunned to find a brittle old man haloed by smoke seated in Steel Hope's chair. Suddenly he felt lost. Carefully he eased himself back down at the table, and only at that moment did he realize the truth, that a lifetime had passed. How could he not have noticed it before? Never one to deny reality, he couldn't accept denial as the reason. It must be something else.

Perhaps because from birth he was never spry, and because boy retainers were never young and prisoners never robust or sovereign—were these the reasons he had hardly given a thought to his own aging? Or was it because ill-equipped healers like him always warned trusting patients that whatever the stage in life, the body was frail? Or because he was separated by more than a half-century from North Star, to whom each dawn created the universe anew, and to be old while in her vicinity was unpardonable?

Now, seeing himself as others saw him, he could no longer ignore his own mortality. But had he in fact done so? Perhaps, unbeknownst to him, it had stamped the letter to Beijing. He was mildly amused by the thoroughness of his self-deception: he had believed that, with Deng Xiaoping's new emphasis on opening China to the world, his hopes for Cinders and the child had prompted the summons to the cadres from the capital. But perhaps the time had come for Mountain Pine to make a friend of death. Then again, perhaps not. Hadn't the old monk predicted that if Mountain Pine conquered tuberculosis, he would live to write a book? Soon he must start.

Suddenly Steel Hope coughed, as if to expel pain. A hand, mottled and veined, thumped his sunken chest. And yet if Mountain Pine shut his eyes, he could still see that prideful carriage swelling a soldier's uniform on parade and inspiring confidence in a battered town. He could still feel Little Panda perched on his shoulders tugging his hair, and truer still, hear Summer Wishes laughing. How bright her laughter had been then, like temple chimes—so different from last evening, when the actress had mimicked those crisp, youthful tones to dampen their fears.

He fixed his gaze on the brackish leaves at the bottom of the cup, and after a while remembered that he'd neglected to tell the part about being in Wen Shui to comfort his dying sister a few days after Mushroom had wisely ordered Steel Hope to take Summer Wishes, who couldn't bear seeing Amber Willows in pain, back to Beijing. That could wait, he decided. Steel Hope needed more time to accept the idea of Loyalty's suicide. The secret of his birth, that the young master and his bookmate were uncle and nephew, would keep.

He allowed the memory of his sister to pull him back to the day of Steel Hope's Grasping Ceremony, to how lovely she had looked in the rock garden wearing that old purple dress of Jade's, which repeated washing had faded to the palest mauve with hints of blue. How odd, when Cinders often had to supply the titles of books he had just put down, that he was able to recapture that color so vividly—not to mention the terror that Jade had instilled in him when the baby ignored every toy and grabbed his ankle instead. But he no longer blamed the mistress; he simply hadn't understood how frightened and tortured a woman she was until long after her death, when he had held his sister's hand while, shedding secrets in her sleep, she crossed over into the Yellow Springs.

He counted the years and credited the fates for treating Amber Willows more kindly at the end. She had lived to welcome her secret son home.

He started to sip his tea. But the sound he made so offended the silence that he invited a scalding, a new hurt, and drained the cup. As his tongue tended the blisters, he wondered which of Loyalty's two fathers was more racked by guilt—the Rightist who had abstained from teaching his wife and son about politics or the cadre who had taught them all too well.

They were still sitting at the table when, amidst the sudden clatter of dishes, Cinders called from the kitchen to apologize for oversleeping, for being the last to rise.

Last? Had she said "last"? How could she be the last? He scrambled to his feet and charged past her into the bedroom. It was empty. The quilts were folded. Though there were no other rooms where Summer Wishes and North Star could possibly be, he was about to call out their names when he spied the unlatched window. Below it, on the dirt floor, melted snow had left clotted black patches.

Turning about, he collided with Steel Hope, who took hold of Cinders, insisting, "You must believe me. She would never, never hurt the child."

Cinders' frantic eyes turned to the man she trusted more.

Mountain Pine nodded, repeating, "Never."

Suspended in the air like the Sword of Heaven, however, was the unspoken word—"intentionally."

"You stay here and make breakfast," he said, smoothing her hair. "We'll find them and bring them home."

Her hands to her mouth, she shook her head violently. A tear fell.

"No, you must stay here," he said. "What if they come back while we're out?" Then, before another tear could escape, he turned away to put on more layers.

Outside, the snow had stopped, but the wind still howled and hissed. The sky lowered like an iron shroud. Huddled arm in arm, with their clothes lashing about them, the two old men bent into the gale, following the footprints specked with dirt from the earthen floor until they reached the birches, where snow blown from the trees had covered the prints, large and small. Mountain Pine assured Steel Hope that this didn't matter. There was only one place Summer Wishes would have wanted to go, and he knew the way.

Their progress was slow. Not a word passed between them, for breathing in the bitter cold air, sharp, shallow and swift, impeded speech.

The temperature dipped lower. Mountain Pine made fists, motioned for Steel Hope to do the same. He regretted wearing socks. Toes bound with rags were less apt to snap like icicles. As he had done at the camp, they must forget all except keeping upright, placing one foot in front of the other, never stopping.

The cold pierced deeper. Beneath the coils of Mountain Pine's scarf, his face was a mask of ice. He prayed that Summer Wishes and North Star had left the warmth of the hut only moments before they were missed. But what if they had struck out earlier? In the dark?

He barred thoughts from rushing ahead. Better to recall how well they had eaten and compare this time with times past, when the weather had been far colder—when winter after winter he and Baldy and Maestro and Professor were forced to march and march, and dig and dig, day after day after day, despite a hunger that honed senses so keen that one sniff of a belch and they could tell what kind of food an inmate had stolen to fill his belly . . . when weeks went by without a modicum of lard in the whole caldron of soup to grease their innards, and they had squatted at latrines where urine froze before it could splash and endured fiendish agonies for an eternity, time after time, in vain . . . when, with flesh evaporated and bones softened and teeth rotted and fingers and toes lost to frostbite or chopped off by one's own hand in hopes of obtaining a sick slip and a few days indoors; wrapped like mummies in their filthy, sour, lice-infested rags, they had somehow managed to live on—beings who had nothing and asked for nothing except to survive, and who had, after all, survived.

Phantoms emerged before he could banish them, younger and healthier and stronger than Mountain Pine—husbands and fathers, brothers and sons who had paused to rest for just a minute, or at most two, and when spring finally came and the ice thawed, were still resting. . . .

He must not think of them now. He hardened his heart. He made fists. As they neared the charred clearing, he looked up to see the plum tree, and for a moment thought it too was a phantom, limned in ice. He passed a sleeve over his glasses, then, squinting, made out something at the foot of it, a seated shadow. He nudged Steel Hope and nodded. They pushed on.

From the spot where he had waited that night of the fireflies so as not to frighten the desperate mother, he saw clearly. Propped against the trunk of the tree was Summer Wishes. She was dressed only in underwear. On her lap she cradled a bundle of clothes. North Star was nowhere in sight.

Shouting, running, stumbling, again and again, they reached her at last.

A touch and Mountain Pine knew that his true wife was dead. He didn't try to stop Steel Hope from shaking her and embracing her and stroking her and kissing her, all the while crying for her to wake. He tended to the bundle of clothes. He carried North Star home.

I T was late in the evening on June third. Steel Hope spilled the tea wedged in his lap and woke up. Still sunk in the stupor that follows the leaden sleep of exhaustion, he couldn't be bothered to go to the kitchen for a dishtowel. He stared at the blotch instead, watched it seep into the sea-green fabric of the sofa. Would it be Shandong? Or Xinjiang? His bookmate used to dip a finger in the Yangzi and draw outlines of the provinces on the levee, challenging him to name them before their contours were erased by the sun.

He decided that the blotch resembled nothing, was merely a wet stain amid the dried ones. Yawning, he squinted at the wall clock—three hours to go before bedtime at one o'clock. He didn't know why he kept to his old schedule. Any sane man would go to bed now. There were no petitioners at his front or back door to mollify. No guests to entertain. No letters to write. No stacks of papers stamped Confidential, Secret and Top Secret to read anymore. This last thought teased from him a slow, satisfying smile.

Unlike his neighbors—all retired cadres like him, vice-ministers and above—he didn't miss being part of the ruling elite. Let them traffic in headlines culled from foreign broadcasts and in the gossip of their maids. Let them lard their egos and their bellies at official banquets welcoming the most powerful overseas Chinese families home. Toast the Tangs of

Singapore? Only if Matriarch Cassia would skip her annual pilgrimage to the spas of Europe and Sir Archibald Tang, the former Minister of Agriculture and thief, would leave his grave to drink arsenic at the Great Hall of the People. But his good neighbors were above vengeance; they preferred amnesia with every course, like mao tai. He shunned such affairs of high diplomacy and boasted that his most urgent task every day was getting across town before the toothless peddler at the corner of Jianquomen sold out her velvety tofu and fiery Sichuan sauce.

His smile faded. The poor woman had practically swallowed her tongue when, in rejecting her offer to set aside a portion for him, he had threatened to take his patronage elsewhere. Perhaps he shouldn't have shouted. But he had every right to be suspicious of her kindness. Ever since the Paramount Leader's pronouncement that Getting Rich Is Glorious, such favors had inevitably led to dubious requests that perpetuated the venal trade in bribes, which, nowadays, sullied every aspect of life. Still, in retrospect, he wondered if he had been wrong. Perhaps this one time age had dimmed his judgment. Then again, perhaps a principle and not just penny bean curd was involved.

He sighed, knowing better. Racing across town to buy tofu before the supply ran out was, in truth, a childish game he played to while away the mornings. He hated sitting around the house carping to himself about how times had changed, so changed that he was no longer certain of what to hope, think or believe in anymore.

Still groggy, he staggered toward the balcony, expecting to find North Star in the niche bracketed by protruding walls where, dressed for bed and barefoot, whatever the weather, she performed her nightly ritual of remembering. It was empty. Where was she?

Suddenly alert, he remembered. This was not an ordinary night. There hadn't been an ordinary night for seven weeks—not since the students started marching against corruption and for democracy, not since the Party branded their peaceful demonstrations unpatriotic, not since the young took over Tiananmen Square and a million ordinary citizens took to the streets in sympathy, not since talks broke down and martial law was declared and Beijingers came together to defy authority.

*

STEEL HOPE leans over the railing of the balcony. The people are out in force again. They line the curbs and jam the intersections, where abandoned buses, piles of bicycle racks and concrete road dividers serve as barricades, to monitor a convoy of Jeeps, trucks and armored personnel carriers that stretches beyond his view. By now the scene is familiar, and still he reels. What madness! The people versus the Army of the People. Were the ideals he fought for only lies?

Using binoculars, he scans the bridge over which the column of troops must pass to reach the students still camped in the square—among them, North Star. At first he can only make out citizens gesticulating. Then, suddenly, there is chaos. Soldiers scramble out of their vehicles into formation. Unlike other nights, they are not in shirtsleeves, but helmeted, and armed.

An image of his granddaughter falling flashes through his mind and he clutches his heart. No! Not she. She is the best of all those he has cared for. They live on in her. What would be left of them if she too was sacrificed?

He scrambles out of the apartment as fast as his seventy-year-old legs will allow and buzzes frantically for the elevator. But the gods are pitiless tonight. There is no response. He breaks out in an icy sweat. He doesn't dare lose a second. He dares not hurry. A broken bone will end any chance he has of reaching the square. Cautiously, he feels his way down the dark stairway, one hundred and eight steps, past one empty light socket after another. He curses the people who pilfer the People's property.

Out in the yard, confronted by rows of bicycles, he can't remember where he left his, or its license number. What fiend painted every bike black? He thrusts his key at lock after lock.

Whom has he offended lately? The Wangs on the second floor? The Changs on the fourth? The elevator operator? Which one filched his property? He curses them all.

His bicycle was there all along.

On a quiet night, traffic flusters him. Tonight, as he pedals through the astonishing array of conveyances, from child carts to home-rigged ambulances, along with runners, male and female, young and old, all dashing toward the bridge, his confusion borders on panic. Out of nowhere they come and keep on coming, forcing him to ring his bell, which no one heeds, to stop and start and zigzag. He shouts for them to clear a path. His pleas are lost in the hue and cry.

Eventually he succeeds in detouring onto a less congested street. He pedals as fast as he can, but the square seems no closer while the clamor grows louder and louder.

"Protect the students!"

"The youths are patriotic!"

"The People's Army won't shoot, not at us, not at the people!"

Without warning his bicycle swerves out of control, scattering pedestrians like mah-jongg tiles. Spewing apologies, he nevertheless concentrates on untangling himself from the spinning wheels and doesn't focus on his victims until he has righted himself. By then they have regrouped—each with his left hand resting on the shoulder of the person ahead and the right working a cane. He has smashed into a file of the blind—men, women and children, who have vowed to lay their bodies down across the path of the tanks. Spellbound, he gapes, as one after another taps by, reliving the horror and awe that seized him when his Jeep barely missed crushing the sightless Red Devil so long ago. But for that irrepressible hero, he would never have gone to Yenan. Is the man still alive? he wonders. What would he say if he were here now? . . .

A voice shouts, "Senile idiot."

What? He blinks.

"Save the students! Citizens, save the students!"

He climbs back on his bicycle and pedals, mumbling like a mantra, "Must save her, must get to the square, must block all else out."

He pedals until he fears that his heart will punch a hole through his chest, until, sweating profusely and gasping for air, dragging his feet and doubled over the handlebars, he comes to a halt in the middle of a contingent of workers.

"Old man, let me help you to somewhere safe."

He grabs the stranger's arm. "Please . . . take me . . . please . . . the square. Before the shooting starts."

"Don't you know? It's started."

That's impossible. "Are you sure? Where?"

"Muxudi area. A friend from there just called. He said the soldiers have gone crazy. He had to crawl like a worm inside his own apartment not to get shot."

North Star, why didn't you listen to me? I knew it would come to this. He must get to the square. He begs the worker to help him.

The man moans. "But every soldier in China is heading there."

"I beg you."

"You can't do any good. You'll just get in the way."

"It's a matter of life and death." Steel Hope hands him his wallet.

The man laughs. "Keep that for your funeral," he says.

*

H E   S I T S sideways on the rack fastened to the back fender, facing the lampposts that line the Avenue of Eternal Peace, his head resting on the young man's back, his feet skimming the ground as they pass marchers sporting "Dare to Die" headbands, motorcyclists shouting news of the soldiers' movements, citizens manning crossroads, peddlers hauling foreign cameramen on their three-wheeled carts, taxis and buses shuttling sympathizers: ordinary sights since the students rallied and overnight the same people who for years had been ruthlessly stomping on one another to get ahead, in life or on a bus, began caring for one another. His heart aches with pity and pride. And fear. All around, loudspeakers bark, "Citizens, stay home! Students, return to your colleges. The army clears Tiananmen tonight."

From the distance comes the sound of singing—the "Marseillaise." ". . . For justice thunders condemnation, a better world is being born."

From the distance comes the sound of automatic weapons firing.

Sirens wail.

There is no moon. To the east, and the west, the sky glows. Frenzied citizens now dart in all directions.

"They can't get away with this," the young man shouts into the wind. "I live here too!" For a moment, Steel Hope fears the stranger might forsake him to join the runners, but instead he pumps faster, and they spurt toward the plaster statue of the Goddess of Democracy the students erected earlier in the week. That day, he remembers, the sky was clear and there was a gentle breeze. Now the hunger strike has been called off and the overwhelming majority of students have quit the square. Unlike him, until today many in and out of the Party believed that the crisis would end without violence. He harbored no such hopes. Red is the favorite color of both sides, and thus blood must flow.

He has seen the statue before, on his futile trips to the square this week, trying to dissuade North Star from risking all for the unattainable, but only tonight does he notice how the goddess holds her torch high with both hands. Is she trying to shed light on the portrait that hangs on the ancient gates of the Forbidden City across the way? He peers at the Chairman's ruddy face. It is ageless. Even from this distance there is no escaping that hint of a smile and those enigmatic black eyes.

He taps the young man on the shoulder. "Let me off by those tents over there and go where you need to go on the bike."

"You sure?"

"I'm sure."

The immense space looks serene enough in the artificial light, and it is that very absence of alarm—so like the unreadable faces of peasants intent upon the ultimate sacrifice—that sends him hurtling toward the Monument of the Martyrs and the source of the youthful voice, laced with static, that urges her fellow students to remain seated and calm. Whatever happens, North Star says, they must not resist or fight.

He stumbles and falls. Dazed, he looks up to see a slender figure coming toward him through pools of shadow and light, but cannot decide if it is a phantom from his past or North Star until she kneels alongside to take him in her arms. "Are you hurt, Grandfather?"

He shakes his head.

"I was afraid you'd come for me."

"Child, the bullets are real."

She nods.

"You can't win. You can only lose."

Again she nods.

"Do you think I don't know what you're feeling? I wanted to be a hero too. But I've learned that the only heroes China has ever had are dead heroes."

"Grandfather, I never wanted to be a hero, and I'm not anxious to be one now. I'm scared, terribly scared, but I must stay." The tears she somehow holds captive in her sorrowful eyes extinguish all his hopes.

He kisses her frown. "Then I'll stay to hold your hand."

"You can't. I have only you now, no one else, and . . ." She pauses and tucks an envelope in his pocket, then goes on. "There are last wishes you alone can make come true."

The prospect of being abandoned suddenly makes him furious. At her. At all those who have died. At the general, who happened across a magazine story about a Chinese artist and her prize-winning painting of a baby reaching out through a train window. At Cinders, who chose not to stay with them in Beijing but to go to her long-lost father in America, where she might arrange as well for the publication of Mountain Pine's manuscript. At the times, both better and worse, since Deng's reforms. At the world. At the gods. "What about my wishes?" he asks. "What about me?"

She smiles. "Oh, Grandfather, you've often said that my wishes and yours are one and the same. You would never lie to me." It is the same encouraging smile she flashed whenever his eyes couldn't avoid meeting those of the seven-year-old seated across from him on the train speeding toward the capital, away from the wilderness, away from Summer Wishes, who slept beside charred bones in the frozen ground. At the time, the little girl that Mountain Pine and Cinders could not live without, but had nevertheless, for the sake of her education and future, decided to give to his care, had meant nothing to him, less than nothing. He wanted to forget how Mountain Pine had spent years talking about Summer Wishes and, in anticipation of North Star's new life in Beijing, months instilling in the child a willingness to follow the lovely woman anywhere; forget how easily Summer Wishes could cast a spell on children, and believe instead that his wife would still be alive if the child had been intelligent enough to call them instead of stealing with her into the night; if the child had been strong enough to run back for help; if the child had been good enough to refuse her grandmother's clothes.

Now, silently, North Star helps him to his feet. Silently she embraces him. Then, in a voice that sounds as though it emanates from somewhere far off stage, she whispers, "I've only told you of how Grandmother sang her mother's song to me, and looked for a kingfisher on our way to the plum tree. But I've never forgotten what she kept on repeating, over and over, as she was removing her clothes to warm me, and as she held me in the snow. The words didn't make sense, so I told no one. Tonight I understand. Tonight you will as well. She said——"

It's not fair. No! Not now. Not here. "Don't, please don't. . . ."

"Over and over she said, 'I wanted to be a human being.' "

HE MAKES his way mostly through alleyways too narrow for the armored personnel carriers to pass, intent on ignoring the clouds of smoke in the sky, the cacophony of battle, the stink of fear and of valor, distancing himself from the living, the wounded and the dead, until he comes upon a disheveled white-haired man like himself walking beside the tanks that line the street in front of his apartment house. In the man's hand is a broom. On it hangs a torn organza dress, no bigger than a scarf. It is yellow, caked with blood. Waving it in the faces of the soldiers perched on tanks, he cries, "Look, look at what you've done! You've killed my heart, my liver and spleen, my dearest treasure. Look, look at what you've done!"

He climbs the one hundred and eight steps. He can still hear the sounds of battle below, and somehow finds the strength to stagger throughout the apartment shutting the windows and balcony doors to no avail before collapsing in the nearest chair. It almost gives away. He has never dared to sit in it before. When North Star spotted the rare pieces of huali wood in a junk shop, she asked its owner if they had originally belonged to a table or a chair. The man shrugged, then wagered his most prized possession—the set of wooden teeth he was wearing—that every last piece of whatever it was was there, and available at a most reasonable price. Steel Hope had his hand on the door when she pulled him back. "How can we lose, Grandfather? Either way, it's a genuine antique!"

Solving the mystery took them even longer than they had anticipated, for each session sparked bouts of laughter and cheers. The engineer who had built only tunnels was building again! When they finally fitted together a chair in the Ming style, she had set it by the sliding glass doors, pronouncing it "a joint venture that deserves to be seen in the very best light."

Now, seated precariously in the antique with his back to the balcony, he tries to picture her there at seven years old, dressed for bed and barefoot, gazing at the northeastern quadrant of the sky. In the rain. Enveloped by autumn moonlight. With the wind unraveling her braids. The pinkness of her toes under a coverlet of snow. Until the child was no longer a child, he had been oblivious to these devotions, though North Star had initiated the rite of remembering on the very night of their arrival in Beijing. At the time he had agreed to raise her as Cinders and Mountain Pine wished, because breathing required all his efforts, and it was easier to nod than to say no. To him, the girl was little more than an extra suitcase, and once home, he'd turned her over to Mushroom and, as before, devoted all his waking hours to work. As life had hardened the heart of his father, it hardened his. That their blood was the same— that Mountain Pine, her grandfather, was the brother of his true mother— had made no more difference to him than the fact that he was his father's son had made to Stone Guardian.

"North Star deserves a better life than we can give her," Mountain Pine said. "She's special. One day you will know what we've known from the beginning—that she is a blessing from the gods." Why had it taken him so long, until the girl was fifteen, to realize that his old bookmate spoke truly? Even more mysterious was how—between a flash of lightning and a roll of thunder—the reversal occurred. Yet, he remembers it precisely that way....

IT WAS September, and the night skies were scored by rivulets of lightning and windowpanes trembled at the roar. The storm prompted thoughts of Chongqing. How young he had been then. Then, the weariness of which he complained so often had been only talk; for all the while he had dreamed of eclipsing his ancestors. Then, whenever Summer Wishes claimed that the eerie light auguring a downpour could carry messages beyond the Yellow Springs, he had laughed. Now, whenever lightning flashed, he begged her forgiveness.

Forgive me. He had uttered the words countless times since he first uttered them under the tree after she was gone and it was too late. And each time he had prayed that she would never forgive him—not the boy who had stolen the silver pin, not the man who had urged her to strike him—but recall his every wrong, so that the desire for vengeance might vault her over the Great Divide, returning her to haunt him mercilessly.

Forgive me, forgive me. . . .

The faintest of voices asked, "Whatever for?"

He turned. In the niche bracketed by protruding walls stood a familiar silhouette. Had his prayers been answered at last? He almost wept in gratitude when lightning revealed her face. It was that of Firecrackers transformed by the phases of the moon, on the cusp of being recast into that vision of loveliness that had floated across a rickety stage and back into their lives as the bombs fell in Chongqing. Until that moment North Star had represented at best a debt, neither onerous nor negligible, which he owed and had arranged to pay. From that moment on he understood that, if it had been his fortune that whenever Stone Guardian looked at his second son, the Patriarch saw the countenance of his own shame, it was also his fortune that whenever he looked at Summer Wishes' granddaughter he would see the features of the woman he loved.

After he had begun to care for North Star, he discovered that she was not only a reflection of Summer Wishes but an incarnation of the most singular qualities of all her forebears. In her he found the equanimity of Mountain Pine, the originality of Cinders, the soulfulness of Loyalty. Had North Star had sisters and brothers, he often wondered, would she have inherited so great a legacy? But she was an only child, blessed by the gods to be a blessing from the gods.

*

THE MING CHAIR creaks, and he rises and is drawn, pulled by the hand, to her room. On its walls are some of the portraits Cinders painted in this apartment for her first exhibition. Some are of people he knew well, and others he can only guess at—but for that show, all her subjects, no matter what the expression or setting, had been pictured on a train, with both arms reaching through an open window for someone or something unseen.

Above her bed hangs the fan that Cinders held in her hand when she suddenly arrived at the door with all her bags five years ago. Though he had taken North Star to see Mountain Pine in his sickbed earlier that month, Steel Hope was still unprepared for the shock of his death. To lose a bookmate, an oldest friend, a sworn brother, a kinsman all at once was to lose one's bearings: he quit his post at the Ministry to wait for North Star to come home from school, to introduce Cinders to intellectual and artistic circles, to practice his calligraphy and memorize Tang poetry.

He avoids looking at the fan decorated with the poem named "Home-coming" that Mountain Pine had written on his deathbed. He cannot bear to reread it now. Now more than ever, he cannot spare such a friend, someone who was always blind to his excesses; someone who saw his life unfold.

In his need, he wishes. If only he hadn't insisted that North Star finish her education in China. If only the girl hadn't entrusted him with her last wishes. If only Cinders were here to share the agony instead of in New York.

Limp, he leans against the door frame until finally he notices a leaflet tucked in one corner of her mirror. On its cover is a quote from Lu Xun: "Trust Only Those Who Doubt." In the opposite corner of the mirror there is a page torn from a notebook, on which she has written, "Silence is the most hurtful of lies!"

Surely the words are a reminder to herself; but burning with shame, he lowers his gaze.

Beneath the glass that covers the top of the bureau below, she has put the old calendar they discovered in a dustbin on their latest trip into the countryside. Above the numerals is a reprint of an even older theater poster, featuring a beautiful maiden in ancient costume.

On the low table is the phonograph. He places the needle on the record and Summer Wishes sings.

Feeling faint, he lies down on North Star's bed. He prays. He dreams. So many dreams . . .

He flies on the back of a dragon. The Pearl of Potentiality set in its jaws bewitches him and he doesn't flinch when its scales score his flesh. Directly below, a sea of black-haired people stroll arm in arm: on their shoulders tiers of little girls and boys teeter like acrobats on a wayward bicycle. Beyond their view are iron-clad warriors and giant armadillos.

Suddenly, he hears singing.

There she is below. She waves and gladdens his heart.
Firecrackers. The sky glows to the east, to the west.
Stop! He must get off. He must warn them.
The elevator is out of order. . . .

He sits in a grand hall beneath a dome of golden stars. The walls are marble,
vermilion slabs that soar high enough to moor clouds; hewed, it is said, from a
quarry on the black side of the moon. There are no comforts other than the
gnarled cypress stump on which he perches.

He waits. For something? For someone? Seasons pass. Another winter,
another fall. A hollowness he cannot name consumes him.

At last she is here. Like gossamer, she floats across the extravagant width
of this singular room from far left to far right and back to where she first appeared.
She is gone. The silence echoes.

Tendered by unseen hands, a tray halts before him. On it are a looking
glass framed in ivory, pebbles, a toy hammer and a letter. The paper is blue.
Though the calligraphy is as familiar as his own, he cannot read it. He stares at
the reflection of a white-haired man wearing a mask that is his face. It is stiff.
It is unwieldy. It chafes. He rips it off. Underneath lies another. Faster and faster,
he repeats the same motions until, tendons frayed, his limbs dangle like those of
a marionette. . . .

He stops strangers. He explains. He is a faithful magistrate of heaven and of hell.
His years of service to their cause has earned him the honor of sitting in the
highest councils in both these mighty realms. He has a family. They take pride
in one another and in their ancestors. The winter of his days is mellow. He has
no regrets. And as constantly as the dawn graces the horizon, he gleans hope. He
is the man he wanted to be. . . .

He awakes to find his shirt soaked with perspiration. Removing it, he
comes across the letter North Star tucked in his pocket.

My beloved Grandfather,

You must remember Mountain Pine's story about the phoenix
that alighted in the garden of a prince. It is a bird that never
existed. And yet that creature is alive in me. If I must die,
let it be from exploring the heavens, not imperceptibly,
feather by feather, in a cage.

I am humble enough to realize that had I been born at another time I might have joined the chorus singing the praises of the Prince. I am proud enough to realize that nature has endowed me with imagination not merely to serve royal dreams.

In the bottom drawer of my desk are Mountain Pine's diary and some stories I have written, stories you and those we cherish have told, remembering. Promise me they will not be lost.

Your granddaughter

*

AFTER THE tanks roll into Tiananmen Square, he doesn't dare leave the apartment, in case North Star should return or call.

He can guess, but doesn't know, what is happening in the capital. He doesn't own a television and his radio is broken, but from his balcony he can see that fires still burn and soldiers still patrol the streets. He doesn't dare make inquiries, on the chance that somehow she escaped the hidden cameras. There is nothing he can do. There is nothing to fill the interminable minutes. He forces himself to sit and read what she has written.

The words mean nothing to him. His eyes glide over them as if they were as alike as grains of sand. Again and again, he returns to the beginning, until eventually he begins to hear, however muted at first, her voice. Then, with each page, as her rhythm and lilt, her tone and temper become stronger, he becomes calmer, increasingly certain that North Star will escape harm, and that she will live on.

When he finishes reading, the day and night have passed. While only a few of the events are new to him, there emerges to his amazement a story greater than the sum of their days, together and apart. But he is not surprised by the fact that almost all the incidents took place long before North Star was born. Are not memories most vivid, and years less alike, in the distant past?

He looks out the window. In the courtyard, a lone soldier is practicing martial arts. When the youth executes a combination of Swooping Scissors and Throttle the Tiger, he tastes a tear. It is saltier than he remembers.

Why couldn't the three of them have grown old together? It is an absurd question. They were not even allotted the intervening years.

*

THE TELEPHONE RINGS. It is North Star. She doesn't give her name. She says simply, "Meet me. You remember when and where."

Remember? Even as a child she was forever urging him to do so. No doubt Mushroom had told her how to break through his silences at meals. In any event, it worked. He began by telling tales about the illustrious House of Li, about how he and his bookmate befriended a ragamuffin and, much later, about their loyalties. Nevertheless, in those early years, it was their past that had engaged his attention, not her.

So many years wasted. So many years before they began traveling the country in search of articles—once denounced, again desired—that had escaped the torches of the Red Guards. It was her idea to furnish the apartment made barren by the paucity of tasteful furniture after the Cultural Revolution, and afterwards kept barren by neglect, with objects like those that once furnished the home Summer Wishes had made for him in Wen Shui. Every find, a memory. Every memory, a find. More, much more, than things were restored. When Mushroom died in 1987, her parting words were that she had honored her vow. The role she was assigned was done: the bonds between the girl and him had grown as inseparable as those of family.

In boyhood, the happiness that inevitably overtook clansmen upon homecoming had mystified him. Some had never been to the House of Li before. Some hadn't visited since they were carried away in bridal chairs. Some had quarreled so bitterly that they had chosen exile. He had assumed that such happiness was false. Could it be, he wondered now, that the tales the Patriarch intoned at Pure Brightness were more than ritual? That the bonds between father and son, brother and brother, husband and wife, one generation and the next were like birth and death, undeniable?

For who can resist the dream, so different for all and yet for all the same, that haunts every son and daughter who ever lost or who never knew a home sheltered by ancestral roofs and surrounded by garden walls?

He cannot.

*

IN THE MOONLIGHT the ruins of the House of Li, with its reclining pillars and broken pediments, resemble a deserted site where the scattered bones of a dragon lie unearthed. Even the rock from the bottom of Wuxi Lake, the gift of the Emperor, is gone. Reason would have him believe that it was smashed and its shards mingled with the ordinary rubble. But the beauty of a rock that can assume as many aspects as can be imagined by the beholder defies reason; and so he believes that a stranger who treasured the intangibles of life had it removed for safekeeping.

Now, hearing the crickets chirp, he smiles ruefully.

Perhaps there is a reason why, since retirement, he has often sought peace here. No amount of effort could repair the marvels that his ancestors built and others have destroyed. Good deeds do go awry. And mortals cannot escape being casualties of history.

He doesn't have to wait long before she appears.

"Will you help me get away?"

He nods. He has done for her what everyone does every day to accomplish the smallest deed, but nonetheless he has never done before—not even when his best friend was exiled and his weeping wife begged. He has bribed the necessary officials. And he has sent word to those who can be trusted. The kangmates of Mountain Pine will accompany a young man to the frontier. On the other side Cinders will be waiting for her daughter. Though the words of the oath that the young master, his bookmate and the gravekeeper's daughter once took were not realized, their spirits would live together in her.

"Will you come with me?"

He has anticipated every question but that. Nevertheless, without a moment's thought, he replies, "I can't."

"Why not?"

He doesn't really know. Perhaps it is because of the letter Stone Guardian wrote. Perhaps it is because he lacks the desire—or is it courage?—to leave his world with all its ghosts. Perhaps the ruins offer him more than peace. "It's too late for me. What was lost is gone forever."

"Grandfather, take very good care of yourself." She smiles. It is that same encouraging smile. "You must be here to greet me when I come home."

Bette Bao Lord was born in Shanghai in 1938 and came to the United States at the age of eight. Her baby sister, Sansan, remained behind. When the Bao family was finally reunited sixteen years later, the story of Sansan's life became the subject of Mrs. Lord's first book, *Eighth Moon.*

In 1973 Mrs. Lord returned to her native land. Her reunion with her relatives there inspired her to write *Spring Moon,* which was nominated as a first novel for the American Book Award. Her children's book, *In the Year of the Boar and Jackie Robinson,* is the fictionalized story of her first year in Brooklyn as a new immigrant.

She and her husband, Winston Lord, were posted to Beijing from 1985 to 1989, during his tenure as U.S. Ambassador to China. Throughout the weeks of pro-democracy demonstrations in the spring of 1989, Mrs. Lord served as a consultant to CBS News. *Legacies: A Chinese Mosaic,* chosen by *Time* magazine as one of the ten best nonfiction books of 1990, is an account of those years in China.

Mrs. Lord is a governor on the Presidential Broadcasting Board of Governors, the chairwoman of Freedom House, a trustee of Freedom Forum, the Aspen Institute and the National Portrait Gallery, and serves on the Kennedy Center's Community Board. A graduate of Tufts University and the Fletcher School of Law and Diplomacy, Mrs. Lord holds seven honorary doctorates.

She lives in Washington, D.C., with her husband—now the Assistant Secretary of State for East Asian and Pacific Affairs—and is the mother of Lisa and Winston.

A NOTE ON THE TYPE

This book was set in Granjon, a type named in compliment to Robert Granjon but neither a copy of a classic face nor an entirely original creation. George W. Jones drew the basic design for this type from classic sources but deviated from his model so as to profit from the intervening centuries of experience and progress. This type is based primarily on the type used by Claude Garamond (ca. 1480–1561) in his beautiful French books and more closely resembles Garamond's own type than do any of the various modern types that bear his name.

Of Robert Granjon nothing is known before 1545 except that he began his career as type cutter in 1523. The boldest and most original designer of his time, he was one of the first to practice the trade of typefounder apart from that of printer. Between 1549 and 1551 he printed a number of books in Paris, also continuing as type cutter. By 1557 he was settled in Lyons and had married Antoinette Salamon, whose father, Bernard, was an artist associated with Jean de Tournes. Between 1557 and 1562 Granjon printed about twenty books in types designed by himself, following, after the fashion, the cursive handwriting of the time. These types, usually known as *caractères de civilité,* he himself called *lettres françaises,* considering them especially appropriate to his own country. He was granted a monopoly of these types for ten years, but they were soon copied. Granjon appears to have lived in Antwerp for a time, but was in Lyons in 1575 and 1577. For the next decade he lived in Rome, working for the Vatican and Medici presses, his work consisting largely in cutting exotic types. Toward the end of his life he may have returned to live in Paris, where he died in 1590.

Composed by Crane Typesetting Service, Inc.,
Charlotte Harbor, Florida
Printed and bound by The Haddon Craftsmen,
a division of R. R. Donnelley & Sons,
Scranton, Pennsylvania
Designed by Cassandra J. Pappas